SOME KIND OF HELL

CONTENTS

ISBN: 979-8-9885735-1-7(paperback)

ISBN: 979-8-9885735-0-0 (ebook)

Some Kind of Hell

Cover by Maria Spada.

Map of the Continent by Shivnath Productions.

Bloodrune art by Alex Spreier.

To every woman ever told to swallow her anger

"And for Valerius, the Task of the Guardian: So long as you draw breath, the fight is yours to claim."

Teachings of the Church of the Triad

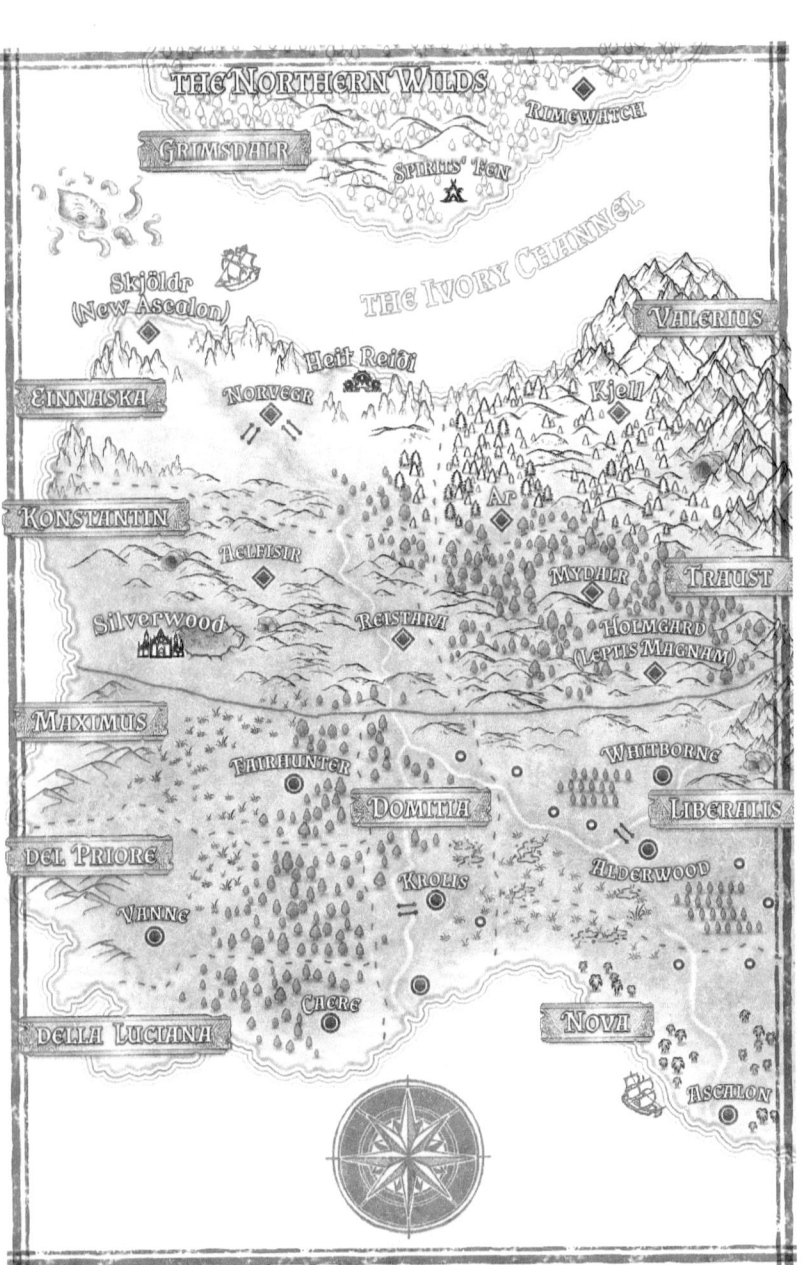

CHAPTER ONE

By this point in her mercenary career, Frelia Valerius was something of a graveyard connoisseur.

You could sit atop a burial mound and feel your ancestors' power through it, see the rune sticks carved with memories and wards against the deceased coming back as a draugr. A Kaldiri grave was a quiet thing.

Volsinii-style graveyards like this one, though, were full of cramped stonework and too many ghosts pressing together. Or at least, Frelia always felt like there were ghosts here. How could anyone rest properly with so many people coming and going, pouring out wine, and generally being a damn nuisance?

Graveyards were still quieter than most of the city, though, and so Frelia frequently found herself there, piss-drunk and talking to her own ghosts.

Tonight was cool, and the wind whipping in off the coastline brought with it the first touch of autumn's bite. Soon it would be too cold up here in the north for the mercenaries she ran with, and they would head south for the winter. And south meant more Volsinii graveyards, more Volsinii accents, more Volsinii everything, until they swallowed the world.

And Frelia was so fucking tired of the Volsinii.

In the fifteen years since the Tyrant's War, the Kaldiri diaspora had carved out what notches of home that they could. Family shrines to the

Triad here, the occasional tavern there. Frelia herself was a relic of what had once been the Kingdom of Kaldr, and these days she felt every inch obsolete.

"Do you need libations again, madam?" came the crooked voice of one of the street vendors nearby. Bakers and sommeliers usually had a cart or two open around here at this time of night for people to pick up grave goods.

Everyone had lost someone in the war, after all.

"*Ja.*" Frelia's guttural Kaldiri accent crackled like ice in the springtime. "Mead, if you've got it."

Her da would appreciate mead a lot more than some Volsinii red wine he'd never drunk in life. The Grimsdalr twins would happily take whatever she handed them, but Frelia liked to think they'd appreciate Kaldiri spirits more, too.

The sommelier dug around the crates he'd brought with him for a moment before emerging with a dusty bottle of mead with a label Frelia didn't recognize.

Nameless mead for a nameless grave, she thought.

It would do.

She paid for it with the rest of the coin from her last job, guarding some self-important merchant guildsman halfway up the coast. It had been mind-numbingly boring, and Frelia swore she'd felt her sword skills atrophy the whole time.

Was this what she'd suffered those endless sword drills and wartime battles for? Standing there and looking intimidating while some raven-starver of a man carted expensive silks and lace across the coast? Frelia was tired, sure, but more than that, she was bored. Her life felt like one decades-long joke, and she was still waiting on the Goddesses-damned punchline.

"In all good conscience, madam," the sommelier said, "I feel I must warn you that a rather... unsavory fellow went in there about half an hour ago." He gestured towards the cemetery gate. "I'm not certain it's safe."

Frelia's fingers curled around the neck of the bottle, and she glanced towards the graveyard walls. They were still intact, and she knew from experience that the graves were laid out in tight, narrow rows. "Unless he can hide a sixteen-foot garmr in there, I think I'll be fine."

She tapped the hilt of the heavy bastard sword sheathed at her left hip. It was the most expensive thing she owned these days, and most of the gold she earned on a job went straight to maintaining it.

"Even so," the man said. "Dangerous to be a woman alone, these days."

Frelia rolled her eye; the blind one behind the eyepatch no longer moved. *Volsinii.*

"Shall I expect you at the same time next week?" the sommelier asked.

Frelia sighed. "Probably."

The man's smile was kinder than most. "I'll have mead again, for you."

Once upon a time, the gates to this cemetery had closed at night, but very likely people kept forcing their way through or picking the locks and getting in anyway. It was a tale Frelia had heard many a time from some disgruntled undertaker or other, when said undertaker found her in there after dark. Eventually they all gave up, hired on an extra guard or two, and left the place unlocked for all the sad drunks who came to say goodbye.

Sad drunks like Frelia.

She hadn't always been sad, she was pretty sure. Even during the war, she could remember absolutely raucous nights when she must've had fun. Cillian Grimsdalr had been alive then, and she'd still had both eyes.

This particular graveyard, Frelia was long since familiar with. The Cost Effectives, the mercenaries she currently ran with, frequently stopped in Norvegr. And even as a child, Frelia had known the once-Kaldiri city's peaked longhouse roofs and grassy thoroughfares. There were a lot more Volsinii here these days—hence the Volsinii-style graveyard expansion—but there had always been enough of them here in the past that there were graves all the way in the back with inscriptions worn away by the wind from the Ivory Channel.

She liked those graves most, since she didn't know where (or if) Cillian or his twin sister, Thera, were buried. Frelia's father had been eaten by a garmr during the war, and Frelia really didn't like to think too hard on where that meant he'd ended up. Her mother and older brother were buried deep in the mountains of what had once been Valerius Territory, and though Frelia knew where their burial mounds were, she had no way of getting there.

So, nameless grave it was.

Frelia picked her way across the grassy, graveyard expanse. The newer graves and mausoleums gleamed in the moonlight, their marble faces inlaid with gold and laden with flowers. The Volsinii took care of their dead almost as well as the Kaldiri did, and it was one of the only things about them that Frelia didn't hate on gut-punch principle.

But the older the graves became, the less well-kept they were. The newer graves didn't have moss and vines creeping over them, or statues of the Triad Goddesses warding off intruders. Frelia touched Lady Twilight's foot as she passed by a particularly ornate statue of the divine sisters—just like every grave-goer before her, if the worn smooth bronze was anything to go by.

And then, at long last, Frelia arrived at her favorite nameless grave.

Whoever was buried here had to have been dead for centuries, since their headstone was neither marble nor flashy. But the carved granite still stood, and Frelia could just pick out a few Kaldiri runes still clear enough to read. She'd crafted a story for this person over her many nights here. Maybe it was a Volsinii man who had married a Kaldiri woman and moved up here, or a Kaldiri woman who had been particularly well-off and wanted to be buried in the more fashionable Volsinii style. Whoever they were, the first libation was always for them.

"Thanks for letting me borrow your grave," she murmured to the deceased. "May you rest easy, wherever you are."

She popped the cork off the mead, and the honey-colored liquid soaked into the grassy soil beneath the headstone. The smell of alcohol hit her and dragged her down to the mud like the kraken itself. Frelia folded her legs into an awkward pretzel, and waited for the world to right itself before continuing.

"Mum," Frelia said, because she always went in order, "I hope you're proud. Da never was."

Frelia had barely known her mother, lost to a plague before Frelia could properly speak. So far as anything feminine was concerned, she'd mostly been raised by the Margravine Grimsdalr, the Twins' mother, and an aunt who knew more about being a woman than Frelia ever would. The third libation was for that aunt, killed in a sudden blizzard like far too many in her family's old territory, and the fourth was for her older brother.

"Diarmuid, I really could have used your help... ever."

He'd been killed in the Winter War before he'd even been able to grow a proper beard.

Then came the Tyrant's War, and two deaths in rapid succession, followed by one in agonizing defeat.

"Da... Thera... Cillian."

Three splashes, three unmarked graves, three punches to the gut that made Frelia struggle to breathe, even still.

"You should all be here, suffering with me." Frelia half-heartedly thumped her fist into the ground. "Or I should be there."

She hoped they'd all made it to Solivallr, or she'd spend her own afterlife dragging them to Lady Daybreak's mead hall whether the Goddesses liked it or not.

"I hate to interrupt," came a smooth, Volsinii accent from somewhere far over Frelia's head, "but word on the street is, a skunk-haired, one-eyed mercenary swordswoman comes out here to pray after the bars let out. Know anything about that?"

Fury gripped Frelia's insides. But that was familiar, comfortable. Normal. She breathed in fury the way she took in air.

Frelia rose to her feet, accursedly unsteadily, but froze at the sight of the voice's owner. He was roughly Frelia's age, with straw-colored hair and a bandolier full of alchemical reagents wrapped around his chest. Worst of all, he wore the stylish leather armor of a Bloodrune Hunter.

Son. Of. A. Bitch.

"Skunks are the other way," was all Frelia could think to say. "They're white in the middle."

The Hunter's brow furrowed. "Oh, they *are*, aren't they?"

It had been a while since she'd bothered to bleach her hair, which was naturally the characteristic inky black of the Valerius family. Her roots were showing, even if they were mostly hidden beneath her hood at the moment. She probably should be better about bleaching it, but it just felt so wrong.

This was a trap, Frelia thought dismally. The question was whether the sommelier was in on it. She didn't think so, given that he'd never bothered to sell her out before, and this wasn't the first post-midnight graveyard walk she'd taken. But betrayal had become a matter of course since the Tyrant's War, and Frelia was used to leaping at shadows.

Her hand settled more firmly on the hilt of her sword.

"Ah-ah," said the Bloodrune Hunter. "None of that, now. There's no need to sully this place with violence."

Frelia's eye narrowed. Did this man think she would hesitate to gut him just because they were in a graveyard? He'd already interrupted the libations; she hadn't even gotten halfway through. All bets were off.

"You already did," she said. "But no, don't know anything about your quarry."

It was only half a lie. Frelia barely recognized herself anymore, and she sure as shit doubted the dead could, either.

The Hunter softly clicked his tongue, "If you're trying to hide, love, might I suggest a better disguise than a bit of lazy hair dye?"

He tapped the crown of his head a few times.

Frelia's bloodrune dug into her side like a sudden, sharp wound. Flashes of a hundred Valerius ancestors in a thousand tight scrapes flashed through her mind, and her leg had lashed out before she'd told it to. The Hunter, predictably, grunted, and his hands snapped to cover his groin too late to avoid the stomp kick.

Frelia tore away from the nameless grave as though chased by Lady Midnight herself. She vaulted headstones and ducked around mausoleums, but clouds had begun to cover the moon, and her sense of direction was scattered without the stars.

She was also so drunk she felt as if she'd vomit onto someone's grave if she stopped moving, which didn't help.

The first flask of alchemist's fire smashed into the headstone Frelia was hurdling, and she squeaked in startled surprise, tripping over her own boots when she landed. Bits of granite ricocheted into her side as delicately carved stone roses snapped off the gravestone.

Frelia scrambled behind a further gravestone just as a second flask of alchemist's fire broke against the grave she'd been standing atop. Acrid smoke filled the air, and more stone broke across the ground.

'No need to sully this place with violence,' he'd said, when he clearly meant his Saints-damned own. How many flasks could he possibly be carrying on that belt? It wasn't infinite, Frelia knew that, but he clearly had no qualms about collateral damage in the meantime.

Frelia scrambled from headstone to headstone, trying to count how many flasks smashed across the names of the dead. *Three... four... shit, was that four?*

She was feeling more intoxicated than she had been the rest of the night, when she'd had nothing more strenuous to do than lift a tankard and flip off men who got too friendly with her backside.

"Oh, come now, Valerius!" the Hunter called from somewhere across the way. "Hiding doesn't suit you, and I so wanted to see those sword skills for myself."

Frelia threw back her head and hissed. She refused to take the stupid bait, not when it was that obvious. But still, it raked at her to sit here and do nothing. She didn't have any ranged weapons on her, and this graveyard was too cramped to cast spells. That had to be why the Hunter was using alchemist's fire, too. Even if he were a mage, it wouldn't help him any; the rows were too close together to draw one's runes properly.

One hit from that alchemist's fire and she'd be done for. Fifteen years of running and hiding would have been for nothing. The Imperium would have what it wanted, and the last vestiges of the Valerius duchy would die with her.

But if there was one thing Frelia Helm's Grace Valerius was, it was stubborn. She had her sword. She had half a working brain. And she had an insistent Bloodrune Hunter after the ancient magic that sang in her blood and had been passed down her family line since the time of the Saints.

No. I won't die here.

She bolted for another headstone just as one more flask whizzed past her ear. It smashed against the statue of the Triad Goddesses she'd passed by earlier, the one where Lady Twilight's foot had been worn smooth by centuries of visitors.

"Is this what you fucking wanted?" Frelia hissed up at them as she huddled behind yet another tombstone. "Thanks for nothing."

For a moment, it seemed almost like the Goddesses' unmoving faces were mocking her. *We gave the Valerius Bloodrune to your ancestor, Frelia dear, not to you.*

But then another flask of alchemist's fire smashed into the statue, and a chunk of someone's bronze hand fell into the muddy grass beside Frelia. The only digit intact was the middle finger.

"Thanks," Frelia called up to them.

She snatched up the chunk of bronze and took off running again. Providence it was.

"Don't you ever get tired of running?" the Hunter taunted.

Yes, daily. Frelia viciously squashed the thought.

Frelia ducked around the corner of a particularly ornate mausoleum at the same time one of the Hunter's flasks caught her boot. It erupted in white-hot flame, and Frelia immediately tugged it off and kept going, the toes of one foot squishing in the cold cemetery mud and the other boot throwing her off balance.

The statue she was looking for was just up ahead; another one of the Triad, this one large enough for an adult to slip under. Frelia shoved herself into the space between the divine sisters, her fingers curling fiercely around the chunk of bronze from another statue, and she waited.

The instant the Hunter rounded the corner, she pelted the hunk of bronze at his heart.

It struck true, slamming into his chest and breaking open his remaining flasks. He immediately began scrabbling at his smoldering clothes, yanking off his armored coat and pulling at the bandolier. But by then, Frelia had drawn her sword. She charged up the row of headstones, blade aimed right for his throat. He fell back, just out of range, and threw the shattered glass and burning potions straight at her. Frelia scuttled sideways like a drunken spider, leaving the flasks to smolder in the grass.

The following scuffle consisted of every nasty trick both hunter and hunted could think of, beginning with hair pulling and ending with

Frelia's arms curled around the Hunter's throat and the weight of her entire body behind them. She wrapped her legs around his abdomen like some kind of demented piggybacker and heaved, while the residual alchemist's fire that dribbled down his front burned through the cheap fabric of her trousers.

Frelia didn't realize she'd stopped breathing until the Hunter quit thrashing, and the graveyard was, once again, silent.

Carefully—deathly carefully—Frelia unwound her legs from around the Hunter, listening hard for his breathing in case it was just a feint. He remained stone solid and immobile, and so Frelia unwrapped her arms from around his neck, too. His body slid off hers and slumped to the muddy ground with a dull thud.

She paused a moment to slather mud across the alchemical burns on her thighs and calves, and then wincingly got to her feet again. She had no idea where her stupid boot was, and there were only a handful of healers in the city who wouldn't ask where she'd gotten alchemical-grade burns at this time of night. No, it would be better to limp back to the Cost Effectives, all the way across town, and have their healer patch her up.

And then make them move again.

Frelia constantly made the mercenary bands she ran with move at inconvenient times. This would be the fifth time in three months that a Bloodrune Hunter had found her—*her*, Frelia Valerius, not just 'some Kaldiri broad with a bloodrune.' *And,* Frelia thought dismally as she scooped up her blade from where it had fallen, *this time there's a dead Hunter for his mates to come sniffing around after.*

She beheaded the Bloodrune Hunter with several hacking, practiced swings. Overkill, maybe, but there could be no missteps. Leaving a Hunter alive would bring on a fate worse than death. The Valerius Bloodrune, etched into her hip like a red tattoo, twinged in what Frelia could almost say was satisfaction.

Maybe the Goddesses had a sense of humor, after all.

As she wiped down her blade on the Hunter's overcoat, Frelia sighed. She couldn't keep asking the Cost Effectives to move towns every time a Bloodrune Hunter found her. There were more of the damn things with each passing year and, between her bloodrune and their Captain's drinking debts, the Cost Effectives were running out of cities to run to.

Krolis? No. Canto, no. Skjöldr... no. Ascalon, definitely not.

She slumped down against another headstone, trying to regulate her breathing again. She wanted to cry, to scream, to punch a hole in the nearest mausoleum. And she wanted her thighs to stop burning so that she could limp across Norvegr with one fucking boot like a cur slinking home from a fight with a wolf, tail between its legs.

But mostly, Frelia just wanted a Goddesses-damned break.

"That too much to ask?" she muttered and, as she sheathed her sword again, her eye fell on yet another headstone across the way.

Quintus Viril.

Frelia froze, staring at the name for an absurd amount of time as her intoxicated mind tried to place it. Then it struck her over the head, and Frelia felt like an idiot.

The Silverwood Military Institute. She'd had no idea the headmaster's family was from Norvegr. Or, well, Gallus himself probably wasn't the headmaster anymore; he'd be truly ancient by now. But he had been in charge, when Frelia had gone to Silverwood.

Wait. *Silverwood!*

It was the Imperium's premier academic institution for those who wanted their kids to grow up killers. It was famously neutral in times of war, since it wouldn't do to alienate half your clientele, and was technically located on a swatch of land gifted from the Konstantin Barony to allow for that fact.

But more important than any of that, Silverwood was public. Its professors were highly visible, and there were never enough of them, if the rumors were anything to go by. Historically, the place had been staffed by old generals and retired royal advisors—both of which were in short supply, after the Tyrant's War.

She couldn't be attacked in the middle of the night and kidnapped by Bloodrune Hunters if an entire school's worth of folks were in the way, and would wonder where she'd gone the next morning. Not like a mercenary could. And she'd survived assassination attempts, Bloodrune Hunters, and two wars—surely teaching couldn't be that hard?

Silverwood, then. She would go to Silverwood, Goddesses help her. The Cost Effectives had more than enough swordsmen to make up for her absence, although none of them were former generals like she was. Tactics were never the Cost Effectives' strong suit, though; she usually got ignored if something was more complicated than "ambush from the high ground, you fucking *dorchyea!*".

Yeah... Silverwood. It was sounding better and better the longer she thought on it.

In the absence of the mead she'd been pouring out earlier, Frelia patted Quintus Viril's tombstone like a dog that had brought back a dead pheasant.

"Thanks, Viril. Sorry Cillian and I stole the headmaster's pocket watch that one time."

She left the Bloodrune Hunter's headless corpse fetched up against a headstone, his own head in his lap. The Wild Hunt could take him, for all Frelia cared.

CHAPTER TWO

IT HAD BEEN A month since Frelia's encounter with that Bloodrune Hunter in the graveyard, but, even through her exhaustion, Frelia knew.

The Silverwood Military Institute wasn't what it used to be.

The place had always held an austere grandeur in its sweeping, stone architecture and stately parapets, but these days it was more grandeur and less austere. Gilt shone in the sconce light, littering the hallways with glints of gold. The simple oak tables and chairs in the dining hall were gone, replaced by better versions in mahogany and ash. Instead of the quiet, beige floor tiles of the academic buildings, the floors were inlaid with mosaics of various monarchs and battles and that damn Volsinii fox. And everything was eye-wateringly crimson.

It stung, but no more than anything else Frelia had lost.

There was the quad that old Headmaster Viril had chased Cillian and Frelia across, the day that the former had cheated on his midterms, and the latter had gotten roped into the chaos. There were the tea gardens, and Thera's favorite old reading spot beneath the wooden gazebo. And there, out towards the lake, was the grassy expanse of lawn that the black magic study group had spread blankets out across when the weather was nice, where she and Vendrick had almost...

No. It was bad enough to be haunted by the ghosts of the Grimsdalr twins; Frelia wasn't going to haunt herself with the ghost of a man that, so far as she knew, was still alive.

"Madam?" called one of the students as she passed him on the quad. "Do you need help finding something?"

Frelia paused and glanced at the kid. He had a Volsinii accent, but that was no surprise. The winning side were likely the only ones with the money to send their kids to Silverwood at this point.

"Is the Headmaster's office still over the classrooms in Salonia Hall?" she asked.

The boy nodded. "Yes, do you need an escort or anything?"

"I've got it. Thanks." Frelia's hand reflexively went for her coin purse, but the student had already turned back to his friends.

She shook her head. *Kids.*

Though it was true she'd once been a Silverwood student herself, the closer Frelia drew to the headmaster's office, the more acutely she felt she didn't belong. She'd scraped her way back down the coast from Norvegr, and bartered a room at the cheapest inn in Silverwood Town last night with three hares she'd caught in the surrounding woods. She'd also convinced them to let her use the baths, and that had been an excellent choice, even if this turned out to be a horrible idea. There had barely been enough meat on the hares to convince the innkeeper to loan her clothes last night so that she could wash the ones she actually owned.

There had been nothing to be done about the reverse skunk stripe of black hair showing at her roots, though.

As Frelia hiked up the stairs to the headmaster's office in stolen boots and clothes well beyond mending, she drew on every inch of her childhood schooling. She'd been raised to be the Grand Duchess of Valerius Territory, for the Goddesses' sake. She could handle a damn teaching interview.

"Just a moment, madam," said an Imperial Watcher as she approached the Headmaster's office, and Frelia flinched instinctively. "Do you have an appointment with the Headmaster?"

"Didn't realize I needed one," Frelia lied coolly.

Of course she didn't have an appointment. That would have required putting her name on something and sending it ahead of her. She didn't have a résumé for the same reason, though some long-forgotten bit of her pride had insisted it was better to show up unannounced than with a chicken-scratch résumé and tattered clothes.

I am the Grand Duchess Valerius, I swear!

Right. That would go over well.

The Watcher sighed deeply. "May I have your name? I will inquire with the headmaster as to his schedule."

"Frelia Helm's Grace Valerius."

There was an enormous pause before the Watcher rapped on the door and announced the Headmaster had a visitor.

A Volsinii-accented voice that Frelia could have sworn she recognized called through the heavy wood: "Send her in, would you kindly?"

Frelia nodded to the Watcher, who was now holding open the door and looking deeply put out, and stepped through the threshold.

Only to stop dead at the sight of the man sitting behind the Headmaster's desk.

His hair was cut stylishly short these days, and he was so thin she almost wanted to demand what illness was wasting him to bone and sucking out what little color had lived in his fair skin to begin with. But those acid green eyes were as calculating as ever as they burrowed into her, and the small smirk that threatened to crack his mask-like facial expression was the same one that had teased her over alchemy homework and on the long walks to class.

"Valerius." There was no inflection in his voice. "It's been a minute."

What was he doing here? He was supposed to be glued to the Imperator's backside or something. Even during their days at Silverwood, he had known he was going to serve the Imperial Court as its Spymaster—nothing less, and nothing more—and it had almost hurt, to be so relegated to the sidelines before the game had truly begun.

The war had been different, though. He'd been an enemy general then, blowing up portions of her battalions with grey magic that left ozone in its wake and set her teeth on edge. Anxiety had always danced in her stomach at the thought of dueling him; mages' duels always came down to a split second. It had nothing to do with the charming, endearing letters she'd burned the day war was declared.

Absolutely nothing.

"Holy shit." Frelia stared at him in consternation. "Caecillion?"

It wasn't Vendrick who answered, but the man Frelia just now realized was standing at his elbow.

"Valerius," the interloper sneered, "I'm surprised you're not dead."

Markus della Luciana was tall and willowy, olive-skinned, and with the grey eyes and dark, curly hair that the entirety of his family seemed to have. He was dressed even more formally than Vendrick, a line of military medals across his left pectoral. Fury spiked in Frelia's stomach at the sight of not one, but two Queenmakers behind the scenes at Silverwood. Was nothing sacred anymore?

The mostly-healed alchemical burns on her legs throbbed. *You know the answer to that, Valerius.*

"Della Luciana," Frelia returned, swallowing her fury like a hot coal, "how are your brothers?"

As if she hadn't killed them both in the war.

Markus' smile tightened. "That's Lord della Luciana to you."

So he still wasn't the Duke of della Luciana Territory? Frelia found that cosmically hilarious.

"And additionally, he's the Count Caecillion," Markus added, glancing sidelong at Vendrick. "I don't know what backwater hovel you crawled from, but—"

"That will do, della Luciana." Vendrick sharply brought the conversation back around before it dissolved into further name-calling. "Valerius, to what do we owe this visit? I don't have your family name on our roster, so I presume it's not for a student?"

Oh, Saints, even the cadence of his voice was the same. Frelia was not prepared for this.

She folded her arms across her narrow frame. "I hear Silverwood needs a new swordmaster."

Silence passed over them, and it was hard to tell who looked more stunned—Vendrick, or Markus. At least the former didn't look disgusted.

Merciful Goddesses, this interview is so screwed.

"Even if we might consider Kaldiri dogs capable of teaching," Markus finally said, "we don't have your résumé."

"Della Luciana, you will remain civil, or I will conduct this interview myself."

Frelia and Markus both stared at Vendrick, who bore it coolly.

"You're not seriously considering hiring this..." Markus paused to find a word that wouldn't get him thrown from Vendrick's office. "...*woman?*"

Vendrick leveled him in a pointed look. "As opposed to whom, all our other distinguished candidates?"

Markus stared at Vendrick so long, Frelia realized that was probably a joke.

"Need I remind you," Markus said, in that harsh, sharp voice that was the equivalent of a Volsinii stage whisper, "she is the reason we lost half our darkbeast corps while taking Northern Volsinii?"

"Hardly," said Vendrick flatly. "I'm well aware of the battles I was in."

Frelia's smile grew tight. "You can just call me a garmur-killer, della Luciana. It's not an insult."

"Oh, honestly!" Markus looked like he didn't know whether to laugh or cry. "Headmaster, I must insist you throw this woman out."

"Your opinion has been noted." Vendrick reached for a spare bit of parchment.

"I will not participate in this farce, Caecillion!"

"By all means, don't," said Vendrick, and Frelia fought the urge to laugh. "And either see yourself to the training yard, where we shall join you in approximately twenty minutes, or send Lancemaster Sabine in your place."

Markus' jaw worked like there was something else he wanted to say, but after a moment, he simply threw up his hands and stalked from the office. The door slammed in his wake, leaving Frelia alone with Vendrick Caecillion for the first time in fifteen years.

She had no idea what to say.

"Have a seat, if you would," he said, and Frelia did so, her stomach churning. "And I apologize for della Luciana's behavior."

"Why?" Frelia couldn't help but ask. "You're not his mother."

"True," said Vendrick, and there was that smirk again, "but I am his boss. And I don't tolerate outright hostility amongst the faculty."

Frelia knew what that meant, alright. "There other Kaldiri working here?"

"A few," Vendrick said evasively, picking up a quill. "Now, your qualifications for the swordmaster position?"

"Graduate of the Silverwood Military Institute," Frelia rattled off, "veteran of the Tyrant's War, veteran of several mercenary groups, including the Cost Effectives and the Red Iron Gang, trained since birth in the old Kaldiri fashion."

Vendrick made notes on his parchment as Frelia's insides warred between her desire to piss off her former alchemy lab partner and to actually get this job. She never mentioned the postwar Northern Rebellion she'd waged alongside Cillian when talking to Volsinii clients, but always brought it up when talking to Kaldiri ones. Technically they were considered "northern Volsinii" now, but nobody Frelia knew actually used the term with anything but sarcasm.

If any of this showed on her face, Vendrick ignored it.

"And why have you come seeking this position?" he asked.

"Like I said." Frelia shrugged. "I hear you need a swordmaster, and I need a job. Seems like a match made in some kind of hell."

Surprisingly, Vendrick laughed, and glanced back up to meet Frelia's eye. Suddenly it was very warm in this office, and Frelia's war instincts screamed at her to run. She cursed every god she knew, blackly and in her mother tongue. Why was she still attracted to this vulture? It wasn't bloody fair.

"And what would you bring to Silverwood?" he asked, and she swore his voice had softened.

She had to poke the bear, put some distance between them again. "I'm the best the old Kingdom ever produced. I'm sure you remember."

"Again, I don't need reminded of battles I served in." Vendrick's smile suddenly didn't reach his eyes, but his voice was still too soft. "And are you prepared to teach at a Volsinii Institution, Valerius? This is no longer the Silverwood you might remember."

Frelia stiffened. As if she needed telling twice. "Are you prepared to let a Krakenguard teach your kids?"

And there it was. Everything that had ever come between them, and set them on their separate courses of destruction.

"Only if she's wise enough not to bring that up," Vendrick answered, and Frelia was both surprised and grateful for the honesty.

"I can't hide what I am, Caecillion." Frelia glanced down at her stolen boots. "But I've worked for plenty of Volsinii since the war, and kept my head."

Silence fell as Vendrick scratched notes across his parchment, and Frelia tried not to fidget. She was unused to sitting still for so long, unused to cushy, safe surroundings and laughter. Something had to go wrong, right? It always did. Maybe she ought to just start planning which direction to run when this went completely sideways.

"Are you prepared to submit to a practical interview?" Vendrick suddenly asked.

Frelia barely dared to believe it. "*Ja,* any time."

Vendrick rose to his feet like a shadow gathering in the corner of a hallway. "Follow me then, if you would."

***

The training grounds, at least, were blessedly the same. Nicer training weapons and sturdier dummies, but otherwise unchanged. Sand was sand, after all; blood was blood.

"I was beginning to wonder if you'd bother to show," Markus della Luciana called from the sparring circle.

Vendrick ignored him. "Grab a training weapon, if you would, Valerius."

A younger Frelia might have taunted Markus as she looked for a wooden sword she didn't hate the balance of. This older one didn't have the energy to shit-talk any more, least of all to someone barely worth the mud she scraped off her boots.

She took up across the sparring circle from Markus in middle guard, just like she had all those years ago as a student herself. Markus warily took up position across from her, his posture rigid and stiff in the Volsinii way.

Vendrick stood by with the evaluation form and a clipboard. "At your leisure, della Luciana."

Markus nodded to Vendrick like a sorely put-upon dinner party host, and then said, *"En garde!"*

"Hau," Frelia replied, and struck.

She was quick and she was strong; the beat parries and clash of blade-on-blade rang throughout the training courtyard with the steady rhythm of all her years of war. The practicum of swordplay had always interested Frelia far more than the psychology, but it was still all too easy to lead Markus through this duelists' dance.

She feinted and parried with practiced ease, batting away Markus' sword to come around to his now-unguarded side with alacrity. Her footwork brought her out of harm's way long before her sword did, and Vendrick eventually stopped tallying all the times that Markus should have been decapitated or run through, and just studied the duel unfolding before him.

Markus had always been a mage knight, with heavy emphasis on the mage, but his sword-work had always been passable in school. It had reportedly saved his hide more than once during the war when he'd over-cast or his spellbook had been torn from his grasp.

But Frelia still felt like the Master of Arms sparring with the lord's child.

Sweat was pooling at her brow, and Markus' face was drawn into narrow, angry lines. She saw him go for her knees, and snapped her practice sword towards his so fast that the wood splintered. She pressed the advantage, sweeping a leg beneath him quickly and violently.

Markus fell hard into the dirt, and recoiled at the splintered blade suddenly at his throat.

"Yield," Frelia bit out.

Markus stared up at her in disgust. "Well," he said flatly, "you remain competent, I suppose."

It was as close to a sign off as Markus della Luciana would ever give her.

"I gave up on trying to score her somewhere around ninety-six," Vendrick said.

One for every garmr she'd ever killed, by Cillian's reckoning. Huh. That was almost funny. Poetic, or something.

"Damn it all," Markus muttered, breathing heavily as he got to his feet. "Just get on with it, Caecillion."

"I see no reason *not* to hire her..." Vendrick's cadence cut off awkwardly.

Frelia tried not to roll her eye. "Beyond the fact that I was an enemy in the war?"

Vendrick's smile was apologetic. "Something like that, I suppose."

Frelia made sure her face was stonily impassive. "Well, if you're prepared to let a loser with a bloodrune teach your kids, I'll take the job."

Vendrick held out a hand. "Then you're hired."

Frelia drew in a deep breath. She'd suffered far worse. She shook his hand, mildly surprised when her own didn't come away bloody.

CHAPTER THREE

EVEN AS HE WENT over the new hire paperwork in his office—mercifully sans Markus della Luciana—Vendrick had a hard time keeping his eyes on the paper and not his brand-new swordmaster.

It had been years since any prominent Kaldiri knights had graced Silverwood's halls, let alone turned up after the war. A few were here as teachers, but most of the fallen kingdom's soldiers had either perished or vanished. Perhaps both.

Vendrick didn't believe in hope, not anymore, but there was no other word for the bubble that had been rising in his chest ever since she'd walked into his office. After all these years, all those failed chances to catch wind of her, had Frelia Valerius risen from her early grave?

It sounded too good to be true, which was why Vendrick had initially suspected a trap. But although the former Grand Duchess was riddled with visible scars, her hair bleached a skull-white blonde that contrasted heavily with the strip of inky black at her roots and washed out the fair skin of her round face, and wore a heavy black eyepatch over her left eye, she'd walked into his office like she belonged there and immediately cursed at him.

So if it wasn't Frelia, it was so good a facsimile that Vendrick probably wouldn't have known the difference anyway. The reality dug into his gut like tiny poisoned knives.

"I'm afraid your salary is mostly a stipend," Vendrick was saying at the compensation section, like he always did, "but room and board are covered by the Institute."

Frelia shrugged. "I don't need much."

"The teachers' dorm is located behind Atticus Hall," Vendrick added.

"I know."

Of course she did; she'd attended Silverwood as a teenager, same as him. But still, he had to do the spiel. It wouldn't do to set her up for failure by assuming she knew something she didn't.

"You're also welcome to redecorate, if you wish," Vendrick continued, as if Frelia hadn't spoken, "but do bear in mind where you are."

"I don't have any Kaldiri knickknacks," Frelia barked, "if that's what you mean."

Vendrick sighed, and set the contract down. Even fifteen years out from the Tyrant's War, and ten from the Northern Rebellion, it was sometimes hard for him to wrap his mind around the fact that the Kaldr of his youth existed no longer. Neither did its nobility, its way of life, and most of its culture.

He couldn't even begin to imagine how painful that must be.

"Are you certain you *want* to work here?" Vendrick asked, as gently as he dared.

Frelia stared for a moment like she couldn't decide how best to throttle him.

"Yes," she finally said, roughly. "Keep going."

"As a martial professor, you are expected to teach one pen-and-paper seminar a week, the rest practical."

"Fine."

"And you will be teaching all of the students, not merely one house. Though your homeroom will be the second year Violet Owls."

"The what?" Frelia's brow furrowed. "What happened to the Northern Kraken and Southern Strix?"

Vendrick paused, just barely long enough to draw attention to it. He'd gotten used to it in the years he'd been headmaster here, but in their haste to scrub all traces of Kaldr from existence, the Imperium had done away with even little things like the Silverwood houses' names—no Northern Kraken for the transported Kaldiri to call home, no Southern Strix for the Volsinii. Now Frelia had no king, no country, no family, not even her bloody Silverwood House.

It was no wonder the Kaldiri hated his people so much.

"There are three houses, currently," Vendrick said carefully. "The Red Eagles, Iron Cranes, and Violet Owls."

Frelia stared at him for so long that Vendrick half expected her to walk out on him again. He held his breath, wondering if he could get one of his black network agents on her tail fast enough for it to matter if she did bolt.

"Figures," she finally said.

"Beyond that, I recommend you familiarize yourself with your surroundings and fellow staff." He smiled, just a little. As much as he dared. "You may find some familiar faces."

He would send notes along to the Kaldiri professors, after their meeting here was concluded. They would see to their own. They always had.

"Classes begin for the fall semester next Wednesday," Vendrick added. "You are expected to comport yourself with the utmost professionalism, particularly while parents walk our halls."

Frelia visibly bristled, but all she said was, "One last thing. I'm not learning a whole new terminology system to teach these kids."

This time, it was Vendrick's turn to shrug. "Personally, I could care less whether the students call it *langenort* or *posta longa*, but recognize you will be painting a target on your back."

"You say that like there isn't already."

Vendrick's chest suddenly ached in a way it hadn't in many years. "Is there anything I should know?" he asked, unwilling to be afraid of the answer but dreading it all the same.

Frelia's eye dropped to where her hands rested on his desk. Her gloves were crisscrossed in gouges and the hems of her shirt cuffs were frayed. "Listen. Caecillion. Eh... Headmaster?"

Vendrick waved her off. "Caecillion is fine."

"Caecillion," Frelia repeated. "Listen. About my bloodrune."

"They're not illegal," Vendrick said at once. "And if anyone gives you a hard time, send them to me. I will personally set them straight."

It was the least he could do. And would probably protect the offending party more than the offended, all told.

"I'm not worried about shitty comments in the mess hall," Frelia said flatly. "I'm warning you about the Bloodrune Hunters. Did you hear about the one who was found decapitated in a Norvegr graveyard?"

"Nasty bit of business," Vendrick said. "I heard they never found who did it."

Frelia clicked her tongue and pointed to herself.

Vendrick's stomach fell three floors to the flagstones in the basement. "They fought you in a graveyard?"

"Didn't even let me finish libations."

Vendrick was disgusted and, more than that, he was furious. "Is nothing sacred?"

"Your Imperator scrapped the church," Frelia pointed out. "I think you know the answer to that."

A hundred reasons why sprang to mind, but Vendrick couldn't voice a single one. Not to a Kaldiri, and certainly not to this specific woman. He was left with nothing but manners and half-truths and dammit, everything had been so much simpler this morning before she'd walked back into his life.

"Regardless," he said, "it's not illegal to have inherited a bloodrune, and the Hunters, believe it or not, aren't sanctioned by the Imperium."

Frelia snorted. "Do they know that?"

"Additionally, they have *never* been permitted on Silverwood's grounds, and that isn't about to start today." Vendrick had always had some choice words (and occasionally, runes) for Bloodrune Hunters who had the audacity to hunt his students or staff. "So if one does bother you here, you are, of course, permitted to defend yourself."

"*Ja,* I wasn't asking."

Vendrick sighed. The longer he spoke with her, the more convinced he became that this was Frelia, alright. "You never do."

"*Don't.*"

He startled, and Frelia seemed surprised that she'd said that aloud.

"Let's just... keep this professional," Frelia added after an awkward moment of the both of them refusing to look the other in the eye. "*Ja?*"

"Right." It tasted sour in his mouth. "My apologies."

"Forget it," Frelia said quickly. "If there's nothing else, I'll take my room key and get out of your hair."

She held a hand out, and Vendrick stared at it as if he'd forgotten what words were.

There was so much more he wanted to ask. How had she gotten here, survived this long, avoided his black network spies ever since the Northern Rebellion? Was she married, was she a parent, was she happy? Had she thought of him at all, or had she pushed him from her mind as swiftly as she'd struck Markus with a blade?

Would she even answer him if he did ask?

"No," said Vendrick, misery like rot threatening to choke him. "That was all."

CHAPTER FOUR

THE STAFF ROOMS OF Silverwood were almost exactly as Frelia remembered the student dorms: standard issue oaken bed, desk, and dresser, and bookshelves built into the back wall beneath the window. Vendrick had rustled up some clean sheets for her before making himself scarce and, after making up her bed, Frelia had deposited her traveling pack on the dresser and kicked off her stolen boots. She shrugged off her road-worn armored coat and flopped down on what had to be the first proper mattress she'd seen in months.

Her back cried out at the fluffy surface, and Frelia realized that perhaps she was getting too old for the 'sleeping on the ground' shit that came with mercenary work. Maybe if she managed not to make a terrible professor of herself, she wouldn't have to anymore.

Sighing, Frelia stared up at her ceiling. It was getting on late afternoon, and, judging by the schedule Vendrick had given her, mealtimes were the same as they'd ever been at Silverwood. Whether they called the houses their rightful names or not, some things just never changed.

She wondered absently if the students were still expected to take on chores like kitchen duty, weapons maintenance, and stable cleaning, or if all the money the Imperium had clearly poured into this place suddenly made that beneath them. Money had to come from somewhere, after all, and they had nobility running the place again.

Nobility like Vendrick.

Goddesses, she was too old and too tired to think about Vendrick fucking Caecillion. Frelia only meant to shut her eye for a few minutes at most, but the next thing she knew, she was somewhere between a dream and a memory.

The students in the advanced black magic class usually met Thursday afternoons in the back of the library after class to help each other make sense of their coursework. But sometimes, in the spring when the weather was nice, they would take their books to the Silverwood lakeside, and spread out blankets across the grass.

It was where they were now, heads bent together over their notes and tossing theories and explanations back and forth. They helped each other solve equations and occasionally headed off each other's mental breakdowns with exams on the horizon.

Besides throwing in the occasional answer, Frelia remembered paying very little attention to any of that. The magic made sense to her, so much as it ever did, and so once she'd finished her homework, she'd spent most of her time doodling in the margins of her notebooks and trying not to stare at the boy beside her.

And he made it damn difficult. They'd all discarded their heavy uniform jackets ages ago, and Vendrick had rolled his shirtsleeves up to his elbows to avoid getting ink all over them. He smiled a lot more easily when he wasn't with Octavia Nova, and he'd pulled his long, mahogany hair into a messy bun at the crown of his head. Between the advanced black magic course and their alchemy class, Frelia had been seeing a lot more of him recently than she'd ever meant to, but she was struggling to continue coming up with reasons why that was a bad thing.

It wasn't a secret that, after graduation, Frelia would return to Valerius Territory to serve as its Grand Duchess while assisting her widowed father, and Vendrick would return to the imperial capital to serve as the royal family's Spymaster-to-be, alongside his father. They would perhaps run into each other at formal state occasions that both Prince Hägen and Princess Octavia attended, and exchange the occasional letter until that, too, became suspect.

It would make for a dismal romance.

"So how did you end up with an alkahest here?" Vendrick asked.

Frelia blinked a few times, startled out of her thoughts. Apparently, everyone else had left, leaving Frelia and Vendrick's notes spread across a borrowed blanket and the space between them crackling like lightning.

"That's not an alkahest," Frelia said, "it's just filtered aqua fortis."

Vendrick paused, his brow furrowed deeply above his thin nose. His hair was falling out of its bun at this point in the afternoon, hiding his eyes again. Frelia had to resist the urge to reach out and push it back.

"That's... how you write the symbol for aqua fortis?"

"Well how do you do it, Count Caecillion?"

"I'm not the Count yet." He made an embarrassed noise that didn't hide the blush creeping up his neck. "And like this."

He reached for her quill, idle beside her notes, and his hand brushed her knee as it passed. Even through her tights, it sent a bolt of something fierce and unfamiliar through her, and so Frelia rearranged herself so that her legs were folded beneath her uniform skirt.

He wrote the alchemical formula across the top of her notes in neat, spidery strokes, leaning into her personal space to get at the margin of her notebook. He smelled like woodsmoke and parchment, and Goddesses-dammit, was there anything unattractive about him?

Besides the whole Volsinii thing.

"That looks the same," she muttered when he set down her quill again.

"No, that looks like a formula. Yours looks like—oh." He cut himself off as he glanced back over to her. "You have, er." He paused, coughed, and started over. "There's something in your hair."

Frelia froze. Thera had done her hair this morning in two neat twintail braids that barely reached the nape of her neck—what in the hell could possibly have gotten stuck in it?

"Here, hold still," Vendrick said. "I've got it."

Frelia stared at his unbuttoned top button as he leaned in, and tried not to let her mind wander too far down his throat. A moment later he was back at a much more respectable distance, a pear blossom in his fingers.

"I didn't realize these were in bloom yet." Vendrick set the flower at the edge of Frelia's notebook. "We really are getting close to graduation, aren't we?"

It was hard to say which of them moved first, but suddenly Frelia was looking up at him, and Vendrick was looking down at her, and the world had ceased to move around them.

"One more round of exams." Frelia noticed Vendrick's eyes flick downwards to watch her lips move. "Then we're all back home."

There was a version of this story where he kissed her then. Where they forgot their alchemy notes and spent a while just like that, learning exactly how their mouths fit together beneath the dappled spring sunshine beside Lake Silverwood.

But it was the version where they weren't Frelia Helm's Grace Valerius and Vendrick Caecillion, and so what actually happened was that Octavia had shouted for him from somewhere across the field, Vendrick had shut his eyes and cursed softly, and then they both packed up their things and did not speak of it again.

The following week, Vendrick sat beside Markus in the black magic study session, and Frelia tried not to feel hurt about it. The week after that, he stopped coming at all, claiming there was simply too much political business with his imminent return to Ascalon.

Frelia hoped he'd fail his damn exams, the bastard.

She was startled awake by heavy, pounding footsteps in the hall, and the lengthened shadows across the room announced that the sun had fallen low in the sky.

"Helheim," Frelia muttered as she fought the creaking in her bones to sit up.

She didn't need to be thinking about this, let alone *him.* Silverwood was already making her soft, and she hadn't even taught a damn class yet.

Voices washed by her door, no doubt on their way to dinner in the mess. Frelia knew she ought to get up and go, herself—particularly since she didn't have a single gold to her name to find dinner elsewhere if she missed the mealtime—but she remained fixed on the narrow bed, staring at her dirty stockings like they held a single answer.

CHAPTER FIVE

THE SILVERWOOD CAFETERIA WAS, like the sparring grounds and the mealtimes, the same as it had been before the war. The furniture had fewer nicks in it, sure, but there was only so much one could dress up communal benches and the long, thin tables. Frelia mused, privately of course, that it was still set up Kaldiri-style. Probably just because the lack of chairs granted some extra space, but it was another tally in the "Goddesses might have a sense of humor after all" column.

"Excuse me, madam?" came a disembodied voice. "May I see your identification, please?"

Frelia sighed and dug around in her coat pockets for a moment before producing her room key. All the Silverwood dorm keys were the same—brass monstrosities on a keyring from which also dangled a charm of the Silverwood Crest. Frelia held it up so that the woman seated on a stool just beside the cafeteria door could see it clearly.

"Erm," said the woman, who could only be the on-duty monitor. "That's not quite what I meant."

"I'm the new swords professor," Frelia said, stowing her key again. "I don't think they've had time to make my papers yet."

The monitor's lips pursed—no doubt at Frelia's Kaldiri accent—but she seemed to decide it wasn't worth the trouble, and waved her through.

Frelia kept her face like stone as she trekked across the enormous dining hall. All around her, students and professors bustled about, greeting friends from last year and new ones yet-to-be.

She fell into line, and felt an old pang of loneliness in her stomach. It was such a constant feeling that she typically didn't even notice it anymore, but something about Silverwood twisted the knife. She had never stood *alone* in the cafeteria lines, before. Cillian ought to be talking her ear off about something, or she ought to be comparing bruises with Thera. This... emptiness was uncomfortable. More so than all the emptiness that had come before.

She tried to push it down further as she passed the chalkboard menu on the wall. Garlic-and-herb fish sauté, mixed greens salad, cioppino with freshwater mussels and cod, sourdough rolls.

Fucking Volsinii, all of it. Where was the venison, the hunter's stews, the Emmentaler? Silverwood was lakeside, sure, so there had always been fish on the menu, but for the Saints' sake, was it too much to ask for a damn *varenyky*?

Frelia tried not to audibly sigh as she asked the chefs for the cioppino. Of course it was too much. Anything Kaldiri was 'too much.'

Chatter began in the line behind her as a chef handed her a bowl and silverware. She heard the phrase 'northern Volsinii' more than once, and it took every ounce of common sense she had not to snap at the students behind her. They were kids. They didn't know better.

Or so Frelia had to tell herself to keep from going insane.

Vendrick—despite her best efforts, Frelia still thought of him as simply 'Vendrick'—had asked if she were certain she wanted to work here. It wasn't a stretch to say Silverwood was by far her best option at this point, but everything about the place just fucking *hurt*. And she resented that, after all these years of never exchanging a word, Vendrick could still somehow calculate her reactions with infuriating accuracy.

Was she that predictable? That had to be it; it wasn't like he *knew* her. Not anymore.

Eyes dug into her back as she headed towards the professors' table, and whispers about her accent, her eyepatch, her sword, burrowed into her ears. It inevitably pissed her off, but at least it was better than the emptiness.

It was nearing the end of the dinner hour, so the professor's table was mostly empty. A few folks gave her the side eye as she approached, and just as Frelia was about to fling the damn fish stew over someone's head and go back to mercenary work after all, she spotted the back of a familiarly tailored jacket.

She did a double-take, not trusting her own sight. But she'd know that style of mage's coat anywhere, and even if it were forest green instead of cleric white, she had spent a good chunk of the war staring at it.

A former cleric would probably be a safe dinner companion. At least in the sense of, they'd also lost something deeply important to them and therefore wouldn't side eye her like these Volsinii. Good enough for government work, as the Volsinii said.

"This seat taken?" she asked as she skirted around the edge of the table.

"Oh, I er, beg pardon," said the man wearing the green cleric's robe, and then he looked up. "It's—"

And suddenly Frelia was staring down the bespectacled gaze of Edmund Blightsen.

He was a kind-hearted, portly man, fair-skinned and balding, but with an impeccable sense of style, especially for a professor's budget. Here, at least, was one person who would understand the razor's edge the losing side walked, and the useless fury building in Frelia's gut. Edmund had been the son of the Kaldiri king's seneschal, once upon a time, and he was also the only person Frelia knew with a penchant for apologizing to inanimate objects. She hadn't spoken to him in years, though she'd heard through the grapevine that he had survived the Battle of Skjöldr.

He stared back at her for a moment before he took off his glasses, cleaned them on a fistful of his robe, and then jammed them back on his face.

"Frelia?" he asked, quiet and incredulous.

"Hey, Edmund." Frelia tried to smile, but her mouth didn't seem to work right. "Been a while."

She barely had the time to set down her tray before she was enveloped in a crushing hug—or at least as crushing as Edmund could muster. She stiffened at the casual contact and unannounced affection.

"Oof!" Frelia grunted, though she did sling an arm around Edmund's shoulders. "You only get this one because you probably thought I was dead."

"I did! What are you doing here?"

"Haven't you heard?" Frelia said. "I'm the new swordmaster."

Edmund let go of her to rub at his eyes, and then clean off his glasses again. "Well, Saints." He threaded his glasses more carefully behind his ears this time. "Your students will never know what hit them."

The dissonance of sitting down to a meal in the Silverwood cafeteria had been bad enough before she'd run into another of the old Kaldiri king's guard—better known as the Krakenguard. Now the world felt like it was spinning off its axis, like she were drunk, or worse.

"How long have you been teaching here?" Frelia asked as she poked at the cioppino with her spoon.

"Just about fourteen years," Edmund said with forced lightness.

Well, shit. Frelia knew Edmund had been captured when Skjöldr fell, but that would mean he came here after he was released. No wonder he'd never showed up to fight in the Northern Rebellion. Frelia tried not to hold that against him.

Much.

Edmund noticed her silence, though. Of course he did. The seneschal's son had learned to read moods before words on a page, Frelia was pretty sure.

"I'm... so sorry about Cillian, Frelia."

It was still a javelin to the gut, even after all this time. A physical ache where her best friend and unblood brother should be.

"Don't be," Frelia muttered. "You didn't do shit."

Edmund, after all, hadn't started the Tyrant's War.

"And Thera, too," he added, oblivious to the murder he was committing. "I... well, I can't imagine."

"*Don't.*" It came out more sharply than Frelia intended.

It was a second war wound, the loss of her unblood sister. In a kinder world, Thera would have married Prince Hägen ten years ago, and Frelia would have been teaching their little ones how to play knights and dragons between meetings at the summer moot. Instead, Frelia had been sleeping in the dirt and killing people for gold, panicking whenever the telltale Valerius black began to show through her blonde hair dye.

The Imperium had a lot to answer for, and it was a bitter existence to know they never would.

"I'm sorry," Edmund said again, and it grated on Frelia's ears. "I just... I never told you."

A lot of people had never told Frelia they were sorry for her losses, but that didn't mean she wanted to hear it.

"So why does it matter now?" she asked, something high and tight in her throat.

"I..." Edmund swallowed audibly. "I lost them too."

Frelia supposed that was fair enough, but she didn't want to talk about the Grimsdalr twins' ghosts here, where she'd only ever known them alive.

"So what's Silverwood like now?" she asked in a blatant attempt to change the subject. "Besides offensively Volsinii."

Edmund's laugh was just as gentle as she remembered. "Maybe don't say that so loudly," he said, glancing pointedly down the table to where a cluster of other professors sat. "But all in, mum's the word. We don't give away that we served in the Tyrant's War, and nobody asks us about it. We can't hide that we're from Kaldr, though. No need to bother."

"The accent gives it away," Frelia agreed, staring moodily into her soup. "And I already warned Caecillion I'm not relearning an entire school of thought for these kids."

"I doubt he'd have asked you to," Edmund said. "He's not the sort."

Silence fell, and Frelia glanced up to find Edmund staring at her with such kindness that she felt the driving urge to punch him.

"I'm sorry." Edmund reached out to squeeze her hand. "I'm sure it can't be easy on you, seeing him here."

Frelia was suddenly acutely aware that one of the very few upsides to all your friends either dying in a hopeless war or scattering to the winds after surviving was that nobody said shit like that to her anymore. She didn't know how to handle it, any more than she knew how to handle the reality of what Edmund had experienced.

He'd been at those black magic study sessions, after all.

"Stop apologizing," she snapped, jerking her hand away.

Edmund's smile wavered. "You know I can't do that. Too much of the world is broken."

"*Ja,* well that doesn't mean you're responsible," Frelia said. "Or that I want to hear it."

They ate in tense silence for a long moment, and Frelia choked down a few more of the slimy mussels in the stew. She knew she shouldn't turn down food when it was offered, but Goddesses above and below, she hated the texture. She wanted something strong to bite into, the way food was supposed to be.

But Frelia also knew that Edmund wasn't going to break the silence on his own, so she grabbed for the first inane thing she could think of. "Do you know where I could get my hands on some toiletries?"

Edmund took a small sip of water. "The marketplace in town should have them cheaper than the commissary here. Why?"

"I am in desperate need of a shower."

Edmund laughed a little. "And for your, er, predicament, I take it?" He gestured to the crown of his balding head.

Frelia sighed. She'd known she needed to re-bleach her stupid hair for a while now, but she couldn't bring herself to do it. Not again, not now that she was back at Silverwood and apparently staying.

"Do you think it'll matter?" she asked instead.

Edmund paused. "What do you mean?"

"If I let it grow black again." Frelia poked at something she hoped was a piece of fish. "Do you think it'll just bring the Hunters down on my head?"

Edmund studied her for a moment. "I think," he finally said, "that if it does, Caecillion will have plenty to say about it."

"Oh, shut the fuck up." Frelia rolled her eye and resolved to look like a backwards skunk for a while.

"Language," Edmund said mildly. "Sorry, I know how you are, but we're supposed to maintain a certain façade in front of the students, and I doubt you want to be fired on your first day."

"Do you see any students paying attention to me?" Frelia gestured vaguely across the cafeteria.

"Unfortunately," said Edmund, "that doesn't mean they're not listening."

That reminded her. "Caecillion said I'll have the second year Violet Owls. Do you know which ones those are?"

"Their table is in the middle." Edmund pointed towards the room behind him. "The kids with the purple uniform accents. I don't know too many of them, offhand—I have the Iron Cranes, you see—but their prefect for the second year, is. Um."

He stopped.

"Their prefect for the second year *is...?*" Frelia prompted.

Edmund set down his fork and seemed to mentally brace himself for the next words out of his mouth.

"Faustine della Luciana."

Frelia's spoon clattered so loudly against her tray, several people turned to stare. "Markus della Luciana has a child at Silverwood?"

She hadn't thought her graduating class was getting that old, but she hadn't exactly sent her Volsinii classmates Yule cards lately. Or the Kaldiri ones, for that matter.

Edmund shook his head quickly. "Not Markus." He glanced over his shoulders, and then said, very quietly, as if he could summon the man by his nom de guerre alone: "Ironfang."

Cold dread sluiced down Frelia's spine. If there was one being in this postwar hellscape that Frelia Helm's Grace Valerius despised, it was General Ironfang della Luciana. He was the reason why the Northern Rebellion had failed, why Frelia had lost Cillian, why she no longer had the title of Grand Duchess, and why she had spent most of the Tyrant's War fighting monstrous creatures from the depths of Helheim, or so the legends went.

And Frelia was supposed to teach his daughter how to fight? As though the girl's father hadn't murdered half the people Frelia had ever held dear? It had to be some sick cosmic joke, and Frelia would be damned if she passed on the hard-earned skills of the Valerius family to General Ironfang's daughter.

Then again, if she didn't, she might as well slip out of her room tonight and leave her brand new key on the desk. But that would mean more hard nights on the road, more skinny hares poached in forests and charred over fires, more Bloodrune Hunters turning up in places they didn't belong.

Even if it was Volsinii, the cioppino was the first hot meal she'd had in weeks that didn't taste like game meat.

Frelia whipped her head around, zeroing in on the teenagers with purple uniform accents across the dining hall. If Ironfang's daughter were the prefect, she would have—ah, there it was, a vibrantly violet half-cloak thrown over her left shoulder.

She was a slight girl of maybe fifteen, with wildly curly brown hair that was valiantly attempting to escape the chignon she'd pulled it into. She had the same olive-toned skin that most Volsinii did, but other than the grey eyes that Frelia knew her father also had, Faustine barely looked like the bastard at all.

"Do you, erm." Edmund winced at himself. "Want an introduction?"

"No, I do not want to meet Ironfang's fucking daughter," Frelia hissed between her teeth.

Something hard fell across Edmund's round face. "The girl has done nothing wrong, Frelia."

"I know that," Frelia barked.

"So it really isn't fair to judge her by her bloodline," Edmund continued, as though Frelia hadn't spoken. "You know she had nothing to do with—"

Frelia slammed her hands on the table and stood to go. "Thank you for the lecture, Brother Blightsen, but I'm too old to be told to behave around the fucking winning side."

Edmund recoiled as though she'd struck him. It was a low blow, and they both knew it, but it was too late to take it back. Frelia might have grown up with Edmund Blightsen, once upon a very long time ago, but she barely recognized him now. Who was this man who told her to watch her language with an affected accent and taught at a Volsinii institution as if he hadn't bled beside her in the Krakenguard? As if the Imperator hadn't dismantled the Church of the Triad at the very first chance he got, and stripped him of his sacred order.

Fucking hell, even Vendrick Caecillion seemed to get it more than Edmund did, but Frelia shoved that thought into the furthest corner of her mind.

"I'm not a cleric anymore," Edmund finally managed, looking like a kicked dog.

Frelia resisted the urge to tear her hair out. *Goddesses-fucking-dammit, Frelia, you had* one *possible friend and you've gone and ruined it.* Why was nothing the damn same anymore?

"And I'm not a fucking duchess," she said, instead of any of that. "What's your point?"

Edmund's jaw opened and shut a few times, but he said nothing, and looked back down to his dinner. Disgust pooled in Frelia's gut, and she stalked from the room, eyes digging into her back as she went.

CHAPTER SIX

THE SECOND YEAR VIOLET Owls were whispering amongst themselves when Frelia strode into her homeroom the following Wednesday morning. The classroom was as eerily familiar as the rest of Silverwood: the same flagstones and plush rugs with the school crest, same heavy wood tables and chairs set up two-by-two. There were seven students in all, on Frelia's homeroom roster, plus several dozen more across her other classes. She was somehow going to need to remember all their names.

But she could do this, right? Frelia didn't get nervous, least of all about wrangling kids. There had to be another explanation for the roiling in her gut.

"I am Frelia Helm's Grace Valerius," she announced as she strode up the rows, and silence fell almost immediately, "to whom you will refer as nothing less than Professor."

It might help her get used to the concept.

She reached the massive teacher's desk, and turned to face her students. They stared at her with polite attention, though some looked a little taken aback. Had these kids never seen a mercenary before?

"I will be your swordmaster this year," Frelia added. "Good morning, Violet Owls."

"Good morning, Professor Valerius," they chorused.

Good. At least they had some manners.

Frelia pulled her class roster out from her armful of notes—most of which were on loose paper that she'd wrapped together with a spare bootlace—and began the attendance rundown. Many of the students had Volsinii surnames, but there was a Free City name or two, and one that was definitely Kaldiri.

But then Frelia arrived at della Luciana.

She announced the family name and glanced up sharply. Her face was stone as the teenage girl from the cafeteria raised her hand and said, "Present."

Fucking *Helheim*, Frelia really was about to teach Ironfang's crotch goblin how to duel, wasn't she? And a baby Secundus and Ossani, too. The Goddesses had to be mocking her.

"You will attend this seminar every Monday beginning next week," Frelia said once attendance had finished, "and spend the rest of the week in practicum. I expect everyone in the training grounds armed and ready when class begins, or it will be laps for all of you. Am I understood?"

Tittering spilled across her classroom. She caught the words 'Northern Volsinii' more than once.

"*Ja*," Frelia barked, rolling up the sleeves of the new blouse Markus had all but forced her to purchase (with an advance on her salary, no less). "I would be from Kaldr, if it were still f—" She just barely caught herself. "—even here."

The Violet Owls seemed surprised she'd admit it so openly. It was written in the lines of their young faces, the horrified looks in their eyes. Frelia had to hold back the rueful smirk threatening to break across her face.

"And *yes*," she added, "I'm aware I only have one eye. Now, is there anything else you wanted to whisper about?"

"No, Professor Valerius," her class chorused.

"Good," said Frelia. "With that out of the way, I have an announcement. I will be spending tomorrow and Friday dueling each of you."

"You will?" said a student with shaggy blond hair, the one who had answered to Christel Vilulf.

"Well *ja*." Honestly, this was so basic. "Can't teach you without learning what you already know. Sign-ups will be on my desk after class. You will have a free period, minus your duel. Understood?"

Nods, and a few "Yes, madam"s.

"Good. Now, take out your notes. We've work to do."

Her students took surprisingly furious notes, given that the only things new to them should have been the terms. Frelia spent the rest of the period explaining the basics of swordsmanship, outlining the three basic kinds of attacks, the various cuts, parries, and ripostes. Frelia wrote the undoubtedly unfamiliar Kaldiri words on the chalkboard, and occasionally drew an actual blunt sword to illustrate some mechanic or other.

It was fine; this was fine. She had all year to break them of their bad habits.

***

As the students and the professors settled into their first day rituals, Vendrick had an important one of his own:

Security detail.

A paranoid man by both nature and nurture, Vendrick saw to the defenses at the Silverwood Military Institute himself. From the locks on each student dormitory door, to the fences surrounding the practice fields, to the siege-defensible stone walls that surrounded the main campus, nothing escaped Vendrick's scrutiny.

Nothing.

It was also why he knew the day laborers repairing the archery field fence were running behind schedule by several days, and that the repairs to the bailey had been thousands of gold over budget, but at least they were done. And the alumni autumnal donation campaign would most likely cover the unexpected expenses. At the very least, the Ossani and Secundus families would attempt to one-up each other's generosity. Anything from non-noble student families would cover the rest.

Probably, anyway. It would do as a plan for now.

It was rare these days that Vendrick traveled campus with his spellbook, but it thumped familiarly against his hip now as he made his way across Iuvenlis Quad. He had long since memorized the most salient runes in his repertoire, but he was a grey mage by practice and nature. He would probably always require the rune diagram in front of his nose to make sense of white or black magic.

And warding was very much a white magic. Boons and banes always were.

The main Silverwood Gate was an ostentatious thing of wrought iron and stone. When Vendrick had first assumed the headmaster's mantle, it hadn't actually been worth its weight in metal, so far as defenses went. It was pretty, and that was about all.

It had been the first thing he'd gotten fixed, right after he'd fired the Saints-awful cook who had been there when Vendrick himself had been a student.

"Good morning, Headmaster," called the Watcher on duty at the main gate. He had a dusting of freckles beneath a ginger fringe badly in need of a trim.

"Good morning, Dolfi," Vendrick returned. At least, he was pretty sure that's who this was. "How's the morning watch?"

"Eight of the morning's watch, and all is well," the Watcher said automatically. He said nothing about his name, so Vendrick figured he'd been correct. "But what brings you out here this morning, Headmaster? Isn't it the first day of classes?"

"Indeed," Vendrick said.

The plinths that held up the gate columns came nearly up to Vendrick's shoulders, and Vendrick was not a short man. He could make a fool of himself attempting to climb it in a waistcoat and formal trousers—

Or he could simply cast magic.

He slipped his spellbook out of its holster, holding the heavy tome open in his left hand. He flipped through the pages with easy familiarity, looking for his warding runes. He organized everything first by cluster, then by first stroke, which was a great help in battle when one needed to improvise on the fly. Out of battle though, Vendrick could simply take his time.

"Err, Headmaster?" Dolfi put forward after a long moment. "Is everything alright?"

Vendrick didn't look up from his work. "Just fine."

The man shifted nervously from foot to foot in Vendrick's periphery, his halberd shaking ever-so-slightly. "You're not... going to cast something, are you?"

This time Vendrick did shoot a look Dolfi's way. "Why else would I have my spellbook, man?"

"Well, see, that's my point," Dolfi said. "Technically you're not supposed to have that, and I should be confiscating it and reporting you to Captain della Luciana."

Vendrick disguised his knee-jerk eyeroll by craning his neck to look at the main gate's keystone several dozen feet overhead. "The captain is well aware I do this every year."

Vendrick drew in a breath and familiar, arcane energy jumped to his right hand. It crackled like lightning in the early morning sun, dangerous and intense. He raised it to the level of his eyes with the poise of a maestro, and then began to draw a rune with the purple light.

"Oh," said Dolfi, drawing the word out. "You're warding it."

The rune wasn't complex, with the diagram right in front of him. Vendrick made quick work of its twisted arms and jagged turns, completing the ward rune with a flourish. The magic pulsed before his eyes for a moment, and then the matching rune on the keystone began to glow, as well.

"That will do." Vendrick snapped his spellbook shut, and began to pass under the gate again. "Thank you, Dolfi."

"You know, Headmaster," the Watcher began what probably passed for 'thoughtfully' from him, "you re-draw those every year, but nothing ever happens."

Vendrick spared Dolfi a glance over his shoulder, waiting for that remark to sink in. When it clearly didn't, Vendrick said, "Exactly," and continued back towards campus.

The ward runes on the eastern, western, and southern gates went by in much the same way, although the southern gate simply led to the training grounds and thus didn't have a Watcher on duty to pepper him with questions.

And they always did, without fail. Vendrick would find it annoying, if he didn't know better. He was the former Imperial Spymaster, a Count with an immaculate Senate record, and his late father had been a personal friend of Ironfang's. By all accounts, if anyone had the right to cast a very obvious ward around the Silverwood Military Institute, it was Vendrick Caecillion, even before he'd become the Headmaster.

And yet, Markus fought him on it every year.

It's a waste of your time, he'd said at their security meeting last week, just like he did every year. *A waste of our resources, and a waste of thought, honestly. You know nothing ever happens here.*

Your opinion has been noted, Vendrick had returned cooly, just as *he* did every year. *And I shall continue to run this school and safeguard its occupants however I see fit.*

It was so much fuss over a bit of light spellwork. That alone would make Vendrick suspicious, but given who was making it, Vendrick upgraded his response to wary. Markus della Luciana may have been one of Princess Octavia's Queenmakers, once upon the Tyrant's War, but that didn't mean Vendrick had ever trusted the man.

Vendrick's little sister's voice drifted across the back of his mind: *Well, you don't trust anyone.*

And for good reason, he told it. Trust was a good way to get something broken—limbs, regents, said trust itself—and his little sister was lucky she found deception tiresome, or he wouldn't trust her, either.

He'd ruthlessly and unceremoniously rebuilt the Caecillion family black network after his father died, and a few of Vendrick's spies were at Silverwood, posing as staff. The rest were scattered across the Imperium, bringing news of the world beyond to the spider sitting in the middle of his ever-expanding web of contacts.

And still, there was too much Vendrick didn't know. He couldn't piece together why Markus cared whether the school was warded, and by extension why that would matter to Ironfang, so seated on the Imperial Throne and with not one, but two, of his children in residence at Silverwood. Vendrick couldn't say what it was that drew Ironfang's delegates to Silverwood every year for Yule, either. A general merciless enough to become Imperator didn't get there by accident, and Silverwood wasn't technically a Volsinii institution. It stood on sovereign territory gifted four hundred years ago from the Konstantin Barony, and existed as a sort of no-man's-land between countries. There would be little point in the Imperator acknowledging the institute beyond a gesture of goodwill towards his future military strategists and generals.

All of this led Vendrick's mental wanderings, as ever, back around to the Unseen.

The best word he had for them was 'cult,' although it wasn't the most useful in polite company. That the Church of the Triad's three major Goddesses had shifted to other, singular churches was not surprising—it wasn't as if worship had merely stopped when the conglomerate church had been dissolved. Devotees of Lady Daybreak and Lady Twilight were of little concern to Vendrick; those Goddesses were largely benign.

It was the ones who worshipped Lady Midnight that worried him.

Tradition painted her as the goddess of endings, a vengeful deity whose wrath would end the world. In kinder ages, she had been depicted as simply the natural end, without which life holds very little purpose.

But the fact that the brutal warlord who had become Imperator worshipped her made Vendrick figure it wasn't natural endings that drew him in. Particularly since the first thing Ironfang had done upon taking office was disband the Church of the Triad, defrock its clerics, and proclaim his patronage of the Unseen Church in downtown Ascalon rather loudly. A fair number of senators, predictably, had followed suit.

So. Volsinii had a doomsday cultist for an Imperator, several more in the Senate, and Vendrick was stuck at Silverwood. Fantastic, truly. Definitely where he'd wanted to be at this point in his life.

It was the better option, the little voice in the back of his head where his conscience had once lived reminded him.

Better, sure, but not good.

His warding brought him to the edge of Lake Silverwood, where it jutted up against the practice fields. Across the water, Vendrick could make out the edges of Silverwood Town, its docks shining with lights even at this hour of the morning. Fishmonger superstition, or so he'd been told the only time he'd asked.

Ghosts can't sneak up on you if there's a fire burning.

The water was a natural bulwark, given the size of the lake, but Vendrick still drew a rune on the rocky shoreline anyhow. It took him a moment to find it, since the large boulder he typically used had apparently been shot by a stray ballista shot last spring and moved dozens of feet forward.

It nearly touched the water, now, and several gulls startled off its summit as Vendrick approached. He drew his spellbook and began to cast the ward rune again, purple, arcane light blooming at his fingertips.

The rune in the boulder responded in kind, glowing brightly against the grey slate, and by the time Vendrick had finished, the gulls had returned to their perch with prey in their neck pouches.

He watched them crack clamshells against the boulder and swallow the innards for a moment, and then departed for the archery practice field to see about progress on the fence.

The gulls left a growing pile of shells in his wake.

CHAPTER SEVEN

THE FOLLOWING MORNING, FRELIA arrived at the training ground to discover that several geese had decided the nearby brush was prime waterfront property. They snarled at her presence like dogs guarding the King of Kaldr, and Frelia stared down their beady, black eyes with distaste.

She had served, in no particular order, as a general (twice), a Grand Duchess, a mercenary, and a garmr-killer. She was not stupid enough to pick a fight with a goose, least of all the ones that lived around Lake Silverwood.

With a wary eye on the nearest of the devils, Frelia crept across the sandy training ground as quietly as she could. The geese hissed in cacophony, but seemed reluctant to leave their nests. That was fine. She could work with that.

Frelia reached the shed that housed the racked training weapons, and loaded herself up with an armful of wooden instruments. *Rapiers, sabers, lance for me... anything else?* Her eye fell on the practice shields, racked on the wall of the small shed, and her gut twisted.

I should probably...

No. She'd deal with shields in the advanced class, or something. She couldn't avoid teaching the kids how to fight with sword and shield eventually, but she didn't have to deal with it today.

She scrawled a quick note—*Training grounds infested with geese. Sword duels to be in Iuvenlis Quad at the same times. Professor V*—and slipped back outside. She shut the shed door behind her with a foot, and surveyed the grounds again.

Dozens of beady, passerine eyes stared at her, and Frelia felt the hair on the back of her neck stand on end. But her bloodrune stayed silent at her side, and so she drew in a deep breath, cracked her neck, and took off running.

The old alchemical burns on her thighs throbbed, although they were mostly scars, now. Frelia managed to get across the sand and slam the gate to the training grounds shut before anything came flying after her.

She left her sign on the door, and hoped word would spread between the kids and they'd all show up where they were supposed to be relatively on time.

She doubted it, but she hoped. *Fucking geese.*

Frelia set off at a brisk pace towards Iuvenlis Quad. The bells were already ringing the hour, damn it all. In the back of her mind, Frelia wondered where the hour even tolled from, any more. In her day, the bells had been atop the chapel, but what good was a chapel without a Church of the Triad? There were no clerics to keep it.

"Going somewhere with those, Valerius?" came a cool voice from over by her blind side.

Frelia glanced sharply left, only to find Markus della Luciana in full Watcher armor striding her way. His circular, segmented steel breastplate gleamed in the morning sun, and the heavy leather strips on his sword belt thumped against his kilt as he scurried along. He was very clearly trying not to jog to keep up with her, so Frelia increased her pace.

"*Ja,*" she called back over, "Iuvenlis Quad."

"You are not authorized to carry a weapon anywhere beyond the training ground," Markus snapped.

"And my classroom," Frelia reminded him. "However, the training ground is infested with geese and I don't have a death wish."

Markus blinked at her. "It's what?"

"There are geese," Frelia said again. "Nesting in the brush."

"Oh." Markus looked like he wanted to keep arguing with her, but for as incompetent a Queenmaker as he had been, he wasn't a complete idiot. "You still should have cleared the change in rooms with facilities."

"I wish I'd had the time," Frelia lied. "My class is starting."

"Professor!" came a small voice from behind them.

Frelia turned to see one of her Violet Owls hustling towards her—the farmhand-sturdy girl Frelia refused to believe was fifteen. What was her name again?

"Ja?" Frelia called back.

"Do you want help carrying those to the quad?" the girl asked.

Frelia glanced down to her armful of wooden training weapons. "Couldn't hurt."

She passed a few of the swords over to—*Karina!* That was her name—and looked back to Markus. "Do I report the geese to you, or facilities, or... I don't know, the Volsinii Bureau of Waterfowl?"

Karina giggled, and Markus' face pinched into something vaguely resembling a shrew. "The facilities department will do."

"Great," Frelia said. "Will do after my actual job."

"Is there a Volsinii Bureau of Waterfowl?" Karina asked.

Frelia shrugged. "Wouldn't surprise me."

"No," Markus said crisply, "there is not. And kindly do not injure anyone in the quad, Valerius."

Frelia pulled up short to shoot Markus an incredulous look. "Do you expect these kids to learn sword fighting without bruising?"

"I expect," Markus said, "competent teaching."

Frelia refused to grimace as he peeled away towards the library.

She and Karina walked in silence for a few more minutes before the girl said, "Um, Professor? Captain della Luciana is mean. As in, *really* mean."

"I noticed," Frelia said flatly.

"Professor Ossani says not to pay him too much attention," Karina added. "The Captain is, um..."

Frelia knew where that sentence ended, alright: "Upset about not being the duke and making it everyone else's problem?"

Karina blinked. "Yeah, how'd you know?"

Frelia was not dealing with politics today. "Lucky guess."

They arrived in Iuvenlis Quad and Frelia commandeered one of the benches to serve as a makeshift weapons rack. She leaned the sabers and lance against it, then turned to Karina for the rapiers as well.

"Which ones are we using, professor?" Karina asked.

"All of them," Frelia said. "But we'll start with the rapier."

Karina very quickly proved herself two left feet with a rapier, and only fractionally better with a saber. By the time Frelia took up the lance, the blonde girl had a welt on her arm that was purpling, and looked on the verge of tears.

Frelia's eye widened. *Not good.*

"What are you planning to concentrate on next year?" Frelia blurted out.

Silverwood believed in a rounded education for years one and two, and a concentrated curriculum for year three. Little mages would make their spellbooks, little swordswomen would perfect their craft, and little cavaliers would train with every horse in the stable twice over.

"I don't know yet," Karina said with a note of apology. "Not swords, obviously."

Frelia felt eyes on her back, and looked over to see her next student duels walking into the grassy quad. A teenage boy built like a brick shithouse, and his shaggy, blond-haired friend built like an elm sapling.

They eyed her intently, and Frelia knew, whatever she said was going to get passed around the school like gossip in the court.

Fuck. She was so bad at anything delicate. Where was Cillian when she needed him?

Dead, said the voice in the back of her head, and Frelia appreciated it even less than she usually did.

"I'm not judging you," Frelia said after a moment. "I'm wondering what to focus on with you. Not everyone's suited to fencing, after all."

Karina's mouth fell open into a tiny, surprised *oh,* and then Frelia called out—"*Hau!*"

Lances always had the advantage against swords. They were longer, stronger, and required less skill to wield. Frelia wasn't so much dueling her students with it as testing how they'd hold up in an actual fight. Karina Hunter would be instantly skewered, apparently.

Saints, who the fuck had taught these kids last year? Markus?

"Alright, that's enough," Frelia said, and Karina immediately relaxed her guard. "I have what I need, Karina, and you are free for the rest of the period."

Karina nodded, and went miserably over to the bench to "rack" her training saber. "Did... I fail?" she asked.

Frelia recoiled. What an absurd question. "No, why?"

Karina looked over to her classmates, and found them deep in conversation, so she shuffled closer to Frelia to admit, "I know I'm really bad at swords."

"So?" Frelia cocked an eyebrow. "The assignment was to duel me, not to win. You'll get full marks."

"Oh." Relief broke across Karina's face like the sun through a storm cloud. "Okay!"

Frelia dismissed her with the Silverwood hand sign for retreat. "Have a good day, Karina."

"Thanks, Professor Valerius!"

She practically skipped across the quad to go talk to the other two Violet Owls. The larger boy broke away from the group and Frelia realized he must be next up.

"Hi, Professor!" he called over.

Frelia studied him for a moment, trying to place him on her roster. She gave up quickly. "Sorry, still learning everyone's names—you are?"

The boy pulled up alongside the bench rack, and broke into a smile. Merciful Saints, he was already taller than Frelia. "I'm Siegmund."

The Ossani kid. Right. Frelia resisted the urge to rub at her forehead, or ask him whether he knew what happened to his hopefully-not-father Nemo in the Tyrant's War. Frelia had been half the reason he'd been killed at the Battle for Mydalr.

"Thank you," Frelia said. "Choose a rapier and we'll begin."

Within two minutes, Siegmund was firmly fixed in Frelia's mind as *the lapphund kid*. He looked like the puppies she'd grown up alongside, with paws too big for the rest of him. He'd fill out his huge frame one day, but for now he had exuberance and gangly limbs to spare, and only slightly less hair than the dogs. She should probably remind him that the dress code said students had to be clean-shaven.

He was also leaps and bounds ahead of Karina, which was no surprise. The Ossani were a Volsinii noble family; they'd have trained their children to fight from a young age, especially if they wanted them at Silverwood as teenagers.

He didn't last much longer against the lance than Karina, but he held his own. A stab through his side in a real fight, instead of a skewering. Or something like that, anyway.

She asked him the same thing she'd asked Karina: "What are you planning to concentrate on next year, Siegmund?"

"Wyvern corps!" he supplied immediately.

Frelia nodded. Wyvern cavaliers needed skill in wyvern handling, obviously, plus lances, tactics, and reconnaissance—same as their horse-bound counterparts. A sidearm would do him well if he were ever dismounted.

"Then you're nearly there with your sword skills," Frelia said. "Keep up the work."

Siegmund did that Volsinii thing where he wanted to look surprised but knew he wasn't supposed to. "Wait, really?"

Frelia swore she felt a vein pulse in her temple as she resisted the urge to ask if she'd stuttered. "*Ja,* really."

"Oh, cool." Siegmund sounded genuinely surprised. "Last year, Professor Catianus said I was lucky to pass."

Frelia didn't recognize the family name as anything other than generically Volsinii. She was beginning to understand where Karina's tucked tail came from, though. "Well, either you've improved over the summer," Frelia said, "or Catianus' standards were too high."

The Violet Owls were children who'd grown up in peacetime, after all. Frelia (and any other professor, for that matter) *should* be far better trained and experienced.

Siegmund bounded off towards his friends, and the kid with the shaggy, blond hair approached the weapons bench. "Good morning, Professor," they said in their strange, not-quite-Free-Cities accent.

Frelia pinned this one's name immediately as Christel Vilulf.

They were an odd one. Whip-thin and broad-shouldered, they had apparently appeared last year in the mess hall, muddied and road-worn, a week into classes and without even a proper uniform. They were quiet and did little to draw attention; there were even rumors that the Headmaster had pulled some strings in order to enroll them. Christel studied her with wary blue eyes; suspicious in a way most of Frelia's students weren't.

"Morning," Frelia said. "Find a rapier you like, and we'll begin."

Christel tested a few of the wooden rapiers before selecting one and taking up across from Frelia in the grass. From the way they held the weapon, Frelia could see they were self-taught.

"*Hau,*" Frelia called.

Christel lunged forward with grace but no style. Their wooden blades clattered noisily in the midmorning sun, and although Frelia riposted, Christel came back around with lightning quickness.

With *battle* quickness.

"You've seen combat," Frelia remarked over the clattering training swords.

A thin sheen of sweat had appeared at Christel's brow, but they didn't wipe it off or break their guard. "If it's all the same, Professor," they said, "I'd rather not talk about it."

"You don't have to," Frelia assured them. "I can just tell by the way you fight."

After a few more rounds of rapier, they switched to sabers. Christel was even more comfortable with a broadsword, treating it like an extension of their arm. Put a shield on their other arm, and they could've held their own against any Valerius recruit, back in the day. So, Christel was self-taught in the Kaldiri style?

No, it would make more sense for one or both of their parents to be Kaldiri.

"Who taught you to fight?" Frelia asked.

"My mum." Christel focused intently on Frelia's practice sword. "You kind of fight like her."

Mum is Kaldiri, then. Frelia had been right.

She switched to the lance and Christel immediately took several steps back. "Good!" Frelia crowed.

Christel was the first one to know how to handle a lance, as a swordsman. Another strike against Catianus' teaching style, apparently.

They eyed the wooden training lance with suspicion. "Why are you fighting us with a lance, Professor?"

Frelia hefted the weapon into middle guard. "You won't always fight a swordswoman in a real fight. And it's less dangerous to practice against a lance than spellcraft."

Christel seemed to accept this, and they didn't wait for Frelia to call out the new duel. They launched themselves into the fray with footwork that was awkward but passable, with strikes and lunges that had bad habits Frelia would need to help Christel break this year.

"Enough," Frelia called after a few more exchanges. "You'd survive a real fight with a lance at least long enough to run away."

Christel flinched, and Frelia suddenly had a bad feeling about why the teenager was so familiar with combat.

"That was an apparently poor joke," Frelia added. "You're dismissed, Christel. I have what I need from you."

They shuffled their weight in discomfort. "Aren't you going to ask me what I want to concentrate in?"

Oh, right. Frelia should probably keep track of that for all of them. "*Ja,* what is it?"

Christel snorted. "I mean, swords."

"Good choice," Frelia said, and Christel inexplicably laughed.

After Christel's duel, Frelia had a few minutes to jot down notes on Karina, Siegmund, and Christel before her next student arrived. He strode across the quad like he owned it—spine straight, shoulders back, a polite, neutral expression on his face. He had to be highborn, or failing that, well-off.

Frelia double checked her roster again. She'd already dueled the Ossani kid today, and none of the rest besides della Luciana were noble, so that left Secundus.

A bloodruned noble family from the heart of the Imperium.

"Good morning, Valente," Frelia guessed.

For a moment, he almost seemed like he hadn't heard. Then he deigned to say, "Good morning, Professor Valerius."

"We'll begin with rapier," Frelia said, "then move to saber, then take your pick and I'll use the lance. Now, remind me—what does your family's bloodrune do?"

Valente's face pinched, and he looked over his shoulder towards the on-duty Watchers looming across the quad. "That's not a polite question, Professor."

Frelia cocked an eyebrow. *Fucking Ironfang and his damned Watchers.* "Well, they're not illegal, so I just need to know, does it go off in combat?"

"Oh." Valente suddenly seemed to realize why it would matter. "That... makes sense, then."

"*Ja,*" Frelia said, trying and failing not to sound annoyed. "Mine is a combat rune; that's why I warned you all at the end of our first class."

She'd told the Violet Owls (and every class she'd had after them) that the Valerius Bloodrune was known to make weapon strikes harder, and she couldn't control when it activated. She would do her best to pull back, but they needed to remain vigilant whenever sparring with her, or any other bloodrune bearer with a combat rune. She'd shown them the signs, and done all she could to prepare them.

It'll feel like when mages cast magic—the smell of ozone, and then an astral snap like the world is being ripped open.

None of the students had offered anything about their own bloodrunes, if anyone had one (and Secundus almost definitely did). And it wasn't like Frelia got a list of kids to keep an eye on during sparring, either. She wondered how in Helheim the professors were supposed to teach their students without knowing where to watch for deadly force?

"I wondered why you were telling us something so..." Valente seemed to look around for a courteous word. "...personal."

Frelia forced herself to breathe. Much as she wanted to, it wouldn't do any good to snap at a teenager who didn't know of a world before Ironfang's imperium. "Because I'm not trying to kill any of you."

Valente's jaw fell open, and he quickly shut it again while looking around to see if anyone had noticed besides Frelia. "Can the Valerius Bloodrune do that?"

"Oh, *ja,*" Frelia said. "I wasn't allowed to touch a weapon as a child without being tested for the family rune."

And why was she telling him this, anyway?

"And anyway," she hastened to add, "do I need to watch for yours or not, Valente?"

"No, Professor." Chastised for the moment, Valente looked to his feet. "The Domitia Bloodrune isn't a combat rune."

Domitia, that was right. The Huntress. Why that one had gone to the Volsinii, Frelia would never know. Maybe they'd been a lot less polite a millennia ago. Better trackers.

"Fair enough," Frelia said. "Let us begin."

Valente was about on par with Siegmund. Noble born and bred, trained since childhood in how to fight. He was passable with both rapier and saber, and like Christel, would last long enough against a lance to run away, in a real fight.

"What are you planning to concentrate in, Valente?" Frelia asked after they'd finished.

"I'm not sure yet," he said as he racked his rapier against the bench. "I like black magic and I like cavalry."

It wasn't as disparate as it sounded. Black magic was what everyone thought of when they thought of war magic—gouts of fire, bolts of lightning, pillars of frost. It was annihilation, and obliteration.

It was also the only kind of magic Frelia had ever been any good at.

"Well, last I checked, the Volsinii military has mounted mages." Never mind that they'd been the bane of Cillian's wartime existence. "If that's your goal, I recommend going the black magic route and keeping horsemanship as your elective."

Valente blinked at her. "Why?"

What did he mean, *why?* What were they telling these children in academic advising? "Because it'll be a lot easier to build a spellbook while you have your professors and the Silverwood library on hand?"

Valente's brow pinched. "How do you know? You're not a mage."

Do not strike this child, Frelia. You need this job. "I can cast enough runes to tell you how to build a spellbook."

"You can?"

Rather than continue to argue with a fifteen-year-old, Frelia shooed him away and laid her lance against the weapons rack bench. She drew in a deep breath, and then held her right hand at the level of her eyes. She only had one rune that wasn't a direct attack, so it had to be that one.

It was strange to draw the Grimsdalr Blink rune without a sword in her hand. In the war, she'd used it to pelt herself onto the backs of monsters taller than houses and crack them open with a hatchet. But she didn't see any reason why it wouldn't work horizontally as well as vertically. And Frelia wasn't the sort to lab-test a hypothesis, anyhow.

She hadn't cast the blink rune very often since the war, but the jagged lines of her oldest friends' family secret was baked into the muscles of her right arm. Icy blue arcane light dripped from her fingers as she drew one looping line, another, *another*, and then a jagged one sharply down the center in the air before her.

The instant the rune was completed, the once-familiar spark of magic jerked behind her navel, and then Frelia was being shot across an icy, kaleidoscopic world as if from a cannon.

She reappeared across the quad, skidding to a halt just in time to avoid colliding with an irate Markus della Luciana.

"What in Hypogia do you think you're doing?" he demanded.

"Proving a point," Frelia muttered, brushing dirt off her skirt as she got to her feet.

"Whoa, Professor!" Valente shouted from across the quad. "Can you teach me that one?"

Frelia opened her mouth to tell him that wouldn't be a good idea, but Markus beat her to the punch: "Absolutely not!"

Valente visibly flinched, across the quad, and Frelia had the absurd urge to put herself between Markus and her student.

Well, maybe not that absurd. It was her family's Sacred Task, after all. *So long as you draw breath, the fight is yours to claim.*

"That rune," Markus spat with the fury of a god scorned, "is Kaldiri filth with no place in a Volsinii institute of learning."

Which meant it wasn't illegal. That was something.

Frelia put her hands on her hips. "Pay him no mind, Valente," she said without taking her eyes off Markus' back. "He's just bitter I used it to kill his pets, in the war."

For the della Luciana family had always been the beastminders of the Volsinii military. And Frelia had been an outstanding beast-killer.

Markus froze mid-stride, and whirled on Frelia. "Need I remind you," he hissed, "that you are at Silverwood by the grace of Vendrick Caecillion and little more?"

"Nah, you've hit your quota for today, I think." Frelia began to walk across the quad again, her shoulders as rigid as any Volsinii Duchess'.

Markus' voice came from behind her: "You will be receiving a citation for this!"

Frelia would not give him the satisfaction of turning around. But she did ask, "Why?"

"We aren't supposed to cast magic in the quad, professor," Valente offered, somewhat apologetically. His eyes were flicking between Frelia and Markus with confusion, like he couldn't understand what he was seeing.

Markus' smug grin was just begging to be smacked off his face. "It is rule four-hundred-and-twelve in the student handbook."

"Well," Frelia said, "I'm not a student, and I never got the handbook, anyway."

"It should have been amongst your onboarding paperwork." Markus put delicate emphasis on the operative word.

Frelia's eye narrowed. "Well, it wasn't."

"Perhaps you should take that up with Caecillion," Markus said haughtily. "And ignorance of the law is no excuse."

Frelia's gut told her that Markus had probably filched that out of the stack of onboarding paperwork she'd found on her classroom desk. But Frelia had no proof, and nothing to gain by needling an Imperial Watcher.

After all, she knew a losing battle when she saw one.

"Fine," Frelia said. "I will stop by the Watchers' office to deal with the citation right after I talk to facilities about the geese."

Markus opened his mouth to argue, but couldn't seem to find anything to pick at. "You're on thin ice, Valerius."

"Good thing I grew up with eight months of winter," Frelia muttered, and then turned back to Valente. "You're dismissed. I have what I need from you."

Markus posted up outside Iuvenlis Hall while Frelia took notes on Valente's progress and waited for the next Violet Owl to arrive. She wondered where he'd gone after barking at her about the training grounds, if he was just going to loom over her shoulder all day like a bad opera villain.

"Professor Valerius!" came a voice with an accent that made her heart twist.

She glanced up just in time to see one of her Owls sprinting across the way. His hair was in disarray and his uniform jacket was mis-buttoned, and Frelia wondered whether he'd overslept, or always looked about like this.

"Sorry I'm late!" he added.

Yep, always like this.

"Was that the Grimsdalr Blink rune?"

Frelia froze in the middle of picking up her rapier. "Was that what?"

The boy had reached the weapons rack bench, and Frelia didn't have to look at her roster to know which one he was. The lone Kaldiri accent had stood out to her on day one. It was Owen Gundalf, the kid with a Grimsdalr Territory name.

"The thing you cast." Owen jerked a thumb over his shoulder like he could point to where Frelia had reappeared in the quad. "Was it the Grimsdalr Blink?"

Frelia cringed again, and reflexively looked over her shoulder. She marked one Watcher near Salonia Hall, and Markus at Iuvenlis behind her. Neither had moved, so Frelia prayed they were out of earshot.

"Keep your voice down," she said quietly. "I've already pissed off della Luciana today. Also..." She made a snap decision. "...yes, it was."

"Holy shit." Owen's jaw fell open and he leaned forward to say. "Then you're really General Valerius? My da is going to freak out when I tell him!"

This child spoke way too fast to keep up with. "Uh," Frelia said, "then don't?"

"No, I mean in a good way," Owen said. "He, um..."

Finally, the teenager had the good sense to realize where he was standing and who could be listening. He looked around the quad, from the passersby to the Watchers, and then back at Frelia.

Owen then put his hands around his mouth to stage whisper, "He served in the Northern Rebellion."

Frelia's eye widened. She didn't recognize the family name Gundalf, but that didn't mean the man couldn't have been one of Cillian's house knights. Probably one with money but no title, if he could safely send his kid to Silverwood now.

"Did you really kill ninety-six garmur?" Owen whisper-added.

"Don't ask questions about the war," Frelia said, loudly enough that Markus couldn't claim she wasn't trying. Then she dropped her voice and added, "Yes. Plus some assists I don't remember the exact count of."

"Holy shit!" Owen said again, loudly enough that a passing professor told him, "Language, Owen."

He straightened up. "Sorry, Professor Sabine!"

The lancemaster sighed as she passed them by. "This is your final warning."

"I know, I know," Owen said. "I'll try not to let it happen again."

Sabine caught Frelia's eye in such a way that told Frelia this was a frequent problem with Owen. She nodded to the lancewoman, and resolved to half-assedly tell the kid off when another professor was in earshot.

Owen was ill-suited to rapier—Frelia disarmed him twice in the first three rounds—but much more comfortable with saber. He managed to land a hit on her forearm, although he immediately whooped in triumph and promptly got himself disarmed again.

Then Frelia went back to the bench for the training lance.

"Can you do that twirly-thing my da does?" Owen piped up.

She froze, her hand half-wrapped around the lance haft. "Can I do what?"

Owen switched to holding his saber like a polearm, and attempted to baton-twirl the wood across his back. He dropped it with a mangled curse that Frelia figured was good enough for government work, to use the Volsinii phrase.

"Oh," said Frelia. "*Ja,* hang on."

Cillian, she thought, *I hope you're watching.* He was a much better lancer than Frelia had ever been.

She took up a spot across from Owen, lance properly in hand, then flipped it around her off hand, across her back, and snatched it back up with her right hand to smack the butt of the training lance hard into the dirt. She hoped no one could tell she'd almost dropped it twice in that little demonstration.

"That's it!" Owen howled excitedly, and then looked over his shoulder. "Professor Sabine, can you do that?"

Frelia hadn't realized the lancemaster was still in the quad. The Volsinii woman paused in speaking with the Watcher at Salonia Hall. "Can I do what, Owen?"

Owen looked pleadingly to Frelia, who sighed, and repeated the uselessly flashy lance move.

Professor Sabine sniffed—"I've told you, that Northern Volsinii nonsense has no use on a battlefield."—and turned back to the Watcher.

"Aww, but it's so cool," Owen muttered to his boots.

Frelia stared at Professor Sabine's back as though she could admonish the woman with just her thoughts. There was a perfect motivational opportunity for a kid in need of one, and the lancemaster wouldn't even use it?

"Tell you what, Owen," Frelia said, dropping into middle guard. "If you get a hundred on one of your exams, I'll teach you how to do it."

Owen's face lit up—"You're on, Professor!"—and he dueled her with the exuberance of a child at Yuletide.

It didn't help his grip any, but he got points for effort.

"What are you planning to concentrate in?" Frelia asked as Owen gathered up the books he'd scattered near the weapons bench.

"Siege weaponry, I think," Owen said, "or maybe archery. But Professor Serrana said at the end of last year that either way, I should have a sidearm. And I always liked swords best, so..."

He trailed off as he caught sight of Frelia's last two duelists of the Violet Owls. Faustine della Luciana, Frelia could name even without the violet house prefect's cloak—she had the same curly, brown hair and grey eyes as most of the della Luciana family. Which meant the other small, mousy girl had to be Ellie Mattingly, the only other name on the roster.

Frelia studied Owen for a moment. He was frozen in place, and if he were a garmr, Frelia would have heard his heartbeat a mile off. Her gut instinct was that he was afraid of his house prefect, but that was probably her own experience talking.

"You're dismissed, Owen," she told him.

"Hi, Professor Valerius!" Ellie called from across the quad. "And Owen, aren't you supposed to be helping Professor Serrana set up this week?"

"Uh, er, yeah." Owen blushed a furious crimson. "I'm going!"

Oh, he had a crush on Ellie. *Got it.*

He took off for the archery range as Ellie and Faustine got closer, the former handing off her book bag to the latter so she could head over to the weapons bench. Ellie was visibly overwhelmed at the sight of all the training weapons, and Frelia wondered what the matter was. Was she even allowed to ask a Volsinii kid that?

She settled for, "Everything alright?"

Ellie swallowed audibly. "I'm fine. Thank you, Professor."

She was very clearly not, but Frelia wasn't here to argue with fifteen-year-olds. "Then choose a rapier you like, and we'll begin."

Skill-wise, Ellie sat somewhere between Owen and Karina—not great with a blade, but not completely awful. But by the way she held the hilt, Frelia could see the girl was deeply uncomfortable with forged steel.

"What are you planning to concentrate in?" Frelia asked as they switched to saber.

"Oh, I've been on the white magic track since the end of last year." Ellie stuck out her tongue as she concentrated on blocking Frelia's sword thrusts. "I just need one more year of martial credits before they'll let me drop it entirely."

"Ah," Frelia said, "that explains it."

White mages were the healers, the diviners, the extra oomph behind a cavalry charge or swordswoman's advance. Once upon a time, it had also been the clerics.

"Explains what, sorry?" Ellie asked just as her saber went clattering into the grass.

"You are visibly uncomfortable holding a weapon."

Ellie tried to hide her wince by stooping to pick up the practice sword. She was too young and too few Senate caucuses deep to do it properly. "I'm sorry. I promise I'm trying."

"It's not a thing to apologize over," Frelia said. "Just work on it."

Ellie didn't seem convinced. "Professor Catianus said last year I'd be lucky to survive a battle, at the rate I'm going."

"*Ja,* the more I hear about him," Frelia said, "the more I think Catianus was an idiot."

Ellie laughed in surprise, then clapped a hand over her mouth to stifle it in wide-eyed shock.

"White mages should never be on the front lines," Frelia tsked. "And I presume you're also in black magic courses to learn enough runes to defend yourself?"

Ellie nodded vigorously.

"Then *ja,* there's no reason for you to be in this class," Frelia said. "Do you need me to speak with your advisor?"

"It's a school requirement," Ellie said, but something new had entered her voice. Something less like fear. "But I appreciate the offer, Professor. Genuinely."

"Well," Frelia said, switching to the lance once again. "Then do your best, child—and if you're never comfortable with a blade, you'll know white magic was the correct choice."

Ellie managed to hold Frelia off long enough to get a hit in, and Frelia felt a weird sort of pride take root in her gut. They may have been

Volsinii, but they were just kids. And besides, she was basically just their Master of Arms. Maybe she could just focus on keeping these kids alive in a fight, and the world could sort itself out for once. She would have been the Valerius Master of Arms, after all, if her brother had survived long enough to be Grand Duke.

The thought lasted all of thirty seconds after Ellie's duel, for the next one up to spar was the della Luciana kid.

CHAPTER EIGHT

FAUSTINE DELLA LUCIANA WAS ill at ease with a rapier. Not in the way that some of her classmates were—she was clearly trained and practiced, holding the rapier in middle guard with perfect posture. But in those grey eyes—the same ones Ironfang and Markus had—lay turmoil.

Frelia wondered whether it was Catianus who had taught her to be afraid of fencing, her father, or both.

"I'm ready, Professor," Faustine said.

"Hau," Frelia barked, and lunged.

Faustine stutter-stepped into her first parry—that was a habit that would need breaking—and their first rounds echoed noisily across the quad. The kid was definitely a duelist. Great, that meant she would probably concentrate in swords.

That was just what Frelia needed.

They switched to saber, and Faustine racked the rapier like she couldn't be rid of the thing fast enough. Within a handful of exchanges, Frelia could tell, Faustine would easily have been top of her swords class, if not for Christel. Combat experience would always trump training.

"You'll be concentrating in swords, I take it?" Frelia tried not to sound annoyed as she swapped her saber for the training lance.

"Oh, er, probably not." Faustine sounded surprised to be spoken to. "My father wants me to join the wyvern corps."

Frelia opened her mouth to ask whether *Faustine* wanted that, but was suddenly struck with a rumbling, roiling pain in her stomach.

So long had it been since she'd felt the sensation that at first, Frelia wondered whether it was indigestion. With porridge for breakfast, that wasn't likely. But as the world narrowed into focus again, Frelia's teeth began to rattle, and then her very bones.

And she knew in an instant what was happening.

It had once been as familiar to her as her own heartbeat. At first they'd thought it was simply because garmur were enormous creatures; of course they'd shake the ground as they walked. But even the smaller ones set Frelia's teeth on edge and made her bloodrune vibrate as if it wanted to burst from her skin.

But what was a garmr doing at Silverwood?

"Professor?" Faustine interrupted her train of thought. "Is everything alright?"

Frelia whipped her head around, looking for another bloodrune bearer. Even a kid like Valente would do, but he had disappeared after his duel, and Frelia didn't see anyone else useful on hand.

There had only ever been nine Bloodruned Families, after all. And that was before Ironfang had massacred the Church.

Frelia forced herself to look back at Faustine. "Do you feel that?" Frelia asked, despite knowing the answer.

Faustine's brow pinched. "Feel... what, sorry?"

"Rumbling," Frelia growled, and she plucked the lance from its resting place. A wooden weapon was better than nothing.

Frelia's gaze skittered across Iuvenlis Quad. Across the doors to the academic buildings, across the Watchers keeping guard, across professors as they hurried to their next classes. It should have been a normal school day, but the insistent rumbling told Frelia something was very wrong, here.

"Ellie." Frelia glanced over to the white mage. "Take your friends and anyone else you find, and get out of here. *Now.*"

The teenage girl went very pale. "Professor?"

"Faustine," Frelia added, "take a wooden sword, go with them. Ellie can't fight."

For a moment, Faustine looked like she might protest. Then she tossed the wooden sword to Ellie and said, "Go get Owen and Siegmund."

"Right!" Ellie dashed off towards where her classmates had disappeared to.

"I didn't say to—" Frelia began, but a flash of black fur caught her attention as it scuttled beneath a row of hedges.

All else fell away as Frelia bolted after it.

"Professor!" Faustine called. "What are you doing?"

She could see it, weaving around roots and low branches. Black fur, four legs and a tail, and several burning, green eyes like fire from Helheim itself. It was probably about the size of a wolverine, but bigger than anything Frelia had ever skinned.

She'd skin this thing too, if the hide could actually be used for anything after she was through with it.

"Valerius," Markus barked from somewhere on her blind side periphery, "I must insist you—"

The garmr was running out of hedge. The instant its head appeared on the path, Frelia drew back her foot and punted the damn thing like a kickball in a game of Chase-the-Draugr. Pain lanced up her leg as the creature went flying across the quad.

It smashed into a brick wall, squealing and shaking like a wet dog as it righted itself. It stared Frelia down with menace in those unnaturally green eyes.

She glared right back, and didn't take her eyes off it to hiss, "*We've got a problem, Captain!*"

The garmr pelted towards her, jaws wide and spittle flying. Frelia sidestepped towards the hedge, but the garmr caught the edge of her long skirt with its jagged teeth. It shook its head with the mouthful of fabric like it was playing tug-of-war, and not even for the first time today, Frelia cursed that she didn't have her sword on her.

She stabbed at the garmr with the butt end of the training lance, cracking the sturdy wood into its eyes. The garmr shrieked and its bite loosened just enough for Frelia to stab at it again and backstep. Her skirt came free with a horrific ripping noise.

"Valerius!" Markus shouted again. "What are you doing?"

"Fighting a garmr; what does it look like?"

She'd mostly fought the enormous ones in the war—the walking siege weapons that were as tall as buildings. These little ones were a nuisance she'd usually left to the rearguard. And just as Frelia was debating whether to attack or let the monster come to her, Markus shouted from behind her:

"Valerius, *stand down!*"

Frelia whipped her head around to stare at him. She knew what the Volsinii had called her in the Tyrant's War, alright. *The mad darkbeast-killer.* "The fuck you mean, stand down?"

Did he not know the damage these things could do? *Of course he does; he's a beastminder.* All around them were students with bite-able legs and no skill to hold a monster off. A kennelmaster knew better than to loose teething puppies on people, and needle-teeth didn't even hurt; what the fuck was Markus thinking?

Dammit, if she only had a sword!

"You do not have the authority to deal with this," Markus began, and Frelia could not believe her ears. "Nor do you have actual steel with which to—"

"Professor, behind you!"

Frelia sidestepped again, and a moment later, a second wolverine-sized garmr blew past her and into the academic quad.

Because of course there was a second one. The logical part of Frelia's brain knew garmur hunted in packs, but the rest of her wanted to have a word with the damned Goddesses.

"Faustine!" Markus growled.

Across the way, Faustine's fingers curled in on themselves, not quite fists, not quite a nervous habit. "I can help."

"Out of the question!" Markus snapped at her. "I am the beastminder he—!"

"Then act like one!" Frelia roared.

She felt a sudden twinge of magic near her left hand, and Frelia immediately jerked away from it. An astral sword fell to the dirt, its magic translucent in the morning sun.

"What the hell—" Frelia whipped her head around, but cut herself off a second later.

Vendrick Caecillion was standing in the eaves of one of the academic buildings, purple arcane energy blooming at his fingertips as he finished concentrating on the spell. He caught her eye, and with his free hand, made the Silverwood hand sign for 'advance.'

Frelia growled in frustration, but snatched up the sword anyway. Kaldiri beggars couldn't be sore losers.

"Caecillion, you are not needed," Markus snapped.

"I never am," Vendrick returned.

Newly armed, Frelia took off after the garmr again. One saw her coming, and Frelia was just fast enough to get the sword into position as it charged. She sliced into the creature's shoulder as it passed. Black ichor splattered the grass and the hem of Frelia's ruined skirt.

"Watchers," Markus shouted, "form up!"

Lancemaster Sabine fell into step beside the other Watcher in the quad, one of the wooden sabers in hand, and Frelia wondered if she had been a Watcher before she became a professor. *One to keep an eye on, then.*

They triangulated one of the wolverine-sized creatures between them, Markus at point as he cast a rune in red-gold arcane light that Frelia swore she recognized from the Tyrant's War. The Krakenguard mages had tried to label them like dog commands—sit, stay, come when called, go get 'em—but her focus had always been on how best to kill the monsters, not how to read the beastminders' runes.

Still. Something about the spell didn't sit right—and her gut was rarely wrong.

On her blind side, claws picked up speed as they clacked against the stone paths. Frelia brought her left arm up reflexively—too late, she realized that unlike the last time she'd fought these things, she had no shield.

The garmr bit into her arm with enough force to snap it, and Frelia felt her bones crack a half-second before a deep, splitting pain erupted from her fingertips to her shoulder. She viciously shook her arm, but the garmr held on.

The wound began to burn, and Frelia's vision swam with bright, fathomless pain. She reversed her grip on the astral sword and kicked at the garmr. It howled, but held fast.

She kicked again, made enough space to slash into its flank with an inelegant slice. The garmr howled again, this time dropping off her newly-broken arm and back onto the ground. Frelia pivoted, bringing Vendrick's astral sword down with all the force she could muster one-handed.

It turned out not to matter.

Ancient magic seared into her side—a sharp, arcane snap just beneath her ribs—as her bloodrune activated. The sword cleaved into the garmr as though swung by a god, the weapon strike tearing into hellish flesh as easily as a hot knife through butter. The sword buried itself deep in the garmr's ribs, and the monster collapsed, chest heaving.

Frelia yanked the sword back out with some trouble, and set to sawing the garmr's head from its shoulders. Ichor splattered across her skirt, reeking of bile and dead things.

Decapitation done, Frelia turned to face the quad again, her left arm hanging uselessly at her side and fury singing in her blood. The other garmr had gotten loose from whatever the Watchers were doing, and it was snarling at Faustine. Spittle flew from its teeth as Faustine tried to backstep. Her eyes were wide as saucers.

Did they not teach her to beastmind? Frelia couldn't believe what she was seeing. Wasn't that the thing the della Luciana lorded over all the other noble families? Surely even the littlest one would know how to handle one of the damned things?

If she didn't, then wouldn't that mean Faustine had never been safe in her own home?

Markus was furiously drawing runes in red gold light, but the magic they produced just seemed to glance off the garmr's inky black hide. It stalked Faustine, its beady little eyes intent on its prey.

"Della Luciana!" Frelia shouted at him. "What are you doing? Kill it with fire!"

"I will not have my methods questioned by a—"

A knot of grey magic zoomed past Markus' left arm, leaving a trail of astral energy in its wake like a tiny comet. The knot buried itself right between the garmr's eyes, and ripped itself out of the back of its skull like a cannonball.

Frelia knew that spell, alright. She'd seen it on the battlefield enough times during the war, and it was the single grey magic spell Cillian had ever attempted to learn. Although Cillian had given up long before he could reliably produce the complicated rune, Vendrick didn't even need to consult his spellbook as he puppeteered the Singularity pellet. With a deft flick of his fingers, the pellet looped back around and smashed through the garmr's skull again crosswise.

Markus was turning purple with rage. "Caecillion!"

"You were taking too long," was all Vendrick said.

Frelia limped across the quad towards the still-twitching beast. Fire and decapitation were the only things that would reliably down a garmr, and she wasn't about to take any chances.

She never had.

Frelia didn't have enough grip in her broken arm to go at a garmr's neck a second time, so she passed the sword to Faustine. "Get ready to saw this thing's head from it's body. I'll hold it down for you."

Faustine's eyes were still wide as she clutched the astral sword. "Are you okay, Professor?"

"Of course not," Frelia barked, "my arm's fucking broken."

She grabbed a fistful of the fur in the garmr's jowls and caught its hindquarters beneath her boot, aligning the monster flat against the ground. "Stay steady," Frelia grunted at Faustine. "Doesn't matter if you miss the first time, just don't hit me."

"This is outrageous." Markus was coming towards them now, fury in every line of his features. "You will not demolish evidence of—"

The sword sank into the garmr's back, off-center but with enough force to expose its rancid spine. The stench rising from the corpse was like a mountain of battlefield dead had baked in the summer sun and been left there to rot. The garmr gurgled loudly enough to jangle the rumbling still going deep in Frelia's bones, and it bucked beneath Frelia's boot.

"Sorry," Faustine squeaked. "I... I've never killed anything before!"

Had this child never even been hunting? *Helheim.* "Again," Frelia ordered.

Faustine squared up a second time, and this time she dug her loafer into the garmr's neck and leaned all her weight on the blade. She sawed at its neck for a few seconds before Markus snatched Faustine by the scruff of her neck like an angry mother cat.

"Oi, oi," Frelia snapped. "Don't manhandle my student."

"I will deal with my little sister however I see fit," Markus snapped. "And you, Faustine—you know better than to touch a darkbeast corpse."

Faustine had gone limp in his grip. "It's not dead, though?"

Unnatural flame erupted at the center of the garmr's back, and Frelia hastily released the creature before it burned her. She scuttled backwards as black fire licked the garmr's hide and searched for the purchase that would make even a hell-beast burn. Damn, Frelia had forgotten how good it was to have a genuine battlemage at the back line in a fight.

She squashed the thought. Viciously.

"Captain della Luciana," called Vendrick from across the way. "A word, if you would?"

CHAPTER NINE

FAUSTINE STARED AT THE still-twitching corpse in disbelief. She'd seen darkbeasts before, of course, but Faustine had always been told they were none of her concern. She'd never been this close to one that wasn't restrained, and especially not a dead one. Did they always smell so bad, when they burned?

"Hold a moment, Caecillion," Markus snarled at the headmaster, and then whirled on Professor Valerius, who was unconcernedly ripping her sleeve away from her broken arm. "This was an unnecessary, absolutely unhinged display of Kaldiri brutality! I will have you know that I had this situation perfectly under control, and I do not appreciate having my methods questioned by the likes of you."

Professor Valerius stopped ripping her sleeve to stare at Markus. How she was still standing was a miracle, at least to Faustine. "You call that 'control?'"

"Some of us put the horse before the cart." Markus released his grip on Faustine's school jacket, but she knew better than to think she was off the hook. "And of course you'd support this barbarity, Caecillion. You were always—"

"Oh, no," the headmaster interrupted dryly. "I hire experts and then allow them to do the things they're experts in. Truly, I must support anarchy."

Faustine desperately wanted to ask what the Headmaster meant. What was Professor Valerius an expert in, exactly? Staring down monsters that bit people? Darkbeast kickball? Fashionable eyepatches?

"We hired her to teach swords!" Markus shouted. "Not hunt monsters with some sort of knight complex."

"Look, della Luciana," Professor Valerius said, "I know I killed your pets in the war, but we have garmur corpses that need taken care of, here." She gestured with her broken arm and immediately hissed and clutched it to her chest again. "Also, I have never been accused of knighthood in my life."

Oh, no. Was she... the *General* Valerius? The one Faustine's father had routinely complained about, any time Markus brought up darkbeasts? Surely the mad darkbeast-killer of the Kaldiri army couldn't be Faustine's new swordsmanship professor?

There had to be a law against that kind of cosmic irony.

And yet, Faustine was equal parts fascinated and terrified. Professor Valerius didn't seem crazy, any more than she seemed able to gut a sixteen-foot darkbeast with a sword and a spell. She was just... a woman. Lean, scarred, and clearly built to swing a sword.

"And another thing," Markus continued, and merciful Saints, he was really gaining steam, now, "Caecillion, I thought you knew better than to set evidence on fire! If the corpse were intact, I could have dissected it to determine its origin. But as it stands, I have nothing to work with."

Faustine glanced between the two darkbeasts corpses. "The other one is just decapitated?"

"You will be silent," Markus snapped at her, and Faustine tried not to wilt.

She was in trouble, wasn't she? The question always was, for what? She could usually guess what she'd done to upset her father or her siblings, but this time, there were too many options. Was it that she'd apparently aided General Valerius? Was it that the darkbeasts were dead? Was Markus just having a fit of pique?

Headmaster Caecillion had folded his arms across his narrow chest, and was staring Markus down with the look that quite literally scared the piss out of students. "Are you quite finished, della Luciana?"

Markus huffed. "For the moment."

"In that case—" Nothing about Headmaster Caecillion's face or posture changed, and he didn't raise his voice, but somehow that just made him scarier. "—do remind me—*what in Hypogia am I paying you for?*"

Markus blinked. "I beg your pardon?"

"Thought you might say that, so I shall remind you." The headmaster's voice was a thin whipcrack of reproval. "You are paid to guard the Silverwood grounds, its faculty, its staff, and its students. And yet, *somehow,* two darkbeasts have made it into the center of campus beneath your notice, and one of my professors has since injured herself doing your job for you."

Oh. When he put it that way, it did sound rather damning, didn't it?

Faustine suddenly had a very bad feeling about this fiasco. The della Luciana family ran the Empire, so there were always agendas and machinations looming in the background of her existence. But surely Markus couldn't possibly be this stupid?

"Furthermore—" Headmaster Caecillion turned to call to "—Professor Sabine!"

The lancemaster turned from where she was talking to the other Watcher who had been in the quad when the monsters had shown up. "Yes, headmaster?"

"I distinctly recall that when I hired you," he said, "you were informed that you do not take orders from Captain della Luciana any longer."

A shadow passed over Professor Sabine's face. "Are you seriously chastising me for leaping in to assist during an emergency situation, but not Valerius?"

"Figured it was coming next," Professor Valerius muttered.

"The problem is not your willingness to act," Headmaster Caecillion said crisply, "it's that you seem to be under the illusion you're still an Imperial Watcher. However, we shall deal with it later as I am enacting lockdown protocol this instant."

He spoke so calmly. Like crises happened every day.

Faustine could barely process it. Her father would be yelling at everyone in a twenty foot radius, and her sister, the duchess, would have been barking orders even as she suited up with all her armor. What was Headmaster Caecillion even made of, to be so composed right now?

"Sabine," the headmaster continued, "you will inform the classrooms in the quad that students are to go straight to their dormitories and lock their doors. Their professors are to escort them there, then proceed directly to the faculty meeting room. Have prefects and professors spread the word from there."

Professor Sabine nodded, just the once, and then she slipped into the big doors of Salonia Hall.

"Captain della Luciana," the headmaster continued, "you are to post an Imperial Watcher on each dorm floor while the staff deliberates additional safety measures. Valerius..." The headmaster turned to Faustine's swordmaster. "...I presume that's broken?"

"*Ja,*" Professor Valerius said flatly, clutching her arm at an unnatural angle.

"Then, Valerius, you can—" The headmaster began, at the same time Faustine heard herself ask, "How are you just standing there?"

All three adults turned to look at her—Markus, with annoyance, the headmaster with flat, unreadable interest, and the Professor with pain in her eye.

"What do you mean?" Professor Valerius asked.

"I mean..." Faustine stared at the horrid angle of the woman's broken arm. "Doesn't that hurt?"

"Oh, *ja,*" said Professor Valerius, "like a bitch."

Faustine's jaw dropped as Markus instantly hissed, "Valerius!"

How can she just... say that? Faustine wondered. The first rule of being a Volsinii was to never admit pain, physical or otherwise, unless you were quite literally dying and talking to a doctor, and maybe not even then.

"Then, Valerius, head directly to the meeting," the headmaster said. "Inform whichever professors you find on the way to get their students to their dorms. Blightsen should be in Brekka Hall, one-thirty-seven at this hour; stop by there to get your arm seen to."

"I'm not an invalid." Professor Valerius stared at the headmaster like he'd grown a second head. "How long does that sword you conjured hold up?"

Faustine startled when she realized it was still shimmering a few feet away in the grass. It caught the light and refracted it in tiny rainbows, painting the lawn in a riot of color. The astral sword was too pretty, for an instrument of war.

"Realistically? Until I dispel it," the headmaster said. "But you clearly need medical—"

Professor Valerius cut him off by snatching the sword up and slicing a strip of cloth out of her skirt. Markus made an offended noise while the headmaster instantly averted his eyes. Professor Valerius ignored them both, twisting the broad swatch of cloth around her arm in a winding, figure-eight sort of thing that took Faustine way too long to realize was a makeshift sling.

The Professor cursed under her breath when she reached the end of it, though. "Someone tie me up."

Headmaster Caecillion graciously held out a hand, and Professor Valerius twisted so that he wasn't completely on her blind side while he tied a strong knot in the fabric at her shoulder.

"This is ridiculous, Caecillion," Markus said. "There's no need for a lockdown."

Oh no, thought Faustine. *He's definitely done something.*

"We have no idea if there are more of these things running around," the headmaster said without looking up from what he was doing. "And I would much rather be safe than sorry."

He finished tying off the Professor's makeshift sling with a flourish.

"That should hold, Valerius," he added. "So long as nothing grabs it."

"Great," Professor Valerius barked. "I will gather the Owls and get to the conference room."

She took off with a rough gesture in Faustine's direction, and it took Faustine a moment to realize she meant for her to follow. Faustine got four steps forward before she felt Markus' heavy hand on her arm again.

"You," he hissed, "will go nowhere."

Professor Valerius turned as slowly and deliberately as a trebuchet. "Faustine will be going to her dorm room with the rest of my students," she said. "If you want to harass her there after the staff meeting, that's your business."

Faustine's jaw fell open in unladylike shock. Did someone just stand up for her? Nobody did that, except maybe that time last year that Siegmund had told Cavalrymaster Corvinus that there was no way Faustine had been cheating on her exam, Valente was the one who had turned it in second.

"Caecillion," Markus snapped, "make her see reason."

"Oh I quite agree with her," the headmaster said. "Now all of you have your orders. Get going before more show up."

"That reminds me," Professor Valerius said, "somebody set the other one on fire."

"Nobody gave you the authority to determine what happens with these corpses, Valerius," Markus snapped.

"We wouldn't have this problem if you'd just lit them on fire to begin with!" Professor Valerius shot back. "The corpses attract more; everyone knows that."

They did? That was news to Faustine.

"That is enough," Headmaster Caecillion snapped. "We will discuss it at the meeting. Move out, all of you."

Professor Valerius gestured for Faustine again, and this time, Markus didn't stop her.

"Go get a wooden sword," Professor Valerius said to Faustine the moment she fell into step. "In fact, grab them all. Better a stick than nothing at all."

Faustine did as she was told, hustling back to the bench to gather the remaining armful of wooden swords. Although she wondered—*what's a garmr?* Surely she didn't mean the darkbeasts. Wouldn't she have just said it?

When Faustine got back to the professor, the woman set off at a brisk pace that nearly made Faustine trip. "Where does your class go next?" Professor Valerius asked.

"Err," Faustine said, "half of us go to Cavalry, and the other half are sort of spread around Iuvenlis and Brekka Hall."

"Damn," Professor Valerius muttered. "Alright, we'll start with Iuvenlis."

Faustine skittered ahead to open the door, but Professor Valerius didn't so much as break stride. The hallways were deserted as Professor Valerius stuck her head into classroom after classroom, telling all the other professors the same thing—

"Garmur in the quad. Get your homerooms to their dorms and then get your ass to the staff meeting room."

They picked up Owen and Karina in Iuvenlis, and Faustine passed them both wooden swords the moment they joined the little party. Karina looked like she might cry, but Owen took a saber without flinching.

"What's going on?" he asked Faustine.

"The headmaster's ordered a lockdown because of the monsters," Faustine told him. Here, at least, she could be useful.

Understanding crossed Karina's face, and she said, "Wait, did you mean darkbeasts, Professor?"

Faustine braced for Karina to be yelled at, but Professor Valerius just kept moving. "*Ja*, that's what you Volsinii call them," the professor said over her shoulder. "But they're the Guardians of Helheim, Lady Midnight's Children. You know. *Monsters.*"

For a moment, Faustine was so stunned she almost forgot how to run. Sure, it was okay to ask questions during class or afterwards, but to ask something like that of a professor in an emergency? It was asking to be brutally lectured, at the very least.

And yet Professor Valerius had just... responded. Like it was nothing.

"I thought garmur couldn't get out of Grimsdalr Territory, Professor?" Owen asked.

Faustine cringed again. Darkbeasts lived up in the Northern Wilds, sure, but the beastminders could summon them anywhere. Didn't Owen know anything?

"Not easily," Professor Valerius said. "Thank the damn Goddesses."

That reminded Faustine—Lady Midnight? Did the darkbeasts—or, well, garmur, as the professor apparently called them—have something to do with the Unseen? Ironfang and Markus and all the other beastminders in the family had never said anything about it, if they were. And that seemed like a very large thing to just ignore.

Although, it wouldn't be the first time the della Luciana family had stepped around a mysterious lump they'd swept under the rug. Or that

Faustine had swallowed her curiosity for fear of what the question would provoke in her elders.

They moved on to Brekka Hall, collecting Ellie from where she'd hunkered down with a group of first years. Professor Valerius' weather eye scanned the paths between buildings before she gestured for her Owls to follow her. Despite the wooden sword in her hands, Faustine didn't feel any safer.

The astral sword glittered in Professor Valerius' hand, ready to be swung at a moment's notice. "We'll swing by the cavalry field, then to the dorms."

But there was something Faustine wanted to test for herself. "Professor?"

"*Ja?*"

Faustine drew in a deep breath. She knew it wasn't polite, and she knew she shouldn't be asking about it, but for how much her father and Markus went on and on about them, Faustine wanted to know.

"Was that your bloodrune, that went off?"

Professor Valerius finally stopped hustling, and turned to look at Faustine. But instead of the anger Faustine was expecting, all she could see in the Professor's face was worry.

"Why?" Professor Valerius asked.

"I was just wondering," Faustine said hurriedly and oh, no, this had been a terrible idea. "And, well, I've heard of bloodrunes before but never seen... one..." She trailed off at the grim look on her professor's face.

"I warned you all about the Valerius Bloodrune yesterday in class," Professor Valerius said. "Did you think I told you that for my health?"

"I've never seen one either," Karina piped up. "What did it do, Faustine?"

"She swung her sword like normal," Faustine heard herself say, "but when she hit the monster it just... kind of...?" She mimed slicing something in half.

Professor Valerius sighed. *"Ja,* 'for Valerius, the Task of the Guardian—so long as you draw breath, the fight is yours to claim.'"

It sounded like something the woman had told herself many, many times.

"What does that mean?" Ellie asked.

"That I hit *very* hard," the professor said. "Now all of you, keep moving. There may still be garmur afoot, and it isn't safe out in the open like this."

As they continued towards the practice fields, Faustine could almost see the general the woman had once been. Professor Valerius directed them in Silverwood hand signs Faustine could suddenly see the merit in, paused at corners to peek around them with her sword in middle guard. Her back was straight and stride confident, but she didn't linger.

It was sort of amazing to watch. Like Faustine's oldest sister, Duchess Orsina, but without all the nastiness.

When they reached the cavalry field, Professor Corvinus was nowhere to be found, but Christel, Siegmund, and Valente were wide-eyed and hiding in the eaves of the big oak tree on the edge of the field.

"Give Christel a saber," Professor Valerius said. "Valente a rapier, and Siegmund what's left."

"Professor!" Siegmund shouted. "What's happening?"

Professor Valerius filled them in as she ushered the entirety of the Violet Owls across the practice fields the back way to the dorms. Faustine had to jog to keep up with the Professor's pace; the woman's boots seemed to eat the ground as she moved.

"How'd you know this was here, Professor?" Christel asked, picking their way between brambles with more dexterity than the rest of the class combined.

"Used it to sneak out of the dorms when I was here," the Professor said, and Faustine's jaw was not the only one that dropped. "I wouldn't recommend it anymore, though, they've put the—ah, yep, there it is."

An enormous sewer grate was nestled in the hillock just behind Atticus Hall. It smelled awful, like garbage left to rot on the side of the road in the middle of summer, and Faustine's brow furrowed as she tried to place where she'd smelled that stench before.

The basement of della Luciana Manor.

With a sinking feeling, Faustine realized she'd been right about why Markus had been making such a fuss earlier. Why he wouldn't want the corpses set on fire. Why he would want Professor Valerius as far as possible from the darkbeasts.

Those were Markus' beasts, weren't they? It wouldn't be the first time Ironfang had told him to cause trouble on campus, but Faustine had no idea what the point was, this time. Nobody ever told her what the point was, and then they said it was for her own good, so most of the time she just had to guess.

The last time Markus had been told to make trouble, it had been to drive Professor Ysra to quit so that the Unseen could take his bloodrune. He'd stormed off in a huff, to hear Markus tell it, slamming his key on the headmaster's desk and telling him that he could not work with the Imperial Watchers breathing down his neck.

The Unseen waiting in the woods beyond Silverwood had captured him the instant he left campus, and made it look like he'd simply fallen in the lake.

Markus' intelligence had been wrong, though. Professor Ysra wasn't a Konstantin cousin at all, so he had no bloodrune for the Unseen to steal. Their father had been so furious, Faustine had heard his screaming from down the hall.

That had been the year before she'd been enrolled at Silverwood.

"Swiftly, now." Professor Valerius' thick, Kaldiri accent cut into Faustine's thoughts. "Around the edges of the grate—Owen, do *not* cross it directly. Merciful Saints, child!"

Owen sheepishly hopped off the middle of the grate and back onto the grass, and the Violet Owls kept pace with their professor as she charged up the hill.

This close to Atticus Hall, there were other professors and students about. Everyone was carefully streaming into the dorms, and Imperial Watchers were stationed at every major door, holding them open with a hand on their weapon.

"Are all of you in Atticus Hall?" Professor Valerius asked.

"Yes," Faustine heard herself say. "It's the only student dorm."

"Then whoever is on the first floor, you go in first." Professor Valerius began to fall back, towards the rear of the group. "Then line up based on who's on second and third. Once you're in your rooms, hitch your desk chair under the doorknob and find something heavy to put in front of your windows—then wait."

Saints, Professor Valerius sounded almost as calm as the Headmaster had.

"Oh, and change your clothes, too," the professor added. "Put them in a pile outside your room; we'll burn them later."

Burn them? None of the beastminders ever did that.

"Isn't that wasteful?" Karina asked.

"Better that than dead."

Ellie maneuvered her way to the front of the gaggle of students, and Faustine's stomach twisted. "Professor," Ellie asked, "shouldn't you be up front?"

"Not much point; I don't know where you all live," the professor said. "Christel, take point until we get to your room."

"I'm on the third floor." Something hard glittered in Christel's blue eyes. "I can stay to drop off everyone else."

"Fine," the professor said. "Ellie, lead the way."

Ellie and Karina disappeared into the rooms on the first floor, wooden practice weapons in hand. Professor Valerius didn't let anyone else move until she heard the locks click on their doors, and then she physically pushed them forward.

Siegmund, Owen, and Valente slipped into their rooms on the second floor next, locking the doors behind them even faster than Ellie and Karina. The hair on the back of Faustine's neck was starting to stand on end, and was starting to feel extremely exposed out here in the open.

Professor Valerius nodded to the Watcher on duty as she ushered Faustine and Christel up to the third floor. Christel's room was right near the stairs, so they slipped inside and locked the door.

Which left Faustine alone with the professor.

She would never get another chance to ask questions, not freely like this. If Professor Valerius were going to answer, Faustine should be asking more questions, if only for the delightful feeling of getting an answer without being yelled at.

But she suddenly had no idea what to say.

"Professor?" Faustine asked quietly.

"Yes?" The woman's voice was hard and taut—but not unkind.

"Um, thank you," Faustine said. "For telling Markus off, earlier."

Nothing about Professor Valerius seemed to change, but her voice was softer when she said, "He's always been a git. Don't let him get to you."

Faustine stopped them in front of her door, quickly unlocked it, and slipped inside. Her mind was buzzing with the professor's instructions—*change clothes, lock your door, barricade the windows*—but the one about Markus was impossible. Didn't she know that was the whole point of having an older brother?

CHAPTER TEN

FRELIA HAD NEVER HUSTLED to a staff meeting so fast.

Not this shit again, she thought. *This cannot be happening again.*

Her broken arm was burning, and she was so anxious, bile was biting the back of her throat. But the kids were safe, the rumbling hadn't returned, and when she skidded practically sideways into the staff meeting room, Edmund Blightsen was thankfully already there.

"Frelia!" His sleeves were rolled up to his elbows and Frelia could see the echoes of the wartime medic he had once been. "I heard you needed medical attention, but, um."

"What?" Frelia collapsed into the chair nearest Edmund that wasn't occupied by someone else's butt.

"You look..." Edmund paused, looking around for a polite word. "...rather banged up for a broken arm."

Frelia stared at him for a moment, confused. What else was she supposed to look like? It was combat, not the Silverwood winter ball.

It took one of the Volsinii professors muttering 'indecency to even change' for Frelia to realize what Edmund meant. *Oh, like they've never seen a damn kneecap,* she thought sourly.

"*Ja,* well." Frelia set the astral sword on the table in front of her. "That's what happens when you need to make a sling out of your own clothing. If I'd had a cloak, I would have used that."

"What exactly happened in the quad, Valerius?" asked the old man, Magicmaster Marcellius. He'd been teaching black magic since Frelia had been a student.

Frelia shrugged as Edmund set to work untying her sling. "I was dueling my students in Iuvenlis Quad—"

"About that," came Lancemaster Sabine's cultured, clipped voice, "why in Hypogia were you doing that in the quad? As opposed to, oh I don't know, the training ground?"

Frelia shot the woman a dirty look. "Quad wasn't infested with nesting geese."

A grimace ran through the room, and even Sabine made a conciliatory noise in the back of her throat.

"Then all of a sudden I..." Frelia trailed off, and despite everything, she looked around the room for someone else like her. But there were no Grimsdalr scions here, no Einnaska, Traust, or even Secundus or Nova.

She was utterly alone—the only bloodrune in the room. Nobody was going to believe her about the rumbling; they never did. Not even the Krakenguard had, until Cillian, Thera, and Brigitte had confirmed it.

"...I just felt like something was off," Frelia said instead. "Eyes on the back of my neck, you know?"

That did get some nods from the room—Ossani, Serrana, and Corvinus had all served in the war, after all. They knew exactly what she meant.

"Then I noticed the garmr under the hedge, and..." A sharp, sudden pain spiked in her arm when the sling came undone under Edmund's fingers. "*Skitr*, Edmund! Warn me next time."

"Sorry," said the healer sheepishly. "I'm, um, going to heal your arm, now."

He carefully laid Frelia's broken arm on the meeting table. Beside the glittering astral sword, Frelia could feel its unnatural angles acutely.

Blood began to ooze lazily onto the table, and Edmund slid the ruined strip of her skirt-sling beneath her arm.

"These are deep," Edmund muttered, probing the bite marks with gentle fingers. There were twin puncture wounds around the broken bit of her forearm.

"Garmur," said Frelia dully.

Edmund made a face like he understood, and then his spring green magic began to light the room with a hazy, arcane glow. Frelia watched in fascination as the muscle and bone in her arm slowly began to work themselves back together.

"I thought there were supposed to be wards against darkbeasts?" asked the ever-nervous Tacticsmaster Vitellus.

"There are," came a dry voice from the door. "And even if I hadn't redone them yesterday, I just checked them all again. They're perfect."

Vendrick's face gave nothing away as he strode into the room, his black, mages' coat swishing at his heels. He strode towards the head of the table, where Magicmaster Marcellius and Wyvernmaster Gellir quickly parted to make room for him.

"No holes anywhere," Vendrick added at the growing silence.

Frelia looked at Edmund, but the white mage was still fixated on her arm. *Is nobody going to say it?* she thought. As Vendrick paused by the astral sword still at Frelia's elbow, Frelia realized, she was going to have to.

"Then the shout came from inside the house," she said.

"What?" said Archerymaster Serrana.

"Haven't you seen *Men of the Forest?*" Roguemaster Olsen asked. "It's the third act—when Gerim is murdered, the shout comes from inside the house."

"Meaning what?" Lancemaster Sabine said with all the weary gravity of a Volsinii matron whose dignity had been affronted.

"Meaning," Vendrick said, even as he drew a small rune in the air over the astral sword, "the monsters were already here when I re-upped the wards."

Understanding filtered across the room, and the astral sword winked out.

"You have two della Luciana at Silverwood right now," Frelia said. "Why don't you ask one of them how a garmr got in here?"

"I do not enjoy being accused, Valerius," came Markus' snippy voice from the door.

The assembled faculty stared at her, and Frelia wondered whether it was because she was supposedly sassing a Prince of the Imperium, or because none of them had thought to do it. Markus' reputation had preceded him, here at Silverwood. He was a nuisance to put up with, not a genuine threat.

"If I were accusing you," Frelia said, "you'd know."

"This was my next order of business anyway," Vendrick said. "Have a seat, Markus."

A sharp intake of breath overtook the room, like a wave cresting the shoreline. The Captain of Silverwood's Imperial Watchers pointedly remained standing.

"Or don't." Frelia got the sense Vendrick was trying not to roll his eyes. "Well, della Luciana, what do you think?"

"I think Valerius is a brutal woman not fit to—"

"Oh, *enough*, della Luciana," said Axemaster Ossani, and Frelia was stunned that of all people, a former Imperial soldier was coming to her defense. "We all know you don't like her. What do you think about the darkbeasts?"

"Did you do something?" asked Roguemaster Olsen. She was nearly as old as Marcellius, now that Frelia could get a decent look at the woman. Silver-haired and sharp-eyed.

"Oh, I didn't summon these." Markus harrumphed. "If I had, they'd be far better trained."

Frelia's eye narrowed at him, and she winced as Edmund moved to a new part of her broken arm.

Something in Vendrick's facial expression twitched. "Any ideas where they came from, then?"

"The Northern Wilds, presumably," Markus said.

"But that's half a continent away, across the Ivory Channel." Edmund finally spoke up. "How could they have gotten here without being noticed?"

"They can't cross water," Frelia added. "Least, not very well."

For a brief moment, Frelia's mind was miles away in a muddy battlefield in Grimsdalr Territory. Then Edmund cracked the bone in her arm back into place with enough force to make her eye water and searing pain double back up her arm to her shoulder.

"Further," said Archerymaster Serrana, "I've never heard of a darkbeast this far south that wasn't summoned by our beastminders."

She left unspoken that Volsinii had not had a need to call for the beasts since the Tyrant's War.

"It's absolutely possible," said Markus. "Historically, darkbeast territory stretched from the Northern Wilds all the way to the northern reaches of Nova Territory. But we were... let's say encouraged to lessen the Imperial Watch's presence in the northern territories after the war, so here we are."

No need for a fucking Watcher garrison up there if you'd just left the Grimsdalr alone, Frelia wished she could say.

"Well, this isn't historical," she said instead, "and there's no Kaldiri territories to stop them. So what do you propose we do about the garmur, eh beastminder?"

Markus shot her a vicious look he didn't even bother to hide. "I shall dissect the intact corpse in the alchemy lab and see if I can determine its origin. From there, we can bury the remains."

Frelia slammed her hand so hard on the table that it startled Edmund, still at work on her other arm. "If we don't get those things on a pyre, they're just going to attract more."

"That's a myth," Markus snapped.

Was he being stupid on purpose, or was there something darker there?

"No, it's not," Frelia barked. "It's how we lost Brigitte Konstantin."

Silence fell hard and fast across the room, like nightfall in winter. Brigitte had been the Baroness-Konstantin-to-be, a bright, bubbly spot of laughter and puns. Frelia would never forgive herself for the archer's death, when it had been so preventable.

Cavalrymaster Corvinus surprised everyone by saying, "I second burning them." At the looks he got from his Volsinii coworkers, he added, "What? Better safe than sorry."

Markus shot him a look. "That is wholly unnecessary, Corvinus."

"I believe I'm the judge of that," said Vendrick coolly. "And I third the burning—after della Luciana has examined the body, of course."

"What if there are more of them, Caecillion?" It was the first thing Alchemymaster Caelia had said all meeting. "What are we supposed to do then? Valerius was lucky she even had a training weapon—only the mages here can defend themselves, and only with runes they've memorized. To say nothing of the students!"

There was a sunken, haunted look to the woman's eyes, and Frelia wondered whom she'd lost to a garmr. If it had been during the Tyrant's War, or well before.

"I have been thinking of that, as well," Vendrick said. "And I—"

"I shall call in reinforcements from Ascalon," Markus interrupted. "We can have a Watcher in every classroom by next week."

Horror wrenched Frelia's stomach at the idea of *more* of the bloody Imperial police crawling the campus. There was no way she could teach anything useful with a Watcher in every classroom, let alone carry a knife or fight. They would all be eaten by garmur and it would be Markus della Luciana's fault for bringing Ironfang's eyes into Silverwood.

"More police will *not* help," said Roguemaster Olsen. "It will only make the students jumpy—and their parents, for that matter."

"Well, do you have a better idea?" Markus fired back.

"*Ja,*" she said. "Let us professors carry weapons, for starters."

"Oh, that's asinine. You are teachers, not soldiers, and I for one—"

"Except we *are* soldiers," interrupted Axemaster Ossani. "Or were, anyway."

"I certainly wouldn't mind the extra hands if those brutes show back up," Lancemaster Sabine said.

"The only reason that garmr got as far as it did is because I didn't have real steel," Frelia snapped. "If I were a governess in Caere, yes, arming me would be ridiculous. But this is a military school on the Konstantin Frontier and I teach swords."

Markus leveled her with a reproving look. "On the what?"

"You know what she means, della Luciana," Edmund said quietly.

"For what it's worth, I agree with Valerius and Olsen," Tacticsmaster Vitellus said. "If those monsters made it all the way into the center of campus once, and we don't know how, I don't see why they couldn't do it again. I'd feel much better with a proper weapon."

"Oh don't be ridiculous," Markus said. "This was clearly an isolated incident. There's no need to—"

"Clearly?"

All eyes turned to Vendrick. He was surveying Markus with a calculating look Frelia had only ever seen across a battlefield.

"What about this," Vendrick added, "is *clearly?*"

"We have walls," Markus began, holding up one gloved finger, "wards, a full contingent of Watchers, and we are, as Blightsen so helpfully pointed out, half a continent away from the nearest concentration of darkbeasts. There's no reason to think this isn't an isolated incident."

Vendrick stared at Markus for long enough that the rest of the faculty began to shift in their seats, perturbed. Frelia wished she could figure out what was going on in the man's head, but her war instincts had been screaming at her all afternoon to get a damn sword and it wasn't helping.

"Here is what we shall do," Vendrick finally said. "Professors shall be permitted to carry with them a personal sidearm. Students shall be permitted to carry a personal sidearm no longer than their forearm and which cannot explode—"

"We're not arming students, Caecillion!" Sabine shouted.

"Certainly not," Vendrick agreed, "I don't want students running around with full-on axes and swords; they're not trained enough. However, they cannot be escorted from room to room indefinitely—we haven't the staff. Also, frankly Sabine, this is a military school. Combat experience is invaluable."

"He's... not wrong," Serrana said. "We no longer pursue the low-level mercenary jobs third years used to do."

"Because they're dangerous," Sabine snapped.

"Combat is dangerous," Frelia pointed out. "That's kind of the point."

"This is absurd," said Markus, and he was lucky Frelia's arm wasn't intact yet or she might have clocked him. Nothing about *any* of this was absurd except the fucking monsters on campus. "Why would you not just have students go to their rooms after classes and have meals brought to them? There's no need to arm them, for the Saints' sake."

Edmund looked up from his work on Frelia's arm. "Are they prisoners?"

"Truly." Vendrick nodded to him. "At that point, why would we not just send them home?"

"Oh, come now," Markus said. "I will write to my father for reinforcements and—"

"And will you also request a sizeable donation for renovations to the current Watchers' Barracks and the food to feed this new army?" Vendrick interrupted swiftly. "Or are you volunteering to donate your salary to the cause?"

Markus' jaw hung open for a few seconds before he snapped it shut again.

"We haven't the budget or support staff for more Imperial Watchers, and it's that simple," Vendrick added. "So, therefore, we shall arm and defend ourselves, maintain additional wards, and Markus, your current contingent of Imperial Watchers will focus on the perimeter rather than the occasional intoxicated student."

Markus cringed, but relief spread in Frelia's stomach. Thank the Goddesses nobody else wanted more guardsmen, either.

"I will arrange nightly patrols, for which professors will be expected to take at least one per week until this mystery has been solved," Vendrick continued, and despite night patrols being, objectively, the worst possible watch, no one so much as groaned. "No, there will not be additional pay due to the aforementioned budgetary concerns. And, also..."

He turned those green eyes on Frelia, and her stomach tightened in six different ways.

"It occurs to me," he said, "that we have the most celebrated darkbeast-killer of the Tyrant's War on our staff."

Frelia's eye was wide, and wary. "And what about it?"

"We add a mandatory seminar for all the students," Vendrick added, "Darkbeast killing."

The room exploded in protests—from the Volsinii professors who didn't want that knowledge handed down, and the Kaldiri remnants who knew exactly what Frelia's method of garmr-killing entailed. What it would mean giving up.

But Frelia could only see the Grimsdalr Blink rune in her mind's eye—the last tangible thing she had that connected her back to Cillian and Thera—spread out amongst the student body like the broken pieces of a mosaic. A secret the Grimsdalr family had kept for a thousand years, revealed now because it was suddenly convenient to the Volsinii. Frelia wasn't even part of the Grimsdalr family; she had prodded Cillian into teaching her the blink rune in the middle of a war.

But it had been his secret to give, then. Not hers.

"No."

All eyes in the room turned to stare at Frelia in shock.

"It's not my place," Frelia added, more quietly than was her usual.

"Not your place to save lives?" Magicmaster Marcellius didn't seem angry, exactly, just confused.

Frelia grimaced, and tried to find a way to tell him she'd be pissing on the memories of her dearest friends.

"Isn't your kill count over a hundred?" Vendrick asked.

"It's ninety-six," Frelia said automatically, and she felt Markus' pissed off stare bore into her back. "But, no, I mean, the Grimsdalr blink. It's not my place to give away their secrets."

The room quieted down again, and a few of the Volsinii had the decency to look embarrassed for demanding such a thing. They knew damn well none of them would ever have handed over a family secret, regardless of circumstance.

"I never expected sense from you, Valerius," Markus said. "What a pleasant surprise."

Frelia leveled a withering look at him. She wanted to say that he could have the secrets of the family his had murdered over her dead and decaying body, but she had a feeling that was probably his preference anyhow.

"Then don't," Vendrick suddenly said. "Teach the students what to look for, instead. How best to go about taking care of the big ones versus the small ones, how to determine the correct artillery—that sort of thing. You know plenty of useful information, I'm sure, without desecrating the memory of your comrades."

Frelia stared at him in outright shock, unmoored and adrift in the sea of grief Silverwood had turned into. She didn't even realize Edmund had moved away until suddenly her left arm was whole and unencumbered.

"You do realize you're speaking of a rebel general?" Sabine asked acidly.

"I speak," said Vendrick, "of a classmate. Two, in fact."

He had known Cillian. Had classes with Thera. And although he couldn't outright condone them, he was offering Frelia a way not to piss on their memories.

It was more than she could have hoped for, let alone expected.

Of course she couldn't get away with not teaching the kids, not with their homes under attack. Her own ethics wouldn't allow her to stand idly by while people died. But if she didn't have to teach them Cillian's way... she could make something work.

"I'll..." Frelia swallowed past the lump in her throat. "Put something together."

"I want to review your curriculum before you so much as think about teaching it," Markus interrupted at once.

"Fine," Frelia said, distantly.

"And I shall review after della Luciana is finished," Vendrick said. "So that's the current plan, the future provisions... is there anything else we require?"

"What are we going to tell the parents?" asked Ossani.

Vendrick sighed, and pinched the bridge of his nose. "I shall compose a letter."

Frelia didn't envy that job.

"Beyond that," said Vendrick, "let us get a patrol schedule worked up for overnight shifts. I'm thinking two—one until midnight, and one until dawn."

Guard patrols were familiar, rote. Frelia let them wash over her like Edmund's magic, her brain already twisting together how in Helheim she was supposed to teach these kids how to kill garmur.

For it was, after all, the Grimsdalr Sacred Task to guard the Northern Wilds. The Valerius Sacred Task was simply to fight.

CHAPTER ELEVEN

FAUSTINE HAD BEEN PACING her room and nervously looking out her window most of the afternoon, but by early evening she'd gotten bored enough to crack open her homework. Crises, apparently, were only interesting when you were in them. Afterwards, you were just anxious and bored waiting for your heart to stop pounding.

She became so engrossed in her white magic homework that she forgot all about Markus until a pounding came at her door.

Faustine yelped and knocked over her inkwell by mistake, cursing as she scrambled across her room looking for a handkerchief. She found one wedged between the bedframe and bedside table, and had to wrap both hands around it and yank to pry it loose. By then, the knocking had resumed again—louder this time, and more insistent.

"I'm coming!" Faustine shouted, and then immediately winced at herself. Did that sound too impertinent?

Too late to worry about it now.

She threw the handkerchief onto the spreading pool of black ink, then went to her door.

"Unbelievable," was the first thing out of Markus' mouth when Faustine opened her door.

Faustine's stomach dropped, and although she didn't want to ask, she knew she had to. Markus loved few things as much as an audience—and he was just like their father, that way. "What is?"

He shut the door behind him with an ominous thud.

"How dense must you be to drag Frelia Saints-damned Valerius into our business?" Markus demanded.

"I'm... sorry?" Faustine froze, from her stockinged feet to the tips of her ears. "I just thought..."

"You are not meant to think," Markus continued, throwing the bundle he'd been carrying onto Faustine's bed. "And here, I spent all that time building those two darkbeasts, only for Valerius to swoop in and decapitate one—and never mind what you did. Do you have any idea how far back you've set Father?"

All the heat drained from Faustine's face. "Why didn't you tell me you were going to—?"

Markus leaned over and smacked her cheek, hard.

Faustine recoiled, hot shame boiling her cheeks. She hated that Markus had figured out lately he was 'allowed' to do that. One of the nicest parts of being at Silverwood last year had been that Faustine was free of their father's discipline, but now Markus was picking up right where Ironfang had left off. It made Faustine want to curl into herself and cry.

But then, a small voice in the back of her mind whispered, *Professor Valerius stood there with a broken arm and argued with not one, but two of the Imperium's most terrifying Queenmakers, and she hadn't cried.* She hadn't so much as flinched. And that was even before she'd dragged the Owls across campus with her broken arm in a makeshift sling.

Faustine wondered how the woman could move forward like that.

When it became apparent Faustine wasn't going to burst into tears, Markus snapped, "You should know better than to interfere with me."

"I didn't know!" Faustine insisted, although she knew it wouldn't get her anywhere. "And I didn't know the professor was General Valerius, either."

"It's obvious." Disdain dripped from Markus' tongue. "How many other Valeriuses do you think there still are in the world?"

Faustine wanted to scream. This kind of thing happened all the time, whenever her father or older siblings got annoyed with her for not keeping up with a conversation. They had fought in the Tyrant's War fifteen years ago; Faustine hadn't even been born for most of it. How was she supposed to know which noble families were still around?

But instead of provoking Markus, Faustine just rubbed at her newly-reddened cheek. "I thought all the Northern Volsinii families with bloodrunes were dead."

"Not all of them." Markus heaved a put-upon sigh, and oh, Saints, she'd done it now. "Faustine, remind me—what are you, again?"

Faustine hated this question. It never heralded anything but a lecture. "A della Luciana," she said dully.

"And what does that mean?"

A lot of things, but Faustine knew the one Markus wanted. "That what we do, we do for the family."

"Correct," said Markus. "Now, with that in mind, I have a way for you to redeem yourself."

Faustine's stomach seized. "You... do?"

Markus nodded, and pointed to the bundle he'd dumped on Faustine's bed. "Put this on, and follow me."

He disappeared out of her room, and Faustine turned to the clothes. It was a set of leather armor probably nicked from the Watchers' armory, plus a dark cloak that was too hot for the season. There were no boots or gauntlets.

Sighing, Faustine got changed into what turned out to be ill-fitting armor (it was too big in the bust and too tight at the hips), and pulled the cloak over her shoulders. Her eye caught on the window, and for a moment she just stared at the rolling hills and bits of lake shoreline.

What I wouldn't give to be anywhere but here.

The thought startled her. Where had it come from? Faustine had given up on escaping her family name a long time ago.

"Well that certainly took you long enough," Markus harrumphed when Faustine joined him in the empty dorm hall. "Come along, sister."

He took off towards the north end of the hall without so much as looking back, and Faustine hastened to keep up with his long-legged stride. The Watcher on duty for her floor nodded to Markus as they passed, but the woman didn't look at Faustine, either.

You're invisible, she could almost hear her oldest sister say. *That's what we girl-children are good for, you know.*

Still. Faustine had never seen the campus so deserted. Markus led her out of Atticus Hall and down into the quad, and Faustine spotted some professors scurrying over to their dorm, plus a few more armed and apparently patrolling. But there was no sign of the students anywhere.

It felt wrong, somehow. Like an empty opera house.

Markus led the way to the Imperial Watchers' Barracks, and it was only once they set foot inside that anyone bothered to look at Faustine. *She doesn't belong here,* the Watchers' eyes said. *Why did you bring this failure of a girl?*

Faustine swallowed against the growing lump in her throat.

Markus unlocked the door to his office and he shoved her impatiently inside. Faustine's lunch threatened to come back up her throat as she crossed the threshold. Whenever she was called into Markus' office, she never knew whether it was something school-related or whether it was a family affair. She hated the uncertainty, and she was pretty sure Markus did that on purpose to make her uncomfortable.

He was too much like the rest of their family, that way.

"Shut the door," he demanded, and Faustine obeyed.

She wanted to ask what they were doing here, but knew Markus would either tell her on his own good time, or she'd be left stumbling in the dark behind him and guessing. But she would never make the mistake of asking. Not when he looked angrier than Faustine had ever seen him.

He stomped over to a lectern nestled between a bookshelf and a weapons rack. It was the same kind of podium that Faustine's professors taught from, only this one held a swordsmanship manual that looked completely unused.

"You will recall," Markus began, "what I have told you about Valente Secundus?"

Faustine swallowed hard. "You want his blood. That's why you switched me into the Violet Owls last semester."

Never mind that she had been happy in the Iron Cranes, or that it meant she basically had to start her reputation over with a new professor in order to be made prefect by her second year, like Father had demanded.

"Indeed." Markus' grey eyes flicked reflexively towards the closed door. "And you have, so far, accomplished absolutely nothing on that front."

Markus conveniently left out that he hadn't given her anything to take blood with. Was that another thing she was just expected to find, somehow? Where would she even get a syringe, besides the infirmary?

"I'm still working on it," she said.

"Well clearly, you need to be reminded of what's important," Markus said.

No! Faustine's eyes widened, and she braced for pain.

Instead, Markus flipped open the swords manual on the lectern, and held it open to a page. "Go on," he barked.

Nervously, Faustine crept towards the open book. Her vision swam with diagrams and lettering that felt a lot more like a magic tome than a martial one, but the page was just a diagram of the Vom Tag sword stance. Faustine could see the little man's hands holding his sword above his head.

Could see Professor Valerius' in her mind's eye, doing the same thing at every corner the Violet Owls had come to, earlier.

"Time's up," Markus muttered, and then he jammed his thumb into the little swordsman's face.

A heavy click came from deep within the lectern, and out of the corner of her eye, Faustine saw the bookshelf swing forward, just a little.

"I thought Orsina had been teaching you code, Faustine." Markus didn't even pause his reprimand as he pulled the bookshelf further into the room. Its hinges were whisper-silent. "Or is that yet another thing that's fallen to me?"

The bookshelf had swung open to reveal an honest-to-the-Goddesses secret tunnel. It was dark, but there was a magelight flickering at the bottom of the stone walled passage. The air was cooler there, but held the undercurrent of something foul.

Leave it to Markus to make something like a secret tunnel terrible.

Faustine expected him to shove her through the doorway, but Markus instead gestured impatiently for her to get moving. She ducked her head and did so, hurrying across the threshold and onto the stairs. Markus followed a moment later, shutting the bookshelf behind him with a thud. A moment later something clicked, like a lock resetting.

"Move," Markus barked, and Faustine realized she'd been standing still.

Markus pulled the magelight off the wall when they passed it, and shadows danced off the stony walls as he hurried onwards. Faustine began to feel the weight of the earth pressing down on them, constricting her lungs and distorting her own breaths, until stepping into the flat, open room at the foot of the stairs was a relief.

Until she saw the darkbeast.

She froze mid-stride, and Markus got several steps ahead of her before he noticed she wasn't beside him. The darkbeast was chained to an operating table, belly-up and with its head chained separately from its body. It was the decapitated one from earlier this afternoon, near as Faustine could tell. Same wolverine-like body and four green eyes set into its forehead.

It smelled even worse than before.

"Hold this." Markus didn't even wait for Faustine to acknowledge him before he was shoving a silver tray full of medical instruments into her hands. "Do not drop it, and do not touch anything."

Oh. Faustine swallowed hard. "Am I to be your assistant?"

"Well you're certainly not the surgeon."

Faustine made a face at Markus' back as he washed his hands in a nearby sink and pulled a kerchief over his mouth and nose.

He didn't offer her one, though, so Faustine had to ask, "Can I have one of those?"

Markus rolled his eyes, but found another kerchief for her. He set it down on a clean portion of the operating table before bustling off to find whatever else he wanted for this endeavor. Faustine carefully set down the silver instrument tray and picked up the kerchief. It was stained in the corner with something black and unidentifiable.

Faustine hoped it was ink, and tied the kerchief around her own nose and mouth.

She'd seen Markus work, of course, and assisted Orsina and their father with other darkbeast-related things. But Faustine had never been present for a dissection, before. She wondered what it was that Markus was hoping to find, or if he even *could*, amongst the black fur and purple flesh of the creature.

The first cut Markus made flooded the room with the same rank stench from the sewer grate behind Atticus Hall. Faustine's eyes watered, and she struggled to blink the moisture away. She couldn't touch her eyes, although Markus had at least thought to give her gloves.

He worked methodically, barking at her for this scalpel or those forceps. Faustine didn't know the names of all the instruments, and Markus snapped at her more than once for handing him the wrong one—hadn't he clearly said the five-eighths inch hemostat and the curette with the hook?

Faustine just tried to memorize which one did which thing faster than Markus could demand them. He snapped at her less as he kept on, although Faustine didn't know whether that meant she was getting better or he was just more focused on the darkbeast.

She wanted to ask him how it had gotten down here, and why it had been up in the quad. There were cages in the back room that Faustine could just make out through an open door down a short hall. Were more darkbeasts in there?

"*Ahhh.*" Markus breathed quietly, almost reverently, and set down his scalpel. "There you are."

He stuck his whole hand into the darkbeast's open chest cavity, and Faustine's eyes widened in horrified surprise. For a moment, she held her breath as Markus dug around viscera and Saints-knew-what-else, but a moment later, his eyebrows relaxed.

He pulled a large, red crystalline thing from the dead darkbeast.

"What is that?" Faustine asked, horrified.

"Its bloodstone, obviously." Markus shot her a withering look. "Thank the Saints it's still intact."

He set the lump down on the silver tray, and went back to digging around the darkbeast corpse.

Faustine stared at the crystalline lump in fascinated horror. It was about the size of her palm, and black, sticky ichor clung to its crevices and curves. But even through the muck, it shone a dull, ruddy red in the magelight, and if Faustine squinted and tilted her head just right, she could almost make out a small, glowing rune set deep into the middle of the rock.

"With any luck, I can use it for a new darkbeast," Markus added, and Faustine got the sense he was mostly talking to himself. "These things are the devil to create and I'm running low on supplies."

Something seemed to occur to him, and he looked at Faustine again.

"We wouldn't be in this mess if you had just gotten Secundus' blood when I initially told you to. I'm too low on Grimsdalr blood, and you know that."

Faustine swallowed the urge to argue with him and instead said, "Well what about Professor Valerius? She's got a bloodrune too; couldn't you use her blood?"

"I shall deal with her in due time." Markus switched back to pulling apart the Y-shaped incision he'd made, pinning back skin with forceps like an embroiderer ironing her work. "But for now, you're just going to keep an eye on the frigid bitch."

Faustine felt like she might throw up. She'd mostly brought the professor up to make Markus think about something else; she wasn't volunteering to spy on the woman! Professor Valerius had done something that, in fifteen years of Faustine's life, her father and older siblings never had.

She'd defended her.

Nobody did that, and especially not about anything serious. Professor Valerius may have been Kaldiri, and she may have been one of father's most detested enemies, but she was fair and honest.

Ja, she'd said. *Like a bitch.*

Who just came out and said that?

"It's perfect," Markus continued. "You can continue to gain Valente's trust and keep us informed of Valerius' maneuverings, right up until Father has need of either bloodrune."

Part of the reason Faustine hadn't made any progress about Valente was that, frankly, she didn't want to spy on her classmates, or steal their blood, or whatever other terrible thing Markus and Ironfang wanted her to do. She didn't like Valente very much, but that didn't mean he deserved to be chained to a wall in Markus' secret lab room.

So Faustine did what she did best, and tried to avoid doing things by talking about it too much.

"You still haven't said how I'm supposed to make Valente like me," she said.

This time when Markus leaned towards her, Faustine flinched before he'd even gotten close. She was out of his range, and she watched Markus' internal debate about whether to yell at her flicker in his eyes.

"You'll have to improvise," Markus hissed instead, turning back to the corpse. "Now, Valerius is too brash by half, but she is observant. Don't give her anything to suspect you."

Faustine braced herself. "Like what?"

"Like implying I'm involved, you dunce."

Faustine was pretty sure Professor Valerius was smart enough to figure that one out on her own, but knew better than to say so.

Ooooh, Markus was just so difficult! Their eldest sister, Orsina, enjoyed needling him, but Faustine mostly wanted to get out of a conversation with Markus—or any of her siblings, for that matter—as fast as possible. It was the least painful method of dealing with the lot of them, when you were the youngest and least likely to inherit a single thing.

"So," Markus said, "you will continue your assignment with Valente Secundus, and work your way into Valerius' good graces, such as they are. You are to inform me of anything useful or suspicious that you learn about either of them. If you could get their blood, that might be enough to appease Father for this morning's disaster."

Despair began to creep into Faustine's chest. How in the world was she supposed to get Valente's blood, let alone the professor's? She wasn't a white mage in training and, even if someone got hurt during swords class, the blood would be dry and useless long before Faustine could get it to Markus.

"I will be informing him, of course," Markus added.

This time, Faustine really did cry, although she managed not to make a sound as the tears streamed down her face.

"Good," Markus said, "you understand the gravity of the situation you've destroyed."

Of course she understood. Faustine wasn't stupid, even if Markus and their father liked to think so. She knew better than to disappoint Ironfang.

She wanted to say she'd get right on stealing the professor's menstrual rags and straddling Valente with a knife during training, but all that came out of her mouth was, "Was there anything else you wanted me to do?"

"I think you have plenty." Markus heaved a massive sigh, and scraped something off the darkbeast's innards. "I shall continue observing Caecillion in the meantime, although I imagine he'll mostly be chasing Kaldiri tail for a while."

Faustine blinked, surprise cutting off some of the silent tears. "He'll be what?"

"Saints above, Faustine," Markus said, exasperated, "I thought women were supposed to be observant about this kind of thing?"

"He doesn't seem any different when he talks to her!"

"I didn't ask your opinion on whether Father's old Spymaster seems like anything," Markus said flatly. "He's a very good liar. But to the point, yes, he's been in love with Valerius for probably a decade, and she's likely no better. It's part of the whole 'traitor to the crown' business we've been attempting to pin on him for that same decade."

Faustine's brow furrowed. It was hard to picture the grim headmaster as anything other than, well, that. Faustine couldn't reconcile the idea that he was in love with the blunt new swordmaster any more than the idea that Professor Valerius could be in love with him. It just didn't sound right. Headmaster Caecillion had once been her father's Imperial Spymaster, the infamous Viper of Ascalon, and Professor Valerius was the Wolf of Kaldr, or so Ironfang's stories went.

How did people that cold and that deadly love?

None of it made any sense, and Faustine knew enough about tactics to know that that meant she was missing one of the bigger pieces of the puzzle. It rankled her, that Markus and her father and everyone else seemed to think her incapable of higher order thinking.

"Although..." Markus rubbed something black and viscous off on a nearby cloth. "Perhaps Valerius' sudden intrusion is a good thing. Caecillion will be distracted enough to slip up, at the rate he's going."

Faustine was pretty sure the point of a Spymaster was that they didn't slip up, but she wasn't up for a third attempted smack, today. So she bit her tongue and didn't ask why there were darkbeasts in the quad, or why Markus needed bloodrune-bearers' blood so badly, or why his hands were shaking while he tried to dismantle the evidence of his work.

CHAPTER TWELVE

IF YOU TOLD HER outright that Frelia seemed more comfortable at Silverwood after the garmur attack in the quad, she'd have said you were full of shit. And then—privately in the back of her mind—she'd have said you were right.

She felt a lot more at ease dealing with monsters from legend than academic bureaucracy and her students. Such was her lot.

And so, after four separate attempts to get a curriculum approved by both Markus and Vendrick, it was why she was the most relaxed she'd ever been standing in front of a class that Wednesday evening.

Garmur Killing 101. Vendrick had thought the name was funny, but Markus, like just about everything else Frelia had put forward, had vetoed it. Twice. Eventually Vendrick had vetoed Markus' veto and said, to his face, that it was simply because he was tired of discussing this, and which one of them was the headmaster here.

It was, hands down, the funniest thing Frelia had ever seen a Volsinii do.

She tried to hold onto that thought, instead of *Merciful Saints why are there so many eyes.* Vendrick had pushed to open the seminar for professors, as well, since most of them were Volsinii and had never been on the business end of a garmr. Frelia hadn't been in much of a place to argue, so here she was. Teaching the entire second year of Silverwood, plus a handful of professors, what in Helheim a garmr even was.

"This is not a class on the anatomy and physiology of monsters," Frelia said from the lectern in the biggest lecture hall Silverwood had. "And it's not a class on their history in warfare, either. This is a class on how to kill the bastards when one comes charging at your face. Am I clear?"

"Yes, Professor Valerius!" chorused the students.

The handful of professors—Frelia noted Magicmaster Marcellius and Lancemaster Sabine near the front of the class—nodded as well, although a few made faces that said Frelia had done something wrong, somehow. She didn't exactly care.

"Good," Frelia said anyway. "First off, a question—before two showed up in the quad, how many of you had actually *seen* a garmr?"

The handful of professors immediately put their hands up, but that was no surprise. Frelia knew for fact that Lancemaster Sabine and Edmund had both served in the Tyrant's War, and Marcellius had been an old man fifteen years ago. She was more interested in the students.

Faustine raised her hand—*zero surprises there*—but so did Owen. He *had* to be a Grimsdalr knight's kid, Frelia was almost certain of it, now. Johanna, the Iron Cranes' house leader, also raised her hand, and so did Nikolaus from the Red Eagles.

Kaldiri kids, all of them—except for Faustine.

"Johanna," Frelia called, and the girl sat up straighter in her seat. "Tell me—what do they look like?"

"Oh," she said. "Um. Black fur, green eyes, and kind of like a forest animal. Deer or wolves or that kind of stuff."

"But bigger," Owen piped up, eager to please as ever. "And usually there's something wrong with them—too many eyes or two sets of antlers or something."

"Correct," said Frelia. "Now, who can tell me where they come from?"

Frelia watched as Owen visibly bit down on the inside of his cheek. As much as he wanted to be helpful, someone—his parents, probably—had drilled into him what he could say at Silverwood, and what he couldn't.

"The Northern Wilds, isn't it?" Sabine was examining her nails as though the entire lecture bored her.

"*Ja,*" Frelia confirmed. "That, or a beastminder summoned one. Then they can crop up anywhere."

It was the first time in the lecture Frelia had to pause for students to take notes. Quills and fountain pens scratched across parchment, echoing in the lecture hall like this was any other lesson, any other time.

Although it rankled her, Frelia swallowed her instinct to tell war stories from Heit Reiði, or Mydalr, or Skjöldr itself. She knew when to poke the sleeping dog, and when to let it lie. Markus had made it very clear what she was and wasn't allowed to say about the della Luciana Beastminders, after all.

"Who knows the legend behind the garmur?" Frelia asked instead.

Owen ducked his head and scribbled on his parchment. Nikolaus tapped his forefingers together and refused to make eye contact with anyone. Johanna started digging around her bookbag for something.

So. The kids knew their history. But knew better than to admit to it.

Fantastic.

Frelia hated the Imperator a little bit more with every passing moment.

"Once," Frelia began, "it is said, there were three divine sisters—Daybreak, Twilight, and Midnight. Lady Daybreak taught humanity to work the land and gave us fire, and it is from her that all things begin. Lady Twilight taught us to rest and the secrets of the sea, and it is from her that we learned balance, and measure. From Lady Midnight came endings—death, decay, and winter—for everything has its natural end."

"Professor?" Cora's hand went up—the Red Eagles' Prefect, doing her civic duty. "We're, um, not really supposed to talk about the Triad?"

"*Ja,* I'm aware." Frelia waved off the Imperator's orders like a buzzing horsefly. "However, you cannot understand what a garmr is without first knowing their legend."

She'd fought Markus tooth and nail about it, and even Vendrick had reservations about allowing her to tell what were very clearly Triad stories. In the end, they'd agreed to let her tell it under the condition that she kept proselytizing to the absolute minimum (not that Frelia was much of a preacher anyway) and treated it as a bit of historical trivia. Like studying legends from the Rippling Isles or the Free Cities.

Whatever. Frelia knew her place in the Waking World, and it wasn't appeasing Imperator Ironfang.

"Now for a time," she continued, "the three sisters watched over humanity together. But Lady Midnight, who ruled over Helheim and never gave up her dead, grew jealous of humanity's love for her sisters. Beginnings were all well and good, and life was lovely in its own right, but they only held meaning because of endings.

"And so she created her own beings—the garmur. She made them black as night itself and unrelenting as death, and they were meant to safeguard the entrance to Helheim. But in her jealousy, Lady Midnight made them hungry, too. And so garmur will eat, and eat, and never grow full. They are voids, and seek only to sate their hunger and serve their mother—though neither will ever be satisfied."

A shudder ran through the room, then. Even old man Marcellius drew his cloak a little more tightly around him, despite the warm autumn evening.

Then Karina's hand shot up. "What's Helheim, professor?"

"The land of the dead," Frelia said.

"Oh." Across the room, Valente's brow furrowed. "Do you mean Hypogia?"

"Uhh..." Frelia cocked an eyebrow and looked to Edmund.

The man was sitting halfway up the rows, still in his green-dyed cleric robe. "Yes," he said quietly. "Hypogia is what the Volsinii always called it. Helheim, the Kaldiri."

"Thanks, Blightsen," Frelia told him, and Edmund nodded before turning back to his notes. "Anyway, humanity grew tired of losing their friends and family to Lady Midnight's beasts, so they begged Lady Daybreak and Lady Twilight to do something about it. But the sisters could not kill their own kin any more than they could stop things from ending. So..."

"You know this is just a story, right?" Sabine interrupted. "Darkbeasts are no more supernatural than bears or sea snakes."

Frelia fixed the lancemaster in a gaze steady enough to fire arrows with. "Can stories not inform the way we view the world?"

Sabine's mouth opened like she wanted to protest, but then she shut it again. "I'm just saying," she said after a moment, "you don't need to go filling the students' heads with ecclesiastical nonsense to teach them how to keep an eye out for large animals."

Frelia had figured Sabine was here as Markus' plant, but that pretty much confirmed it. She fought back an enormous sigh.

"When *you* are teaching the class how to fight garmur," Frelia said, "you can do things *your* way. For now, we do them mine."

Someone in the back row made a strangled noise that was probably a giggle, and a rustling overtook the lecture hall.

"As I was saying..." Frelia began to pace the front of the room, unable to stand still and make herself an easy target. "...Lady Daybreak and Lady Twilight could not kill their own kin any more than they could stop things from ending. So they struck an accord.

"The Triad divided Helheim between themselves—Solivallr for Lady Daybreak, and the souls of the brave; the Sapphire Fields for Lady Twilight, and the souls of the diligent; and hell for Lady Midnight, and the souls of the wicked. And for a time, the garmur dwelled in hell with their mistress, and the world was peaceful once again."

"That... can't be the end of the story?" Faustine clapped a hand to her mouth, as though she hadn't meant to say that out loud.

"It isn't," Frelia said. "As the Sapphire Fields and Solivallr swelled with good folk and the Soul Warriors, Lady Midnight grew dissatisfied. If her sisters were so terrified of endings, then she would show them the end."

Frelia paused, just for a breath, to study the room. Most of the students were listening with visible intent, and it twisted Frelia's gut. This legend should not be new.

"The garmur burst from Helheim to ravage the land," Frelia continued. "And this time, the Bloodrune Saints begged Lady Daybreak and Lady Twilight for the power to push them back. So Lady Twilight poured her divine blood into the hollow of a shield, and each of the Saints drank from it. And it is from here that Bloodrunes come—they are the Goddesses' pity, sorrow, and power, all in one."

They were a lot more than that, but Frelia was already playing with fire. Just because there wasn't an Imperial Watcher standing in the back of the room didn't mean their ears weren't in it.

"The Saints took to the battlefields—to sword and bow, lance and spell. And for fifteen years, they and their kin pushed back against Lady Midnight and her terrible children. And Lady Midnight's fatal error was in underestimating humanity. Her garmur were much bigger, much stronger, much harder to kill—and yet, when she found herself cornered against the mouth to Helheim, she did not yield... Yes, Ellie?"

The Violet Owls' white mage put her hand back down. "Then why are there still darkb—er, garmur, in the world?"

"I'm getting to that." Frelia felt herself smile, just a little. Judging by the way Ellie flinched, it was probably ghastly. "Legend has it that the Bloodrune Saints sealed Lady Midnight into hell, never to leave, but her children were caught in the in-between. Not quite alive, not quite dead. There would always be garmur, then, in the Waking World."

Her smile fell as she cut the cadence off awkwardly. Here was the part where a cleric would build the story into a crescendo, where she would tell the gathered folks about the Bloodruned Saints and their duty unending. About Frelia's ancestors, and Cillian's, and Valente's, and every other bloodruned person's.

About their Sacred Tasks, and their defense of the world since time immemorial.

But Frelia could no more say any of that than she could cut off her own hand.

"So," Frelia said instead, and she willed her voice to remain level, and loud, "if we assume that legend is at least partially true, that's why they're big, hungry, and angry."

Frelia held up a finger for each attribute.

"It's also why they're smart enough to learn," she continued, "and hunt in packs."

"Wait," said Owen, "they hunt in packs?"

"*Ja,*" Frelia said. "Where there's one, there's always more." She glanced across the classroom and was stunned to find Axemaster Ossani raising a hand. "Uh, Ossani?"

"Even the big ones?" he asked, putting his hand back down.

Beside him, Siegmund's eyes got wide. "There are big ones?"

Frelia sighed. "Okay, diagram time."

She turned to the blackboard behind her, and located a piece of chalk somewhere on the railing. She drew a flat line, and then rudimentary dog-looking things with pointy ears and two sets of eyes. The first one she made no larger than her palm, the second, the size of her forearm, and the third, nearly as large as her whole arm.

"There are," Frelia began, putting the chalk back down, "generally speaking, three kinds of garmur—the little ones, the big ones, and the extra big ones, which I will call archgarmur because it sounds less stupid."

The Violet Owls laughed, but they were the only ones who apparently realized that was meant to be funny.

"The little ones are usually a vanguard," Frelia continued. "There's a swarm of them typically led by one of the middle-size ones, called a Huntmaster. That's a lot of what I fought in the war."

Karina raised one trembling hand, and when Frelia called on her, the girl asked, "Were the ones in the quad... little ones?"

"Correct," said Frelia.

A hush fell across the room. Even Sabine stopped filing her nails.

"But those were huge!" Karina said. "Like bear-hunting dogs, or horses, or baby wyverns, or..."

"Correct," said Frelia again.

Karina's jaw fell open, and on her left, Ellie said, "Oh Saints..."

"You are beginning to understand their utility in warfare," Frelia said, and she tried not to inject anything other than fact into it.

She tried to keep the rumbling feeling from her bones, and the sight of her comrades between garmur teeth out of her mind's eye, and the feeling of their fetid breath on her heels off her skin.

"They are walking siege weapons..."

Skjöldr flashed in her mind's eye, its walls crumbling as bull-like garmur rushed headlong into the ancient stones.

"...destructive, hungry beasts..."

Her father, standing in the courtyard at Heit Reiði, his lance at the ready as he stared down a dozen of the big ones snarling at the gates.

"...that don't care what they kill, or who they eat."

The aftermath of a dozen battles flashed through her mind. Severed arms scattered across cobblestones, viscera splattered against houses and shops, corpses only identifiable by an intact boot or family ring.

Frelia tried to breathe deeply, but she only smelled blood and war and burning hair.

"*That,*" she said, "is what broke into the quad."

That was what Cillian had taught her to face, just like his family had done for generations. What Thera had made witch balls and druid charms to ward against. What both of the Twins had fought since birth.

"How do you fight something like that?" whispered a small, Volsinii voice.

Frelia didn't know where it came from. It could have been any of the students, or even one of the professors. That small, hopeless note Frelia knew very well.

"That is what I'm here to teach you."

Frelia turned back to the blackboard to draw a four-legged garmur in profile. It came out looking more like a bear than a dog, but it didn't matter. She only needed a visual demonstration.

"The little ones don't get much bigger than horses," Frelia said, and pens began to fly across parchment. "The big ones can range from carriage-sized to building-sized. As for archgarmur..."

Frelia trailed off. How could she describe a monster she'd never seen, and wasn't even sure existed?

"Well, if you see one of those," she finally said, "just run."

And fall on your sword if you can't, but Frelia couldn't say that to a room full of fifteen year olds. Even she knew better than that.

"Your best bet, whether the garmr goes on two legs or four, is to sever the ankle tendons." Frelia circled the ankle on each of her diagram's four legs. "That will incapacitate it long enough to blow its head off with artillery." She tapped the head with her chalk. "Not even garmur can come back from that."

"And if there are no cannons nearby?" Professor Marcellius asked.

"Option two," Frelia said, "is to crack open its rib cage so you can light its insides on fire." She moved to point to the bear-garmr's chest with her chalk. "Magically, or the old fashioned way—doesn't matter, it'll burn just the same... Yes, Christel?"

"Why do you have to cut it open to light it on fire?" It was the first time they'd looked up from their notes all class.

"Because," Frelia said, "their hides are greasy enough that fire sloughs right off. They'll singe, but don't burn."

Christel made a disgusted face, but didn't ask anything else.

"Now this next part is almost as important as the actual killing," Frelia said. "Once you have downed the monster, you need to dispose of the monster. Or more will show up."

"That's a myth," Sabine sniffed.

Saints, were Imperial Watchers paid to say that stupid line?

"No, it's not," Frelia barked. "It's how we lost a lot of Kaldiri knights in the war. We didn't know to burn the corpses, at first."

She would never forget curling up on her bedroll the night after the Battle for Kollavik, and waking up hours later to screaming and a camp overrun with monsters. It had been a second massacre, right on the heels of the first. Cillian had nearly lost a leg that night when his war horse had been eaten. He'd instead broken his femur in his haste to dismount, and Frelia'd had to carry him far enough into the forest that the big garmur couldn't follow.

"But we learned," she said, instead of telling the story of one of the worst nights of her life. "We also learned if you cut up a garmr corpse, it'll burn faster. So I highly recommend chopping off limbs and throwing them on a pyre as you go."

"Did we, um, burn the ones from the quad?" Faustine asked, shifting uncomfortably in her seat.

"You'd have to ask Captain della Luciana," Frelia said. "He's the one who insisted on dealing with the corpses."

So, no.

"How many times have you fought these things, professor?" asked one of the Iron Cranes Frelia didn't know.

"Too many." It wasn't Frelia who spoke, but Edmund. His eyes were haunted behind those thick glasses of his.

"We broke no rules of engagement—" Sabine began, and something deep in Frelia snapped.

"I fought them at Skjöldr," Frelia barked. "Mydalr. Kollavik. Fort Frostmaiden. Fort Knaerwood. Fairhunter. Heit Reiði. On the road between forts and settlements. And *yes,* the southern coast of Grimsdalr Territory, Fort Kjalla, and Spirits' Fen."

The silence that followed was deafening.

"So I don't care," Frelia growled, "whether the Volsinii Senate says you broke the rules of engagement or not. For what they have done to my homeland, I will see every garmr burn."

She'd pushed too far. Frelia could see it at once, in the faces of her fellow professors. Sabine was smiling like she had evidence and was going to run to Markus the first chance she got, and Edmund was making slashing motions at his throat with eyes magnified wide as wyverns' behind his glasses.

But the students just sat there in stunned shock, staring at their swordmaster and probably wondering what else she'd lived through. What she'd seen. The brave ones would probably start asking her for war stories, when they thought the Watchers or Volsinii professors weren't listening. The cowards—or, no, that was unfair, they were still children after all—the *children* would probably have nightmares and pretend like they'd never heard of a garmr. Maybe skip her class a few times until they stopped panicking at the sight of her.

But it was too late to take any of it back. Too late to pretend the Volsinii hadn't brutalized her people in the war, to pretend the horror of a garmr attack wasn't still fresh in her mind when she shut her eye.

Too late, to return to the innocence they'd once had.

"I think that's enough for one day," Frelia said. "All of you without bloodrunes are dismissed."

That set the Volsinii kids tittering, just like it always did. The Kaldiri ones kept their heads down.

"Valerius," Marcellius said with kindness forced through the horror in his eyes, "is that really necessary?"

She stopped to look at him—really look at him. Marcellius was horrified, sure, but Frelia didn't know whether it was for himself, for her, or for the student she had once been.

"*Ja,*" Frelia said. "There are a few things those of you with bloodrunes need to know, when you face a garmr."

CHAPTER THIRTEEN

FAUSTINE KNEW SHE NEEDED to leave the lecture hall. She didn't have a bloodrune, and the Professor seemed so on edge that the wrong word would make her bite. But Markus would definitely want to know what Professor Valerius thought was so important about bloodrunes that only those with them should know it.

It was always the thing Markus railed against, after all. *Bloody secretive lot, the bloodruned families.*

All around her, there were students and professors filing out of the big lecture hall in Brekka Hall. Most were unusually quiet, but some—like Owen—were talking even more loudly than normal. Asking about whether anyone wanted to check the commissary, or needed to go to the library.

Valente stayed in his seat, staring down at his notes with a look like he wanted to melt into the floor. Faustine could hear Markus' voice in the back of her head telling her to *make friends, dammit.*

"Are you okay?" she asked Valente quietly.

"Of course." He sniffed. "I am just following orders."

Right. Of course he was.

Faustine turned back to her own notes and began shoving them into her canvas book bag. She missed the heavy, booted footsteps that approached from the front of the classroom, and startled when she sat back up to find Professor Valerius with her arms folded across her sternum standing at the foot of her desk.

"Go on, Faustine," the professor said. "I'm sure your brother will want to know how this went, anyway."

"Professor Sabine is probably already on it," Faustine mumbled, getting to her feet.

Professor Valerius snorted. "You said it, not me."

The professor wasn't stupid. She waited until Faustine had trudged out of the lecture hall to turn back to Valente; Faustine could feel it when the woman's' eye left her back. And dammit, Faustine was missing important information. She knew she was.

Wasn't there a door to the upper floor of the lecture hall, though? Maybe she could sneak in through there to listen. Professor Valerius had a voice that echoed across the training ground; she could probably catch something the woman said. It would be better than going back to Markus empty handed.

That decided, Faustine turned towards the stairs—

"Oi, Faustine!"

—and froze.

Owen waved cheerfully from the door out of Brekka Hall. "We're going to the commissary for snacks," he shouted. "Do you want to come?"

"Oh, um, no thank you." Faustine's stomach protested loudly.

Christel raised an eyebrow. "You sure?"

"Yes." Faustine forced herself to smile, and she knew from experience it was a pretty good fake. "I wanted to find a classroom to do some homework in after the darkbeast class, anyway."

She held up her heavy canvas bookbag and shook it for good measure.

"Uh, okay," Owen said. "Good luck, I guess?"

"Thanks!"

Faustine took the stairs up to the second floor two at a time. She had class up here on Tuesdays, and tried to focus on the doors she didn't normally see opening. *Two-oh-four, two-oh-five... ah ha!*

She set her heavy bag down beside the door labeled two-oh-six, and pulled her hand back into her sweater sleeve. She carefully checked over each shoulder, then twisted the knob, tense and ready for the hinges to squeal.

But they slid smoothly, and Faustine slipped back into the lecture hall with not a moment to spare.

"...felt really weird after I left my duel," Valente was saying. His voice drifted up the stadium-style rows and straight to Faustine's ear. "I don't really know how to describe it, Professor."

From her vantage point behind the desks in the second floor balcony, Faustine could just see the back of Valente's head. He was still seated at his desk, and Professor Valerius still had her arms folded, but now she was leaning sideways against what had been Faustine's desk. If she looked up at the wrong angle, Faustine would be caught, and it made her stomach twist.

"Let me guess," said the Professor. "It felt sort of like your entire body was vibrating, and your bones wanted to grind themselves out of your skin?"

Faustine recoiled, but Valente stayed silent for a long moment.

"Yeah," he finally said. "That's... kind of... Saints, yeah."

"We always called it the rumbling, because that's what it feels like," Professor Valerius said. "It's what happens when bloodruned folk get near a garmr."

"Who's we?"

Funny, Faustine also wanted to know that.

"The, um." For the first time since they'd met her, Faustine and Valente both saw their professor stumble. She had talked around things and corrected her speech mid-sentence before, but she'd never gone completely blank like this.

A moment later, Professor Valerius sighed. "The Krakenguard."

Faustine filed the word away to tell Markus later.

"But anyway," the professor continued, "that's how I knew there were garmur in the quad so fast. I *felt* it, long before I saw them."

"Was..." Valente seemed to be on the verge of something. "...was it like that during the Tyrant's War, too? During all those battles you mentioned?"

Professor Valerius shut her eye. "*Ja.*"

Shit. If Faustine had been taken aback before, she was *horrified*, now. What *was* a bloodrune, to do that to a person?

"Do you know your family's Sacred Task, Valente?"

His head whipped towards the doors, and then he said, very quietly, "And for Domitia, the Task of the Huntress: You shall pursue that which you most fear."

That all sounded... church-y, to Faustine's untrained ear. Sure, she'd been to the occasional Unseen service with her father and older siblings, but the Unseen weren't really a 'gather on Sundays to hear a sermon' type.

Still. Ironfang's interest in darkbeasts would make sense if he also worshipped Lady Midnight, based on what Professor Valerius had been saying. But why had no one else ever told Faustine that? Did Markus even know?

Faustine's hands tightened in her sweater sleeves as the weight of the unspoken settled over her shoulders like her prefect's cloak.

"Good." Professor Valerius nodded to Valente. "Hold onto that as we move forward."

Faustine could practically hear Valente's furrowed brow when he asked, "What do you mean?"

"Until we know how those monsters got into the quad," Professor Valerius said, "you and me are Silverwood's first line of defense. We will know garmur are coming long before anyone else does."

She set a heavy hand on Valente's shoulder, and he jumped.

"Sorry for your lot."

"I didn't even *think* of that..." Valente's voice was dropping as the realization cracked across his head. Faustine strained to hear more, and crept out from behind the desk, just a little, trying to hear.

"You don't have to charge headlong and defenseless into hell," Professor Valerius said. "You just—"

Faustine's loafer crunched a loose piece of paper, and Professor Valerius' eye snapped up towards the balcony. Faustine froze, and prayed she was still hidden enough behind the desk and chairs. Her heart hammered in her chest as Professor Valerius stared hard at the second floor balcony.

"You just need to tell someone if you feel the rumbling," the professor said, looking back to Valente after what felt like an eternity. "Preferably a professor, not a Watcher, but beggars can't always be choosers."

"Why not a Watcher?" Valente asked. "Isn't that what they're for?"

"Because Captain della Luciana would rather beastmind the damn things than kill them," the professor said. "And he doesn't have that luxury in a confined space like Silverwood."

From what Faustine had heard of her oldest brothers, Saints rest their souls, they could have managed it. They'd practically been darkbeast-whisperers, to hear Galeria tell it. Could even bring the big ones to heel in the middle of a bloody battlefield, if they needed to.

Markus... was not nearly so talented a beastminder. And everyone knew it.

"Okay," said Valente. "I'll try to find you, if I feel it."

"Doesn't have to be me specifically." Professor Valerius was looking around the lecture hall like a wolf who had scented prey, the angles of her round face lethal as they twisted in the lamplight.

Faustine needed to get out of here, now. But if she tried to open the second floor balcony door, the professor would surely see or hear it, now that she was on alert. Could Faustine curl into a ball beneath a chair and wait out the professor's inevitable search once Valente left? *Maybe...*

Then Faustine remembered her bag, sitting outside the door, and mentally cursed herself. She would have to get out of here and find a classroom before the professor found her.

"Anyway, if you don't have any questions, that's all, Valente." Professor Valerius said. "You're dismissed."

Shit!

"Actually, I did have one?" Valente said.

Faustine could have kissed him.

"Why did you tell everyone else to leave just to tell me about the rumbling?" Valente asked, and now that he mentioned it, Faustine was wondering the same thing.

Beyond how Church-of-the-Triad-heavy everything related to bloodrunes usually was, what about it was so secret that everyone else didn't deserve to know?

"One," said the professor, "because if everyone finds out you're a walking alarm bell, you end up treated like one."

That... actually made a lot of sense. Faustine wasn't so afraid of darkbeasts as most of her classmates, but if she were like Karina or Arielle who had never seen one...

Yeah. Valente would suddenly and stressfully become the most popular person on campus.

"Two," Professor Valerius added, "if you hadn't felt it yourself—would you even believe me?"

Faustine blinked. What an odd question.

"Err," said Valente, "probably not. Your description would sound kind of... I don't know, overdramatic?"

"Exactly."

Had it? Maybe Faustine really was stupid, because she'd just taken the professor's description of the rumbling at face value. Was she not supposed to?

Faustine shook her head, and tried to creep back towards the balcony door without turning around. She kept her eyes on the ground, careful to step around the loose notes she'd crushed before, and kept her ears peeled for anything else.

"You're dismissed, Valente. Go find yourself something to eat. Apparently if you hurry, you can catch Owen at the commissary before it closes."

Wait. If the professor had heard that, what else had she...?

Shit, shit, shit!

Faustine lunged for the balcony door, and prayed Valente's laugh covered the sound of the hinges. Faustine snatched up her bag and sprinted down the hall. She wrenched open the first door that wasn't locked, and dropped onto the nearest desk chair.

She pulled out her tactics homework and tried to make it look like she'd been here since the end of the original lecture. How did she normally do homework, anyway? Did she put the textbook to the left of her work, or the top? Should she have grabbed a drink from the commissary after all?

She heard heavy boots coming from the hallway, and tried to focus on the tactics homework. *You are put in command of an archery unit for an upcoming battle. The terrain is extremely flat, and dry due to lack of rain. If the enemy is reported to have a full infantry contingent as well as archers of their own, how would you best prepare for a battle likely to take place in the next few days?*

"Faustine."

She startled at the sound of her name, and looked up to see Professor Valerius in the doorway.

"What in Helheim are you doing in here?" the professor added.

"Err." Faustine's heart was pounding so hard, she wondered if the professor could hear it. "Studying?"

"In the dark?" the professor pressed.

Faustine shrugged. "I didn't think it was *that* dark yet."

The sun was setting, now, clearly visible out the windows on the other end of the room. If she intended to stay here too much longer, Faustine would need to light a sconce or runelight or something. But for now, she hoped, it was fine.

"Plus, the library is always crammed this time of year," Faustine said. "I prefer the quiet."

The professor's eye narrowed, and Faustine's palms started to sweat. She wished she could wipe them on her skirt without making it obvious.

"One thing I hope you learn from me, Faustine," Professor Valerius finally said, "is that in all things, there are hunters, and there are prey."

She leaned over the lectern, rummaging around the back of it for a moment before straightening back up with the room's tinderbox in hand.

"*Don't.*" She took a step forward.

"Be." Another.

"Prey." She tossed the tinderbox onto Faustine's notes, where it landed with a thump so heavy Faustine almost startled out of her seat.

Professor Valerius left the room again, and Faustine didn't stop shaking until long after her footsteps had receded into the growing twilight.

CHAPTER FOURTEEN

VENDRICK'D HAD A HUNCH that Garmur Killing 101 was not going to run smoothly, given how hard Markus had fought him on the curriculum. But Vendrick had at least hoped Frelia could teach more than a single seminar before Markus dragged her into his office by the scruff of her neck.

Fantastic. This was just what Vendrick needed this morning.

"What did I tell you?" Markus snapped. "This dog should be muzzled before she—"

"You will speak of and to your coworkers with civility," Vendrick interrupted calmly, "or remove yourself from my office."

"And let go, dammit." Frelia swatted at Markus' hand, clenched around her bicep.

He released his grip, but didn't move from the doorframe. He was, quite literally, throwing his weight around and Vendrick didn't like it. Frelia didn't either, judging by how she sidestepped around the chairs on the opposite side of Vendrick's desk so that she could keep an eye on both men.

It was too early in the morning for this argument. Vendrick wasn't even through his first cup of coffee yet.

"If you're prepared to be civil..." Vendrick fixed Markus in a hard stare. "...then tell me—what in the world are you barging into my office for?"

"I have class in twenty minutes," Frelia muttered.

"Have you not heard what happened last night, Vendrick?" Markus snapped, and Vendrick winced at the use of his given name. "It's all the students can talk about!"

"Caecillion will do," Vendrick reminded him, "and say that I haven't."

Of course he knew; who did Markus think he was dealing with? But if the captain wanted to throw accusations around, Vendrick was going to make him come out and say them.

"She was telling war stories, Vendrick!" Markus shouted.

"I was not," Frelia argued. "I said I'd fought garmur at several battles during the war. That's not the same thing, and it's also my credentials!"

"Point to Valerius," said Vendrick. "They'd be asking why she was teaching the class otherwise."

Markus looked affronted, but he pressed on. "She also scared several of the students within an inch of their lives. Who in their right mind tells a room full of fifteen-year-olds that darkbeasts eat people?"

"They do eat people!" Frelia screeched. "Am I supposed to pretend like they aren't monsters? Or should I have said, 'just fall on your sword to spare yourself the indignity of being eaten alive if you see one' and left it there?"

"Point to della Luciana." Vendrick sighed. "In the future, be more tactful, Valerius. You needn't lie to them or cause a panic."

Frelia's eye twitched, but she didn't get the chance to say anything because Markus was shouting, "And furthermore, she told Triad legends!"

"Moot point," Vendrick said. "We approved the original legend of the darkbeasts as historical context, provided she stopped before the part regarding the Bloodrune Saints."

"Which I did," Frelia hissed. "It's not like all the second years can tell you who the nine bloodruned families are."

"Were," said Markus crisply.

A vein pulsed in Frelia's temple, and her right hand curled into a fist at her side.

Saints, this was getting bad. Vendrick needed to—

"She also singled out the bloodruned students and told them lies about their status afterwards," Markus said smugly.

For the first time in the entire argument, Vendrick was taken aback enough to set down his fountain pen and study the two more closely. That didn't sound like Valerius, in that she both knew the cost of such a thing, and was a deeply practical woman. She didn't have any agenda beyond keeping the bloodrunes and their bearers alive.

"I beg pardon?" Vendrick said.

Frelia met his gaze head on, and didn't look away. "I told them anyone with a bloodrune has a few other things they should know about garmur. Not everyone needed to know we're walking alarm bells."

"You are?" Vendrick asked at the same time Markus said, "You're what?"

"We can feel the garmur coming long before we lay eyes on them." Frelia bounced on her heels, her sword jangling in its sheath at her side. "It feels like a rumbling in your blood."

Vendrick blinked as he processed this new information. "Is that why nothing at Mydalr was a surprise to your side?"

"*Ja,*" said Frelia warily. "We had me and the Twins on hand at Mydalr."

"Oh this is ridiculous," Markus said. "See what I mean, Vendrick?"

Vendrick ignored him. "Why didn't you mention this at the staff meeting, Valerius?"

"Because no one has ever believed me unless they felt it themselves." Frelia snorted like something was funny. "They just called me crazy."

"You *are* crazy," Markus muttered.

"*Ja,* well, you can thank your da for that."

Between the two of them, Vendrick was getting a migraine. "*Enough.*"

The warring parties across his desk fell silent.

"It sounds to me," Vendrick began, "that Valerius kept to the agreed-upon curriculum and perhaps could have more tactfully addressed a few things. This does not warrant barging into my office and making a scene, della Luciana. Particularly since Valerius has classes to teach this morning and we have..."

Vendrick looked down to the scheduling sheet he'd been working on before this chaos.

"...*no* substitutes. Either bring me accusations of substance, Captain, or kindly see to your own duties this morning."

Markus stared at Vendrick like he could bore a hole through Vendrick's chest.

"Last I heard," Vendrick added, "you still had no idea how those darkbeasts got into campus. Has that changed?"

It was so satisfying to watch Markus go purple with rage. Vendrick was a practiced hand at it, but it never got old.

"This is not the end of this," Markus hissed.

"It never is, with you," Vendrick agreed.

Markus stormed out of Vendrick's office, his Imperial Watcher's cloak a bloody red smear in the air behind him. Vendrick reached for his coffee cup and took a small sip, eyeing Valerius over the rim. Was she witnessing this properly? Did she suspect anything beyond two Queenmakers arguing? She wasn't stupid, but she wasn't Volsinii, either.

She turned to go, and Vendrick was forced to ask her back, "Have you spoken with Blightsen since last night?"

Frelia paused midway across his office. "Why would I do that?"

Vendrick's eyebrow rose as he set down his coffee cup. "He's the school counsellor and I am required to ask?"

"I don't need to talk to Edmund about it." Frelia's fists tightened at her sides.

Survey says otherwise, Vendrick thought, but he wasn't an idiot. "It's not unreasonable to find the past upsetting," he said instead. "That's all."

"Upsetting," Frelia hissed, "is 'I left the laundry out in the rain and now I have to do it all over again.' Fighting garmur is 'watching all of my friends die by being torn apart, eaten, and then shat out again by a monster.'"

Vendrick studied her carefully for a moment. It kept him from dwelling on that lovely mental image. Her shoulders were taut, her fists clenched, and she'd spat most of that out through gritted teeth.

"But you don't need to talk to the other Kaldiri on staff," he remarked.

Frelia made a disgusted, very Kaldiri-sounding noise that Vendrick honestly didn't know when the last time he'd heard was. Probably from her, in school. "Talking to Edmund isn't going to help," Frelia muttered. "I served with him, remember?"

"And?"

Frelia rolled her eye. "And, he'll probably piss himself in terror if I bring up Kollavik or Mydalr; he was a healer for the Saints' sake. I'm fine, Caecillion. I just..." All the annoyance fell away from her, and it left behind a hollowness Vendrick couldn't name. "...I wasn't expecting to have to remember. That's all."

Watching all of my friends die by being torn apart, eaten, and then shat out again by a monster, she had said.

Vendrick wondered how many times that had actually happened. More than once, he was thinking, if she could draw it up so readily to clothe herself in the fury it granted her.

Did Grimsdalr die that way? He wanted to fire back. But he knew it would start a fight about how the man had actually died, and it would be antithetical to Vendrick's entire purpose.

Which was, chiefly, that he needed an ally here at Silverwood, and he needed one badly. Frelia Valerius may have once been his enemy, but that was exactly why she was the best candidate now. She wasn't Volsinii; she had no patience for their political games, and she wouldn't play them. So if there was one person whose opinion he could trust, it would be hers—if he could just get her on board.

So instead of needling her, Vendrick said, "I did hear, however, that you have some choice commentary for the Volsinii Senate about the war."

"Who doesn't?" Frelia asked flatly.

"Okay, that's fair." Vendrick snorted. "But keep it to yourself, next time. Markus is looking for any excuse he can to get you fired."

Frelia cocked her head, studying him with the intensity of a wolfhound who had sighted its quarry. "Why bother to stop him?"

"If I could bring your attention to the previous bit about substitute teachers...?" Vendrick jerked a thumb over his shoulder as if to point at it.

She spluttered into hoarse laughter, and the sound warmed his very bones. It was good to hear her laugh again, to see that stony mask moved off-center. She seemed more like Frelia that way, and less like a hollow shell of herself.

Vendrick shook his head as though he could physically dislodge that thought.

"Also, by the way, Caecillion..." Frelia looked over her shoulder to the open office door.

"You may shut it," Vendrick said carefully, "if you like."

Frelia nodded, and crossed the rest of the way to close the door. She turned back to face him to say, quietly, "You have a mole. That's the only way a damn garmr is making it anywhere near the center of campus, and Markus knows it."

Saints, Vendrick had missed working with professionals. His spy network was only so helpful while spread so thin across the continent. He had a few folks posing as kitchen and janitorial staff here at Silverwood, but it wasn't like he could be seen talking to them all the time.

Part of him wanted to ask what she knew, what she guessed, but the other part of him screamed that even if she still faced darkbeasts head-on and had a crooked smile, she might not be the Frelia Valerius he had known, at all. He didn't think there was someone masquerading as the old Kaldiri general, but that didn't mean it wasn't possible.

But, said a little voice in the back of his mind, *there are ways of determining if someone is who she says she is.*

"Valerius," Vendrick said, "humor me with a question, would you?"

"Humor you?" She stared at him in disbelief, and Vendrick wondered what she even saw, anymore.

Vendrick sighed. "Say it's for old times' sake."

"Do you want me to duel you?"

Oh, he didn't have the patience for this today! "Didn't work out well for Grimsdalr the first time, no?"

The olive branch snapped, and they stared at each other over his desk like circling felines.

Damn.

"Keep his name out of your Goddesses-damned mouth," Frelia hissed.

"Answer the question, and consider it done."

It would be a start, anyway.

"Fine." Frelia crossed her arms across her lean frame. "What?"

Vendrick honestly hadn't expected to get this far, and so his mind completely wiped itself clean of everything except the most obvious one. "Where and when did the black magic study group meet, when we were Silverwood students?"

Frelia physically recoiled. "Where did *what?*"

"I did say humor me," Vendrick pointed out.

Frelia stared at him like she was in physical pain. "Thursday nights in the back of the library," she finally said. "Or sometimes out by the lake, in the spring when the weather was nice."

She suddenly wasn't looking at him.

Ah. So she remembered that day in the spring of their third year, as well. *Capital.* Vendrick released a breath—and with it, the tension in his shoulders. "Thank you."

"Why the fuck would you ask me that?" Frelia muttered, mostly to his office door.

"Do you want the honest answer?" He was stalling, and he knew it.

"Are you capable of giving one?"

Despite everything, Vendrick laughed. She really was the same as she'd been, all those years ago. It warmed something deep in his Spymaster's soul.

"Because," he said, "I needed to confirm that you were you."

Frelia froze, her knuckles turning white against her palms. "You think I'm an imposter?"

"Not anymore." It was only years of working in the Senate that kept Vendrick's face straight. "That was the point of the question."

"I killed two garmur in front of you," Frelia snapped, "and you wonder if I'm me?"

Well, when she put it like that, it did sound sort of ridiculous, didn't it? The only thing the General Valerius was more famous for than being stubborn as the northern wind was darkbeast-killing. She was a consummate professional, that way.

"And what do you care if I'm Frelia Valerius or someone wearing her face, anyway?" she added. "I can teach Ironfang's fucking daughter either way, can't I?"

Ironfang.

It struck Vendrick over the head. *All roads lead to Ironfang*, he thought. And just like that, Vendrick had found the skeleton key that would unlock Frelia Helm's Grace Valerius.

"Well, for starters," Vendrick said, "the darkbeasts only showed up *after* you arrived, and your wartime record is a hell of an alibi, wouldn't you say?"

Frelia's hands smacked down on the top of his desk, jarring paperwork and inkpots. Vendrick didn't flinch. "I did not bring those cursed beasts here."

"You, as in Frelia Valerius? Of course not." Vendrick stared down the amber eye that had haunted him all these years. "You, as in someone theoretically wearing your face? It'd be a brilliant cover story."

She leaned on his desk now, her face looming over his head in the early morning sun. "Is that possible?"

"For Ironfang's people? Absolutely." Vendrick refused to smile. It would give him away. "So, you'll have to excuse my double-checking. It's a habit I've found I can't break."

She looked like she wanted to ask him something. It was on the tip of her tongue, *right there*, waiting to be breathed into being.

Come on, Frelia, Vendrick mentally urged her. *If you're still you, I know you'll want to fight the bastard.*

"Fine." She suddenly straightened back up. "Am I good to go teach?"

Vendrick couldn't keep the surprise from his face. He had expected her to push, to press, to demand answers and reasons. Did she not trust him enough to talk further? That would explain a lot, and the more he thought on it, the more he figured it was probably true.

Dammit, was war not enough of an in with her anymore?

"Of course," Vendrick said, "if you've nothing further you wished to discuss?"

"Just thought I'd ruin Markus' day," Frelia muttered, and she disappeared from his office so fast, it was like she'd never been there at all.

CHAPTER FIFTEEN

FRELIA FELL INTO THE rhythm of Silverwood life about as well as she had the first time—which was to say, poorly. There were many late nights and early mornings; she lifted the ban on beverages in her class just so that she could drink some damn coffee. Markus had not been thrilled, but Frelia had pointed out that if they were going to be assisting the Watchers in patrolling the place, there were going to have to be some concessions.

It was mostly that Professors Sabine and Ossani agreed with her about the coffee, Frelia figured, that had lifted the ban permanently.

"Try not to let him get to you; della Luciana just likes to throw his weight around," Edmund said to Frelia one night as they patrolled the quiet campus. "And I can help you with your darkbeast lesson plans later this week, if you'd still like help?"

He and Frelia had sort of buried their argument from that first night in the cafeteria in the time-honored, Kaldiri way—by one of them bringing it up haphazardly, and the other punching them in the shoulder and telling them to shut up.

"I'm *this close*—" Frelia held up one gloved hand, her thumb and forefinger a half-inch apart "—to taking them to the training ground and teaching them the war songs, Markus della Luciana be damned."

"You really shouldn't joke about that, Frelia," Edmund said with a nervous laugh, glancing over his shoulder as if the Watcher Captain might appear.

"It's not a joke."

Edmund's eyes widened, comically large behind their frames. "Then you really shouldn't be saying that. I know you miss the war songs, but it's not safe."

Frelia had warred with herself about this, but ultimately had wound up caught between 'the Grimsdalr war song is about garmur' and not wanting to wake up dead.

Or worse, fired.

"They're practical!" she argued anyway. "Are you really trying to tell me you never get the black magic song stuck in your head?"

"I never said that." Edmund glanced over his shoulder again and, upon confirming that the path was empty, sighed. "What about your sword classes? Are those going any better?"

"I guess." Frelia kicked at a loose cobblestone as they rounded the corner of the academic quad. "I just keep running into the language barrier."

Most of her students had picked up the obvious—the parts of the sword were *stark/swach,* as opposed to *forte/debole, Vom Tag* was your basic guard up stance, *hau* was the word for strike—but nothing was ever done quickly when it took half the class to get everyone on the same page.

Professor Valerius, one of her students had said the other day, *why aren't you using the right words?*

Mine are relics of a lost age, Frelia had said, pressing the tip of her longsword into the sandy training ground floor. *Just like me.*

"Then why not learn the Volsinii terms?" Edmund asked.

Frelia had already picked up a handful of them, but still, she recoiled. "Why in Helheim would I do that?"

"It would probably make your life easier." Edmund already sounded on the verge of an apology.

Frelia spat on the cobblestones. "Not worth it."

Edmund studied her a moment with an old sadness in his eyes, and then said, very quietly, "They're just words, Frelia."

"No. They're not."

Silence passed over them for a few turns, broken only by the chittering of birds overhead in their nest, up in a classroom window too high for regular cleaning. Frelia knew she was being unreasonable, and also that she didn't care.

"It's not a moral failing to fade into the background, you know," Edmund finally said. "Sometimes it's just... necessary."

Frelia pulled up short, and Edmund got several paces ahead of her before he realized. He turned back to face her, his shoulders already hunched as he braced for her incoming ire.

"You affect a Volsinii accent." Frelia worked to keep her voice low. "You teach white magic without mentioning any of the Goddesses. You tell me to learn the Volsinii words for swordsmanship like I haven't known the Kaldiri ones as long as I've breathed."

Edmund flinched, but said nothing.

"You were a cleric, Edmund!" Frelia flung her free hand in a useless gesture. "You know how they used the garmur, and they broke apart your church—don't you fucking hate them?"

Edmund's face twisted as tears began fogging his glasses. "I'm not like you, Frelia. I'm not built for that kind of rage. I can't—"

"You're wrong."

Edmund flinched. "I... beg pardon?"

"Everyone is built for their anger." Frelia ground her molars together to keep herself from shouting. "It's the part of you that knows, deep down, that you deserve better than this shit."

"Frelia, if I thought of it like that, I'd be angry all the time!" Edmund said, desperate now.

"Why do you think I am? Sheer spite?"

Edmund scratched at the back of his neck. "I mean... yes?"

Frelia supposed she'd walked into that one, but she still didn't appreciate it.

"I'm no one, Frelia," Edmund said, his hand twisting on his torch like it were the last thing tethering him to reality. "You had the bloodrune, the title, the history, but I..." He sniffed, his voice growing thick. "I'm not really Kaldiri, am I? So how angry do I really have the right to be, that there isn't a Kaldr anymore?"

"You grew up there," Frelia argued. "It was home, wasn't it?"

"Yes and no," Edmund said, so softly Frelia almost didn't catch it. "I grew up there, but I never felt like I belonged there."

Frelia gaped at him like a stupid fish beached on Lake Silverwood's shore. "Of course you did," she said. "You were with us at the moot every summer!"

"And the rest of the year? When Prince Hägen and Princess Reina were busy with their tutors, and all I had were my parents or the servants' kids who didn't want to play with the funny-looking half-Volsinii boy?"

Frelia could sense a deep, dark hurt blossoming on the edges of Edmund's words, and knew she was not equipped to deal with it. "Well, I didn't think you were funny-looking," she said. "And neither did Hägen."

Hägen the healer, who, despite never formally taking up the cloth, had been trained like a Church of the Triad white mage for most of his life—right alongside Edmund. Although he'd never said it, Frelia suspected that was why Edmund had even joined the Krakenguard in the first place. Loyalty to Hägen—not Kaldr, the crown, or anything else.

You would do a lot for your best friend.

"You, the Twins, and Hägen were unique that way." Edmund took off his glasses to scrub at his eyes for a moment. "Now, please, can we talk about something else? News about how long you're doing the darkbeast classes, perhaps?"

Frelia sighed, frustrated at both Edmund dodging the point and at her extra seminar. "Good question," she said. "Caecillion's mentioned a few times that it's just a first semester thing, but I'm not holding my breath."

Edmund winced in sympathy pain. "What would be left after a semester of what they're allowing you to say?"

"No idea," Frelia said. "Practical training, I guess."

She could always set up dummies and targets twenty feet off the ground, but at some point, there was only so much training you could do. When it came down to it, either you could stare down the face of death and slash it open, or you couldn't. And no amount of muscle memory would override the sheer terror of watching a garmr chew on your friends, no matter how big the beast was.

Frelia paused, something else coming to mind that she'd been meaning to ask someone. Unfortunately for Edmund, he was all she had.

"How long has Caecillion been at Silverwood, anyway?" Frelia asked. "Wasn't he supposed to be Ironfang's Spymaster until death do they part, or something?"

"Six years, or so? He arrived a while after I did." Edmund paused, and then dropped his voice very low to add, "And to tell you the truth, I think the Imperator sent him away. But I'm certainly not going to ask him; I prefer my organs where they are."

Frelia froze in the middle of the path. "Ironfang what?"

It went against everything she knew about both Vendrick and Imperator Ironfang. Duty was everything to the Caecillion family, and nobody liked dangling that kind of thing over your head quite like a general-turned-Imperator.

Besides, Vendrick had chosen home all those years ago, hadn't he?

"Exactly." Edmund nodded. "It's completely unsettling. Wasn't he supposed to be the Count of Caecillion and take over for his father?"

Frelia fixed her eye on an overgrown hedge in need of trimming. "I doubt Caecillion ever really knew what he wanted."

"But I suppose," Edmund added, too kind to make fun of her, "he is deeply paranoid, and there's no need of a war dog when there's no war."

Frelia shot him a tired look. "Tell me something I don't know."

"Um…" Edmund's eyes flicked nervously around the throughway. "Your hair's coming undone?"

Frelia harrumphed, and handed him her torch. "Hold this."

She tugged the tie out of her hair and combed through the braid she'd put up this morning. Edmund was right; it was falling apart.

"I don't remember you struggling this much, before," Edmund said.

"Course you don't," Frelia muttered as she began weaving her bleached ends together again. "Thera Grimsdalr used to do my hair."

CHAPTER SIXTEEN

LATE SUMMER TURNED TO autumn proper, and as the days grew shorter, the professors began piling their students with homework. Between the magic classes she barely understood and the darkbeast-fighting classes Markus insisted Faustine recount in full detail afterwards, Faustine was so exhausted and overworked that when fall break showed up, she almost missed it.

But a della Luciana was not allowed to have off days.

That wasn't to say Faustine didn't have days where she wasn't at her best—those happened all the time—but rather that at no point in her fifteen years of life had she ever been allowed to simply do nothing. There had always been work to do, training to keep up with, social responsibilities to maintain.

And so that was why, instead of sleeping in and maybe swimming in the lake with Ellie and Karina over autumn break, Faustine was still in the library with Christel and Siegmund. All three were in practical danger of failing their white magic exam next week without serious intervention.

Ellie had gone to lunch hours ago, followed by Valente and Karina (the last of which left in frustrated tears), and so Faustine, Christel, and

Siegmund were all that remained of the second year white magic study group.

"Do either of you understand how bone divining works?" Siegmund's voice echoed in the silent library, and the librarian at the desk shot them a dirty look.

Christel and Faustine both winced, and Christel made a 'quiet down!' gesture at Siegmund.

Siegmund grimaced. "Sorry," he stage-whispered.

"And I don't think it seems that complicated?" Christel squinted at their notes for a moment. "You just kind of..." They mimicked drawing a rune in the air without any arcane energy behind it. "...and then just..."

They moved as if to roll a set of dice, and then cried out in sharp pain.

"Fuck." Christel slumped forward, clutching their shoulder.

The librarian looked up again, but this time Faustine waved her off. "They're okay, sorry!"

"Hit my foot," Christel muttered.

"Keep it down, kids," the woman muttered, turning back to whatever it was she was doing at her desk.

"Christel?" Siegmund was leaning halfway out of his chair. "You okay?"

A snap of arcane energy burst from where Christel was holding their shoulder, and then their eyes rolled back into their head. It felt just like when Professor Valerius had cleaved that darkbeast in the quad.

Arcane energy like someone's cast a spell, and then the stench of ozone.

Faustine's stomach fell through her boots as she rose shakily to her feet. "Christel?"

There was no response.

She came around the table, dread pooling in her throat, to get a look at Christel's back. And there, leaking through their shirt with blood and arcane energy, was a hazy set of concentric circles that had to be a bloodrune.

Faustine clapped a hand to her mouth to silence the scream she refused to make. She would have to tell Markus; there was nothing so important as getting him more blood for the darkbeasts he was trying to make, after he'd lost those two earlier in the year.

Oh, Goddesses, she was going to have to tell Markus.

She didn't know what would become of Christel, but it would be nothing good. And the idea that something awful could happen to the stoic, golden-haired person who was supposed to be one of her Violet Owls didn't sit right with Faustine.

Why did this have to happen with her here?

"Holy shit, Christel!" Siegmund's voice brought Faustine sharply back to center. "Is that... is that a bloodrune?"

"Keep your voice down!" Faustine hissed.

"Ow," muttered Christel. "The fuck just happened?"

Faustine reached out to touch the rune on their shoulder, almost without thought, but quickly jerked her hand away. "Did you know you had this?"

"Had what?" Christel snapped.

"That's what Professor Valerius warned us about," Siegmund said. "She said that if hers went off, there'd be a flash of light and a... do you remember how she said it, Faustine?"

"Magic snap," Faustine said, distantly. "But she also said hers would make her weapon strikes harder. Did... did yours even do anything, Christel?"

All the color drained out of their face.

"I..." Christel glanced wildly between Faustine and Siegmund. "I think I need to lay down."

"But you're bleeding," Faustine said.

"What did I tell you?"

The librarian had suddenly appeared at their table, looming like one of the terrifying statues that guarded family mausoleums and government buildings in Ascalon.

"You are being entirely too loud and there is no spellcasting in the library! All of you need to leave, at once."

"Sorry," Faustine said automatically. "We just, um..."

"We were getting ready to go anyway," Siegmund added, shoving his books and notes haphazardly into his bag and throwing Christel their uniform jacket.

"Right," Christel added, shakily moving to pull the jacket over their shoulders. "I think we can still make it to lunch if we hurry."

Faustine watched the librarian's line of sight as it skittered across the three of them. She held her breath as the woman's sharp gaze slid over Christel, but if the librarian saw anything out of the ordinary, she said nothing about it.

"And don't come back today." The librarian departed from their table, her heels clacking ominously across the flagstones in her wake.

Faustine, Christel, and Siegmund hurriedly finished shoving their things away, and then hustled out of the library. Christel winced as they shouldered their book bag, and Faustine realized their coat was too big.

Siegmund grabbed the bag from Christel, throwing it over his own, and then looked to Faustine. "What do we do?" he whispered.

"I'm thinking," Faustine whispered back as they entered the stairwell. "How do you feel, Christel?"

"Shitty," was all the swordsman offered.

Faustine knew that she should take them to Markus. Bloodrunes were supposed to be registered with the Imperial Watchers, and if Christel hadn't known they had one, they wouldn't be in the archives yet.

But her stomach twisted at the idea of delivering her friend into the jaws of the beasts. There had to be another option, even if it wasn't the one Markus would want. She could always make up a story about how she couldn't go straight to him when he yelled at her about it later.

"Let's find Professor Valerius," Faustine heard herself say. "I bet she'll know what to do."

Markus would think it plausible. The woman had a bloodrune, and he'd said to get on her good side, anyway. Maybe she would stop watching Faustine like a hawk all the time if Faustine could 'prove' she wasn't like the rest of her family and, Faustine didn't know, had respect for the bloodruned families, or something?

Christel sounded too relieved for Faustine's jangled nerves. "I bet she would," they whispered.

"Oh, good idea," Siegmund said. "Anyone know where she'd be right now?"

"Uh..." Shit, Faustine hadn't thought of that. Without their class schedules, it was impossible to guess where most of the professors would be. Professor Valerius might be in Silverwood Town, or hunting in the forest, or the professors' dorms, or...

"Let's try the training ground first," Christel interrupted Faustine's spiraling panic. "If she's not there, I bet someone there has seen her, at least."

Faustine felt herself nod alongside Siegmund, and then the three of them veered sharply in the direction of the training grounds.

***

Frelia wiped the sweat from her brow and reset her feet into the fool's stance. She had been mindlessly drilling the fundamentals today, because they were easy, and they were important, and they didn't require too much thought on a troubled mind. She just needed the sandy training ground floor, a weapon, and a sparring dummy.

Her sword low in the fool's stance, she slashed upwards at a cross angle, flipped to the *ochs* stance at the height of its arc, and then smashed downwards the other way. She repeated the motion on the other side, her shoulders burning with exertion as she swung the blade into the training dummy's chest over and over.

The wood was cracking, now, and the stray thought that *maybe I should find some lunch* drifted across the back of Frelia's mind. She'd made it to fall break, and with the students released from their classes, maybe she should use the afternoon to catch up on grading papers or figure out the written exam for next week, or something.

She reset herself into the fool's stance again, sword low to the ground. In a real fight, a lot of people took it as a provocation. *How dare you lower your guard around me, Kaldiri bitch!*

It was the last mistake a lot of Volsinii knights had ever made.

Cillian had never understood Frelia's love of the fool's guard—but then, he was a lancer. He never would. He hadn't needed to bait people the way Frelia had; he just had to get close enough to run them through with his lance while his horse galloped onward.

You have it easy, Frelia had always told him.

Nothing's stopping you from getting on a horse, you know, he'd always teased back.

"Professor Valerius!"

Frelia tensed in the middle of the half-square drill, her fingers tightening reflexively on her sword as she turned towards the noise.

Siegmund was frantically waving from near the training ground gate. Behind him, Christel was leaning heavily on a terrified-looking Faustine as they hurried through the fence. Frelia swore she could smell blood on the air, but it didn't look like one of them had broken something, or worse.

Frelia shoved the tip of her practice sword into the sandy training ground floor. "Everything alright?"

"No." Faustine's voice was high, and tight.

All the heat drained from Frelia's face, and despite the warm autumn wind, she was suddenly cold. "Is it garmur?"

Frelia avoided the chapel on principle these days, but she'd passed by it the other day and sworn she felt her bones vibrate. Just a little. She hadn't been able to find Valente to confirm it, and she needed to stop thinking of him as 'the other bloodruned soldier' anyway. He was a kid, and a Volsinii one at that.

But still. The rumbling didn't lie. Frelia just needed to know whether it was what she felt, or not. Had these three found whatever was lurking in there?

But all three Violet Owls just shook their heads. "No, thank the Saints," Siegmund called back. "It's, um, about Christel."

"Can we, er, talk to you, professor?" Christel called over in their strange, not-quite-Free-Cities accent. "About... something private?"

Frelia blinked a few times, and resisted the urge to shove her finger in her ear to clean it out. "I'm not sure how much help I'll be if it's not about swords," she said. "But sure, go for it, I guess."

Her students met her in the middle of the training ground. A couple of geese still stared at them from their nests, but facilities had taken care of most of the bastards.

They were alone, out here.

Christel glanced over their shoulder, taking stock of the empty grounds in the same way Frelia's old mercenary friends would. It twanged painfully against something in her chest, that a kid like Christel would need to know how to watch their back. Faustine and Siegmund were both just looking expectantly at Frelia.

"Look," Christel said after a moment, "you're Kaldiri, right professor?"

Frelia had no idea where this was going. "What gave it away, the accent?"

Siegmund laughed, but Christel swallowed audibly. "Then do... do you know about the other bloodrunes? Besides yours?"

If this were a blatant trap to get her fired, Markus della Luciana was going to have to try harder than that. "Course I do," Frelia said, because there was no sense in lying. "Why?"

This time all three kids looked around, nervousness written in every line of their faces. "Because, um," Christel continued. "What do you do when someone... you know... has one?"

Frelia blinked a few times. "What do you mean, what do you do? Nothing. They're not illegal."

Though they might as well be, in Ironfang's grand new empire of shit. If he weren't going to do a thing about the Bloodrune Hunters, it was going to be a long road home for anyone cursed enough to get their attention. Valente's family at least had money and status and history of loyalty to the Volsinii crown to hide behind.

That hadn't been enough to save all the Volsinii bloodruned families, though.

"No, no!" Distress crossed Christel's face, and they turned ashen pale and glanced hopelessly to their friends.

"What we mean is," Faustine said, so quietly Frelia nearly couldn't hear her, "what do you do when it shows up?"

Dread pooled in Frelia's gut as she suddenly understood.

With a quick overhead glance to the gate, Frelia said, lowly and urgently, "Which one of you?"

As if she couldn't already tell. Christel looked like they were about to faint.

"Me," Christel said quietly.

"Which rune was it?" Frelia pressed.

"Um," Siegmund said. "We have no idea."

Helheim, that was right. None of these kids had grown up with the Church of the Triad.

"Well what does it look like?" Frelia asked. "Is it a whorling knot, a broken heart...?"

"Uhh...." Christel looked to Siegmund and Faustine, and Frelia's stomach sank even further into her boots.

There was only one reason Christel wouldn't yet know what lived in their blood and on their skin.

"It's kind of a bloody mess right now," Faustine offered. "But I think there were circles?"

Frelia's jaw fell open as she finally placed Christel's shaggy, golden hair. Their thin frame. Their sword style.

It all belonged to the Traust daughters, in Frelia's memory. Geir and Ulfhild and little Astrid.

So *this* was why Vendrick was rumored to have pulled strings to enroll them. What did the old Spymaster care, though? There was little point in tracking the old Bloodruned families, without a church to make it matter.

Frelia's heart twisted in her chest, as though it would burst, still-beating, from the cavity. "Did this just happen?"

Her students nodded.

"I was looking over the white magic textbook for this year," Christel said. "I was looking over... divining bones, I think? And then it just kind of..."

They made an explosive, outward gesture over their shoulder, and then grimaced.

Fuck. This was not good. This was so not good. Christel needed to go to ground, now. Frelia could mourn the dead already buried later, once the living were safe.

Her father's study, back when it and Valerius Lodge had been whole, jumped into her mind's eye. It was where Frelia had weathered her own bloodrune's awakening, cozy and insulated from both winter's cold and prying eyes.

"How long ago did it show up?" she demanded.

"I don't know," Faustine offered, "maybe twenty minutes?"

"*Skitr.*" That meant they had another forty minutes if they were fortunate, and Frelia had never been accused of being lucky before. "We'll be cutting it close."

"Cutting what close?" Christel asked.

Frelia hustled over to where her longsword was still stuck in the ground, and yanked. There was no time to worry about the training dummy or cleaning the blade, right now; she'd have to deal with them later.

"Come on," Frelia said. "We need to move, now."

She would figure out where to put Christel on the way. She couldn't exactly have the kid sleep in her dorm bed for the next three days, nor could she hover around the students' dorm rooms. Maybe she could take them to Edmund, in the infirmary? Or, no, there would be too many people in and out, too many possibilities for exposure.

Shit, shit, shit!

Siegmund planted himself between Frelia and Christel. "Professor, what are you talking about? Where are we going?"

Frelia shoved her sword through her belt, and forced herself to breathe. "Bloodrunes aren't just tattoos and pretty lights," she said, and it echoed of another voice, another time, a million years ago in the shadow of the mountains. "They're ancestral magic, handed down through families alongside shit like eye color and bad taste in romantic partners."

No one so much as snorted.

"And Christel," Frelia added, "you have just thrown open the floodgates to your ancestors' memories. You're going to be hit over the head with memories you don't have, people you've never met, things you've never experienced. If you're lucky, it'll just knock you out and you'll sleep for three days."

"And if I'm not?" they whispered.

"Then you'll have nightmares, sleepwalking, and worse," Frelia said. "So you need to hole up somewhere safe, and we need to go right now."

That finally got them moving. Faustine tugged at Christel's arm, and the three of them scrambled to catch up with Frelia.

"Can't Christel just stay in their room?" Faustine asked.

"Yeah, we could bring them food and stuff?" Siegmund added. "I know people who've done that when someone in their house gets really sick."

Frelia shook her head—"No, someone needs to watch over them. Preferably someone who knows what to look for."—and dragged open the training ground gate with enough force to make the hinges squeal.

What to look for, she thought, *and the stories to make the pain matter.*

Once upon a time, a Bloodrune Awakening was something of a celebration, in the same way a wake was. At Gyastfylnacht, the parents and their friends would drink, siblings and friends would play games, and all would watch over the little one while their ancestors drove through their minds like wartime charioteers. Thera had told Frelia once that the party was supposed to keep the ancestors happy, or at least neutral. Nobody wanted to watch their own birthing, or feel their great-great-great uncle's lifeblood leave his body on some battlefield somewhere.

Frelia wasn't sure whether that worked or not, but she did know that if you were drinking and carrying on, it was much harder to fall asleep. And if somebody was always awake, then somebody would always be there if the awakening went wrong.

"Well can you tell me what to look for?" Siegmund asked. "Faustine can't stay with Christel all weekend because, y'know, she's a girl and people will get weird. But I could. We hang out all the time anyway."

Frelia stopped walking.

Siegmund couldn't stay awake all weekend. He couldn't help Christel if something go wrong with their bloodrune, awakened as late as it had been. He couldn't tell Christel the legends they would need to know, the family history, or answer questions about how bloodrunes worked. Valente could, maybe, but Frelia couldn't dump this on another student. It was bad enough that Faustine and Siegmund were here. Faustine would run to Markus the first chance she got, and Siegmund's family, though famously runeless, would have paid someone thousands for the information Siegmund had simply just stumbled into.

Dammit. Christel needed help, and they needed Frelia's help, in the absence of their own mother.

And Frelia needed somewhere to hole up that wouldn't get her fired on suspicion of impropriety, or whatever the Volsinii liked to call it when nothing bad actually happened but everyone thought it had, anyway.

"No," Frelia said to Siegmund. "You can't stay awake for three days straight, and I'm guessing you don't know whether what Christel is feeling right now is normal or not."

"What about the infirmary?" Faustine offered.

"We can't tell the Volsinii teachers about this thing!" Christel hissed. "They'll turn me over to the Bloodrune Hunters! Or worse…"

"No they won't," Faustine began, but Frelia was no longer listening.

It's not illegal to have inherited a bloodrune, said a smooth voice in the back of Frelia's mind, *and the Hunters, believe it or not, have never been permitted on Silverwood's grounds, and that isn't about to start today.*

"Blightsen won't turn you in," Frelia said. "But the infirmary isn't secure."

Damn it all, she knew what would be.

The headmaster's suite. Unlike the rest of the faculty, the headmaster actually had his own kitchen, bathroom, and living room separate from his bedroom. That would be secure enough to keep watch over Christel, and keep tongues from wagging.

Except you'd still need to be there, Frelia reminded herself.

"We're going to the headmaster," Frelia said. "Volsinii or not, he won't allow the Hunters anywhere near his students."

CHAPTER SEVENTEEN

VENDRICK HAD NEVER HANDLED sleep deprivation particularly well. It was a necessary evil for a Spymaster, soldier, and Imperial advisor, but the fact still remained that no amount of tea or coffee had ever been enough to fix the fuzziness that followed the day after (or the rest of the week). The situation did not improve when he retired from politics, particularly given he'd only taken on a new form of it.

As the lunch hour approached and Vendrick continued to stare at the same set of paperwork as he had all morning, he decided that skipping lunch to take a nap was probably a better use of his time. It was fall break anyway; the students would be anywhere but the academic buildings.

He shut the door to his office and locked it with a practiced flick of his wrist, then stowed the key in one of his many interior jacket pockets and set off down the hall. The Headmaster's suite was a stone's throw from his office, on the top floor of Salonia Hall and deliberately separate from the other faculty and staff.

His mind drifted across budgetary issues and parental complaints about the fiasco earlier in the year, and Vendrick found himself in a tired haze for most of the walk.

But, at the top of the stairs to the headmaster's suite, he found the door unlocked.

Adrenaline cleared his mind in a way nothing else had all morning. Saints, he was in no mood to deal with an intruder. Readying his spellbook, Vendrick pushed open the door and prepared to quick-cast something suitably nasty.

The living room was empty, but the door to his bedroom was ajar. Vendrick padded carefully across the carpeted floor, only to find his younger sister and what appeared to be half of his wardrobe strewn across his bed.

Vendrick sheathed his spellbook ruefully and took back his previous thought; he probably would have preferred an actual intruder.

"May I help you, Clarissa?"

Her curly brown hair was piled atop her head in a messy yet elegant bun tied off with green ribbon, and she looked to him with alarm in her eyes. She was a talented enchantress who worked at the famous magic shop, the Ebon Ring, and therefore knew just about everyone of consequence in Volsinii high society. Last Vendrick had heard, she was still in Liberalis Territory on family business, and she usually was much better about informing him of her whereabouts.

He didn't like this.

"Vendy." She held up one of his vests and shook it for good measure. "Brother dear, this is six years out of style."

"It's a waistcoat," Vendrick argued. "Do they even do that?"

"Ugh!" Clarissa tossed it onto the bed, alongside what was most definitely half his wardrobe, now that Vendrick was properly in his bedroom. "You have no fashion sense, I swear to the Saints."

Vendrick had been wondering whether he ought to check if it were really Clarissa, but an argument this old could only come from his actual sibling. "We've been over this."

"Oh, I know you don't care." Clarissa tossed yet another shirt onto what was undoubtedly her rejects pile. "But *I* care *for* you. How are you supposed to court a woman wearing clothes from six years ago?"

"Court a...?" No, he wasn't about to ask. He'd had enough of the blind dates she'd set him up on about ten years ago. "Clarissa, why are you eviscerating my closet when there are about four hundred better uses of your time?"

Chief among them the things he'd assigned to her.

"Oh, don't worry, I'm also here with news about Liberalis Territory and Northern Volsinii. I just figured I could kill two birds with one stone when I heard Frelia Valerius had risen from her early grave." Clarissa put her hands on her hips and surveyed his half-empty closet. "This should about do it, I think?"

A vein twitched in Vendrick's temple. "And are you prepared to do all the laundry you're forcing on me, with half my wardrobe apparently out of commission?"

"Oh, Saints no, Vendy," Clarissa said. "I've arranged for replacements. You should be getting a trunk in a day or two."

"Clarissa, Saints above, if you—"

"Oh don't worry, Vendrick, I know your aesthetic. It's still all mostly black. Now." She whirled on him, and brought her hands together with a resounding clap. "About Liberalis Territory."

Vendrick's eyes narrowed. "Don't change the subject."

"Fine." Clarissa sighed. "I'll let you go through my rejects pile and keep whatever you can't bear to be parted with, and I'll donate the rest."

"Just cancel the order, Clarissa. I don't have time to be fussing with this. If you've heard about Valerius, I know you've heard about the darkbeasts, too."

"But I've already paid for it!" Clarissa protested. "And I'm late for your birthday, anyhow. I also brought you some cheesecakes from Bakery Cafaro, so you can't say I did nothing for you this year."

Vendrick regarded his sister with a long-suffering look she knew very well. "Why do you do this to me?"

She put a hand to her heart as though offended. "I'm helping!"

"Even if my fashion sense were a concern," Vendrick said, "there are much bigger issues, Clary."

"Mmm," said Clarissa, pursing her lips, "I don't think that's true. You could do with some loosening up."

For a moment, Vendrick debated whether he had the mental capacity to explain to his little sister that a seventeen-year-old crush did not warrant this level of intrusion on his thirty-six-year-old life, and that her matchmaking schemes had long since pissed him off.

...

No, he didn't.

Vendrick turned on his heel. "I'm leaving. Lock the door behind you, and there's food in the kitchen if you're hungry."

"Vendrick!"

Clarissa sprinted across his room, moving to cut him off at the door.

"Really, Vendrick, it isn't like your clothes—"

She nearly ran into him when Vendrick stopped to shoot her the other look she knew well. Clarissa suddenly realized she had made a terrible mistake; he could see it in the jadeite green of her eyes.

"Clary," he said, "this living vicariously through me has got to stop."

She suddenly found her riding boots fascinating. "Well, I'm dying alone. So I have to, you see. Non-negotiable. Sorry."

Vendrick heaved a put-upon sigh. "You could also just, I don't know, date someone?"

"Dying alone!" Clarissa threw up her hands.

"You and della Trova broke up years ago. You needn't worry you seem... well, unseemly."

"*She* wasn't worried about it," Clarissa muttered.

"And that's why you're the classy one."

Clarissa gave a watery laugh. "I really am just trying to help, Vendy."

"I know. But could you find less obtrusive ways to do it?"

"I don't think so." Clarissa wrinkled her nose. "That seems far less fun."

Vendrick leveled a dirty look at her, and she laughed so hard she started coughing.

"Well," he said over it, because Clarissa would only put up with so much fussing, "report, I suppose."

"Oh!" Clarissa was on the move again, back towards Vendrick's decimated closet. "It was the damnedest thing, really. Lady Liberalis was perfectly respectable, of course. Invited me in for tea, happily ate up the lie that I wanted to meet with her court alchemist about medicine for mother."

"Clarissa, we have the most impressive black network this side of the Free Cities, and you went with *that* lie? When was the last time you even spoke with our mother, anyway?"

"I needed an excuse to look around! And I'm going to visit her after I see you, so I don't want to hear it, Sir I-haven't-been-home-for-Yule-in-years." Clarissa was rummaging about in her travel bag. "Also, guess what I found?"

Vendrick sighed. "Something of note?"

"Worse." Clarissa thumped a heavy, leather-bound tome onto the unoccupied end of Vendrick's bed. "A mystery."

Vendrick picked up the book gingerly, as though it might burst into flames in his hands. He stared at the thing, gently turning its pages. Familiar drawings and notes splayed across the pages, instructions jumping at him like fleas from the Ascaloni shoreline.

"Clarissa... what was my war spellbook doing in Liberalis Territory?"

She folded her arms. "I was hoping you would know."

They stared at each other for a moment, the last two scions of the House of Caecillion. It was bitter work, running a spy network, and even worse when the only person you could trust about it was your sibling. It was a good thing they mostly got on, or Vendrick might very well have lost this cold war years ago.

"What else have you found?"

"Well, for starters," Clarissa said, "there's only one half-empty teacup in here. I'm so proud of you, Vendy!"

She was lucky she was the only family left he actually liked, or Vendrick would have throttled her years ago. "About the Unseen, Clarissa."

She sighed. "I just—"

A heavy knock came at the door.

Clarissa and Vendrick exchanged a look honed by many years of cookie-jar-heists and political intrigue. "Were you expecting someone?" Clarissa asked.

"No," Vendrick said, and he made the Silverwood hand sign for hide.

Clarissa nodded sharply, then shooed him out of his own bedroom and shut the door behind him. Vendrick walked back across the living room, and funny, without Clarissa throwing his wardrobe about, it was practically clean in here.

Though his spellbook still thumped against his hip as he reached for the front door, there were plenty of things Vendrick could cast without it, if he had to. "Is there something with which I can assist?" tumbled out of his mouth the moment his door opened.

Standing in the narrow stairwell were a handful of Violet Owls and their swordmaster, looking like Hypogia itself was on their heels.

"Caecillion," Frelia said, and she sounded more haunted than Vendrick had ever heard her, "we have a problem."

CHAPTER EIGHTEEN

Telling Vendrick fucking Caecillion—Imperial Spymaster, besieger of Skjöldr, the Viper of Ascalon himself—about Christel's bloodrune was up there with the Battles for Skjöldr, Spirits' Fen, and Heit Reiði as "hardest things Frelia had ever been forced to endure." It ranked slightly below both parents' deaths and slightly above the time Ironfang split her rib cage open with an axe.

It went against everything in Frelia, right down to her very bones.

The Volsinii had no right to learn something so sacred. No reason to. They had scrapped the Church of the Triad and they deserved to live with the consequences.

But. *But.*

If she didn't tell the headmaster, she had no real way of keeping an eye on Christel. Faustine and Siegmund were no substitutes for a bloodruned woman old enough to both have children of her own and know how to care for them. And Christel's health, safety, and future mental stability had to come before ancient grudges that would never see battle.

Especially because, once upon another life, Christel might have been family. If Frelia's brother Diarmuid hadn't died. If Traust Territory hadn't fallen. If Kaldr hadn't ultimately lost.

If, if, *if.*

"Let me see if I have this," Vendrick began, and as ever, Frelia couldn't read his facial expression. "You require the use of the headmaster's suite to look after a newly awakened bloodrune?"

"Its *bearer.*" Frelia leaned into the word. "And it's not the headmaster's suite, exactly, that matters, it's that I need to do it somewhere secure."

"Yes, you had mentioned that part," Vendrick said. "The thing I seem to have missed is—why? Is Blightsen somehow not capable?"

Frelia couldn't tell if he was fucking with her or not, and it irked her. "The infirmary isn't private," she said, "and Edmund doesn't have a bloodrune."

That's why I said it had to be me, you bastard, Frelia mentally added.

Vendrick's eyes narrowed. Acid-green and piercing, they were easily his most striking feature. They were also the most expressive—you could see the calculations going on behind them, when Vendrick fell silent enough.

There came a sharp pang in her stomach when Frelia remembered that once upon a time, she'd only ever seen that expression over alchemy homework.

"Faustine," Vendrick finally said, "Siegmund."

Both Violet Owls snapped to attention.

"There is a tea kettle and set of cups in the kitchen," Vendrick added, and it was hard to say who was more confused—Siegmund, Faustine, or Frelia. "Kindly go put the water on, would you both?"

They stared at him for a moment, visibly dumbstruck.

"I have a feeling we're all going to want tea, after this," Vendrick added.

Faustine's prefect status seemed to kick in, then. "Er," she said, "of course, Headmaster."

Frelia watched Faustine and Siegmund's backs disappear down the short hall, but it wasn't until they'd both disappeared from view that she felt Vendrick's eyes return to her.

"Let us be frank, Valerius," Vendrick said. "Blightsen is a former cleric. I truly fail to see why he's incapable of taking care of this development."

Frelia shut her eye and drew in a sharp breath. When she opened it again, she found her mark in the headmaster of Silverwood's polite, Volsinii mask.

"Have you heard of Gyastfylnacht?"

She shouldn't be telling him this. She shouldn't be saying a damn word about any of it. Cillian's ghost was looming at her back, now, disapproval in his heavy stare.

But Christel's terrified blue eyes were brighter, in Frelia's periphery.

"Let's say I haven't," Vendrick said.

"I sure haven't," Christel muttered, folding their arms across their thin frame as though to keep warm.

Frelia was going to have to tell Vendrick everything, wasn't she? The things she would maybe have told a runeless husband, one day, but anyone with a bloodrune would simply *know*.

What Cillian, Thera, her da, and all the others would have just known.

"Bloodrunes aren't tattoos or blond hair passed down the family line," Frelia said, feeling both physically present and somewhere very far away. "They're ancestral memory and knowledge, locked in your blood, and bones, and skin. And Christel has just opened the floodgate to all of that."

Finally, gears began turning in that clockwork mind of Vendrick's.

"They may sleepwalk," Frelia pressed on, counting out the symptoms on her fingers, "have night terrors, awaken so disoriented they don't know who they are, convulse in their sleep like a drunk, hurt themselves living out memories from four-hundred years ago, arm themselves to fight a battle that was over before their great-grandmother was born..."

Frelia trailed off, trying to remember what else had happened to various friends and relatives. The stories she'd been told.

"I get the portrait," Vendrick said, not unkindly.

"Gyastfylnacht," Frelia added, refusing to dwell on the pit in her stomach, "is the Ghost Watch. It..."

Damn it all! What could she say?

"Once upon a time, it...?"

It took Frelia a moment to realize, Vendrick was prompting her. She scowled at him, but accepted the conceit for what it was.

"Once upon a time," she said, "a mum might throw a party, and invite all her friends and siblings and their families. They will drink and play games and carry on deep into the night, so that someone is always awake to watch over the littlest one. For three days they will keep this up, until the bloodrune wound seals itself."

"Three days?" Christel yelped, and then clapped their hands over their mouth again.

"At the very least, three days," Frelia told them. "And for that time, you need to be somewhere private, easily watched over, and where you won't be disturbed—or disturb anyone else."

Frelia glanced back to Vendrick, who had folded his hands at the small of his back but otherwise remained unyielding stone. So she looked back to Christel.

"And someone needs to tell you your family stories," Frelia added, quietly, in case Faustine or Siegmund were getting ideas out in the kitchen. "They will make sense of what you see, and feel, and tell you how to live with this new power of yours."

"And Blightsen cannot—?" Vendrick began.

Frelia was done with that train of thought.

"Edmund is a cleric," Frelia snapped. "He will approach it like a cleric. But he doesn't have a bloodrune, and doesn't understand what's going on *here.*"

She tapped her fist against her stomach, on the right hand side beneath her ribs.

"It should be Christel's parents watching over them," Frelia said, "plus the rest of their *volchya.* But we are all they have. And I don't think I need to tell you how much a Bloodrune Hunter would *love* to get their hands on a newly awakened bloodrune bearer who can't defend themself."

Silence fell across the room and over in the kitchen, the tea kettle began to whine.

"No," Vendrick finally said. "I understand that quite well, thank you."

He looked to Christel, who, despite pulling their uniform jacket tightly around their chest, was both shivering and visibly sweating.

"How do you feel, Christel?" Vendrick asked.

"Terrible?" they offered. "Like I'm coming down with a fever, or..."

They cut themself off mid-sentence, and Frelia's eye widened as she felt astral energy coalesce in the room. She burst forward to steady her student just as their bloodrune activated again, spraying the room with arcane light and astral energy.

For a moment, Christel leaned into her hands and convulsed, and Frelia braced herself against the loveseat to bear their weight. Then Christel stopped straining, and their eyes were unfocused as they flicked around the room.

"Geir?" Christel murmured, and Frelia's stomach twisted. "Are you there?"

Frelia shot Vendrick a look, as if to say, *you see?*

"Do you know which one this is?" he asked.

"Traust," Frelia croaked, "but they're all supposed to be dead."

Something seemed to steady in Christel's bearing. "My mother's name was Ulfhild, and my father was Frederick," they said. "I don't know if that helps?"

Frelia bit down hard on the inside of her cheek. "Thought so."

Lucidity came back a little more into Christel's eyes as they focused on Frelia. "Did you know them?"

The weight of all the history—their own history—that Christel didn't know sat, leaden, in Frelia's stomach.

"I knew your mum." Frelia's voice was thick. "She was—"

Christel began to convulse again, and Frelia grabbed a firmer hold of Christel's uniform jacket to keep them upright.

She glanced back to the headmaster, and although Frelia Helm's Grace Valerius did not beg, sometimes she did say, "Vendrick, *please.*"

For the briefest flash of an instant, he looked wounded. But then he was as stern as he ever was, presiding over staff meetings or parent conferences or whatever else it was headmasters did.

She pressed the advantage, like this were any other battle, any other field. "Do you know who Ulfhild Traust was engaged to for years before he died?"

Vendrick shook his head carefully. "Enlighten me."

Frelia shut her eye, and willed her own mask not to break. "Diarmuid Valerius."

"Is... that a cousin?" Vendrick asked. "An uncle?"

"My brother."

Christel convulsed again, and Frelia was grateful to have something else to focus on. *Keep their hair out of their mouth and nose, keep their airways clear.* The usual things, the usual way.

By the time Christel had stopped, Frelia was about ready to promise she'd clean the stables with her toothbrush for a week, if she could just watch over this poor kid who had never asked for their family burden.

Then Vendrick said, loudly, "Clarissa?"

Frelia's brow furrowed, and she was about to ask if he'd hit his head or something when a door behind Vendrick burst open.

Out tumbled a woman in stylish riding clothes, with a spellbook and an easy, dazzling smile. "You rang?"

For a moment, the traitorous part of Frelia's heart squeezed at the realization that Vendrick Caecillion had been hiding a woman in his room. But then the logical part screamed at it that they looked too similar for it to be coincidence, and what did she care, anyway.

"Yes, I did," Vendrick said, and then he looked to Frelia again. "Valerius, may I present my little sister, Clarissa, the Countess of Caecillion."

The woman's—*Clarissa's*—fingers twisted in a highborn, Volsinii wave. "How do you do?"

"Clary," Vendrick added, "this is Frelia Helm's Grace Valerius, the Silverwood swordmaster."

The bubbly energy in Clarissa's eyes was replaced with a gleam nearly as calculating as her brother's. "Oh I *see,*" she said. "A pleasure to meet you, Frelia dear."

Frelia did not like that tone at all.

Vendrick shot his sister a look. "I presume you heard all of that?"

Frelia grit her teeth at the realization that another Volsinii had just heard everything.

"Eh, enough." Clarissa shrugged. "Sounds like you've got a problem."

"No, I have a solution." Something glittered in the acid green of Vendrick's eyes. "Here is what we shall do."

CHAPTER NINETEEN

BY THE TIME FAUSTINE and Siegmund returned to the sitting room with the tea, Christel was fully convulsing. Vendrick found a handkerchief clean enough to stick between their teeth while Frelia and Siegmund dragged a loveseat against the far wall of the sitting room. They could both discuss the next three days, and keep an eye on Christel as they went. They were deathly pale, and their lips moved as though following along to a song only they could hear.

Vendrick had been right about the tea; he was going to need it to get through this minefield.

He introduced Clary to the students and vice versa, and despite more pressing issues, Clarissa still had to go through the whole dance. "Della Luciana," she said, "as in, Imperator Ironfang's youngest?"

"Y-yes, Your Excellency," Faustine stammered.

"Well I'll be," Clarissa said with a bright mixture of surprise and calculation. "And did I hear correctly that you're an Ossani?"

Siegmund nodded. "Of the Tifernem Ossanis!"

"Oh, I've done work for your uncle—or maybe cousin?—Tiberius," Clarissa added. "Do tell him I say hello, would you?"

"Uncle," Siegmund confirmed, "and sure!"

"Okay Volsinii," Frelia growled from her perch on the arm of Christel's loveseat, "now that you've established your hierarchy, can we get on with it?"

"Oh, of course not," Clarissa said immediately, and Vendrick winced. "We've still got two or three small committee meetings before that."

"Clarissa, now is not the time," Vendrick cut in sharply.

She put an affronted hand to her heart. "I always have time to poke fun at the Senate."

Vendrick shot her a dirty look.

"Oh, fine." Clarissa sighed, and dropped into an armchair by the hearth. "Have it your way, brother dear."

Vendrick resisted the urge to roll his eyes by folding his hands at the small of his back and starting to pace. "We shall say Siegmund, Christel, and Faustine were assisting me in the alchemy lab. Valerius happened to stop in at the wrong moment, and we were all exposed to an alchemical solution of..." His hand cycled as he looked for a word. "...indiscriminate origin."

He glanced over to where Christel currently lay immobile on the loveseat. They certainly looked knocked out, and there was no reason to suspect it wasn't an accident. *Dark caps and lavender essence, maybe?* Vendrick wondered. *Raven feathers and wyvern scales?*

"As such," he continued aloud, "the students are confined to their dorm rooms for the next few days while they are monitored for any ill effects."

"That doesn't explain Christel," Clarissa pointed out.

"What are you talking about?" Vendrick glanced over to her. "Christel will have been in their room for three days." He cut a glance sharply to Faustine and Siegmund. "Right?"

Faustine's mouth fell open as she realized he was telling them to lie.

"Don't make them lie like that," Frelia said harshly. "Christel got hit in the face with the cloud of alchemical shit; those two were across the room or something."

"Oh, good thought," Clarissa said. "Then Vendrick quarantined them in here, just in case. Just, you know, since the infirmary doesn't have a quarantine ward."

"It doesn't," Vendrick confirmed. "If plague ever struck Silverwood, we'd be confined to our rooms or, long-term, have to send the students home."

"Um, headmaster?" Siegmund's hands were shaking so badly, he'd put his teacup on the coffee table five minutes ago and hadn't touched it since. "Won't Alchemymaster Caelia be suspicious about this story?"

"She would be," Vendrick agreed, "if I didn't know several troublesome tidbits that would compromise her job status. I'll just pick one to hold over her head for a while, and she won't say a word."

The students stared at him with newfound fear, but Frelia's fierce amber eye was what pierced him most of all. He had dirt on every Silverwood professor, however. Live long enough, and anyone would have at least a few skeletons in their closet.

"Clary, here's where you come in," Vendrick added. "You will—"

"Oooh, let me guess!" she interrupted. "I will go make evidence in the alchemy lab, make sure these two..." She pointed to Faustine and Siegmund. "...get to their rooms, and then rouse Blightsen?"

Sometimes his little sister was alright. "Tell him his expertise is required for a discreet situation in the Headmaster's suite."

Clarissa raised an eyebrow. "Won't he just think there's a pregnant student, or something?"

"No, that would be a delicate situation."

Frelia snorted into her teacup.

"Fair enough," Clarissa said. "Shall I get on?"

Vendrick held up a finger, and then turned to Siegmund and Faustine. They weren't cowering outright, but Vendrick got the sense it wasn't far off.

They both knew, of course, what he'd been before he was the Silverwood Headmaster. Hell, they'd met him at Senate galas and afternoon teas. Plus he'd visited the Tifernem Ossanis more than once, while in Ironfang's service. There was no doubt that the Viper of Ascalon had been used to scare little Siegmund into staying in his room.

He didn't blame either of them for the terror in their eyes.

"I don't think I need to remind you how much danger Christel is in," Vendrick began.

Faustine nodded so hard, her neck cracked. "We understand, headmaster." She elbowed Siegmund, seated beside her on the plush loveseat. "Right?"

"Yeah, we won't tell anybody." Siegmund was more serious than a professor had ever seen him. "Owls' Honor."

"Only..." Faustine's voice caught in her throat.

Vendrick knew where that was going, alright. "If you're concerned about informing the Imperial Watchers, don't be. I will handle that once the immediate danger has passed."

Frelia jerked upright like she'd just been struck by mage's lightning. "You can't tell della Luciana. His sister runs the Bloodrune Hunters."

Vendrick gave her a look, and gestured with a thumb towards Faustine. "It's a bit late for that."

Faustine shifted in her seat as though she were a frog in a pot. "It's... illegal not to disclose an awakened bloodrune, professor."

"And do you have any idea how many hunters I've had to kill since the Tyrant's War?" Frelia fired back.

Faustine's eyes widened as she shook her head.

"Dozens," Frelia said. "If not tens of dozens. I'm not putting Christel in their sights."

"I will handle the reporting," Vendrick said again, even more firmly. "And Valerius, for your own good, you never said that, and we never heard it."

Something flashed in her eye. "Don't presume to know what's good for me, Caecillion."

Clarissa's damnably perceptive ear for gossip practically pricked up at that. Vendrick had to put her off it. Fast.

He spat out the first thing that came to mind: "Now, does anyone have any questions before we set off?"

"Will you let us know how they're doing?" Siegmund asked, uncharacteristically quiet.

"You can see them." Frelia jerked her head towards where Christel lay, unnaturally still for the moment.

"I meant over the next few days," Siegmund said.

For a moment, the room was so quiet you could have heard a spider on the ceiling. Vendrick tried to smile, but it just made Siegmund cringe, so he dropped it, and said, "We shall keep you both informed."

"Thanks, headmaster." Siegmund immediately looked down at his hands, too big for the child's body they were still attached to.

"Well, come on, kids." Clarissa was on her feet like a flash of brilliance. "Give me just a moment to speak to my brother and then let's see about the alchemy lab."

The arm she looped through Vendrick's to drag him into the kitchen was so familiar it was almost comforting. Annoying, but comforting.

In the small galley kitchen, Clarissa turned on him like a double agent. "What do I need to know about the alchemymaster?" she asked, voice low.

Vendrick flipped through his mental paperwork stack before settling on, "Remind her how embarrassing it would be if it were made public just how much debt she's gone into at the brothel in Silverwood Town."

Clarissa nodded. "Anything else?"

"That should do it..." Vendrick pulled a face as he thought on it. "But if not, she also smokes the dried mossblade and replaces it with oregano. Alchemically, they're very similar."

Clarissa laughed. "Okay, easy enough. I'll be back in a bit with Blightsen." She turned to leave, and then paused. "Oh, and Vendy?"

"What?" he said.

"Looks like a certain somebody has to sleep here." Clarissa winked at him.

"Will you get going already?" Vendrick hissed, reddening to the tips of his ears.

She did, mercifully, taking Faustine and Siegmund with her. But with that out of the way, nothing stood between Vendrick and a pissed-off general on the warpath.

"You're not telling the Watchers shit," she hissed at him the instant the door shut behind Clarissa.

And just like that, Vendrick missed his sister.

"I will not be ordered about or cursed at in my own home," he said with practiced calm. "If you'd like to try again, politely, I'm all ears."

The muscle beside her eye twitched, and the tendons in her neck practically stood on end. Vendrick could only watch as Frelia tried to contain her visible fury, to breathe.

"Have you been to Skjöldr, lately?" she hissed. "To Duncregg, Krolis, or Canto? Bloodruned folk go for a hundred gold a head—five hundred, alive."

Vendrick drew very still. He knew the bloodrune hunters did a brisk bounty business on the side, but it was mostly the usual rapists and murderers on their dockets. He knew, because his spies frequently passed said dockets along.

"They tried to get me during libations in Norvegr." Frelia was pressing her fingers into her face like she could claw her skin off. "Do you think it'll matter to them that Christel's a kid?"

No, it wouldn't matter. It had never mattered. And it wasn't the Bloodrune Hunters Vendrick was worried about, it was the money behind them. But he didn't have a way to tell her what they were truly up against without laying all his cards on the table, and then where would that leave him?

With none left to use as leverage, that's where.

Vendrick hadn't become the Imperator's Spymaster by accident. And he hadn't survived long enough to leave the position this side of a coffin by being an idiot, either.

His mind was a swirling spiderweb of half-built plans and possible connections, of theoretical plots and estimations that all depended on how much he could trust the woman standing in front of him.

She'd probably sooner see you dead, the practical part of Vendrick's mind pointed out.

Then again, she hadn't survived this long after the Tyrant's War by being an idiot, either.

"What?" she demanded. "I can see the gears turning back there."

At his confused look, she tapped her skull.

If he asked her another identifying question, she'd start to grow suspicious of them—and moreover, the Unseen would know to expect them. He couldn't go about this like a sloppy drunk on the way back from Augustus Pier; he needed a plan.

He wasn't sure what he would do, if it turned out he were staring down one of the Unseen's agents instead of...

Well. Vendrick wasn't sure what she was, anymore, besides a Kaldiri woman with every right to hate him.

"Valerius..." He would test the waters, gently at first. "Tell me—what do you know about the Unseen?"

She recoiled at the about face. "Never heard of them."

"They're a cult—"

"Thought you banned churches," Frelia interrupted coolly.

"They were never banned," Vendrick said, "the Church of the Triad specifically was disbanded. But, as I was saying, the Unseen are a cult who worship the goddess Midnight, explicitly."

Frelia's entire person froze. It was unnatural to watch. "They what?"

"Exactly," said Vendrick. "Goddess of endings and apocalypse, no?"

"*Ja*, that's..." Frelia broke off to curse in Kaldiri. "No wonder I've never heard of them. That has to be a Volsinii thing; Kaldiri would never be so stupid."

Vendrick refrained from mentioning just how many morons he'd met with her accent and instead said, "So, it's been the damnedest thing. This cult-that-swears-it's-not-a-cult keeps somehow producing Senators, including the current Imperator."

A swirl of emotions crossed Frelia's hard face: first shock, then horror, then cold fury, and then, abruptly, nothing. Her eye was dead and lightless as she turned to study Christel.

"Don't tell me," she growled, and Vendrick knew then that he had her. "They pay the Bloodrune Hunters to bring them the blood of the Saints?"

Vendrick nodded. "Under shell companies, of course."

"Why." It was more a demand than a question, but Vendrick let that slide for the moment.

"My theory," he said, "is that they're collecting the nine bloodrunes. That's why they pay more for live bounties, if I had to take a reasonably educated guess."

Frelia whirled on him so fast, Vendrick barely saw her move. She was just—all of a sudden—standing right there. Between Christel Vilulf's prone, convulsing body, and Vendrick.

A shield between her people and the enemy, always.

"They can't have Christel," she growled.

It occurred to Vendrick, suddenly, that there was an easier way to go about this. He just needed a little give, that was all.

"Valerius, I'm saying I agree with you."

Confusion smacked the fierce expression on her face down hard. "You do?"

"I've no wish to see innocent people—particularly my students—wind up dead or worse." Vendrick tried not to be offended that she looked so surprised, he really did. "And I trust della Luciana about as far as I can throw him—and yes, I know, I'm a mage, it's not far."

She graced him with an amused snort.

"So it's deeply unfortunate that Faustine della Luciana was among the witnesses," Vendrick continued, "because there's no way in hell he won't know about this the instant she's free to roam. Possibly before. But what we can do is minimize the damage he'll cause."

Frelia studied him for a moment. "Trouble in Queenmaker-land, I see?"

"You know, it's almost like Markus didn't support Octavia Nova's claim to the throne at all." Vendrick couldn't help the sarcasm that dribbled from his tongue. "And instead was put into her inner circle at someone else's behest to keep an eye on her."

A pause.

"You know his father will hear about that." Frelia looked like she was trying not to smile.

Vendrick's laugh sounded surprised to his own ears. "I'm certain he already has."

They fell into a much softer silence than the one that had come before. Christel's lips were still moving, and they occasionally reached a hand up as though to grab something. Vendrick wondered what the poor thing was seeing, if apparently the entirety of their family history was in rotation.

"I want to help," Frelia suddenly burst out.

"I beg pardon?" Vendrick stared at her, uncomprehending. "Help what?"

"Don't bullshit me." Frelia folded her arms across herself and cocked her head to stare him down. "There's a reason you're out here in the backwater frontier, and I know it's not that you believe that deeply in education."

Vendrick studied her with renewed interest. *Sharp as ever, aren't you, Frelia?* "For the record, I do, actually. I've no interest in living in an empire full of idiots."

Silence stretched between them, thin and gossamer as a spiderweb.

"But?" she pressed.

"But," Vendrick conceded, "you're correct—there are several reasons, in fact, as to why I work here."

Not all of them fit for release, he thought.

"But I'm not certain what you think I require assistance with," he added, "besides Christel's current condition."

As if on cue, the teenager lashed out like a soldier awoken mid-sleep in the middle of a war.

Frelia caught the punch lightly, and folded Christel's arm back down against their chest without looking at them. "You ever heard of the witch Brenn?"

"The old Kaldiri Spymistress?" At Frelia's nod, Vendrick added, "She was an absolute legend during the Winter War. Why?"

"She was my aunt," Frelia said. "So trust me when I say, I get how people like you think. You don't do something for nothing, and if you broke from your family to leave the Imperator's inner circle, it was for something major."

A predatory smile crossed her face, and Vendrick's throat went dry.

"Something like..." Frelia pretended to think about it for half a second. "...interrupting the Imperator's cult-y side project, maybe?"

Vendrick had to pivot around this dung pile he'd stepped in. Now. "I didn't realize Brenn was a Valerius."

"Seladalr," Frelia corrected. "Mum's side of the family. And don't change the subject. You thought I was an imposter earlier this year and you're dodging me now."

"Okay, to be clear," Vendrick said, "I was checking whether you were an imposter. I didn't figure you were one."

"Well, I'm me." Frelia threw her hands wide; in battle, he could have stabbed straight through to her heart unencumbered. "So what did the great Viper of Ascalon do to have to go to ground at Silverwood, eh?"

For the briefest of seconds, Vendrick wanted to tell her everything. About the Unseen, and everything happening in the Senate, and the rows of corpses he'd had to step over just to reach the ripe old age of thirty-six.

But that impulse was even more dangerous than the other ones he had around her. The ones that wondered if her hair were coarse or fine, if her skin was as smooth as it looked, in the places it wasn't scarred. If he would even be able to feel it beneath his own deeply scarred fingers. If there were a version of the world where he'd be allowed to find out.

He had to be rational, here. Logical. Even if everything in him screamed for connection, for understanding, Vendrick had to be thorough about this. He couldn't afford mistakes.

"A question for you, first."

Frelia rolled her eye. "Fine. What?"

What was something they shared, that only she would know? He'd already asked about the black magic study sessions, but the penalty for failure this time was even higher. He wasn't sure he could stomach having to kill her if she learned too much and turned out not to be the old lab partner who got away.

"How did I lose my cloak during finals week during our third year at Silverwood?" tumbled from his mouth.

Her lips parted in surprise, and then her arms lowered slowly back to her sides.

"You didn't," Frelia said quietly, after a long moment. "You gave it to me one night when I left mine in my room and we were studying in the library. It was the same night you passed out on a stack of books at three in the morning."

She'd given it back to him the next morning, and for days, it had smelled of pine needles and sword polish. The scents he still associated with her to this very day.

"Thank you—" Vendrick began, at the same time Frelia burst out, "I stopped Roland Sferrazza from drawing dicks on your face that night, you know."

"I'm indebted to you, madam."

"Then now it's your turn to answer me." Frelia had gone all tense again, and Vendrick's thoughts were starting to run away from him in opposite directions.

One half was fully invested in the Unseen and the cold war he'd been waging for decades, but the other one was wondering how her brow might smooth out, if he ran a thumb over it. Dammit, he needed a cold shower and possibly Clarissa to smack him.

"When and why did my da come to Silverwood?" Frelia said.

Vendrick only had to think for a moment. "It was at the end of our second year," he said. "Rumor had it you were in enormous trouble for picking grappling as a certification instead of swordsmanship. I distinctly recall stopping by your room to walk with you to class, and suddenly I was staring down a duke."

Einar Valerius was where Frelia's black hair and bloodrune had come from, but size-wise, she must have taken after her mother's family, because her father was an enormous man known as the Warden of Kaldr. Teenaged Vendrick had gaped in horrified shock for an embarrassingly long moment when Einar had opened the door that morning. Then

Frelia had introduced them, and told Vendrick she wasn't coming to class today so he should get going.

"But it wasn't the certification you were in trouble for," Vendrick added, quietly now. "It was not answering his letters to own your decision."

Oh, this hurt. These memories he hadn't thought of in years, suddenly dredged up from the depths like the corpse of a sea monster.

"*Ja,*" Frelia said, unusually quiet. "That was Da."

She shook herself like the war dog they called her, and then straightened back up to meet his eye. She was a head shorter than him, give or take.

"Alright Caecillion, so we know you're you, and I'm me. So tell me—what did you do to get exiled to Silverwood, and can I help?"

Vendrick didn't know whether the thing pulsating in his stomach was panic or something worse, and he did his best to squash it. "No, you can't help with the thing that brought me here."

"What the hell, Caecillion! I—"

"*However,*" Vendrick interrupted, and Frelia stilled, "there is... another matter in which we could use your assistance."

Wariness crossed her features. "Who's we?"

Vendrick glanced over to Christel. They were thrashing again, in the throes of whatever memory Frelia had warned them of. "My spy network, of course," Vendrick murmured. "Did you think I gave them up?"

"That's exactly the shit I mean!" Glee lit up Frelia's face, just for a moment. "Aunt Brenn was the same way."

Vendrick snorted, and despite himself, despite everything, he said, "Saints, you never got away with anything as a child either, did you?"

The emotion drained from her face, leaving behind a frigid mask that wasn't like her. Not the her Vendrick had known, anyway.

"More than you'd think," Frelia said after a moment. "Mum died when I was small. And *don't* say you're sorry for my loss—"

Vendrick's jaw snapped shut, the sentence slaughtered before it had bloomed.

"—just tell me how I can ruin Ironfang's life."

All roads lead to Ironfang. Vendrick had been right about that, after all. He held out his hand, a peace offering, a promise.

"This is a cold war," he said. "It will not be won on battlefields and over war tables, but by proxy, espionage, and finally uncovering something damning enough that Ironfang cannot slither out of it."

He watched for an expression, but so far, her eye just flicked between Vendrick's hand and his face. He knew what she was thinking. It was the only thing she could be:

"So, are you prepared to fight the Volsinii way?"

"There is very little I won't do for my *volchya*." Her grip was as strong as the steel she wielded. "The living or the dead."

Beside them, Christel murmured a song Vendrick hadn't heard since the Tyrant's War:

"This is the end of days, my friends—
It's Heit Reiði."

CHAPTER TWENTY

FAUSTINE TRIED TO CONVINCE herself that she would tell Markus about Christel on the last day of her quarantine, after dinner. That way it wouldn't look odd for her to be out of her room, and Markus couldn't say he hadn't learned about everything at the first possible opportunity.

Only...

Faustine knew Markus wouldn't accept any reason whatsoever for anything he saw as a delay. He would berate her for not sneaking out of her room the very instant she knew Lady Caecillion was gone. No, before that—he would berate her for going to Professor Valerius in the first place instead of him. Was he not savage enough to be trusted, or something?

Nothing Faustine ever did was good enough.

She sighed, and rolled over in her bed to stare up at the rafters. It was kind of nice, the idea of taking these three days to sit in her room and do nothing. The headmaster had said the kitchen would bring meals up to her and Siegmund, and although they needed to keep restroom breaks to the absolute minimum, they could tie a kerchief over their nose and mouth and go about their business.

So for the first time in her life, Faustine had actual free time.

She couldn't go anywhere, but she didn't have to, either. She could just sit on her bed and catch up on homework, and maybe read the Aloysius novel she'd checked out from the library last week. She could even take a nap, and no one would be there to scream at her for how lazy she was being.

These things were true, and yet, Faustine's stomach churned. Every minute she dawdled was another minute Markus would think she'd delayed, and she would pay for.

Faustine couldn't help but think about how Professor Valerius hadn't yelled at them for not coming to her sooner. She'd simply accepted what they told her, and worked from there. It was so strange, Faustine had been thinking about it on and off ever since. Even as Headmaster Caecillion laid out the plan to keep watch on Christel, for whatever that Kaldiri tradition was that the professor had said a few times but Faustine couldn't reproduce to save her life.

Markus will be mad about that too, I'd wager, she thought, dimly. He'd want to know what treason the professor was committing down to the very last detail.

Except, it didn't seem like treason to Faustine. It seemed very practical, actually. Compassionate, even. If a newly awakened bloodrune could make someone sick, then sure, it made sense that families for whom that happened all the time would have some sort of protocol for it. Her and Markus' family had protocols for darkbeast bites, didn't they? What made this any different?

He would have something dismissive to say about that, Faustine was certain. She didn't know what, and she didn't know how, but he would.

She squinted at the ceiling, wondering if she should just get it over with. Before Faustine had gone to Silverwood, Orsina had given her a disguise runestone and told her it was for emergency use only, or she wouldn't be giving her another. The runestone currently lay tucked under Faustine's bed in the same lockbox that held her other valuables (a necklace that had once been her mother's, and an emergency stash of gold, just in case).

It was the same kind of magic the Unseen used to impersonate people, and from what her siblings told her, said magic was good enough to fool military folks who were trained to look for imposters. Surely it would make Faustine look like Ellie or Karina long enough for her to walk over to the Watchers' Barracks and ask for Markus? She didn't know where Ellie or Karina was right now, but it was either in their rooms, asleep, or somewhere they weren't supposed to be anyway, so she'd be doing them a favor.

Right?

She really should just get it over with. Brace herself for Markus' usual Markus-ness and then relax the next two days. (*He'll never let you,* a little voice in the back of her mind whispered, and Faustine told it to shut up).

"That's why I'm anxious," Faustine murmured to the rafters, "I just need to do something. Right?"

Unsurprisingly, the rafters said nothing.

She drew in a deep breath—"Okay, Faustine. You can do this."—and then pulled the covers off.

She lit the jar candle sitting on her windowsill after a few tries, and tried to blame the matches instead of her shaking hands. She set the candle down on the floor next to her bedside table, then dropped on her stomach to pull the lockbox out of hiding. Faustine screwed her eyes shut and tried not to imagine rats or monsters as she shoved her arm under her bed and felt around.

She had to stifle a scream when she touched something furry and damp, but realized a moment later that it was just the edge of her overcoat. A moment later, her fingers brushed the edge of the lockbox, and she jammed her shoulder under the bed trying to fish it out.

Her shoulder screaming, Faustine brought the lockbox over to her desk. She fished around her lowest desk drawer for a moment with her non-screaming arm, pulling textbooks and loose papers and half-broken quills out until she found the small brass key she was looking for.

You're so paranoid. Orsina's voice drifted across the back of Faustine's mine. *The only bauble worth anything in that box is the runestone.*

Faustine shook her head. Orsina could stuff it, especially when she wasn't even here.

The key turned smoothly in the lock, and Faustine carefully pulled open the lid. She breathed a sigh of relief—everything was still here. She pushed aside the coinpurse, and retrieved the runestone.

It was a small, grey rock about the size of her hand. There was a rune inked on the surface that Faustine didn't recognize, but thankfully, she didn't need to know any magic to use it. She took the instructions out, as well—a small, folded piece of paper the runestone had been resting on.

"Okay," Faustine murmured to herself as she unfolded the paper. "Let's see, here."

The rune diagrams swam on the page, and Faustine blinked a few times, trying to clear her vision. Eventually, Markus' familiar scrawl showed up in the bottom left-hand side of the page:

Mentally picture the illusion you want to cast, as clearly as possible. Then make a diagonal incision on your palm, and hold the runestone to it, rune facing you. The magic should take effect by the time you've counted to five.

Great. Faustine wrinkled her nose in disgust. It was always blood, when it came to the Unseen.

Blood, or worse.

She shook her head again and tried to picture Ellie in her mind. Faustine's heart pounded in her ears as she tried to call to mind her friend's blonde hair and small features. Faustine had just been talking to her yesterday, and yet she couldn't remember the color of Ellie's eyes, exactly. Couldn't remember if she wore jewelry or not.

Ugh! It was no good; Faustine couldn't remember well enough to look like Ellie.

Okay, okay, it was fine. She could just impersonate someone else. Faustine mentally ran through the list of the Violet Owls—she couldn't be Siegmund or Christel, and couldn't picture Ellie clearly enough. Karina, Faustine could picture, but she quickly realized that none of her clothes would fit Karina, so that was no good. That left Valente, or Owen.

Wait. *Owen!*

He was always running late and looked messy; it wouldn't matter if Faustine couldn't remember how he usually wore his hair or something. Newly bolstered, she pictured Owen's square jaw and messy brown hair, spinning his mental image together in her mind. She couldn't mimic his accent very well, but that was fine. She just wouldn't talk much, until she got to Markus' office.

Faustine carefully picked up the dagger she'd carried with her since the darkbeast attack, and held it to her left palm. She stared at it for a long moment, nervousness in her stomach like when the healer came by with a needle.

Go on, she tried to mentally urge herself, but all she heard was Orsina and Markus calling her weak.

Faustine slashed a diagonal cut across her hand, and almost gasped at the bright, sudden pain. She picked up the runestone with her other hand, and, pulling Owen to mind again, smooshed the rune into her blood.

She breathed slowly, mentally counting to five.

For a moment, Faustine didn't feel any different. But then she looked down at her hands, and instead of her own thin, tapered fingers, she had blocky, thick ones. Faustine pushed back from her desk, nearly knocking over the chair in her haste to find her compact mirror.

Owen Gundalf's cheerful face stared back at her.

Faustine contorted her face this way and that, raising her eyebrows and poking her cheeks. The illusion didn't waver, but Faustine suddenly realized she should have changed clothes before turning herself into a boy.

"Sorry, Owen," Faustine said, and the voice that came from her was too low to belong to her.

She tried not to look down as she changed into non-uniform pants and a button-up shirt, and turned away from her mirror for good measure. The new angles of this illusory body felt wrong, dysmorphic, but once she was fully dressed again, the compact told her she didn't look that way. If she didn't know any better, she would have believed that it really was Owen Gundalf standing there in her room.

Except his buttons were all done up correctly. So she undid a few and misaligned them.

Better.

She pulled her cloak off the wall, dragged the hood over her head, and then slipped out of her room.

Act like you know where you're going, she could hear Orsina saying. *No one questions a confident stride.*

Faustine mentally scowled at her eldest sister, but tried to emulate the way she'd seen Markus or Siegmund walk. It was a sort of shuffle, like they didn't quite understand that their hips moved. It felt like trying to scurry along to the bathroom while constipated, but the first Watchers that Faustine passed didn't give "Owen" a second glance, so she must have been convincing.

She could do this. She had to do this.

The Professor's voice suddenly burst into her mind: *In all things, Faustine, there are hunters, and there are prey.*

Ironfang was a hunter. Markus was a hunter. Orsina and even Galeria were hunters. Professor Valerius and Headmaster Caecillion were hunters.

But Faustine?

Faustine was prey.

She felt it deep in her stomach as she slipped silently across the twilit Silverwood grounds. Now that she was out of her room and on the path forward, her anxiety had only gotten louder and she felt like she was going to cry.

She didn't want to turn Christel over to Markus. Didn't want anything bad to happen to them. Christel was kind, and funny, and the panic in their face when they'd realized what had happened in the library made Faustine's heart twist into painful knots. Markus didn't deserve to know about the horrible, tragic secret that was cut into Christel's skin.

Someone needs to tell them their family stories, Professor Valerius had said while Faustine was in the kitchen with Siegmund. Faustine hadn't heard much over Siegmund's rising panic, but what she had heard shook her to the core.

Christel needs to know.

Imagine! Someone who actually gave a damn whether you knew something or not! If not for the maids in the Villa della Luciana, Faustine wouldn't have even known what a menstrual cycle was, let alone how to deal with it.

By the time Faustine reached the Watchers' Barracks, she was on the verge of proper tears. But she held it together because she was unable to imagine Owen's face crying, and she didn't know if she needed to to make the runestone work. It jangled against her hip in her pocket, a leaden weight.

"Boy," called the Watcher on duty at the front of the barracks, "it's well past student curfew."

Faustine drew in a breath, and did her best to mimic Owen's Kaldiri accent: "I need to speak with Captain della Luciana."

The Watcher raised his eyebrow. "Regarding?"

She swallowed, audibly. "I think one of my classmates has an unregistered bloodrune."

The Watcher's face lit up like the fireworks over Augustus Pier, and he told Faustine to wait right there. He practically scrambled out of his chair in his haste to rouse Markus from wherever he'd gotten off to. For a few minutes, Faustine just stood there stupidly in the barracks' foyer, trying not to twist the hem of her shirt because that was a Faustine thing not an Owen thing.

For the first time in her entire life, Markus' face didn't pinch at the sight of her. When he rounded the corner, his face was smooth and unbothered, and with a jolt, Faustine realized, that must be what other people saw.

"Owen," said Markus, "what's this about a bloodrune?"

"Can I, um." Faustine swallowed hard. "Can I speak to you in your office, sir?"

Markus' brow furrowed, and Faustine knew at once that her fake Kaldiri accent hadn't fooled him. "You will report right here, Owen," he said. "You have leveled a serious accusation."

"Please, sir." Faustine scrambled to think of something Markus would believe. "I don't think it's... um, safe."

There was Markus' customary sneer, right on time. "You stand in the middle of the Watchers' Barracks. I daresay, there's no safer place on this campus."

Faustine struggled not to laugh. The headmaster's office was safer than this, the training grounds, the cafeteria. The bottom of the damn lake.

"Can we at least walk, or something?" Faustine asked. "I don't really want to stand still."

Markus rolled his eyes—"Fine, follow me."—and took off down a side hallway without even looking to see if Faustine was following.

She scuttled to keep up, forgetting that she was supposed to be walking like a boy.

"Markus," Faustine hissed in her own accent as soon as they were out of earshot of the foyer, "it's me. Faustine."

Her older brother froze.

He turned slowly to look at her, his eyes travelling down to her boots and back up to her face. *"What?"*

Faustine glanced over her shoulder, just to make certain they were alone. "Orsina gave me this for use in emergencies."

She pulled the illusory runestone out of her pocket to show him.

"Put that away!" Markus hissed, and then his huge hand was on the scruff of her neck and dragging her towards his office.

Which was where Faustine had wanted to be in the *first* place, dammit! Why did no one ever listen to her? Apparently, it didn't even matter whose face she was wearing.

The instant they crossed the threshold into Markus' office, he slammed the door shut and whirled on Faustine.

"This had better be good," he snapped.

Faustine swallowed against the lump in her throat. "I wasn't kidding. One of my classmates *does* have an unregistered bloodrune. It just showed up today."

Markus relaxed, just a little. He no longer looked like he wanted to strangle her, just like he'd stepped in something that smelled bad. "Which one, and on whom?"

"Professor Valerius said it was the Traust Bloodrune, and Christel Vilulf."

For a half second, relief broke across Markus' angry face. Then it snapped back to nasty as he realized, "Valerius knows?"

"She was the first professor we found!" It wasn't even a lie. "And she has a bloodrune, so Siegmund just..."

Markus waved her off with a put-upon sigh. "Where is Christel now?"

"The, um..." Faustine looked down to her boots. "The professor made us take them to the Headmaster."

"Shit!" Markus grabbed a decorative vase off the table near his door and flung it at the wall.

It shattered into a million little pieces that glittered in the dying sunlight.

"We have *three days* at most to steal that bloodrune," Markus barked. "After that, we can take blood, but it won't be the rune."

Three days. That was how long the professor said the Kaldiri tradition with the really long name lasted.

You are prey, whispered a voice in the back of her mind.

Maybe, Faustine told it. *But I don't have to like it.*

"I don't... think we'll be able to steal it, then," Faustine said. "The professor and the headmaster were discussing where to keep Christel for the next couple of days. Siegmund and I are supposed to be quarantined in our rooms, too. That's why I look like Owen to tell you this."

Markus roared in frustration, and lashed out at the nearest solid object. His fist connected with the solid stone of his wall, and he howled again, this time in pain.

Serves you right, Faustine thought blackly.

"You can still salvage this." Markus was speaking quickly now, flipping through the swords textbook on his lectern. "It isn't too late."

"*Me?*" Faustine protested. "I can't sneak into the Headmaster's suite to get Christel out! I'd be set on fire with magic, or stabbed, or—!"

"Stabbed?" Markus interrupted as the secret bookshelf door swung open again. "Is Valerius there *with* Caecillion?"

Faustine swallowed past the lump in her throat, and fell into step behind Markus as he tore down the stairs to his lab. "Yes, she is."

Markus heaved an enormous sigh. "Caecillion, you besotted fool."

A fool who outsmarted you, Faustine couldn't help but think. Professor Valerius had been right to go straight to the headmaster; Christel was only protected by her quick thinking and his willingness to listen. If Markus could only steal Christel's bloodrune in the first three days, and it took three days to do the thing the professor had talked about...

No. Headmaster Caecillion was the opposite of a fool.

The instant Markus set foot in his laboratory space, he practically sprinted for the supply cabinet. He jerked the door open and dug around through vials and tools Faustine had no names for until he found what appeared to be an empty syringe.

He held it up to the light, and then said, distastefully, "You will do."

Faustine was so tired, so anxious, so disgusted with herself that she forgot to shut up and asked, "Do for *what?*"

Markus' grey eyes fixed on her, colorless and stormy in the runelight of his lab. "Forget about Valente," he said, and Faustine was so taken aback, she startled. "You can even forget about Valerius, at least for the moment. Use *this*—"

He held the syringe out to her.

"—to get a sample of Christel's blood, and we can still salvage this disaster of a semester."

Faustine took the empty syringe from him. It had a hollow chamber, a thin needle, and a depressed plunger. "How does that help, if we can't take their bloodrune?"

Markus pointed behind him, to a row of test tubes racked on the very top shelf. Faustine followed the line of empty vials to the very end, where a few centimeters of rusty, reddish liquid had pooled in the base of the last vial.

"That is what remains of the Grimsdalr blood Father granted me when I moved here," Markus said. "I cannot use it to make more darkbeasts; there isn't enough. But with *Christel's* blood, it doesn't matter how much Grimsdalr I have left—Traust will get me what I need."

A maniacal gleam had entered Markus' eyes, and, well, if Markus were in a telling mood, Faustine was going to push.

"Why?" she asked. "What's the difference?"

Markus' laugh was fraying at the edges. Faustine could hear it, as it echoed against the walls of his lab.

"Oh, the bloodrunes have *tasks,* you know," he said. "Grimsdalr is for strengthening one's form, Valerius is simply for fighting, and Domitia is for hunting. But Traust..."

A slow smile spread across Markus' lean face, and every instinct in Faustine's smooth little prey brain screamed at her to run.

"Traust is for memory."

CHAPTER TWENTY-ONE

"WELL," SAID CLARISSA AFTER Edmund had come and gone, "now what do we do?"

Frelia sighed and fought the urge to snap something contrary. So far, Vendrick's sister had been nothing but helpful, so really, Frelia could deal with the woman's exhausting personality for three days.

Right? *Right.*

"Don't know about you two," Frelia said, "but *I* have a bunch of stories to tell a terrified child."

All three adults glanced at Vendrick's bedroom door.

"Keep the door open," Vendrick said, "would you kindly?"

Frelia shot him a dirty look. "I'm not going to assault a child."

"Then there should be no problem," he returned smoothly.

Volsinii!

"I'm not responsible for what you overhear," Frelia harrumphed, and she stalked from the living room, leaving behind Clarissa's chatter about dinner or breaking into Vendrick's liquor cabinet.

The woman reminded Frelia too much of Cillian. Too bright, too loud, too much humor in the face of bullshit.

Vendrick had apparently been going through his closet when Frelia had shown up at his door; he'd had to sweep a bunch of clothes into a laundry bin before Frelia could help Christel into bed. The teenager lay there now, propped up on some decorative pillows and sipping from a ceramic jug of water.

"You know there are cups for that," Frelia said.

Christel yelped and almost dropped the jug. "I didn't see any," they said, sheepishly.

Frelia stuck her head back out the door. "Oi, Caecillion."

Two sets of green eyes cut over to her. "Yes?" they both said.

Frelia made a face. "I meant *him*, but I guess either of you works—can Christel have a water cup?"

"Did I not put one in there?" Surprise colored Vendrick's voice. "My mistake, I'll remedy that."

He disappeared down the short hall to his kitchen and Clarissa said, apologetically, "This happens a lot."

Frelia cocked an eyebrow. "Him forgetting things?"

That would be new.

"Oh, no." Clarissa laughed. "Someone shouting 'Caecillion' and both of us answering. You can just call me 'Clarissa', you know. I really don't mind."

"Noted." Frelia knew far too many Volsinii to fall for that one.

"It's not a trick or anything, I do mean it," Clarissa added. "It's a pleasure to finally meet you; my brother's told me so much about you I feel as if I already know you anyway."

What the fuck? "He... has?" Frelia said.

"Well, sure," Clarissa said. "I've heard about all of his Silverwood friends, over the years. Did you ever meet Irirangi of the Kingfisher Clan?"

"A few times, but she was in the Southern Strix, and an archer."

Footsteps came from over by the kitchen. "Found a suitable replacement, so hopefully this will—"

Vendrick cut himself off at the sight of Frelia and Clarissa. His eyes flicked between the two women as though looking for something.

"Thanks." Frelia held her hand out for the cup. "But *ja,* Caecillion, why do you ask about Irirangi?"

"No particular reason." Clarissa shrugged, but Vendrick's stare could have bored holes in her coat. "Just curious."

Frelia was missing something, here. Damned if she knew what it was, though. Did it have to do with the Unseen? Was there a way Frelia could ask?

Nothing jumped immediately to mind. Especially since, it occurred to Frelia, that she didn't know whether Clarissa was involved with Vendrick's private war.

"Man the fort, I guess," Frelia said.

Vendrick winced, although he tried to hide it.

"Oh, it's a *joke,*" Frelia muttered. "And if *I* can joke about it, I don't want to hear shit from either of you."

She went back to the bedroom with Christel's replacement cup, and just barely caught Clarissa's quiet "Did I miss something?"

The water situation fixed, Frelia took the jug from Christel, set it on the bedside table, and then dropped into the kitchen chair she'd dragged in the bedroom for that express purpose.

"I'm sorry," Christel suddenly said.

Frelia's brow furrowed. "For what?"

"Ruining your fall break, for starters." Christel wasn't looking at her, and instead thumbing the sedate fabric of the comforter. "For causing all this trouble. For..."

"Stop it."

Christel's head snapped up, and they looked at Frelia—really *looked*. Part of Frelia wondered what they saw, but the other, louder part didn't want to know.

"We bloodruned folks need to stick together," Frelia added, more quietly. "*Ja?*"

"Yeah." Christel looked back down at their hands again. "Professor Blightsen said I had the Traust Bloodrune."

Frelia was surprised Edmund had said even that much. He'd cleaned and bandaged Christel's shoulder with the terrified fervor of a mouse running from a barn cat, and then made himself scarce the moment Vendrick had thanked him for his assistance.

"That's all the concentric circles *can* mean,"Frelia said. "Besides, you look like them."

Pain entered Christel's expression. "I do?"

Frelia nodded, and suddenly her own chest ached. "You have Ulfhild's hair—Geir's and Astrid's, too—but your grandmother Gudrun's eyes. Probably some of her face, too, but I haven't seen her since the Winter War."

The druidess was responsible for the sparse casualties on the Kaldiri side, after all. Her visions had spared many a Kaldiri knight a fate worse than death.

But not Diarmuid, Frelia thought blackly. *Not Kjeld. Not Jari, either.*

"You're doing it again, Professor."

Frelia's head snapped up. "Doing what?"

"You'll start telling me things," Christel said, "And then get really, *really* quiet. Are you okay?"

Frelia hadn't heard such a stupid question in years.

"Today is not about me," she said. "But tell me if I'm doing that again, and I'll snap out of it."

Christel made a face. "I don't want to hurt you, though."

This time Frelia really did laugh. "We can't always avoid what hurts us, Christel. There's usually something important on the other side." She gestured to their bandaged shoulder. "Like you, knowing what the fuck is on your shoulder blade."

Christel was quiet for so long, Frelia wondered if they'd been overtaken by memories or visions again.

"I only know a little about the Saints," they finally said. "That's where these come from, right?"

They gestured to their shoulder and grimaced.

"Right." Frelia nodded. "You are a descendent of Saint Traust, just like I'm a descendant of Saint Valerius."

"And they sealed the goddess Midnight into Helheim, a thousand years ago?" Christel seemed to debate something, then added, "That was that story you were telling at the first garmur-fighting class?"

"Certain Volsinii made me stop before that part," Frelia said flatly. "But *ja*. Good instinct."

"Can you tell me the rest?" Christel drew their knees up to their chest, curling into a tight ball beneath the covers. "Will the headmaster get mad?"

"I told him I'm not responsible for what he overhears," Frelia said, "because, *ja,* that's what I'm here for. What was the last thing you remember from that class?"

"That." Christel jerked their head to the side. "The Saints fighting the garmur, and sealing the goddess Midnight into Helheim."

"That *is* most of the story," Frelia admitted. "Since the garmur were caught in the in-between at the sealing, and they will always *be,* in the Waking World, the Saints divided the defense of humanity between them. Lady Daybreak and Lady Twilight consecrated that into their most Sacred Tasks..."

Frelia drew in a deep breath, and tried not to remember the faces of the dead as she said:

"Einnaska, to lead them all.

"Nova, to serve as their discretion.

"Grimsdalr, to defend the innocent against Lady Midnight's terrible beasts.

"Valerius, to breathe in the anger of humanity, and breathe out the Goddesses' fury.

"Maximus, to keep humanity on the right path.

"Domitia, to ensure we never forget what can become of us, if we falter.

"Háski, to cut out the rot when it threatens to choke new growth.

"Konstantin, to stitch the world anew.

"And Traust, to remember the fallen, and *never* sink to despair." Frelia sighed. "And so it went, right up until the Tyrant's War."

"That's..." Christel blinked. "...a lot of families."

"It's nine," said Frelia, "and you will remember them all. It's the Traust Clan's *job* to remember—your bloodrune *is* memory."

"Meaning what?"

"Meaning..." Frelia paused. "You know how mine will cut you in half if it activates?"

Christel nodded.

"My job is to stand and defend," Frelia said. "Yours is to weave together the past and future into one eternal present."

Christel's jaw dropped, horrified.

"It's not so much as it sounds." Frelia made a wishy-washy motion with her hand. "You've already started—what did you see, when your bloodrune activated?"

Christel opened their mouth as if to argue, then dropped their eyes back down to the comforter.

"I saw you," they said, "and the headmaster, on the walls of some castle somewhere."

Frelia blinked. "Were we fighting or something?"

"No." Christel shook their head. "Just... talking, I think. You looked pregnant." They grimaced. "Sorry if that's too much information."

Frelia stared at them for a long moment. Traust visions weren't known to be wrong, exactly, but they were malleable. The future was not so set in stone as a lot of folks wanted to believe.

But still. *Pregnant?* There were a lot of things that would have to fall in line before *that* happened, and quickly. Frelia wasn't young anymore. Not old, yet, but not young.

"Traust... gets visions," Frelia finally said. "Your grandmother—Gudrun—fought in the Winter War with my father. He learned of all sorts of troop movements and future battles that both did and did not come to pass. So, heed what your visions tell you, but don't think they can't change."

Christel absorbed this for a long moment. "What do I do if I get another one?"

"I would imagine you won't be getting too many," Frelia said. "You have to actually be *trying* to see the future to get the Traust Bloodrune to activate."

"Oh." Christel made a face. "Is that why I got it while practicing bone divining?"

"That would be my guess," Frelia said. "And also, maybe you should drop white magic. I'll talk to the headmaster."

She doubted Vendrick would put up much of a fight about it, given the circumstances.

"Oh, shit." Christel looked down at their hands. "I didn't even think of that."

"Your bloodrune isn't like mine," Frelia said, not unkindly. "You have the ability to hide it. I recommend doing that."

As much as it hurt her heart to say it, Frelia knew it was the right thing to do. It *had* to be. Christel didn't have the Church of the Triad or decades of sword practice to keep them safe.

It was such a tiny, insignificant thing, the world that could have been. It could fit right in the palm of Frelia's hand, or be crushed beneath her boot.

"Also," Frelia said, "did you hear anything in that vision, or just see it?"

"Nothing that made sense," Christel said.

"Hmm," said Frelia. "Well, count yourself lucky you saw people you know, I guess. Not everyone has that luxury, or so Ulfhild always said."

Christel's eyes lit up at the mention of their mother. "Can you tell me about her? She died when I was small..."

Frelia smiled. Ulfhild Traust was a lot easier to talk about than theoretical futures where she wasn't the last Valerius bloodrune-bearer. "What would you like to know?"

***

"What do you think they're talking about?" Clarissa asked as she and Vendrick reorganized his living room into a makeshift camp.

"Bloodrune things they don't want us to hear," Vendrick said, "I would imagine."

Frelia's voice was resonating through the door to his room, even half-shut, but she kept her volume low enough that, unless he wanted to stand there on the open side all day, Vendrick couldn't hear much.

Just snatches of *it's the Traust family's job to remember* and *so no shit, there I was, on top of a huge hill with Ulfhild and my brother.*

Vendrick had eavesdropped on a *lot* of people over the years, but this one actually made him feel bad for every scrap of information he overheard. Not enough to stop it, mind, but enough that his stomach twisted and guilt pricked at his neck.

Clarissa made a face as she surveyed their handiwork. "I think two pallets should do it, don't you think?"

Vendrick glanced from one bundle of blankets to the other. "There are three of us adults so, no, we'll need a third."

"Only two of us will ever be asleep at a time," Clarissa pointed out. Then she waggled her eyebrows.

"Enough scheming," Vendrick said firmly. "There are plenty of more important things to worry about. Third pallet. Let's go."

"Oh, no, no, no," Clarissa countered gleefully. "I was there when you got her letters, before the war. You *liked* her."

Vendrick immediately glanced to his bedroom door, and counted to five. When no one came bursting out of it, and Frelia's low storytelling voice resumed, he hissed, "Keep your voice down. Are you just *determined* to be annoying today?"

"I mean, always." Clarissa beamed. "But I'm also right, and I'm thinking it's not a past tense thing, no?"

Vendrick grabbed Clarissa's upper arm and practically dragged her into the kitchen. "Stop. Presuming," he hissed. "This is *ridiculous*, I am a *grown man,* for the Saints' sake!"

"Well, if I left it up to *you*," Clarissa said, yanking her arm back, "you would die alone in the middle of your spider's web because you never let anyone in and think everyone else's lives are more important than your own."

She somehow managed to make it sound like both a compliment and an insult.

"*Saints,* Vendy," Clarissa added, "it's not a crime to be happy."

It was such a tiny, insignificant thing, what might have been.

"She hates me, Clarissa," Vendrick said quietly. "And I can't even say I blame her. The fact that she guessed there was more to my being here than simply being bored of Ascalon is just proof I—"

"She figured that out?" Clarissa cocked her head.

Vendrick sighed. "Yes, just now while you were organizing the rest of this nightmare weekend."

She appraised him for a moment like he was one of the artifacts she was paid to enchant. "So is your new-old Kaldiri friend assisting us now? Since I presume you told her everything."

"Not *everything*." Vendrick reddened to the tips of his ears. "And you needn't say it like I'm a monster, thank you."

"Just predictable." Clarissa smiled at him, genuinely this time.

Vendrick's face fell flat. "How dare I both need allies and get along with the same people I always have. *Truly, I—*"

"Oh, stuff it," Clarissa interrupted. "Why don't we break out that wine I brought you and, I don't know, do you have a deck of cards around here, or something?"

Vendrick blinked. "I'm not throwing a *party* about this, Clary."

"It's not a party," she argued, "it's three people. And you can't just expect us to stare at Christel for the next three days."

"I have *work* to do," Vendrick said. "As in, actual Silverwood stuff, on top of what you brought."

"Fine." Clarissa shrugged. *"I'll* play cards with Frelia, then. *You* can be bored at your desk while I raid your liquor cabinet."

She was trying to get a rise out of him, and Vendrick knew it. Ordinarily he didn't bother to mask up so much around his little sister, given that she was just about the only person alive who knew what lay beneath it, but still. Sometimes she just needled him too much.

"Did... Valerius give you leave to call her Frelia?" Vendrick winced at how pathetic that sounded.

"'Course not," Clarissa said, "I just took it. You should try it."

"Clary, we've been over this." Vendrick sighed. "*You* can get away with that sort of thing because you're generally considered cute and nonthreatening by folks who don't know better."

Clarissa's jaw dropped in mock-offense. "I'm adorable!"

"You're the worst. I shall be commissioning a ballad to tell you how awful you are in rhyme."

"Aww, *Vendy,* you shouldn't have!"

"Did she just call you *Vendy?*"

Vendrick's heart jumped into his throat, and he looked over to find Frelia standing in his doorframe with an amused look on her face.

Clarissa cackled. "Oh, he *hates* it."

"If it were within my earthly power to make her stop, I would have by now," Vendrick agreed.

Frelia snorted, shook her head a bit, and then said, "Anyway, Christel's asleep for the moment, so—what are we planning on doing for three days while holed up in here?"

Clarissa seized her chance so fast, Vendrick would have been impressed if he weren't so annoyed.

"We were *just* talking about that!" she said. "We were thinking of opening some wine bottles and maybe playing cards?"

For a moment, Frelia just stood there in his kitchen threshold, completely perplexed. Then she shrugged. "I've heard worse ideas."

"Wonderful!" Clarissa turned a scheming, beaming grin on her brother. "You weren't going to *work* or something, were you, Vendy dear?"

Dammit, she'd outmaneuvered him. "Like I would leave poor Valerius at *your* mercy all evening."

Clarissa snickered, looping her arm through Frelia's. "I am a perfectly—"

"Don't touch me." Frelia swiftly jerked free.

Clarissa's hand fell back to her side. "I'm... sorry?"

Frelia shifted her weight from foot to foot. "I just don't like being touched."

"Oh." Clarissa blinked, uncomprehending for a moment, and then something like understanding brightened her face again. "I understand. Sorry again."

This was going to be a very, *very* long evening.

CHAPTER TWENTY-TWO

SIEGES WERE BRUTALLY BORING when you were the besieged.

Besieger, and there were always artillery trenches to dig and people to fight and a place to retreat to for a damn change of scenery. Not so, when you were the one in the high-walled castle waiting out the enemy. It was mostly officers' meetings and sending other knights to go die out front.

Frelia was sick of Heit Reiði. Sick of its walls, its passageways, its mess hall and its battlements. She had explored every inch of this place over the last few months, knew every single knight in its garrison by name. Knew which cannons and ballistae needed maintenance at any given time, and which alcove to avoid because her da would be in it.

Because he was here too, for some Saints-damned reason. So not only was Frelia trapped in a besieged castle, she was trapped in it with her father. Who refused to let her go fight garmur, which was the entire reason Hägen had stationed Frelia here.

Her da may have been excellent at siegecraft, but he was not good at seeing his daughter as a grown-ass woman with a garmr kill count in the eighties.

So here she sat, twiddling her thumbs, waiting.

"How goes the morning watch?" came a voice to Frelia's right.

She glanced over to find her da climbing the stairs to the battlements, his paladin's armor gleaming in the early morning sun. It was nearly autumn, which in Kaldr meant cloaks but no furs, so while the wind up here was cool, it wasn't bad yet.

Frelia rolled her eyes. "Ten of the morning watch and all is silent."

Her da held out a tin mug of coffee—a peace offering if Frelia had ever seen one. Part of her wanted to refuse, even tip it over the battlements. But the other part of her knew their supplies were growing thin and tantruming like a child wasn't going to help anything.

So she accepted the mug for what it was.

"Getting colder out here," Einar remarked.

"Not cold enough yet," Frelia said. "I think snow would kill them."

She gestured with her free hand towards the sloping fields that stretched towards the Ivory Channel. Currently, it was full of enemy trenches and the corpses of a few garmur their artillerists had taken out, but not yet burned. The corpses made Frelia nervous; she kept waiting for a live one to come shooting out of the forest any minute.

Einar opened his mouth to say something, and then shut it again and squinted at the fields. "Do you see that?"

Frelia whirled on the battlement wall, hand already going to her sword. Right on cue, there were a dozen garmur climbing out of the trenches and the nearby forests.

"Sound the alarm—" She started to say, but then she spotted it, too.

The della Luciana beastminder—always visible in violent, Volsinii crimson—was holding up a white flag. Or, well, his squire was, beside him. The beastminder shouted something Frelia and her da were too far away to hear, and then all the newly-birthed garmur sat on their haunches, or crouched low to the ground, or whatever it was that their sort of creature did.

"I guess we should go see what they want," Einar said, and he threw back the rest of his coffee.

Frelia pointed to the line of monsters sitting just outside their curtain walls. *"That's a fucking trap, da."*

"Perhaps," he agreed. *"Now come on, Little Wolf."*

Twenty minutes later, Frelia and her father, alongside a sizeable contingent of their house knights, rode out of the main gate. They weren't stupid, even if Grand Duke Einar believed in negotiation, so they had their weapons on them and a couple of battlemages hidden amongst their knights.

If Frelia were right and this turned out to be a trap, the Volsinii were in for hell.

"Grand Duke Einar Valerius," called the della Luciana beastminder from where he sat atop a quadrupedal garmr that looked like a stag, if stags could grow to the size of buildings, *"good morning."*

Einar pulled his retune up to an expectant pause, and Frelia shot the beastminder a glare.

"Oh, and the Grand Duchess, I suppose," said the beastminder. *"What is it they're calling you, these days?"*

"The Wolf of Kaldr," came a voice that did not belong to anyone in Valerius blue.

Frelia's stomach fell as more knights fitted themselves between the unnaturally still garmur, but it wasn't because of the sudden numbers. All the new knights wore purpure and sable, and that could only belong to one Volsinii family. The one she had hoped to never see.

"Da," Frelia said, staring at the interlopers like she was somewhere a thousand miles away, *"those are all mages."*

He nodded without looking at her. *"I greet you, della Luciana and...?"*

"Caecillion," Frelia supplied before the Volsinii did.

Vendrick halted just beside the stag-like garmr that carried his commander. His courser was matte black in the midday sun, its hide sucking in light without reflecting a single shred back. The sight of him, *after all this time, punched her in the stomach. Grabbed hold and refused to let go.*

No, no, he wasn't supposed to be here!

"Good morning." There was no inflection in Vendrick's tone.

"I assume you're here to negotiate, ja?" said Einar. "Get on with it, then."

The della Luciana looked taken aback, but Vendrick didn't move.

"My dear duke," said della Luciana, "this is not a parley. This is your singular opportunity to surrender before I take all these darkbeasts, here..."

He spread his arms to gesture to the line of garmur in unnatural repose beside him.

"...and knock down your walls."

Einar started in horrified surprise, but Frelia shouted, "Big talk, from a man whose siege engines we broke last week!"

"Frelia," her da murmured sharply, "I will handle this." He pitched his voice louder to ask, "So why bother to talk at all?"

The della Luciana shrugged. "Caecillion insisted!"

"It's all the siegebreaker training," Vendrick said, and he sounded almost joking. "Makes me believe in things like the rules of engagement and due process."

That line was thin, and Frelia knew it. Vendrick wouldn't insist out of a sense of honor or decorum, even if that's what he said. No, he was insisting on the chance for surrender because of who lay in wait behind the walls of Heit Reiði.

Frelia's heart twisted so hard it hurt. This war was a living nightmare, and she was never waking up.

Vendrick had to know the Valerius family didn't surrender, and especially not from a highly defensive position. He had to know that the Kaldiri dug their heels in and made the enemy pay for every inch they gained. He had to know they would never avoid battle when the alternative was annihilation.

He had to know. He had to know. And yet...

"Well, you've said your bit," said Einar. "And no, it will be war."

The della Luciana beastminder shrugged. "Your funeral. Off you go, then."

Grief burned in Frelia's gut, begging to be unsheathed. "How dare *you dismiss us like you have—"*

"Frelia," said her father, "ech er seiða."

She breathed in sharply, let her mother tongue wash over her until there was nothing left of the girl in blue who had once known the boy in purple.

"Ja," she agreed, and turned from the row of garmur a hair too slowly to miss how they moved to pounce.

If this was war, then so let it be.

"Valerius!"

Frelia awoke sharply, her breathing wild. A heavy weight was pressing against her side, and she reached instinctively for the knife beneath her pillow.

It wasn't there. *Fuck.*

She thrashed against the weight holding her down, ready to scratch eyes out or cast something, should it come to that. But then the voice said, "*Frelia.* You're safe."

She blinked a few times, as though she could bring the world into focus by sheer force of will. She caught sight of dark hair and spindly limbs in the gloom, and then green eyes that made her clutch at her side for the wound she'd sustained that day.

It took her far, *far* longer than it should have to realize she had only her scars, and those eyes weren't burning green, but normal. *Human.*

"Skitr!" Frelia covered her eye with her free hand. "You scared the hell out of me, Caecillion."

"I could say the same," he said, and the weight on her side lessened.

Wait a damn minute.

"Were you holding me down?"

He put distance between them as he pulled back to rest on his haunches. "You were thrashing; I was honestly concerned you'd hurt yourself."

It wouldn't be the first time she'd woken up with a bloody tongue or unexplained bruise, but she didn't know how to tell him that any more than she knew how to explain that his concern felt like a spark against bare skin. Unwelcome, but... warm.

Frelia tried to will her breathing to steady and her mind to come to heel. The Siege at Heit Reiði had been years ago; it couldn't hurt her now. Vendrick wasn't her enemy, anymore.

"Have you always had night terrors like that?" Vendrick suddenly asked.

Frelia's hand dropped from her face, and she stared, unseeing, at some landscape painting on Vendrick's wall. "*Ja*, on and off, as long as I can remember."

When he didn't say anything, she felt the need to add, "Perks of my bloodrune. And several wars, I suppose."

"So they really *do* do that," Vendrick mused. "Fascinating."

Frelia shot him a look. "Where do you think the ancestral trauma *goes*, exactly?"

Never mind where your own went.

"I... can't say I've thought much about it."

"Why would you?" Frelia was tired of both looking *and* not looking at him. Couldn't he just go away? "You're runeless."

"Put another way," Vendrick said, and he sounded on the verge of annoyed, "Octavia never seemed to have that issue."

Frelia made a face in the darkness. "Lucky her."

Every shadow in Vendrick's living room held those nascent, black wings, long, gangly limbs, and burning, green eyes. Or worse, they held memories she had no business holding onto. Frelia needed to move, to fight, but there was nothing to do for it. She couldn't leave to go take a walk or eviscerate a training dummy, what with the cover story the Caecillions had insisted on.

And he was still watching her. With that same, calculated expression he always had. It burrowed deep into her bones and hung there, like the witch balls Thera had made to ward off garmur and hung from rafters.

Frelia was just about to ask what his Saints-damned problem was when he stopped her cold:

"I'm certain I'm hardly your first choice in this, but I'm here, if you wish to discuss anything."

Frelia's jaw dropped, and she stared at him in disbelief.

He hurried to add, "Or I can go get my sister, if you'd prefer? She's keeping watch at the moment."

He thought the problem was *him?* How could a man so intelligent be so naïve?

"I know her even less than I know you," Frelia muttered, and then realized she'd been using present tense. "Knew. Whatever."

Vendrick didn't say anything for so long a moment, Frelia felt like she'd combust under the weight of those bright, green eyes.

Then—"Well, thanks for putting up with her anyway. I've seen her run through the patience of much sterner folks than us."

Call me Clarissa, she'd said. *I really don't mind.*

It echoed, somehow, of *We'll take your hometown back, Frey.* and *Last one up the hill has to drag the sleds back to the house!*

"She's just like Cillian."

Frelia said it so quietly, it was almost lost to her own ear. But it slipped out of her teeth and down her tongue, until it was breathed into being and it was too late to take it back. She braced for Vendrick to tell her not to compare his little sister to a rebel general, for him to tell her off and make her swallow every memory she still had of the Grimsdalr twins like bitter medicine.

To kill them twice. Like they'd never been at all.

But he said, "Do you like cheesecake?"

Frelia startled. "Do I *what?*"

"Clarissa brought some with her," Vendrick said. "And our housekeeper always says, bitter things are made easier with sweetness. So, that's what I've got for that."

He was... *comforting* her? In an extremely Volsinii, hands-off kind of way, but *still*. Frelia was so shocked that all the fight drained right out of her.

"I don't think I've ever tried it," she said. "Is it literally cheese baked in cake?"

"Ricotta, but yes." Vendrick nodded. "So it's not like chunks of Emmentaler stuffed into sweet bread, or something."

Frelia blinked again. She'd been exposed to plenty of Volsinii cooking over the years, so the cake part wasn't weird. But with *cheese* in it? That part made no sense.

"You have no idea what I'm talking about," Vendrick said with a small laugh, "do you?"

For once, it didn't feel so terrible to say, "Not a clue."

He was handsome, when he smiled. Still severe but not quite so grim. "Come try it," he said. "I'll eat the rest, if you don't like it."

"If this is an elaborate scheme to eat cake after midnight..."

"Pfft." Vendrick snorted. "This is my home; I don't need a scheme for that."

He got to his feet and offered her a hand, but Frelia was Frelia, and she didn't take it. Even if he was being softer than usual. *Or maybe he's always this way, when nobody's looking,* Frelia thought.

Did that make her somebody, or nobody?

In the kitchen, Frelia busied herself lighting the jar candle on the table while Vendrick rummaged around his icebox for the mysterious dessert Clarissa had brought. When he set a small box on the counter, Frelia could just make out someone's insignia stamped onto the lid.

"Bakery Cafaro." Vendrick tapped the inked logo with one long, slim finger. "They're legendary in Whitborne."

If a Volsinii said a restaurant was legendary, that typically meant it was one, expensive, and two, fussy. "And your sister just... brought you their shit on a whim?"

"Not exactly." Vendrick slid a finger between the lid of the box and its matching piece. "She insisted because she was late for my birthday."

It knocked something cold into her stomach. Frelia didn't know when the last time someone remembered her birthday was. Leon of the Titanheart when they were still dating, maybe. If not him, then probably Cillian, the last year of the rebellion.

Cillian. Her heart hurt again.

The Bakery Cafaro box held a dozen small, round buns nestled in bay leaves and drizzled with honey. Vendrick set one on a small plate and handed it to Frelia, along with an absurdly delicate dessert fork.

She stared at the little, doughy thing, and poked it with the fork. The dough punctured, but held its shape, and something in Frelia was reminded of the barrow bread she'd thrown on pyres or into caskets as a child.

"This isn't *for* something, is it?" she asked, suddenly suspicious.

"Er." Vendrick was leaning against the unlit stove, a 'respectable, Volsinii distance' away. "Just what I said before, about the sweet and the bitter."

Frelia made a face. "I meant the bread. Is it for holidays or something?"

"Oh, no, nothing like that." He didn't smile, this time, but somehow it was in his voice. "It's just a sweet Clarissa knows I like."

This was ridiculous. She was *being* ridiculous. Frelia had eaten garmur meat during the Northern Rebellion, for the Saints' sake; she could eat a fucking *dessert*. She curved the side of her fork into the cheesecake bun, and brought a small bite to her mouth.

It was soft, the way Volsinii food usually was, and laced with creamy sweetness. Nothing like Kaldiri desserts, which were usually small, hard bricks designed to bake in any weather, if her people bothered to make dessert at all. But the honey was the same—a sticky sort of sweetness that held the hint of something floral.

"What do you think?" Vendrick asked after a moment.

"It's weird." Frelia cut another bite off. "I think I like it, though."

Oh, that grin wasn't *fair*. It did unpleasant things to her insides. "Better try a bit more, just to be sure?"

She snorted. "Exactly."

He piled a second bun onto a plate for himself, and for a moment, all was calm in the tiny kitchen but for the quiet clattering of forks.

"Can you tell me about them?" Vendrick asked. "The Grimsdalr twins?"

Frelia froze, a bite of cheesecake midway to her mouth. Was this a trick? If he wanted to hurt her, there were far easier ways to do it.

"You knew them," she said, cautious.

"Not like you did. I'm curious what about my sister reminds you of Cillian."

Keep his name out of your Goddesses-damned mouth, Frelia had ordered the last time they'd spoken of her unblood brother.

But this time didn't *sound* like a problem. Just like... curiosity.

"Cillian was an idiot," Frelia burst out, like the words had been waiting there beneath the surface all along. "A brilliant, *brilliant dorchya*. If he could've stopped messing with people for twenty minutes, he easily would have graduated top of our class, with honors."

"And that reminds you of Clary, does it?" The corner of Vendrick's mouth twisted, amused.

Frelia refused to focus on his lips. *Nope.* "No, it's that they're both so bright. Full of cheerful laughter in the face of absolute bullshit."

His amusement fell away, and there was the neutral face Frelia knew so well. It was much easier talking to that one than any of his other faces. She knew what to expect from a stone-faced Volsinii.

"Ah." Vendrick stared down at his own, half-eaten cheesecake bun. "Now *that*, I can see."

"Cillian loved all the old tales, too." Frelia didn't know why she was telling *anyone* this, least of all the Viper of Ascalon. "He used to get us all in trouble during moot summers by staying up way past bedtime listening to the skálds at the bonfire. He's why I have..." Frelia's hand went for her shoulder, but stopped when she realized how much of herself she'd have to expose. "Well, I have 'only the dead' tattooed on my back, because of him."

"That's..." Vendrick toyed with a bite of cheesecake he'd cut but not yet eaten. "...from something, is it not? 'Only the dead see the end of war.'"

"*The Ballad of Hana, ja*. It was his and Thera's favorite." Frelia was shaking now, cold despite how warm autumn always was, at Silverwood. "He always wanted to be a hero, like her."

Something small and wet fell onto her hand, and Frelia glanced down to discover it was coming from her.

Horrified, she had to add, "It's why he died."

Vendrick was suddenly in front of her, gently prying her fingers off her fork, one by one, his own dessert forgotten on an unlit stove burner. "Easy, now."

Frelia hadn't even realized she was gripping the fork so tightly.

"And Thera was a hardass." The words tumbled out, and Frelia could hear her accent growing thicker. "Always first into a fight, always last out. She was *so* serious—Cillian's fucking opposite, even if they were twins—and moody about it. But we could usually talk her into our latest nonsense, so long as she could get a good story out of it. She collected experiences the way high shelves collect dust."

Vendrick had freed her hands of their burdens, but hadn't let go. His own hands were gloved even at this hour, but warm.

"She could read a room masterfully, too." Why was she still talking about Thera? "Would have been an excellent queen, if Hägen would've..."

Vendrick's hand was suddenly burning. Frelia snatched hers back, pressing her fist to her heart like it could stop the void there from growing.

"Never mind," Frelia said, much more quietly. "It doesn't really matter anymore. I shouldn't even be telling you this."

Something else fell from her good eye—Frelia could feel it, now—and Vendrick inexplicably flinched.

"That's the worst bit," he muttered. "Isn't it?"

For a moment, Frelia said nothing, and the entire apartment was as still as grass beneath the first frost.

"What," she finally said. "The war? The dead friends? The fact that closure is a lie?"

"That it doesn't matter now." Vendrick took her hand again and squeezed it hard, but he didn't seem to be aware of it. "Any of it."

It occurred to Frelia, then, that he knew what it was to lose a friend. A good one, even. And if, in this dark, quiet space, she could tell him about the Grimsdalr twins, then maybe... maybe he deserved to clear out his own ghosts, a little.

"Your turn." Frelia reached out with her free hand to grasp his arm. The way she would any of her Kaldiri comrades—*and nothing more,* she told herself. "Tell me about Octavia Nova."

He stared at his arm like he wanted to tell her to let go, but couldn't remember the words. "Octavia was... frequently ill as a child," Vendrick said after a moment. "Some of the more uncharitable Senators would complain that she clearly took after her mother, and could we please get an heir who wasn't half-dead?"

Frelia's brow furrowed. "I thought Volsinii didn't come out and say that kind of shit?"

"Oh, not to their faces, certainly." Vendrick's smile was rueful, and much too close. Frelia couldn't find a reason to care about the latter. "But it doesn't really matter while the Senate deliberates and we noble children play in the gardens, does it?"

Frelia couldn't help but smile, herself. Children were children, no matter the territory. It was almost comforting. "We did the same shit at the moot, as kids. Edmund played a very good fire-breathing dragon."

"I... can't picture that," Vendrick said. "Wouldn't he rather have been the knight?"

"Hägen always wanted to be the knight," Frelia said, and the void in her chest threatened to cave in.

Vendrick seemed to sense it. "There was one afternoon where I recall distinctly two of the lesser barons' sons whispering in the corner, 'why do we have to play with Princess Octavia? Everyone's just waiting for her to die anyway.' And Octavia, as one might imagine, burst into tears and ran from the room."

"Um, *ja,*" said Frelia. "Brutal little shits."

There was honesty, sure, but then there was outright cruelty.

"Your words, not mine." Vendrick gestured from her to him, but they stood too close, much too close, and his fingertips brushed her cheek. Lightning jumped down her throat, but Vendrick pretended not to notice.

He had to be pretending, right?

"But anyway, I was—I think six? Maybe seven—and I couldn't stop thinking about how awful those boys were, so I got up and went after Octavia."

Frelia could picture it, too. A little, dark-haired mage boy toddling after the sickly, crying girl. A heart too soft for what its owner would become.

"I found her reading in another part of the garden, beneath this massive olive tree that's supposedly been in the palace gardens since the time of Imperatrix Octavia the Second..." Vendrick trailed off, and then he grinned. "Why don't you take a guess what book she had?"

Frelia bit her lip, and Vendrick's eyes flicked down, just for a second. A *half*-second. *No, not good. Think about the question.* How the hell was she supposed to know? It wasn't like she had a working knowledge of Volsinii media.

"Oh wait, duh," Frelia said after a moment. "*The Ballad of Hana.*"

"What, you mean the sickly child princess looked up to one of the most celebrated female warriors in history?" His hand was twitching, like he didn't know what to do with it. "Perish the thought."

Frelia rolled her eye and oh, this was dangerous. She shouldn't be acting like they were friends again, but now it was too late to stop. "So then what did you do, oh knight in shining armor?"

"First of all..." Vendrick turned bright red, all the way to the tips of his ears. Frelia refused to find it cute. *Refused.* "...I'm pretty sure that if I had to wear armor—let alone bright colors—I'd probably die."

"Probably."

"Secondly..." Vendrick drew in a deep breath. "I asked her where she was in the book. Had a nice conversation about the second moot, right before the darkbeast attack."

Holy shit, that was adorable. And it was *not. Helping.*

"We were friends ever since." Vendrick shrugged, a little self-consciously. "right up until..."

And just like that, their little bubble of truce shattered.

"Well. Right up until we had a funeral, instead of a coronation, and the Duke of della Luciana took the Imperial throne."

Ironfang, he said without saying.

A horrible silence came crashing down, then. Frelia's heart was wobbling in place, shaking beneath the vast wall of ice she'd encased it in all those years ago.

"I was injured by the end of Spirits' Fen." Frelia scrubbed at her eye with the heel of her hand. "Cillian dragged me to the healer's tent and went to go surrender by himself."

Then was captured, paraded around Ascalon in a Triumph, and executed for his crimes against the Empire. But she couldn't say that. Not in Silverwood's halls.

"Then he saved your life."

Anger welled up from the deep pit in Frelia's stomach, and she welcomed it. Drank it in. Shut her eye. "He died playing the fucking hero."

There was pressure on her face.

Frelia snapped her eye back open. She was equal parts shocked and stunned to find Vendrick's gloved hand resting on her cheek.

"It didn't have to be this way." For the first time in a very long time, Frelia knew, without a doubt, that Vendrick was being honest.

It was terrifying.

"I'm..." Vendrick breathed, and she could feel it, from where she stood. "I'm so sorry."

Frelia jerked away so fast it left his hand holding nothing but air between them.

"No, you're not." Frelia shook herself with the force of it. "And sorry doesn't bring back my dead friends."

This had been a mistake. A huge, flaming mistake. Silverwood was making her soft, making her remember again.

She didn't want to remember. She wasn't a Traust; she didn't have to. All she had to do was fight.

And fight, Frelia did very well.

"Thanks for the cheesecake," she muttered, and fled the room.

CHAPTER TWENTY-THREE

VENDRICK DIDN'T KNOW HOW long he stood in his kitchen miserably staring at both of their half-eaten cheesecake buns. He didn't know what possessed him to tell her those things about Octavia, or why he'd been so compelled to touch her, or why she'd let him at all.

He did know he was ruined, though.

How many Kaldiri were dead because of Vendrick Caecillion? And how many Volsinii were dead because of Frelia Helm's Grace Valerius? The numbers had to be staggering.

And yet, in this quiet moment, in his tiny kitchen, all he had wanted to do was hold her until she stopped crying.

It was a dangerous impulse. A stupid one. But there it was, a little kernel of truth hidden beneath hospitality and gentlemanly concern for a woman who could be called, charitably and at most, a friend.

Octavia had always told him it was odd, how well he got on with Frelia. By all rights, they ought to have been at each other's throats. And though Vendrick understood the logic, he'd never been able to articulate exactly why they weren't. Maybe it was the fact Frelia was the only person he'd ever met who consistently told him the truth, or at least what was actually on her mind. Maybe it was that talking to her felt as natural as breathing, most days, or that he didn't have to explain his most paranoid thoughts. She just understood them. Maybe it was just that—okay, fine—it wasn't often that pretty girls had bothered to talk to him back then, and this one had been his lab partner, so she had to.

Maybe it was all of those things, or none of them. He'd never managed to figure it out. It would have been the great puzzle of a Vendrick who had never known war.

He wished he could have told her what he was actually thinking. *I missed you* had danced at the tip of his tongue, daring him to say it, to see how she'd react. The logical part of his brain had reminded him she'd likely punch him, retreat, or both. But that last, hopeful part he'd never quite managed to squash wondered what else she might do...

Because he had.

He'd realized it while playing cards earlier, between the jocularly competitive rounds, glasses of wine, and Clarissa's unending chatter. Vendrick hadn't had many friends, even before the war, and so it had taken him some time to name the feeling.

But there it was. *Loss.*

He had missed having Frelia around, missed their unending back-and-forth, missed having someone he knew would tell him the truth and didn't typically irritate him. And though she was different now, she was still Frelia, buried beneath a decade's worth of armor and disappointments.

And yet, he had no idea how to behave around her anymore. Sometimes it seemed as though nothing had changed, and their friendship had picked right back up where they'd left it. Other times, there seemed to be a yawning chasm between them, and the weight of everything they'd done to one another's homelands threatened to pull them both into its hungry jaws.

Ruined, he thought dismally. He was absolutely ruined for any woman who wasn't a Kaldiri shieldmaiden with one eye. No wonder trying to forget about her had never worked.

His instinct—like that of every well-bred Volsinii—was to apologize. For everything, for anything. For pushing her, for upsetting her, for anything she'd accept contrition for.

But she was right. Sorry wouldn't bring the Grimsdalr twins back exactly as they were, the last time they'd all walked these halls. Sorry wouldn't grant her missing eye back, or erase the forts Vendrick had stormed, or prevent the unending onslaught of monsters his people had loosed upon hers.

Sorry was a useless little word that didn't take into account what exactly it was covering for.

His appetite gone, Vendrick scraped the remains of their cheesecake buns into the trash. He stared at his hands as he washed the dishes and set them to dry. He was just thinking that he ought to drag his pallet into the kitchen so that Frelia didn't have to see him when he heard Clarissa's worried voice.

"...And I don't know what to do!"

"No need to freak out." Frelia's voice, low and rasping, stopped Vendrick dead in the hallway. "What did Christel say it felt like?"

"Like someone had stuck them in a snow globe and shook it around?" Silence.

"That's the rumbling," came Frelia's voice. "It's what happens when us bloodruned folk get near a garmur."

"Merciful Saints, there's a darkbeast here?"

Vendrick's stomach clenched. Were there more of the damned things loose on campus? At a time like this? Faustine must have somehow managed to get word to her brother. It was the only logical explanation for the timing.

Or, thought the little voice in the back of Vendrick's mind, *has Christel figured out where the other one is?*

"I don't think so," Frelia said, and Vendrick's panic cut itself off at the root. "I don't feel anything, so it's probably just a memory."

Another silence fell, and really, Vendrick ought to walk into the living room and make his presence known. But both the scientist and the older brother in him wanted to know how his baby sister got on with his...

Well. Swordmaster.

"Can they do that?" Clarissa asked.

Vendrick could hear, more so than see, the shrug Frelia must've given. "Don't see why not. You can get ghost pain, sometimes. Like I can feel my da's—"

She cut herself off, then started up again.

"Never mind."

Can feel her father's what, Vendrick wondered. *Surely not death?* That seemed inordinately cruel, even for the Goddesses.

"You can feel his what?" Clarissa pressed, more gently than Vendrick could have.

"I said," Frelia snapped, "never mind."

Oh. Oh *Saints.* It was his death, wasn't it? Vendrick had been at Heit Reiði to know the clinical bits—Grand Duke Einar Valerius had died at the siege of the last Kaldiri fort. After successfully holding it for months, he and Frelia had only lost it because Gaius della Luciana had shown up with a horde of darkbeasts in tow. And, given that the Grand Duke's body had never been recovered after the battle but his death had been confirmed, that could only mean one thing:

He'd been eaten by a darkbeast.

And Frelia could feel that? Small wonder the woman was as abrasive as she was.

"Sorry," Clarissa said. "I'm not trying to pry."

"Yes, you are." Frelia said it so matter-of-factly that Vendrick had to stifle a snort.

Clarissa didn't, though—she just laughed. "Okay, I am a little. I'm too nosy for my own good, sometimes. Vendrick will tell you, I'm sure."

It was as good a cue as any. He really ought to get moving, announce himself.

But then Frelia said, "Pretty sure that's what brothers are for."

And Clarissa practically seized the opportunity: "Do you have one?"

"Did," said Frelia. "His name was Diarmuid."

"Oh." Clarissa's exuberance faded. "I'm so sorry for—"

"*Don't.*"

This was going south. Vendrick's good sense finally overrode his Spymaster's instinct, and he picked up his feet to intervene.

"I don't know what I would do without Vendrick," Clarissa said, softly. "He's annoying, and he's fussy, but he's my big brother. So genuinely, I am very sorry for your loss, Frelia."

He could spare her this. Spare them both this conversation.

"My dear baby sister," he said, loudly enough to startle even himself, "was that a compliment?"

Clarissa stuck her tongue out at him. "Don't let it get to your head."

But Frelia was staring at Clarissa like she'd seen a ghost. Maybe two.

"Have you heard of this darkbeast rumbling business?" Clarissa added.

"I'm aware, yes," Vendrick said. "Why, is it happening?"

"Christel's just remembering," Frelia muttered. "I'll watch them for the rest of the night; you two sleep or something."

"Oh, no need." Clarissa's eyes flicked between Frelia and Vendrick, like she could see something had happened but couldn't figure out what. "It's my turn, anyway."

"It's fine." Frelia's voice was like ice. "This is my duty, anyway."

She slipped into the bedroom so fast, Clarissa didn't even have time to stop her.

Clary looked at Vendrick then, mouthing, "*What happened in there?*"

Vendrick just shook his head. The hell if he knew.

CHAPTER TWENTY-FOUR

THE FOLLOWING MORNING, CHRISTEL stood, under their own power, in the doorframe of Vendrick's bedroom and said, "Um, Professor? Is this normal?"

Frelia paused, her coffee cup midway to her mouth. "Depends what you mean by it?"

Christel turned sideways and pointed to their shoulder. "It's... stopped."

Oh. Frelia knew what that was. She opened her mouth to welcome Christel to the other side, but Vendrick said, ominously, "It what?"

Frelia sighed. "Do me a favor, Christel. Go take a look at your shoulder in the bathroom, and tell me what your bloodrune looks like."

Christel nodded, uncertainty in their eyes, but did as bidden.

Clarissa delicately folded her fingers around the handle of her mug. "Should you have sent them off by themself?'

"They'll be fine." Frelia took another long drag of coffee. "All they're going to tell me is that the bloodrune looks like a tattoo now, instead of a scar."

Clarissa looked even more confused, but Vendrick set his coffee cup down to appraise Frelia like a pinned moth beneath a magnifying glass. "Has our watch ended, then?"

Frelia nodded, and shook off the urge to pull her shirt up far enough to expose her own bloodrune. These two didn't need to see that. "I'd bet money on it."

Gyastfylnacht was a lot more tiring than Frelia remembered, as a kid. She wouldn't be upset to sleep in her own bed tonight, away from these Volsinii accents and identical green eyes.

"Oh, fantastic!" Clarissa's beaming smile was genuine, and it still struck Frelia as odd, on a Volsinii face. "I'm glad they're alright—and also that I can get moving."

"Yes, I don't want to see you for at least a month, Clary," Vendrick said. "I did not miss your snoring."

Clarissa stuck her tongue out at him—"Well, I didn't miss your fussing and half- drunk teacups."—and then looked at Frelia. "Frelia, dear, you're a Saint."

Wariness crept into the back of Frelia's mind. "Just descended from one."

Clarissa snorted. "Well, Vendy, I won't be back until Yule, anyway, so you're welcome. I'll bring you all the gossip from Mum and hopefully news about..." She trailed off. "Did you tell Frelia?"

Frelia's wariness bloomed into full-bore suspicion. "Tell me what?"

Vendrick harrumphed. "No, Clary, I've been busy playing host and catching up on the correspondence you brought."

"Well if she's helping us," Clarissa said, "she might have an idea!"

"Of what?" Frelia said, louder.

Both of the Caecillion siblings turned to look at her then, and it struck Frelia that although they did look a lot alike, Clarissa was softer, somehow. Like she hadn't had to fight quite so hard. Vendrick was all hard edges and sharp angles, but Clarissa's face was round and her eyes were a lighter green.

"Do you want to do the honors, Vendy dear," Clarissa began, "or shall I?"

Vendrick sighed and got to his feet. "I'm getting more coffee. Anyone else?"

"Just bring the pot." Clarissa shooed him away, and then turned to face Frelia on the loveseat. "So, I—"

Frelia instinctively backed up as far as the space would allow for.

"Sorry." Clarissa winced. "I figured you'd rather have the loveseat to yourself, but also that you didn't want to sit next to my brother—boys have cooties, and all that."

Frelia snorted so hard into her coffee, Clarissa called for Vendrick to bring a new cup with him from the kitchen, too.

For a moment, it almost seemed like Vendrick didn't hear. Then he shouted, "Now who's leaving half-drunk teacups everywhere?"

Clarissa cackled, but her face dropped so fast into seriousness that Frelia felt the need to do a double take. "So, Frelia," Clarissa said, "any ideas on why Vendrick's war spellbook would have turned up in Liberalis Territory?"

Frelia made a face, considering. Liberalis Territory was the one just below Traust Territory, and above Nova Territory—close to the Volsinii capital, but not as cosmopolitan. She'd preferred visiting Liberalis, both as a child and a mercenary looking for work.

"Well," Frelia said after a moment, "what's in it, for starters?"

"The usual," came Vendrick's voice as he returned with a tea tray. "My grey magic combat spells, plus some odds and ends I found interesting and meant to follow up on when I had the time."

Sounded like every other mage's spellbook Frelia had ever heard of. "Was it stolen?"

"It's supposed to be under lock and key at the Villa Caecillion." Vendrick set down the silver tea tray on the coffee table, took his mug again, and then dropped into his previous armchair. "Only Clarissa, our head housekeeper, and I have a key."

"So it *was* stolen," Frelia surmised, annoyed.

Vendrick made a face. "Or loaned, I suppose."

"Well, Clarissa?" Frelia glanced back to the younger sibling. "Is this all an elaborate ruse of yours to steal Vendrick's old spellbook?"

"Oh, I didn't take it." Clarissa put a mock-offended hand to her heart. "I don't even like Vendrick's spells."

Frelia shrugged, and reached for the coffee press on the tea tray. "Then it was your housekeeper."

"I don't see Grania caring about Vendrick's spellbook," Clarissa said. "Not unless it was in the way of her dusting, or something. She's served our family for ages; she knows better."

"Unless someone put her up to it." Frelia carefully poured coffee as black as death, as sweet as sin, into the new cup. "Someone like—hang on, just spit balling here—Ironfang?"

The man's nom de guerre left a noticeable chill in the air.

"The vault still requires two keys," Vendrick said. "And I have mine here at Silverwood, and Clarissa...?"

She patted her collarbone. "Here."

Well, there were ways into places besides their keys. "How easy would it be to break into?"

"Not terribly," Vendrick said. "It's hidden and double-locked for a reason."

"So you have no idea how it got out, or why anyone in Liberalis Territory would want it?" Frelia clarified.

"More or less, yeah," Clarissa confirmed. "I'm sending our—"

"Professor!"

The adults froze.

Christel swung around the doorframe to the bathroom, their shirt still half-undone. "Professor, is it supposed to look all... I dunno, flat?"

"Like a tattoo?" Frelia asked.

Understanding lit Christel's face. "Wait, yeah!"

"*Ja*, that's what sealed ones look like." Frelia smiled, despite everything, and finally let herself feel a single ounce of relief. "You've made it through Gyastfylnacht. Congratulations."

Christel whooped in exhausted delight, and if she closed her eyes, Frelia could almost hear that same excitement on the wind far, far to the north.

She lives, she lives! The Duke's daughter lives!

"Can, um." Christel shuffled from foot to foot. "Can I go back to my room, now?"

"Not looking like that, you can't," Vendrick said. "And go to the infirmary, first."

He glanced to Frelia with a question in his eyes, and Frelia stared at him stupidly for a moment until she finally gave up on trying to read his mind. "What?"

Vendrick sighed, and Frelia could almost hear how thin his patience was. "Should someone escort them?"

Frelia shook her head. "Their power is sealed, now. Should only show up now when they're asleep or doing the thing that activates it."

There were some other odds and ends, too, but Frelia didn't feel the need to list them all just now, in mixed company, when most of it would never matter.

"Are you sure?" Christel sounded so small, so afraid.

Frelia fixed them in a look she hoped was calming. "You don't see me passing out every other hour, do you?"

Christel, Clarissa, and Vendrick all blinked in surprise, as though the thought hadn't occurred to them.

"You made it through Gyastfylnacht," Frelia added. "Congrats on surviving bloodrune puberty."

Clarissa cackled so hard she wheezed, and Vendrick said, like he was trying not to laugh, "Oh, *really*, Frelia."

Her name barely sounded like itself, in his accent. It was too clean, too cultured, too many clear vowels and crisp consonants to belong to a Kaldiri woman with more scars than sense, these days. It painted a picture of a Frelia that she could never be.

And don't forget it, Frelia thought, dimly.

"Go get yourself cleaned up and get out of here," Frelia told Christel. "I'm sure you don't want to hang around your professors all day."

Christel laughed, and disappeared back into the bathroom.

"So..." Clarissa stared into her coffee mug. "You got those, too? The memories and the visions and such? And then they just... stopped?"

"More or less." Frelia didn't want to get into it all over again. "But I was little when my bloodrune awakened. I don't really remember."

Clarissa's jaw fell open, and for a moment, Frelia couldn't figure at what. Vendrick was similarly shocked, but he recovered his composure faster.

Frelia thumped her coffee cup onto the table, annoyed. "What?"

"You..." Clarissa's voice had dropped to the quietest version of itself Frelia had yet to hear. "You went through what Christel just did... as a child?"

"*Ja?*" Frelia raised an eyebrow. "I think I was four. All the people who could confirm that are dead, though."

"But that looked..." Clarissa looked helplessly to her older brother.

"Dreadful," Vendrick eventually supplied.

Clarissa nodded. "They put children through that?"

Frelia was genuinely lost, now. "How else was I supposed to learn to swing a sword without killing the Master of Arms?"

"At four?" Clarissa shrieked.

"Clary," Vendrick murmured.

They exchanged a look Frelia had no hope of reading.

"I'm... going to go escort Christel." Clarissa abandoned her coffee cup on the table and got to her feet. "I know you just said we don't have to, but I, just..." She stopped, and restarted. "It'll make me feel better."

"Suit yourself." Frelia glanced to Vendrick with what she hoped was visible confusion.

He held up a finger the moment Clarissa's back was turned, and then took a long sip of coffee. He remained stubbornly silent through the good-byes and seeing offs, and when he set his full attention on Frelia again, she realized, for the first time since she'd set foot in the headmaster's suite, they were well and truly alone.

She didn't know whether the shiver that sent down her spine was a good one or not.

"Clary was..." Vendrick stared at his front door, as if waiting to see if his sister would show back up at the sound of her name. When it remained shut, he looked back at Frelia. "Well, she was still at Silverwood when the Tyrant's War broke out. She ended up not needing to serve until halfway through, and by then most of our reserve troops were maintaining captured forts and the like."

"So?" said Frelia.

"So," Vendrick continued, "she's been spared a lot of the terrible things people like you and me have not."

"Bloodrunes aren't terrible."

But even as she said it, it felt sour on her tongue. Bloodrunes were power, and legacy, and history, sure. But they were also pain, and violence, and suffering. One could not be, without the other.

Vendrick, to his credit, deferred. "I'm certain you know better than I."

Frelia sighed, and wished she could thump her head in her hands without exposing her neck to the man. "So, what, she's happy to play Spymaster field commander until the actual war comes around?"

"She's not playing anything." It came down hard and fast, like an axe to the throat. "She *is* my field commander. She's just... too kind for her own good."

So he can criticize his sister, Frelia thought, *but everyone else can't.* It was so normal, it ached somewhere deep in her chest, where Diarmuid's ghost lived.

Frelia made a gesture of surrender. "So what's she sending to Liberalis Territory about your thief problem?"

"Some of our spies." Vendrick seemed to accept the gesture for what it was. "If there's anything to uncover, they'll find it."

Sitting still was starting to put Frelia's teeth on edge. "So what are we doing here in the meantime?"

"Why, teaching of course." Vendrick grinned over his coffee mug. "Certainly not scrutinizing the della Lucianas within an inch of their very lives, and maintaining a watch on Christel and Valente, or something. I'm retired, Frelia."

She wanted to say he wasn't allowed to call her that. That they weren't friends, and she didn't want to be. And it ached, more than Diarmuid's ghost, more than hiding Christel's bloodrune, more than the ghosts and the Imperator and everything else that rankled her. Frelia was no match for the understanding that no matter how similar they were at their cores, it would never be enough.

But instead, she said, "You're a right bastard, aren't you, Vendrick?"

In the liquid, golden light filtering in through the windows, he was breathtaking when he smiled. "So I've been told."

Frelia started to stand, but his hand caught her wrist. It was loose, and she could have broken his fingers if she'd wanted, but it pinned her in place.

"There's one other thing," Vendrick said.

Frelia warily lowered herself back into her seat.

"The best way we've found to determine whether someone is who she says she is," he said quietly, "is a code question. Something that sounds innocuous but only has one, highly specific answer."

Subterfuge normally gave Frelia a headache, but at least this one made sense. "Such as?"

Vendrick paused, his hand flexing on his coffee mug. "I mean," he finally said, "the point of the question is that only you and the person asking it know what the correct answer is supposed to be, so I don't exactly have an example for you."

Frelia harrumphed. "Is this why you keep asking me Silverwood shit?"

Vendrick nodded. "I don't otherwise have a wealth of things only you and I know."

He was so paranoid, it looped back around to brilliant. Frelia refused to be impressed.

"Alright..." She stared at her half-drunk coffee for another moment, racking her brains. "Ask me how my brother is doing, and I'll tell you he sleeps in Traust Territory."

Across the table, Vendrick froze for a moment before he nodded. "Exactly. Perfect example."

"It's not an example," Frelia muttered, "it's the question I'm telling you to ask me when you need to. What about you?"

He took a slow sip of coffee. "Ask me how my magical studies are going," he said after a moment, "and I'll tell you that I've mastered Death."

Frelia snorted. "Dramatic much?"

"Death being a grey magic spell." Amusement danced at the edge of his voice. "No one ever asks after my studies; no one wishes to know the details."

CHAPTER TWENTY-FIVE

"GUARDS UP, *DORCHYEA!*" FRELIA shouted for what felt like the millionth time that morning. "Do you want to get stabbed?"

Her students all immediately shifted their stances—some with more success than others—before resuming their sparring drill. The clacking of wooden practice swords was a chaotic symphony, and Frelia, its maestra.

She sighed, and called for a halt. "What's gotten into you lot?"

Christel was shifting from foot to foot, visibly uncomfortable, but a lot of the others were looking at Faustine. She looked like she wanted to melt into the floor, or something.

"The first winter ball planning meeting was last night," Faustine admitted.

The Silverwood winter ball.

Frelia faintly remembered it from her own school years. Mostly, it was an excuse for the stir-crazy young nobles to dress up and for the clever ones to get drunk after finals week. In Frelia's case, she'd been lucky that Cillian was both. He, Thera, and Frelia had spent much of the evening slipping vodka into their cups, and by the end of the night she'd felt warm and fuzzy to the point that both Hägen's lectures and the biting cold on the walk back to the dorms had barely registered.

Cillian had usually gotten her to dance at some point, which the rest of their friends considered to be nothing short of a miracle. Frelia figured she'd probably snapped something back, but mostly she just remembered how, when he set his mind to it, Cillian could be a pretty decent friend. Maybe the possible marriage that had always loomed in the background of their friendship—first because of their parents, and then because of the rebellion—wouldn't have been so terrible.

She'd probably also said some embarrassing shit those nights, but she supposed one of the very few upsides to losing all your friends in a hopeless war was that no one was around to remember the embarrassing bits.

"The winter ball isn't for another month and a half," Frelia said. "*And* there's finals in the way. Calm down before you give yourselves conniptions."

"Oh, but there's so much to do!" Ellie said. "There are decorations to make, seating arrangements to plan, and meals to determine, and the deputy headmaster is maddeningly unhelpful."

"I'm sure Magicmaster Marcellius is trying his best," Faustine tried.

Karina rolled her eyes. "If it were up to him, we'd all be wearing potato sacks and sitting at gender-segregated tables."

Frelia snorted. "I see some things don't change."

"Wait," Karina said, "you went to Silverwood, Professor?"

"I didn't know that," Siegmund said, and several of his classmates agreed.

Faustine immediately stared down at her shoes. "Is that something we shouldn't know?"

"It's not a secret," Frelia said. "But I know for fact our class portrait isn't hanging in the library where it should be—" Likely because it listed the Northern Kraken and Southern Strix still. "—so I'm not surprised it's news."

"Were you here when the Queenmakers were?" Ellie asked.

"*Ja,* only they weren't called that, then," Frelia said. "Can't recall saying much more than passing 'hellos' to Octavia Nova, though, if that's what you're wondering. Too busy dealing with my own prince."

For all Frelia had been stuck with Vendrick their third year, she'd barely seen his liege lady. Partially because Octavia had taken entirely ranged weapon classes by then, but partially because she simply hadn't... mixed. Frelia wasn't certain Octavia had even had friends who weren't Volsinii nobility.

"King Njal went here?" Valente asked.

Frelia tried not to feel stabbed in the chest that her students knew the late king's father's name, but not his. "Hägen."

A hush fell across the class. All they knew was the propaganda, then.

Ellie shot a glance over her shoulder, as though checking to make sure the gates were shut and the only class in the training ground was theirs. "Was he really as terrible as they say?"

"Of course not," said Frelia sharply. "The Einnaska bloodline doesn't automatically make you a tyrant."

She said nothing, however, about Hägen's older sister.

"Then why do they call it the Tyrant's War?" Christel suddenly asked.

Frelia froze. "If I answered *that,* I'd be fired. At the very least."

She brought her hands together with a resounding clap, feeling sort of like Clarissa as she did so, and her students snapped to attention.

"So. Back to the lesson. It's still about *unterhau.*" Frelia enunciated the undoubtedly unfamiliar Kaldiri word with excruciating diction. "Striking from beneath your opponent's guard."

She reminded them when to use it and when to definitely not, and was just about to turn her students loose on their drills again when the training ground gates clanged open.

"Professor Valerius, madam!" It was Cora, the Red Eagles' Year Two Prefect. She was still dressed for cavalry class in tall riding boots and a helmet. "I'm supposed to tell you that Headmaster Caecillion has called for an emergency faculty meeting. Your presence is requested at once."

Frelia's hand tightened on the hilt of her training sword. "What kind of emergency?"

"Not the darkbeast kind," Cora said. "He also wanted me to tell all the professors that."

Small victories, Frelia supposed. She didn't like the sound of this, but she also didn't exactly have a choice. *Least it's not monsters,* she thought, but it didn't make her feel any better.

Frelia loosened her grip on the training broadsword, and stabbed it into the sand. "Faustine."

The girl snapped to attention across the field as though struck. "Yes madam?"

"You're in charge until I get back," Frelia added. "Keep everyone on task."

Faustine nodded. "Er, right, Professor."

"If I'm not back by the end of the period," Frelia said as she crossed the sandy training grounds, "you'll know a garmr got me."

A nervous skittering of laughter followed.

Frelia sighed—"That was a joke, little Owls."—and followed Cora out of the training ground gates.

"I'm supposed to go get Axemaster Ossani, too," Cora said sheepishly.

Did the girl think Frelia needed an escort to the staff meeting room? "Go on, then."

Silverwood was starting to cool off, Frelia noticed as she hiked towards the center of campus. The leaves were still autumnal red and gold, but the wind was starting to bite. Soon they'd bundle up in scarves and sweaters and not come out again until spring turned the training ground muddy and the fields around the lake green.

"Oi, Valerius!"

She paused just long enough to catch sight of Axemaster Ossani, hustling along from another of the training ground field. His training axe was looped through one side of his belt, his real one through the other.

"*Ja?*" she called.

"Any ideas what this mystery emergency meeting is about?" Ossani asked.

"Not a clue." Frelia turned to keep walking towards Salonia hall.

"Pity," Ossani said, "I thought you'd know, these days."

She froze, head to toe. "What?"

"Oh, you know." Ossani had caught up to her now, and was waggling his eyebrows. "Since you've got eyes and ears on the inside, now."

Frelia stared at him for a moment. He seemed genuine, but that only went so far with Volsinii. "What the fuck are you talking about?"

Ossani shot her an oh-come-now look. "Everyone knows you're sleeping with the headmaster, Valerius. His sister was covering for him all through fall break."

Embarrassed heat just about blasted Frelia's face clean off. "That's not what happened."

"Oh, like anyone believes the alchemy lab story." Ossani rolled his eyes. "Good for you, seriously. He could do with some loosening up, and I've said that for years."

"I don't care what you believe," Frelia snapped, even though she both desperately wanted to squash this rumor and knew it was too late for that. "Why the fuck would I voluntarily hang out with the Viper of Ascalon otherwise?"

"Oh, I dunno." Ossani grinned. "My little sister was in your year at Silverwood, though, so—"

"Shut up, Ossani." Frelia was not getting into this.

"Hey, at least there's no Grimsdalr around to tell you off for sleeping with—"

"I said, *shut up!*"

"A Valerius and an Ossani walk into a bar..." interrupted a voice. "I think I've heard this one before."

Frelia and Ossani both turned to find Markus della Luciana stepping out of Brekka Hall. They then exchanged a look Frelia had no right to expect from a Volsinii, least of all a nobleman who served in the Tyrant's War, but if there was one thing on which the entire Silverwood staff could agree, it was that Markus della Luciana was a twat.

"Well we're waiting on the punchline," Frelia said.

"Good morning, Captain!" Ossani put on the most obnoxious fake smile Frelia had ever seen. "How's the monster search coming along?"

Markus shot them both a withering look. "What on earth are you two doing?"

Ossani cocked an eyebrow. "Going to the faculty meeting?"

Markus' brow immediately furrowed. "What faculty meeting?"

"The one for the faculty that you aren't part of." Frelia tried to push past Markus' bulk, but the Watcher caught her arm.

"I wasn't aware of a faculty meeting this morning," Markus said, and he was clearly trying to sound low and dangerous but stopped at about 'teenage boy mid-puberty'.

"Well, sure," Ossani said. "As Valerius just so helpfully pointed out, you're not in it."

"I get the sense it wasn't pre-planned, either." Frelia yanked her arm out of Markus' grasp with truly vicious force. "Now out of my way."

Ossani's smile intensified. "If you'll excuse us."

Frelia and Ossani got about four steps forward before Markus was jogging along beside them. "I suppose I should see what this fuss is about," he said, like he hadn't been planning to tail them the whole time.

Frelia's eyelid twitched, but she forced herself to bite her tongue and keep her feet moving.

By the time her motley little crew reached the staff meeting room in Salonia Hall, most of the faculty was already gathered, including Vendrick. He looked more harried than Frelia had ever seen him—which, in his case, mostly meant that he wasn't wearing a frock coat and his hair looked like it belonged on a human head instead of a doll's.

The messiness suited him.

Vendrick immediately clocked Markus' intrusion. "Captain?"

"I heard there was a meeting," Markus said coolly.

"A faculty meeting," Vendrick said.

He left unspoken *which you are not,* but Frelia snorted anyway.

"Besides," Vendrick added over Markus' rising protests, "our noon appointment will cover the exact same thing. So unless you have a burning desire to listen to the same information twice, and only plan your portion at the latter meeting, I recommend you go about your business this morning as usual."

Markus gaped at him for a moment like a beached fish.

Goddesses, sometimes it really was amazing watching Volsinii do their thing. Frelia could never have so swiftly and elegantly dismissed someone while making it sound like their idea the whole time.

(Okay, maybe it wasn't 'watching Volsinii work,' but more 'watching Vendrick work,' but it would be a cold day in Ascalon before Frelia admitted that.)

Vendrick's eyebrows rose, expectant. "Good day, Markus."

Frelia was not the only one who stifled a laugh at Markus' retreating back.

She dropped into an open chair beside Edmund and Wyvernmaster Gellir, and for a moment, she was back in the old Krakenguard war room, down in the bowels of Castle Skjöldr. She half-expected Cillian to lean into her personal space to make some snarky comment, followed by Thera's sharp elbow in her ribs at any second.

Then Tacticsmaster Vitellus sidled in, and Vendrick said, "Ah, that's everyone. Kindly shut the door behind you, Vitellus." and Frelia was back, one-eyed, at Silverwood.

"What's going on, headmaster?" Tacticsmaster Vitellus asked as he dropped into the last open chair.

A murmur of agreement rippled through the assembled faculty.

Vendrick drew in a deep breath, and Frelia did not envy his job whatsoever.

"This morning," he began, "I was informed via courier that we are not to expect an imperial delegate at the winter ball this year." His acid green eyes flicked up sharply to observe his audience. "We are to expect the Imperator."

A sharp spike of virulent anxiety, deep in her stomach and beside her bloodrune, dug into Frelia's stomach at the news. "What?" fell out of her mouth.

"Why?" asked Magicmaster Marcellius. "The delegate is a simple formality. An acknowledgement that more than half these students will serve in the Imperial Army soon enough."

Vendrick threw up his hands. "The paper-thin reason I was given is that, with two of his children in residence at Silverwood, Imperator Ironfang may as well come up for Yule."

"Like he has nothing more important to do?" Roguemaster Olsen cocked an eyebrow.

Vendrick turned to her and said again, with excruciating diction, "Paper. Thin."

Silence fell across the room.

"Well," said Lancemaster Sabine, "shit."

"That's the first time I've ever agreed with you, Sabine," Frelia said.

Sabine made a noise Frelia didn't recognize. "And that's the first time I've found you funny, Valerius," she called back.

"So what do we do?" Edmund asked, his fingers nervously toying with the frayed hems of his shirtsleeves.

"Treat it like we do the delegate visit," Vendrick said, and it was the first time Frelia had ever heard him sound remotely at a loss. "Clean the place from top to toe, decorate for Yule, remind the students to be on their best behavior, and go about your business as if the most powerful man in the Empire isn't on his way." Vendrick could only offer his upturned palms. "And as always, should he wish to speak with any of you, you are, of course, granted dispensation to do so."

"Is that normal?" Every eye in the room turned to her, and Frelia had to fight the urge to hide behind her chair. "The delegate, wanting to talk to us professors?"

"It's happened." Understanding flickered across Vendrick's face. "But I get the distinct impression that His Majesty will want to drop into our classes while he's here."

"Got it." Frelia drew in a deep breath and tried to steady her nerves. She failed. Abominably.

"Are we being accused of something?" Roguemaster Olsen asked.

"Not to my knowledge," Vendrick said. "That said, if anyone has a secret stash of dried mossblade or something, I recommend being rid of it before the end of the month. Alcohol in its approved containers, and all that."

Alchemymaster Caelia fidgeted in her seat. "I don't like this, Caecillion."

"Funnily enough," Vendrick said, "I don't either."

He then launched into a lengthy explanation about decorating for the winter ball and protocol for meeting the Imperator and his retinue, and Frelia promptly turned her attention inward.

Fuck. Ironfang was coming here? Where it was supposed to be *safe?* The campus on the ass-end of nowhere, miles from anything cosmopolitan? Markus and Faustine had been bad enough—they were technically Volsinii royalty, sure, but neither was going to inherit the throne, barring something drastic. Their older sister was the head of the Bloodrune Hunters, and Frelia could just see Ironfang using this visit as an excuse to drag Orsina along with him.

Never mind that Frelia had come to Silverwood to avoid the Bloodrune Hunters and the Volsinii Imperium, not walk straight into them. There was that cosmic joke again, always coming back to bite her in the ass.

"And that concludes our faculty meeting for this morning." Vendrick's smooth, clipped voice cut Frelia abruptly out of her worry. "Thank you all."

Frelia stood to leave alongside the rest of the faculty, but Vendrick added, "Olsen, Valerius, Gellir, and Blightsen, kindly stay back another moment."

Frelia knew what that meant, alright. She dropped back into her seat, staring at a fixed point out the window as her Volsinii colleagues streamed out around her.

"I don't know why you're lumping me in with this lot," Olsen harrumphed even before the Volsinii had fully cleared out. "I was old when the Winter War started; I sure as hell didn't serve in the Tyrant's."

"I was just a Konstantin wyvern knight." Gellir's eyes were wide and terrified. "I wasn't..." He looked at Frelia and Edmund, cut himself off, and started again. "I didn't..."

"None of you are in trouble," Vendrick interrupted, not unkindly.

"Edmund and I are." Frelia couldn't break her unseeing stare from the world beyond the window.

This is the end of days, my friends, Cillian's ghost sang in the back of her mind. *It's Heit Reiði.*

"No, you're not," Vendrick said, more firmly this time. "Both Blightsen and Valerius have been acquitted of their military service in the Krakenguard as of the Ascalon Accords of Twelve-Fifty-Three."

Finally, *finally*, Frelia could tear her eyes away from the bright blue, autumn sky, and bring them back to this dark, wooden place. To Vendrick's sharp angles and sinister silhouette.

"And the Northern Rebellion?" she asked.

Gellir, Olsen, and Edmund all refused to look at her, but Vendrick held her gaze like he could use it to see straight into her soul. She wondered what he'd even find there. A wall of ice?

"If Ironfang wanted to arrest and execute you, Valerius," Vendrick said, "he wouldn't have waited ten years to do it."

"That's not good enough." Frelia's fingers tightened against the hilt of her sword—her only comfort in this black world. "Based on what your people did to Cillian, I should run, now."

"Frelia..." Edmund tried.

"By Volsinii law, triumphs may only be conducted immediately after a decisive victory." Vendrick spoke quickly, over Edmund's feeble attempt to deal with the very real possibility Frelia painted. "He's far too late for that, and the Senate wouldn't allow it. You've also outlasted the end of the war through the Ascalon Accords, and the only reason you aren't personally named in them is because your post-war status was not confirmed until earlier this year."

Silence fell.

"Basically," Vendrick added, "it wouldn't be worth the headache to arrest, try, and execute you. Yule would stall the process long enough for a good lawyer to—"

"You know what I get paid!" Frelia spluttered a laugh. "What makes you think I can afford a lawyer, let alone a good one?"

Vendrick leaned over the table, just a little. Enough that all eyes in the room went to the shrinking space between him and Frelia. "Do you have any idea how many lawyers in Ascalon owe me a favor?"

Olsen's eyebrows rose, and Edmund ducked his head in secondhand embarrassment. Gellir stared, wide-eyed, his focus shifting between Frelia and Vendrick.

You are not helping the rumors! Frelia wanted to hiss, but bit her tongue. There were more important things to worry about, like not getting thrown in prison for daring to exist, for starters.

"Besides, Ironfang won," Vendrick said. "If anything, he'll just gloat that you have been..." He trailed off, probably trying to find a polite way to put it.

"A backwater mercenary since then," Frelia finished for him.

"Well." Vendrick made an apologetic face, and straightened back up. "Yes."

Olsen studied Frelia with a wary, rogue's eye. "I don't envy your lot."

"No one ever has," Frelia muttered.

"The reason," Vendrick said, seeming to realize the conversation had derailed, "I have asked you all to keep back is that I fully expect Ironfang to pay each of you a visit individually. He does nothing without an ulterior motive."

"Speaking from experience?" Gellir asked.

"Of course," Vendrick said. "I was his Spymaster, once upon a time."

"I thought that was supposed to be hush-hush?" Olsen asked.

"What, like it's a secret?" Vendrick snorted, amused. "I'm sure Ironfang or his men will fish for something incriminating to hold over your heads."

"Just like Markus?" Edmund pointed out.

"Where do you think he learned it from?" Vendrick's smile was rueful. "So, my point being, don't let them. Give the shortest response you can that answers his questions, and don't offer up any information you aren't directly sure of. Feel free to send him or his Watchers to me as often as possible. Any questions or concerns?"

"Besides everything?" Frelia asked.

Vendrick nodded. "Besides that, yes."

"Think I'm set," Frelia muttered, at the same time Olsen said, "We're Kaldiri; not stupid, Caecillion."

"None of this has anything to do with intelligence, Olsen." Vendrick eyed his Kaldiri faculty as they all got out of their chairs to go. "It's politics."

"If you say so," Edmund murmured, and he caught Frelia's eye as they turned to go.

Frelia started to ask him what he wanted but heard, "Valerius, could you hold another moment, please?"

Oh, Frelia did not like the looks she was getting from the other Kaldiri professors. Not. At. All.

She waited until they were alone in the meeting room to whirl on Vendrick. "You are not helping the rumors, you know that?"

His brow furrowed. "Which ones?"

"The ones where we did nothing but have sex over fall break?"

Vendrick made a face like he wanted to say something honest, but his manners were getting the better of him. "Oh, Saints, there are *plural* about that? Which ones did you hear?"

"The ones about how clearly we're having a wild affair because I was in your room after a 'lab accident'—which, by the way, apparently no one believes. What about you?"

"Mostly the ones about how the laboratory accident seems awfully coincidental." He made a face. "I've always said this school is just a royal court without an Imperator, and you know, I'm standing by that theory."

Frelia snorted.

"Well, rest assured, my dear Lady Valerius, I will not show up outside your door with a bouquet and a fistful of poetry."

"I dare you to try."

Vendrick put a mock-offended hand to his chest. "How else would you know that I am deeply serious about this affair-that-isn't, in no small part because neither of us are married?"

That time, Frelia really did laugh. She felt eyes on her back, like Cillian was somehow disappointed.

"So what did you actually call me back for?" Frelia asked.

All the amusement drained from Vendrick's eyes, and a sharp pang stabbed Frelia's stomach at the loss. "I couldn't say this in front of the others," he said, "but you know the real reason Ironfang's left you alone this long, don't you?"

Frelia's brow furrowed. "What do you mean?"

"It's not that it's inconvenient to arrest you," Vendrick's voice dropped so low Frelia had to lean in to hear him. She refused to entertain the possibility that her resultant shiver was in anything but horror. "And it's not that you've been acquitted."

"Then what..." It struck Frelia over the head then, and she felt like an idiot for not realizing it sooner. "Shit, it's the bloodrune, isn't it?"

Vendrick nodded, and he sounded almost... apologetic. "It has to be. Nothing else makes sense."

"His daughter runs the Hunters, though," Frelia said. "If he wanted it, he could send her to take it at any time."

"Precisely," Vendrick said. "So why hasn't he?"

Frelia considered it for a moment. "Don't suppose I'm lucky enough that 'because I'll kick her ass' is a deterrent?"

Vendrick made a wishy-washy motion with his hand. "That's enough to deter something spur-of-the-moment, but I doubt it would do much long term. No, Ironfang and his Unseen cronies are planning something. I intend to use the winter ball to figure out what."

A slow, creeping smile spread across his face.

"Care to join me?"

Frelia's laugh was a bark that had once echoed across the Thundering Peaks. "Thought you'd never ask."

CHAPTER TWENTY-SIX

ALL THROUGH THE REST of their swords hour, Faustine fretted.

She fretted about keeping her classmates on task, given that most of them hated Professor Valerius' sword drills. She fretted about the test she had in aerial cavalry later today, and she fretted about whether Owen and Karina had remembered to study for said test.

But mostly, she fretted about Christel.

Markus was frustratingly vague about how she was supposed to get close enough to stab Christel without them noticing. He mostly offered nonsense solutions and told her not to compromise her future marriageability, which was honestly more frustrating than him just telling her to figure it out herself.

"What do you all think the faculty meeting is about?" Owen suddenly asked.

"Dunno." Siegmund used Owen's momentary distraction to disarm him. "Not darkbeasts, though, thank the Saints."

"Maybe I'm just terrified of them," Ellie said, wincing as her sword was batted out of her hand, "but what could constitute an emergency *except* something like a darkbeast?"

"I know," Faustine said. "I'm trying to remember what normal even was. A broken sewer pipe somewhere, maybe?"

"Why would that warrant taking the professors out of class, though?" Valente asked.

"I don't know," Faustine said, an embarrassed flush creeping up her neck, "I'm just guessing."

"I, um."

Everyone turned to look at Christel, who had cut themself off almost as quickly as they'd begun.

"You what, Christel?" Karina asked.

They shook their head. "Never mind."

"No, no." Valente was suddenly in Christel's personal space, wagging a finger like a lord at a scullery maid. "You know something."

Valente, leave them alone. The order was on the tip of Faustine's tongue, but it lodged in her throat like treacle and refused to move.

"If they don't wanna talk," Siegmund said, "they don't have to."

Valente snapped back something nasty, but it occurred to Faustine, then, why Christel was clamming up.

They hadn't heard a rumor, or anything of the sort. They'd *seen* something with their new gift.

Faustine's stomach twisted in horror and disbelief. No, no, they needed to drop this, *now.* "We're getting off task," she blurted out.

"Oh, the professor won't be back for at least half the class." Karina waved her off. "The staff meeting room is in Salonia hall; it'll take half her time just to get there."

"What were you going to say, Christel?" Ellie asked, more gently than Valente and more kindly than Karina.

Maybe that's why Christel swallowed, audibly, and said, "I heard a rumor that the Imperator will be here for the winter ball."

Gasps went around the Violet Owls, and everyone turned to stare at Faustine.

"Why are you all looking at me?" She squeaked. "I haven't heard anything about it!"

Her father was seriously coming here? To Silverwood?

Silverwood was supposed to be safe. Sure she was stuck with Markus, but she could mostly avoid him. Here at school she didn't have her father looming over her, or the head housekeeper arranging meetings with potential in-laws every twenty minutes, or Orsina telling her how to behave (like she didn't know) and Galeria telling her all the things about marriage Faustine didn't *want* to know.

She knew about the babies and the running of the household and expectations of a noble-born Volsinii woman in good company. She didn't *want* to know about the politics, the affairs Galeria said were inevitable, or the illegitimate children a wife was expected to manage, one way or the other.

Was it so much to ask for someone to make a promise and bloody well keep it?

Ellie's voice shocked Faustine back to the training ground: "He didn't tell you?"

Faustine swallowed against the lump in her throat. She had to be careful what she said, here; the truth wouldn't do. "Maybe his letter got lost or something?"

There were eyes on the back of her neck, now, and Faustine turned to see Christel and Valente staring at her with something unreadable in their eyes. Oh, no, was she that transparent?

Prey, said the little voice in the back of her mind. *Prey, prey, prey.*

"I wonder if your brother knows," Valente said thoughtfully.

"I would think so." Faustine looked back down at her boots.

"Unless his letter got lost, too?" Ellie pointed out.

"They talk a lot more than Father does to me," Faustine said. "I'm sure Markus has heard about this already, if it's really true."

"I'm... sorry, Faustine," Christel suddenly said.

Faustine's head jerked up. "What are you sorry for?"

"I mean..." Christel made a face. "I didn't mean to upset you, or anything."

"I'm not upset," Faustine lied.

For oh, she realized as she said it, that was a lie. She was upset. Not just that nobody in her family had bothered to tell her father was coming to Silverwood, but that Father coming to Silverwood meant this fairy-tale dream was over. She couldn't simply be 'Faustine' or 'the Violet Owls' Prefect' if Father was here.

If Ironfang were here, she'd be 'princess' and 'child number six' and 'the Imperator's youngest' and... and...

"Let's... get back to swords," Faustine managed.

"Okay," said Owen. "Duel me?"

The Violet Owls paired up again, and Owen didn't say a thing as the tears rolled down Faustine's cheeks except 'Hau.'

***

Professor Valerius didn't show back up by the end of class, so the Violet Owls decided via popular vote that they should duck out early to get to their next classes and maybe have time to get a coffee from the commissary on the way.

It was all *very* senatorial. The professors wouldn't even be mad, probably.

Faustine trudged over to the weapons rack to put away her training sword. She should probably go talk to Markus, ask him whether he knew anything about this. But then she'd have to explain why *she* knew, and "I heard a rumor" wouldn't be good enough, and—

"Hey, Faustine?"

It was Siegmund, standing there with Valente. The Ossani, and the Secundus boy. If anyone understood what was going on in Faustine's head, it would be one of them. They had noble fathers with high expectations, too.

"Hello," Faustine offered weakly as she grabbed her books from the floor beside the weapons rack.

"It's just a rumor," Valente said, dismissive even when trying to cheer someone up. "I'm sure there would have been a giant announcement if the Imperator were coming here."

He forced himself to laugh, and Siegmund joined in a moment later.

"Can you imagine?" Valente added. "The Imperator, wasting his time at Silverwood?"

For three bloodrunes converged in the same place? Faustine thought dismally. *Yes, I can.*

Oh, *no*, was this because of *her*? Or, well, because she'd told Markus about Christel? Faustine thought she might be sick.

"My father's done..." Faustine tried to find a word, and none of them seemed to fit, so she went with the most ridiculous: "...sillier things with his time."

Siegmund elbowed Valente in the ribs. "Do you want us to cover for you in Tactics?" Siegmund asked. "We can tell Professor Vitellus that you threw up or something."

Faustine clutched her books more tightly against her chest. Siegmund would be a hunter, one day. Once he no longer had to answer to professors or parents or his older brothers.

"Would you?" she asked, a small breath on a short wind.

"Sure." Siegmund shrugged. "Long as you promise to help me with the history homework later."

Faustine's smile was watery. "Deal."

Valente nodded smartly. "We'll tell the others. Go take a nap or something; you look ghastly."

Siegmund elbowed Valente again, harder. "Be *nice*, man."

"What?" Valente rubbed his side, grumpily, and Faustine wondered, for a moment, where his bloodrune was. On his shoulder, like Christel's? His hip, like the professor's?

"Thanks," Faustine got out. "Both of you."

Siegmund beamed—"Sure!"—and Valente merely bowed like the Senator's son that he was.

Faustine got four steps out of the training ground, towards the direction of the dorms, when Christel caught up to her.

"Listen, Faustine," they began, "about—"

"I know," she interrupted.

Christel blinked. "You... *know?*"

"It's the thing Professor Valerius told you about," Faustine added. "That's how you heard."

She stared at Christel for a moment, willing them to understand.

But all they did was furrow their brow. "I mean yeah, but that's not..." They swallowed. "Don't you want to know why your father is coming?"

"I can—" Faustine started to dismiss them, but then realized with dawning horror that if Christel had seen something Unseen-related, Ironfang would have her head for not bringing that information to Markus as fast as her feet could carry her. "Well. I can guess, but what *did* you see?"

Christel glanced over their shoulders—first the one, and then the other—and then said, so quietly Faustine almost didn't hear them, "Your father is coming here to make monsters."

Faustine shivered. "You mean darkbeasts?"

"If they are..." Something horrified crept into Christel's eyes. "...then they're the ones Professor Vee called the big ones. Archgarmur."

Faustine's stomach plummeted to her boots. "What exactly did you see?" she whispered urgently.

An arcane light shone deep in Christel's eyes, and a voice that was not theirs said, "Thought and Memory."

CHAPTER TWENTY-SEVEN

As winter bloomed across the Imperium, Silverwood made frenzied preparations for the end of the semester. Classes were called off to redistribute the students to other tasks, like mopping the dining hall and dusting places no one had been certain existed previously. As frost set in, the student body grew exponentially more anxious. There were panicking teenagers in alcoves, debating with their friends about asking dates or what to wear. Even the most dedicated students were losing focus, and their professors collectively speculated as to whether making them run laps was even a deterrent anymore, there was so much nervous energy floating around.

And that was just the normal winter ball anxiety.

The announcement that the Imperator was going to grace the school with his presence for Yule had been met with a predictable mix of terrified glee and surprised horror. Alchemymaster Caelia actually resigned a few days after the announcement, and Vendrick himself had to absorb her classes. Frelia had only been spared taking some on by continuing to teach the darkbeast seminar, as it had come to be known.

Even so, when Edmund had asked her for help cleaning out the alchemy lab one Saturday afternoon, Frelia couldn't find it in her to say no. Felt too much like kicking a sled dog pup.

"You're a *Saint*, Frelia," Edmund insisted. "Seriously."

"Dunno what you're talking about." Frelia waved him off for the millionth time. "You're buying me a pint later."

They were going through the cabinets one by one, and taking stock of what needed to be refreshed or replaced either by the end of the semester, or before the beginning of the next. The master ingredients catalog sat on a lab table with a mysterious scorch mark that Frelia was pretty sure she'd seen Professor Terzah put there, once upon a time. If the list was anything to go by, Edmund had only been about a third of the way through when he'd recruited her.

Edmund had been chatting all afternoon to fill the silence, and Frelia was vaguely proud of his restraint when it took him until nearly three o'clock to say: "So I heard an interesting rumor about you, the other day."

"Which one?" Frelia asked around the quill in her mouth. "The one where I'm an evil creature born of Helheim and descended upon Silverwood just to make her students run laps, or the one where I'm a Kaldiri murderer who eats the children who wander too far into dark forests?"

Edmund squinted at the jars arrayed on the table before him. "The one where you're apparently having a wild affair with the headmaster."

Frelia snorted, and did her best to remain impassive. "First of all, I don't think Caecillion can do wild *anything*."

"But Frelia..." Edmund's tone was dangerously close to teasing. "He's asked you to stay back after every staff meeting *and* you were in his room all through fall break."

"For the millionth time," Frelia began, genuinely annoyed, "the lab accident happened right over there."

She pointed to a burn on the far wall that still hadn't been painted over.

"And you know why I was in his room over fall break," she added, more quietly but just as annoyed.

Edmund sighed, and Frelia was uncomfortably reminded of his father just before an oncoming lecture. "Frelia," he said. "I sat across from you and Caecillion during those black magic study sessions in school. He *adored* you, and it wouldn't surprise me if he still does."

"Oh, shut up." Frelia made a tired noise that couldn't quite be called a sigh. "That was one eye and two major wars ago."

She was so fucking tired of rumors. Especially the unfounded ones. It would be one thing if she actually were secretly dating the headmaster, but she wasn't and Edmund damn well knew it.

The former cleric paused, and the concern in his voice was so gentle Frelia wanted to break it. "You keep time with your scars?"

She looked up from her scratch pad. "You don't?"

"I don't honestly think I have enough." Edmund paused, then added apologetically, "That could just be because I didn't go into mercenary work after the war, though."

Frelia opened a new cabinet, and grimaced at all the empties. "*Ja*, well, they aren't all from mercenary work."

"I know, but—ah, Helheim."

He cut himself off with a great crash, and Frelia's head immediately snapped up. Edmund was torn between staring in disbelief at his empty hand, and a broken jar of Dark Caps on the flagstone floor.

"Don't move." Frelia abandoned her cabinet. "I'll get the broom."

"I'm alright," Edmund said, and Frelia knew a lie when she heard one. "I just... it just slipped. No need to make a fuss."

Frelia paused midway through pulling the broom and dustpan off the wall. "Are you okay, Edmund?"

He stared so deeply at the mushrooms and shattered glass on the floor that, for a moment, Frelia wasn't certain he'd ever look up.

Then he said, so softly she nearly didn't hear him, "No, I'm not. But thanks for asking."

Frelia wasn't cuddly by nature, and so when she reached out to pat Edmund's back, it was awkward, and too hard, and probably not comforting at all. But Edmund gave a watery hiccup, and reached up to squeeze Frelia's hand anyway. He held it so hard, her knuckles began to turn white, but he didn't let go until Frelia tugged it free to start sweeping.

She said nothing, sweeping glass and ruined mushrooms into the dustbin for a long, drawn-out moment. He either would tell her or he wouldn't, but she wouldn't poke the raw wound festering just below the surface of his skin. Edmund deserved better than that.

"My da died today."

Frelia's stomach dropped through the alchemy lab floor. Edmund's father had been the Einnaskas' seneschal for nearly as long as Frelia had been alive. As was common in Kaldr, he'd been an old war buddy of King Njal's, and stood beside the King until the very end, or so the stories went.

And Njal had died halfway through the Tyrant's War, leaving Hägen an orphan, an only child, and King of all Kaldr.

"You'd think I'd be used to it, after all this time." Edmund sniffed loudly, then took his glasses off and set them carefully on the lab table to scrub at his eyes. "But somehow it always sneaks up on me."

Frelia knew the feeling. It wasn't like Cillian's, Thera's, and her father's deaths, or the Battles for Skjöldr or Spirits' Fen, weren't the same day every year, either.

"Tell me about him," Frelia said, and it echoed in a Volsinii accent in the recesses of her mind.

Edmund curled in on himself, Dark Caps forgotten. "You knew my da."

"Not like you did," Frelia said, before she'd really even processed it.

Edmund hiccupped, and Frelia abandoned sweeping for a moment to thump him on the back a few times. It was all she could think to do.

"Ow," Edmund said, trying and failing to twist around and rub his back. "I know that's supposed to help, but you hit hard, Frelia."

"Sorry," said Frelia, who had been trying not to do exactly that.

Edmund sighed. "I suppose I'm just thankful your bloodrune didn't activate."

"It normally doesn't if I'm not holding something," Frelia offered. "It wants a weapon, I guess. Also you've stopped hiccupping."

Edmund laughed a little, and, for a moment, the alchemy lab was still. If she listened just right, the winter wind outside howled just as it did all the way in the north.

"Do you remember," Edmund said after a moment, still hiccup-free, "that time that I yelled at Reina Einnaska?"

Frelia's brow furrowed. Her child-self had been terrified of Hägen's older sister, not only because she possessed the bloodrune that could bend other bloodruned folk to her will, but also because she had been tempestuous and cruel, an indulged child who grew into a tyrant of an adult.

Sweet, gentle Edmund Blightsen had done *what?*

"I see from your face that you don't," Edmund said with a little laugh. "Hägen and I were six, I think? So Reina was nine and just *so...*" He looked for a word.

"Full of herself?" Frelia supplied.

"Bossy," Edmund landed on. "And she was going on about how Hägen was never going to make a good king if she died, he was too soft, and couldn't fight, and was going to constantly put the court in danger watching his back, and just... awful things."

Frelia's lips twisted into a thin line. It may have come from Reina's mouth, but it was something a lot of Kaldr had thought about the king's bloodruneless second child.

"Brat," she said.

"She was," Edmund agreed. "And, Crown Princess or not, she was making poor Hägen cry and I just... let her have it. He was the kindest person I'd ever met, and all the clerics said he was a natural with white magic, and all *she* could do was kill things."

Frelia studied him for a long moment. "I'm having a hard time picturing you yelling."

"Okay, so it was more the verbal equivalent of a strongly-worded letter," Edmund admitted sheepishly, scratching the back of his neck. "But my point remains! Reina was so taken aback she just kind of..."

He mimicked the long-dead Crown Princess with frightening accuracy, staring at Frelia with his mouth half-open in perfect offense.

Frelia laughed but, somewhere deep beneath her ribs, everything ached like she'd just run all the way from Skjöldr.

"At this point," Edmund continued, "my da swoops in and steers me out of the courtyard by the arm. He says absolutely *nothing* as he drags me down the halls and the back castle steps—you know, the ones that lead down to the water—and at this point, I've already said goodbye to about six people in my mind."

Frelia snorted. "Your da was terrifying like that."

Built like a brick wall and twice as thick, Orm Blightsen had been used to scare many a misbehaving child into company-worthy behavior with the force of his reputation alone. Not Frelia and the Twins, who would typically otherwise be disciplined by Grand Duke Valerius or Margravine Grimsdalr, but other kids, certainly.

Kids like Edmund, or Hägen. Kind ones.

"And he sits me down on the steps," Edmund continued, "folds his arms, and then he says, 'That was a good thing you did.'"

Frelia fumbled with the dustpan, cursing in Kaldiri.

"I know," Edmund agreed, and he dropped to a crouch to steady it for her. "Here, I had been prepared for the tongue-lashing of my life, and instead I'm being... well, not quite commended, exactly. He tells me that, no, I shouldn't yell at the Crown Princess no matter how mean she's being, and yes, he would be taking my paints away for a week because technically I'd misbehaved, but ultimately, I had done the right thing. 'We stand up for our *volchya*, Edmund, even and especially when it's hard.'"

It wasn't often that Edmund spoke Kaldiri, but some words were just untranslatable. It made Frelia's heart ache as she swept the glass and ruined mushrooms into the dustpan.

"That's the Kaldiri way," she muttered.

After all, hadn't that been the entire Tyrant's War? Defending the too-kind King Hägen in her parents' stead, like a new tooth growing in to replace the old? Frelia stared at the hands grasping the broom handle, scarred from all her years of battle.

Grief welled up in her throat and threatened to choke her. "I always knew your da was soft, deep down."

"It was my mum's doing," Edmund agreed.

"Is she...?" Frelia didn't even know how to ask after the seneschal's wife who used to bring the moot children pastries and teach them watercolor painting while their parents deliberated in the next room over.

"She's alive, living in Olicana under her maiden name." He smiled, just, so sadly. "I visit her during the breaks, when I can. But the Volsinii know who I am, and it's just... dangerous."

Frelia wanted to howl, to slash something, to make somebody, *anybody* bloody pay for *something*. Here, Edmund had living *volchya*—something Frelia would kill for, *had* killed for—but he couldn't see her. Not really. There was no fighting 'we lost the war,' and no fighting 'to keep you safe.'

Skjöldr, Heit Reiði, Spirits' Fen, and every other lost battle were proof enough of that.

And yet somehow, unthinkably, Edmund drew in a deep breath and settled into the sort of otherworldly calm that Church of the Triad Clerics had been famous for, once upon a time.

"How do you *do* that?" Frelia asked.

"Do what?"

"*That.*" Frelia gestured towards him. "Settle out, in the middle of Goddesses-damned bullshit."

"Oh." Edmund straightened up, handling the dustbin with practiced care. "You see a lot of awful things as a cleric, and you have to learn not to let it harden you. I used to offer it up as prayer to the Goddesses, but..." He paused to dump the ruined alchemy ingredients into the trash can.

"...I don't think they ever heard me."

Frelia grimaced, and shut her eye. "*Ja,*" she agreed after a moment. "I don't think they ever heard me, either."

"I think the Kaldiri are cursed." Edmund glanced over to where Frelia had taken up leaning against a table leg. "Even half-breeds like me."

Frelia flinched. That was sacrilegious, and coming from Edmund? It would have been unthinkable, fifteen years ago.

"I know." Edmund was looking at his hands, his scratch pad notes, the tables—anywhere but Frelia. "How could a former cleric say such a thing?"

He drew in a shuddering breath.

"I believe there *are* Goddesses," he said, "but I don't believe they're kind. Not after everything I've seen."

Frelia forced herself to speak from deep beneath the icy fury that was as much a part of her as her own name. "I can't forgive them, either."

"You don't need to forgive," Edmund said quietly, "just to let go."

Frelia's eye narrowed. "And what is the *fucking* difference?"

Edmund slowly picked up his quill to mark down the missing Dark Caps. "Forgiveness is 'I see all you've done, and I am choosing to see better in you,'" he said. "Letting go is 'I see what you've done, and I am choosing not to let it hurt me any more.'"

For a moment, neither of them said anything, and the only sound in the alchemy lab was the quiet scratching of Edmund's quill against paper.

"Can you do that?" Frelia asked quietly. "Just... choose?"

It was automatic, her anger. As dependable as the sunrise, and just as blistering. She no more chose the fury that lived in her chest than she had chosen her black hair or her bloodrune.

"Just as much as you can choose to see better in someone," Edmund said gently. "It's that simple, and that hard."

It barely even registered as possible, and a tiny bubble of *what if* bloomed somewhere deep in her chest. Forgiving Vendrick Caecillion wasn't an option, and it never would be. She could work with him easily enough, but letting go of how furious the Tyrant's War made her? Letting go of her dead friends and family, of her dead title and broken future?

Actually, that didn't seem like an option, either, and dammit, she wasn't going to dwell on this!

"Who are you thinking of?" Edmund asked quietly.

Knowingly. The little shit.

"Today isn't about me," Frelia said, and this time it was her eye that snapped to the floor.

Edmund squeezed her arm, and she jumped. "You know," he said, "if I'd known you were with Leon's mercenaries, I would have written you."

"Don't take it personally." Frelia didn't look at him. "I avoided everything after the rebellion collapsed. Cities, Bloodrune Hunters, classmates, just... everything, I guess. 'Til I wandered into Leon's mercenaries."

For a moment, Edmund said nothing, and Frelia stared at Lake Silverwood through the window as though it held the answers to her existence.

"If you just wanted to avoid everything," Edmund finally asked, "why come back to Silverwood at all?"

Frelia tried to disengage, to go back to her half-empty cabinet of alchemical ingredients and be anywhere besides this conversation. "It puts me in front of people who would notice if I went missing."

Edmund studied her for a long moment, and he looked so small, all of a sudden. Dwarfed by his fashionable waistcoat and glasses that were almost too big for his face, and by the weight of the Tyrant's War and all his long-dead friends.

"Do you want my opinion?" he asked.

Frelia was pretty sure he was the only person to ever ask first. "Sure."

"I think it's because you were happy here, once."

Frelia stared at him as if he were the one talking to ghosts in his head.

"That's why I came back, after all," Edmund added. "Silverwood was home just as much as Skjöldr ever was and, hey, it doesn't have General Verona presiding over it now."

It... made a lot more sense than Frelia wanted to admit.

"Also," Edmund continued, "I wanted to make sure I instilled a sense of empathy in the Volsinii kids who were too young to understand war."

It occurred to Frelia that she didn't exactly know: "What happened to you, after the Battle of Skjöldr?"

Edmund was quiet for so long a moment, Frelia almost told him not to bother.

"I was captured on the main thoroughfare after the war song changed," he finally burst out, quietly and with a sharp glance over his shoulder like he expected Ironfang himself to appear there. "The Volsinii held me prisoner for a few weeks, and by the time they let me go, I had no resources to run their blockade on the Ivory Channel, so I stayed with the Church until they came for that, too. Then I went to Silverwood."

He drew in a shuddering breath. "I'm... sorry, Frelia."

"It's probably for the best, given how Spirits' Fen turned out."

Edmund reached out, and held his hand over her arm. "I'm still sorry you had to go through it. I remember how often you and the Twins were in the medical tent. I should have been there, I know."

He was offering not to intrude on her personal space, Frelia realized. So she nudged his hand with her elbow; it was as much contact as she was really capable of handling at that moment.

In many ways, Edmund was the last vestige of her life before the Tyrant's War. Of the Frelia who had gone to Silverwood, grown up with the Grimsdalr twins, and had a living father, too.

"Should is a dirty word." Frelia jerked her arm away.

Edmund let her retreat. "No arguments there."

Her hands suddenly itched for something to do, and so Frelia moved back across the room to where she'd been counting out ingredients. She lined up the empty jars on the countertop below the cabinets, tried to steady herself on the salt and silver smell of the alchemy lab.

"And don't call yourself a half-breed," Frelia added.

"It's not an insult if it's true."

"Yes, it *is* an insult," Frelia snapped. "Just like it doesn't matter who calls me a bitch, or how true it is."

She was, and she knew it, but she wasn't about to let that stop her.

Some of the fire that must have lashed out at Reina Einnaska came right out of Edmund. "Who's called you that?"

"Who *hasn't?*" Frelia snorted derisively. "The Twins, my dead knights, the other professors or the students when they think I'm not paying attention, Leon..."

Well, actually, there was one major player missing from that list, but Frelia wasn't thinking about him.

"How is Leon, anyway?" Edmund asked. "And his mercenaries, for that matter?"

"*Our* mercenaries," Frelia corrected automatically. "And fine, last I heard. Though he's probably drinking himself stupid right now, if I had to take a guess."

"I've only ever heard Leon's name attached to them," Edmund offered apologetically.

Frelia kept lining up bottles on the countertop. "They were 'his' only because I didn't want my family name on it to draw fire. The Cost Effectives, out of Duncregg-or-whatever-the-fuck-it's-called-now."

There was a long silence, and Frelia started noting down amounts of hawthorn branches and moth wings.

"I like the name."

"Leon likes to think he's clever, *ja*." Frelia tried to breathe, but her shoulders shook with the effort. "Likes to think he's a lot of things."

Edmund paused, and then folded his arms around his torso as though to keep himself warm. "Forgive me if I'm overstepping, but... were you together?"

Frelia made a face at the ingredient jars that Edmund mercifully couldn't see. Damnable clerics and their thrice-damned *emotional intelligence*.

"I just think you'd get on like a house on fire, is all," Edmund hurried to add when Frelia didn't say anything. "He's... well, he always reminded me of Cillian. I didn't mean to–"

"Yes," Frelia interrupted with a tired sigh, "we were, for a while. It was after the Northern Rebellion and he'd been exiled. I'd lost everything; he'd lost everything."

The scrape of her quill across the scratch paper made Frelia wince.

"And, *ja,*" she agreed, just to fill the void, "he is a lot like Cillian. Right down to the need for a drink and a good time."

Edmund let the next silence linger before he asked, "So what happened?"

"We dated for a while, if you want to call it something that lofty when you're mercenaries sleeping in the dirt and killing people for gold." Frelia squinted at the spidery handwriting announcing the blackish leaves in the jar she held were dried bitterroot. "Eventually broke up because we got into a fight while trying to have sex, believe it or not."

Edmund's jaw dropped. "That's a terrible time to break up! Sweet, merciful Goddesses..."

"I wasn't trying to!" Frelia said hotly. "I was just trying to make him slow down for once in his Midnight-damned life, and suddenly everything came flying out of both of us. All the 'you never did this' and the 'you always do that' shit they tell you not to argue with. And as we're yelling, I just realized, Leon..."

A pause stretched between them, thin as the spiderwebs in the jar at Frelia's elbow.

"Leon what?" Edmund asked softly.

"Leon just... wasn't the man I wanted there." Frelia marked down the empty bottles of wolfsbane and foxglove on her list, her gut twisting as she remembered the fields of those flowers that had once lain between Valerius Territory and Skjöldr. "And when I told him so, he stopped yelling and told me that was a relief, because I wasn't the person he wanted there, either."

"My Goddesses, what an awful thing to say!"

"Honestly, we had a good laugh about it while we found our clothes." Frelia shrugged. "Still friends to this day."

Edmund's brow furrowed. "Then why do you sound so sad?"

Frelia set down the quill, and finally glanced over to Edmund. "Even if I don't love him like, well, a lover, I still care about Leon. Just got too hard to watch him destroy himself, after everything we'd survived until then."

She grimaced. "Also I got tired of picking up his bar tabs."

"So who did you want there?" Edmund's voice was gentle. "Cillian?"

"Fuck no." Frelia made a gagging noise.

Edmund's voice was calm as he went right for her gut. "Caecillion, then."

"I don't know," Frelia lied, turning back to the jars. "Maybe."

She'd tried. She had genuinely, aggressively tried. Leon had been more than simply there, after she'd lost the rebellion, her home, and Cillian in one fell swoop. He'd survived Silverwood, the war, and the loss of his homeland, too. He understood the previous seven years at a level most never would have, even if he wasn't Kaldiri.

But he wasn't raised to fight the harshest winters, like she was. Wasn't built for war, like she was. Didn't even out her worst tendencies and take her abrasive jabs in stride. If anything, he absorbed and threw them back in a terrible game of catch. They'd fought more than they'd done just about anything else, in those days.

And then Leon had re-discovered drink, and Frelia couldn't stand watching another of her friends throw himself headlong into battle and the bottle.

"I know I don't have much room to tell you not to get involved," Edmund said, and something more horrifying than malevolent gods and dead family crept into his voice, "but be careful with Caecillion, Frelia."

"Or what?" she asked flatly. "I'll get my heart broken again? I don't think there's anything left in there to break."

She knocked her knuckles against the left side of her chest, as though she could rattle the organ in question.

"Believe me," Edmund said, "there's always something. The Goddesses may let you be happy, for a little while, but I think it's just so they can twist the knife later."

Frelia tried to test that theory against everyone she knew—memories of sledding with Diarmuid on the hill beside Valerius Lodge as children, of sitting on balconies deep into the night and talking with Thera, of lazy moot summer afternoons playing board games with Cillian and avoiding the heat—and then against their deaths.

She honestly didn't know if Edmund had a point or not.

"I think if the Goddesses cursed us," Frelia said, "then I don't care what they think."

Edmund's laugh was watery. "That's a Valerius statement if I've ever heard one."

She shrugged. "I can only be what I am—and damn the Imperium for trying to make me into anything less."

"Does Caecillion do that?"

Frelia looked down at her jars, at the spidery handwriting she knew to be Vendrick's after staring at it on the school forms all year. "No," she finally said. "He's just the Volsinii Spymaster who got a lot of my *volchya* killed."

Make it make sense, she wanted to ask—Vendrick, Edmund, the Goddesses, *anyone.*

"The Tyrant's War was fifteen years ago," Edmund said, not unkindly. "We aren't the people we were then."

Deep in her soul, Frelia felt something crack.

"Rebellion was only ten," she muttered. "Sometimes I look over my shoulder and still expect Cillian to be there."

"I get it," Edmund said quietly. "Sometimes I still dream I'm late to white magic lessons and Hägen is knocking on my door."

They stared at each other for a long moment, the swordswoman and the white mage of King Hägen's Krakenguard.

"We're in Lady Midnight's hell, aren't we?"

Edmund grimaced. "I think you might be onto something."

CHAPTER TWENTY-EIGHT

DESPITE THE IMPENDING IMPERIAL visit, her bloodruned hide to worry about, and a winter ball to plan for, Silverwood's professors were still just that—professors. So despite the million other things Frelia needed time for—like creating her final exam, or planning what the fuck she'd do about Ironfang at the winter ball—she was, instead, wasting an entire week of afternoons on academic advisement appointments.

Okay, maybe not wasting—the kids did need the guidance—but she'd suggested moving them to after winter break at the last faculty meeting and been outvoted. Twice. By Markus specifically.

"...I just don't know, Professor," Owen said for the hundredth time. "I really like cannons and siege weapons, but I feel like concentrating in cavalry could be a better way to go?"

"It's about whether you want to be in the siege-breaking units," Frelia said, for the two hundredth time, "or whether you want to be in the melee."

"Will I really ever need to do either, though?" Owen asked. "Who even is there to wage war against anymore?"

Frelia had to stop herself from saying the Unseen. "There's always the Rippling Isles, out for revenge, or the Wilds up north—which you very well know."

Owen shuddered. "I... don't want to fight garmur, professor."

"Then pick cavalry," Frelia said. "Siege weaponry and heavy artillery are who they call in to fight garmur when someone like me isn't around."

Owen blanched just as a knock came from the classroom door.

"Looks like that's your time," Frelia said. "Give it some more thought, and if you're still hemming and hawing by Friday, for Lady Twilight's sake, flip a damn coin."

Owen laughed as he gathered up his books. "I don't care what everyone says about you, Professor. You're really funny."

Frelia half-wanted to ask what they did say about her, but it was probably better not to know.

Owen let himself out the main doors, and Faustine slipped in through the gap made by his passing. She clutched her books to her chest like a shield, nervous in approaching Frelia's desk despite having class five times a day in this room.

This was Frelia's last appointment for the day. She could do this. "Good afternoon, Faustine."

Faustine seated herself across Frelia's desk. "Good afternoon, Professor Valerius."

Frelia had never been one for preamble and she wasn't about to start now. "So, have you given any more thought as to what you'll concentrate in?"

Faustine cast her eyes down to her boots. "I'm sorry, Professor. I still have no idea."

Frelia could not do this.

Since the end of fall break, Faustine had been even more skittish than usual, and it had only intensified since the announcement that Ironfang was coming to Silverwood. Frelia had asked her once or twice if everything was alright, but the girl always brushed her off. Frelia was beginning to think she either ought to call in the cavalry and have Edmund approach her, or resign herself to the fact that Faustine simply didn't wish to tell her professors whatever it was that was very obviously bothering her.

The stinging irony that she was worrying about Ironfang's daughter was not lost on her, and Frelia's lack of patience didn't help with the child's screaming indecision.

"Faustine." Frelia pinched the bridge of her nose and tried not to snap. "You have talent in just about every martial weapon, passable mounted skills, and a firm grasp of tactics. You can, quite literally, take the exam for anything martial."

"That's just the problem!" Faustine burst out.

Frelia froze. *That* was not like Faustine.

She removed her hand from her face and leveled a heavy gaze at her student. "Is there something I should know?"

Faustine quickly looked back down at her boots. "I'm sorry, Professor Valerius. I shouldn't have shouted."

Frelia nudged the teapot towards her. "Have some tea, Faustine."

Some of her students would take a cup of tea during their advisements, and some wouldn't, but Frelia always had it around. She supposed that some habits simply died too hard. It was damn cold growing up in the north.

Faustine didn't look up. "I'm not thirsty, Professor."

"You'll feel less awkward with a drink in your hands."

"I don't... um." After a moment, Faustine reached for the teapot. "Okay."

Frelia stifled a smirk as Faustine fixed herself a cup of bergamot tea, dumped in a few sugar cubes and splash of milk, and took a long, drawn-out sip.

"So we've established," Frelia said after Faustine had resituated herself, "that you can do anything martial. Question is, what do you *want* to do?"

Faustine stared into her teacup. "Father wants me to join a wyvern corps."

"An excellent choice." Loath as Frelia was to agree with Ironfang on anything, it would be a good choice for the kid. "You have the constitution and the lance-work. You'd just need to brush up on your wyvern maneuverability. Very attainable. But."

Faustine seemed to brace for something. "But?"

"I didn't ask what Ironfang wants you to do," Frelia said. "I asked what *you* want to do."

Faustine let out an exhausted breath, crumpling in on herself around her teacup. "To be honest, Professor, I don't want to be so far from a fight—or, honestly, so high off the ground."

"So the wyvern corps is out," Frelia said, throwing Ironfang's preferences aside. "What else do you like?"

Faustine took a bracing sip of tea. "I've thought about swords and daggers. A lot, actually."

"Another excellent choice. You've become quite adept with a blade this semester."

Faustine grimaced. "You're not just saying that because you concentrated in swords, are you?"

Frelia barked a hoarse laugh. "Oh, I didn't choose swords. I concentrated in grappling."

Faustine nearly choked on the sip she'd just taken. "I beg pardon? *Grappling?* Like Karina?"

"Why is that so surprising?" Frelia asked, amused.

"Because... well..." Faustine was struggling to find the words she wanted. "You're really good at swords!"

Frelia cocked an eyebrow. "Are we only allowed to be good at one thing, now?"

Faustine turned bright red. "No, I just mean... well... Karina's a lot... bigger than you?"

Frelia took pity on the girl. "Remember that disarm unit from earlier in the year?"

Faustine nodded.

"All grappling techniques. There's a lot of crossover, actually."

"Oh," said Faustine, perking up a bit in her seat. "That unit was really fun."

Frelia was reminded, not for the first time, that usually all her students needed was a bit of encouragement, and they'd find their own way forward.

"My da wasn't as thrilled," Frelia said. "I spent a whole week after the exams composing a letter to let him know. My friends insisted on reading it over four times before I sent it, just to be safe."

Frelia remembered, faintly, Thera's quill scratching out this turn of phrase and that, telling her for the Saints' sake, not to infuriate her da any further. Cillian had just cackled from atop Frelia's bed, telling her he wished he'd had the guts to stand up to his grandfather and pick a class that didn't require a lance certification, just to piss him off. He just liked horses too much.

Frelia couldn't read Faustine's expression, and the girl took ages nursing her teacup before she spoke again.

"Was your father angry with you?"

"Disappointed, more like," Frelia said. "He wanted me to follow his footsteps and become a paladin. Thought I was a natural with lances."

Faustine wrinkled her nose. "I can't picture you on horseback like that."

"That's because I hate being cavalry," Frelia said. "Both feet belong on the ground, thank you."

Faustine's laugh was short and hiccupping, and she grew serious again quickly. "So then what did your father say, when you told him?"

"Oh, I ignored several letters back," Frelia said, grimacing a little. "Last time I ever did *that*. And then one day, Da just... showed up at Silverwood, and dragged me out to the lakeside by the ears."

Faustine's jaw dropped, but Frelia wasn't finished.

"He asked me what in Lady Twilight's name had gotten into me." And also several other things that didn't bear repeating, especially in Volsinii Standard. "What was I thinking, certifying in grappling?"

"So what did you tell him?" Faustine seemed almost afraid to ask.

Frelia made a face. "Let me preface that by saying one, I was not an easy child, and two, my older brother was technically too young to serve in the Winter War, but went anyway."

Faustine blinked at the new information. "Okay."

Frelia shut her eye. "I told my da that doing what he wanted was what got Diarmuid killed, and I wasn't going to do the same."

Faustine stared at her professor, her mouth open in a little round 'o'. "You said that to your *father?*"

"Wasn't the worst thing I ever said to him, honestly." A deep, painful melancholy began to bloom in Frelia's chest. "But that's how it goes, sometimes."

Both Frelia and Faustine stayed silent for so long a moment, the only sound in the classroom was their breathing.

"Was your father always like that?"

"Not always," Frelia said, suddenly somewhere far away. "Sometimes he was perfectly happy to leave me to my own devices. Took my friends and me sledding every year in the foothills, when we were little."

She smiled, just a little, at the mental image of her very large, very intimidating-looking father wrangling her, Diarmuid, the Grimsdalr twins, and their older brother Kjeld on the snowy mountainside.

"And he told me he was less angry that I hadn't picked swords or cavalry," Frelia added quietly, "than he was angry that I wasn't owning up to my choices."

"I'm sorry for your loss, Professor," Faustine said. "For both of them."

"Don't let anyone catch you saying that." Frelia's eye snapped open and fixed Faustine in a pointed stare. "Not *ever*. Not to me."

"What good is an education if I never use it?" Faustine burst out, and suddenly a lot more came tumbling out. "The history books don't make sense! They crisscross and backtrack and I know the truth has to be somewhere between what they say and what you know."

"Faustine." Frelia drew in a somewhat shaky breath. "Don't empathize with me. You don't want your loyalty questioned by the Shadows of your father's Imperium. You have a bright future ahead of you—and fuck Ironfang, he's wrong. You were never meant for the wyvern corps."

"No," Faustine agreed, "I know exactly what I should be."

***

"Assassin?" Markus shouted. "Really, Faustine? Whatever happened to the wyvern corps?"

He stared at her from across his lab table, and Faustine tried not to cringe at the twisted lump of flesh at his elbows. She wondered what it used to be—an owl? A barn cat?

"I don't want to be three miles away from battle!" Faustine shifted her weight from foot to foot, trying to channel Professor Valerius' stoniest facial expression. It was only half-working. "I want to be in it."

"This is Valerius' doing, isn't it?" Markus threw up his hands in disbelief. "I knew I should have set up your advisement appointment with me."

Faustine smacked her thigh in frustration. "I came to the conclusion myself, Markus."

He appeared not to have heard her. "Do you have any idea how many good men we lost to that bitch in the Tyrant's War?"

Faustine didn't know why, but it tumbled from her mouth before she could stop it: "Enough to give you pause in harassing her, so you make *me* do it for you."

Markus froze over his unliving creations, and Faustine realized she may have just stabbed too far.

"That woman," Markus said, his voice low as he pulled off his surgical gloves, "is a Kaldiri dog—"

"So you've said," Faustine interrupted.

"—and Caecillion denied Father's request to transfer you out of her class out of sheer spite."

"He denied it because I didn't want to leave." Faustine had no idea where this was coming from. "I've learned more this year from her than I ever did from Catianus."

"Oh, don't think I haven't seen you signing up for Blightsen's white magic seminars and Olsen's dagger salons, too."

"I'm *learning*," Faustine spluttered. "Isn't that what I'm here for?"

A smack sounded across the stony lab, and Faustine's face was suddenly on fire.

"Don't be smart." Markus righted the rings on his hand. "And *don't* forget why we're here."

Blood trickled from Faustine's nose, and she glared at her older brother as she let it run. "Oh, right, of course. We're here because you lost that darkbeast Father still talks about, so he can't make any more of the big ones."

Color rose in Markus' pale face as an artery in his neck bulged. "And so that you will make some noble git a miserable family man. Can't forget *that* part; it's all you girl-children are good for."

Why are you always so horrid? Faustine wanted to ask, but what was the point? That was all their family was good for. Being horrid, and stealing bloodruned folk out of their beds.

Kids like Christel and Valente.

Professors like Valerius.

There are hunters, and there are prey.

Faustine had never felt more sick to her stomach. Was Markus right, and this was all she'd been made for?

"And let me guess," Markus barreled on, "you haven't done a single thing about the Traust Bloodrune, have you?"

"I'm working on it!"

"As you have said for weeks," Markus snapped. "If you're going to do something, you had best hop on it before Father arrives and we've nothing to show for it."

Something new stood out to Faustine then, that she hadn't quite noticed before. "What do you mean 'we'?"

Markus shot her a look like she was an idiot, and gestured to the lab table at his hip. "This is your family legacy as much as mine, Faustine. And I should think you'd want to ensure it lives a thousand years."

Faustine swallowed, and forced herself to look at the huge lump of unidentifiable flesh on the table, its furrows and crevices, its sickly sheen and disgusting pallor. Her brain refused to make sense of what she was seeing; there was nothing remotely resembling a head or body or limbs.

I would sooner put a creature like that out of its misery than let you torture it one more moment.

The thought was so sudden and vehement it scared her, but it was true. The truest thing Faustine knew.

"Why didn't you tell me Father was coming?" she asked.

Markus didn't pause in pulling his surgical gloves back on. "Figured you'd learn soon enough."

"I still would've liked to know before the professors announced it," Faustine insisted.

"Why?" Markus eyebrow rose. "What about your life does it change? You weren't going home for the break."

It changed Faustine's entire life, couldn't Markus *see* that?

"And, if you've nothing useful," Markus added, "you may go."

For some reason, being dismissed like a servant rankled her. It shouldn't have; that was how Markus (and their other siblings, for that matter) usually did it. But still, was it so much to ask to be treated like someone worth knowing?

"No," Faustine said. "I'll let you know when I've anything for you."

She marched back up the stairs to his office, ignoring her brother shouting "And lock up behind you!"

She did, though, pulling the bookshelf shut and making sure it was slotted properly into its spot on the wall before picking up her books and slipping out of Markus' office. She'd been at the library late, studying and avoiding her brother and her classmates and, well, everyone.

The Watchers barely even acknowledged her presence as she moved through the barracks, and when she exited the building, the night air was cold. She tried to breathe in deeply, but the chill stung her lungs and she could swear she still smelled the rank alchemy of Markus' lab in her own snot.

"It's far past curfew, you know."

Faustine froze mid-stride, and turned to see Headmaster Caecillion coming up the cobblestoned path. He was dressed in a heavy cloak, a lantern smoldering in his hand, and if not for its dying light, she might not have even seen him at all.

"Err, sorry, Headmaster," Faustine said automatically. "I was in the library and then Markus said he wanted to speak to me, and then, I..."

She trailed off at the stern look on his face. She couldn't read it, and Faustine's stomach twisted as she wondered whether he believed her. It was the truth, and all she had, but still.

"I was just getting back to the dorms," Faustine added, stupidly.

Silence.

"You're bleeding, Faustine," the headmaster finally said, tapping his nose.

"Oh, um. It's the dry air this time of year." She ducked her head under the guise of searching for a handkerchief in her bag. "I get nosebleeds all the time."

"I see."

Faustine glanced up to find Headmaster Caecillion holding out a dark handkerchief to her, neatly folded and pressed. "Oh, um, thank you," Faustine mumbled, taking the cloth and holding it to her nose. It smelled of parchment, like he normally kept it pressed between the pages of a book.

"Does Markus do that often?" Headmaster Caecillion asked.

Faustine froze. "Do what, sorry?"

The headmaster tapped the side of his face, the same place where Faustine's cheek still twinged. "Strike you."

It suddenly occurred to Faustine that if the headmaster could see through *Markus'* lies, he could probably see through hers, too. Markus might not have been as accomplished a liar as Father or Orsina, but he was still leagues ahead of Faustine.

"If it's all the same to you, Headmaster?" Faustine said, looking down at her shoes. "I'd really rather not talk about it."

She expected him to fight her about it, given how poorly the headmaster and Markus got on, but Headmaster Caecillion only nodded. "I'm sure you wouldn't. Allow me to escort you back to Atticus Hall, then."

Faustine didn't know if that meant she was in trouble or not, but she knew better than to ask. "You don't need to waste your night chaperoning me, Headmaster Caecillion. I study late all the time."

"It's no trouble," he said. "Besides, I'm the night watch, tonight. That's part of why I'm here."

They fell into step through the quiet, darkened paths of the Silverwood Military Institute. Headmaster Caecillion was easily a full foot taller than Faustine, but rather than looming over her like Father did, Faustine felt a bit like she had an overprotective shadow.

It was sort of nice.

"How's your sister, Her Grace, by the way?" the headmaster suddenly asked. "I'm not sure I've seen her in years."

"She's fine, so far as I know," Faustine said, surprised at the question. "I don't see her much, either; the Bloodrune Hunters keep her busy, and all that. I think I last saw her over Yule, the year before I started at Silverwood."

"I see," said Headmaster Caecillion, and Faustine got the sudden sense that she'd done something wrong, somehow.

Or maybe that Orsina has.

"I suppose the age gap would make socializing a bit difficult," he added.

It was sort of amazing that, around the Viper of Ascalon, Faustine could feel safe enough to say things she never would around her own siblings. "Yeah, we don't have very much in common."

"I'd imagine not," said Headmaster Caecillion, and then he paused. "You know, I was just like you, when I was here in school."

Faustine pulled up short. "You were?"

It was hard to imagine Headmaster Caecillion as weak and afraid, like Faustine always was. Surely he had never been prey?

"The old librarian was constantly shooing me out of the library after midnight," the headmaster said, and oh, of course that's what he meant.

The studying. "The other Southern Strix told me—daily, really—that I ought to sleep more."

Faustine stared at him, uncomprehending. "The other what?"

Headmaster Caecillion barely paused long enough to draw attention to it—but he did pause. "There were only two houses, in our day. The Northern Kraken, for students from Kaldr, and the Southern Strix, for students from Volsinii. Students from anywhere else were assigned randomly, like how it's done today. Is that news to you?"

"A little." Not for the first time, Faustine wondered what else she didn't know.

"I suppose my point is," the headmaster said as he started walking again, "there's a time and place for everything. Also, do as I say, not as I do."

Faustine laughed, only she sort of felt like crying.

When they came to a crossroads that she moved to take just a hair too slowly, Headmaster Caecillion glanced over to her. "Faustine? Is everything alright?"

Faustine wasn't sure when she'd started crying, but she knew she couldn't stop. It was as though a dam had broken somewhere deep in her soul, and no amount of stiff upper lipping was going to make it seal itself again.

"I'm okay." Faustine blew her nose in the handkerchief she'd have to wash to return. "I don't want to be a bother."

"You're not a bother," the headmaster said firmly, and he guided Faustine over to a nearby bench.

Faustine dropped onto it without protest, pressing her hands into her mouth and trying to stifle her sobs. The headmaster continued to loom, but he wasn't staring at her or anything, and for that, Faustine was grateful.

Saints, she hadn't cried like this since her mother died.

It felt like an eternity before the tears slowed, and by then, Faustine's legs had gone numb, where her skirt and tights didn't protect them enough from the cold. When she finally looked up, the headmaster was holding out another handkerchief, and Faustine knew better than to ask why he had more than one.

"Thank you," she said instead, and blew her nose so loudly something in the nearby bushes startled.

"Do you wish to tell me what's wrong?" Headmaster Caecillion asked, although his attention was focused on whatever had just moved. "I'm well aware I'm not anyone's first choice for it, but I'm happy to listen just the same."

Faustine's insides were completely torn. She knew what she was 'supposed' to do: be a dutiful daughter, marry whomever she was told, concentrate in whatever she was told, and graduate from Silverwood ready to support her father and the Unseen however he decided was best. She was supposed to steal Christel's blood, and help Markus make monsters, and hate Professor Valerius, and just be prey.

But she wanted so much more than that, it burned a hole clear through her chest.

"I want to concentrate in assassination," Faustine finally managed. "Markus is furious, and my father will be, too, when he hears. They want me to join the wyvern corps when I graduate."

"A difficult decision, then." Headmaster Caecillion folded his arms across his chest as he looked back at her. "And not an easy one to come to."

Faustine blew her nose into the disgusting handkerchief again. "That's basically what Professor Valerius said during my advising appointment earlier."

Headmaster Caecillion regarded her for a moment, then leaned forward conspiratorially. "Did she also tell you about how Grand Duke

Valerius was less-than-thrilled when she picked her concentration in school?"

A giggle burst up through Faustine's body like a bubble rising to the surface of Lake Silverwood. "Did he really just show up out of nowhere to discipline her?"

"I presume he came from the old duchy, but yes." Headmaster Caecillion shook his head, and Faustine caught a flash of something unnamable exposed on his face. "Bloody terrifying man. Three times the size of any of us, and he stormed right through the students' dorms to the end of the hall. I suddenly understood a great many things about my Kaldiri friends that day."

Faustine recoiled at the idea that a man like Headmaster Caecillion would be afraid of anything, let alone a long-dead Kaldiri duke.

Oh, maybe he had been talking about more than just studying in the library.

"Is that a surprise?" The headmaster cocked an eyebrow. "I daresay, you've met our swordmaster. How do you think she turned out that way? Dice rolls and astrology?"

It was nice that Faustine could just tell him the truth. "It's... just hard to think of you as scared of anything, Headmaster."

"Is it?" Headmaster Caecillion smiled, but it was only half, and looked unbearably sad. "I can assure you, there are plenty of things I'm afraid of."

Faustine could not have heard that correctly. "But you're the—!"

She just barely had the presence of mind to cut herself off.

"The Viper of Ascalon?" he supplied wryly.

"I'm sorry!" Faustine clapped her hands to her mouth.

"I'm not surprised you know that, with your pedigree." Headmaster Caecillion sighed. "Though if you know that, it should stand to reason that there would be things that terrify even me."

The Shadows of your father's Imperium, Professor Valerius had called them. Faustine had figured the professor meant the Unseen—though how she knew about them, Faustine had no idea. She'd debated telling Markus all afternoon, because he and their father would want to know there was another wrench in the grand plans they didn't bother to inform Faustine of.

"There are many dark corners on this continent, Faustine," Headmaster Caecillion continued. "Choosing assassination means that you will grow quite familiar with them. Are you prepared for that?"

Faustine stared down at her boots: the same ones she'd replaced her chewed-up loafers with, at the very beginning of the year. "I just don't want to be helpless anymore. You know?"

For a long moment, the headmaster said nothing. Silence fell across the road the way rain swallowed the countryside.

Then Headmaster Caecillion said, "Am I correct in assuming that, if you know about the Viper of Ascalon, you know why I became such?"

Faustine was too ashamed to look at him. "Your family has always been Spymasters, haven't they?

"No, actually. We've simply served the Imperium in whatever way she needs." Headmaster Caecillion shrugged. "Though you are correct that my father was Imperator Claudius' Spymaster before I served your father. That just isn't what I'm referring to."

"Oh." He must have meant the other thing the Caecillion Family was famous for. "You mean your grey magic."

It wasn't a question.

"Precisely. Are you aware of how grey magic functions?"

"I'm sorry." Faustine buried her nose in the handkerchief. "I'm hopeless with magic."

"That's not something to apologize for," the headmaster said. "I'd just hate to bore you with things you already knew."

How... It took Faustine a moment to find the right word to apply to the ominous headmaster. ...*thoughtful.*

"Grey magic," he continued, "takes the caster's life energy and uses it to destroy. It is a difficult style of magic to master, a precise balance to maintain, and frequently results in scarring, arcane accidents, and worse."

Faustine's eyes widened. "If it's so dangerous, then why use it? Wouldn't black magic be easier?"

"It would be," Headmaster Caecillion agreed. "But black magic wasn't what I was created to wield. When my tutors discovered where my talents lay, I was presented with a choice: the easy road, or the one I was born for."

There are hunters, and there are prey. He sounded just like Professor Valerius.

"Now, your father will either come around, or he won't," Headmaster Caecillion said. "You need to be ready for either eventuality."

"I think he will," Faustine said. "Just... not quickly."

"Fathers can be like that," he agreed, and she thought he sounded sad again.

"Thanks for walking with me, Headmaster," Faustine said. "I think I get it, now."

"I live ever to serve." Headmaster Caecillion smiled—*really* smiled—and for once he looked like an encouraging professor, instead of like he was plotting a murder. "Now, do you wish to head back to the dorms, or did you want another moment to collect your thoughts?"

There was one other thing Faustine wanted to know first. "Headmaster Caecillion, how did you know which road you were born for?"

Just like that, his smile was gone.

"It's the one that doesn't gnaw at you while you walk it."

CHAPTER TWENTY-NINE

IN THE END, FAUSTINE realized she'd been thinking too hard. She didn't need to orchestrate an elaborate scheme at all. She just had to tell Christel the truth—or part of it, anyway.

"Sorry, you need my what?"

"Your blood," Faustine said again, this time even quieter. They were outside, between Brekka Hall and the mess, but there were still other people around. "The headmaster asked me to get a sample so that he can take a look at it. Something Professor Valerius told him about—" She cut herself off. "Well, you know."

Christel made a face. "Why can't he come get it himself?"

Faustine shrugged, and she hoped it came across as remotely genuine. "He said it was less suspicious this way?"

"I guess." Christel shook their head. "Yeah, okay. How do you want to do this?"

"Just come by my room after dinner or something," Faustine said. "Or I can stop by yours?"

"Siegmund and I were gonna play cards later," Christel said. "Can you stop by his?"

Faustine swallowed. She didn't know how to ask Christel not to bring Siegmund into it, given that Siegmund already knew, so there went her best argument. "Uh, sure. Which room is his?"

"He's between Cora and Valente on the second floor."

So, that was how Faustine came to be standing in front of a boy's dorm room door, thoroughly nervous and for none of the usual reasons. She drew in a deep breath, trying to steady her nerves, and then knocked.

Siegmund showed up in the doorframe a moment later, blocking most of it with his massive shoulders. "Oh, hi Faustine. C'mon in."

He removed himself and Faustine could suddenly see the rest of his room. It was messy, the way most people's were, but at least Faustine couldn't see anything that looked organic on the floor. Christel was sitting cross-legged on Siegmund's hastily-made bed, playing cards in hand and several more scattered across the blanket.

Faustine tried to act normal. "What are you playing?"

"Crowns versus Crooks," Christel said. "Want us to deal you in?"

"I, um." Faustine froze, words failing, and tried again. "I'm just here for..."

"We know," Siegmund interrupted. "But you can still hang out after if you want to."

Christel made a face as they considered. "Probably *before*. Doesn't blood need to be iced, or something, if it's out of you too long?"

"...Yeah," Faustine managed around the lump in her throat. "It does."

"Then yeah, come play with us!" Siegmund clapped her on the shoulder so hard that Faustine stumbled. "You work too hard, Faustine. It's ok to take a break, y'know."

"Don't listen to him," Christel said, jokingly conspiratorial, "all he takes are breaks."

"Hey!"

The part of Faustine that genuinely *was* just a Silverwood student smiled—"Okay, I can play a few rounds."—but the part of her that was a della Luciana made it feel like a crime—"But then I need to get moving."

"That's the spirit!" Siegmund crowed.

"Do you want a snack or anything, Faustine?" Christel pointed to a canvas bag sitting on Siegmund's desk. "We picked up some from the commissary."

"Oh, no thanks, I'm okay." Warmth had begun to spread in Faustine's bones, and she wanted to hold onto the feeling for as long as she could. "And also, I'm not sitting on your bed, Siegmund."

So that was how Faustine came to be sitting in Siegmund's desk chair and playing cards with the person she was supposed to be stealing blood from. She tried to put that from her mind and just enjoy the game, but it chilled the warmth in her bones and left her shivering.

She didn't want to betray their trust like this, and didn't want something horrible to happen to Christel because of her. She liked the swordsman, the way their brow screwed up over their cards when they were thinking, and the kind way they did everything, even lose.

And she liked Siegmund, too, and his boisterous enthusiasm for practically everything, and wished that the Ossani had a bloodrune that Father would want so that she could at least marry someone who wasn't terrible. The options thrown at her before had always been grim and much, much older than her.

Why couldn't Markus steal the blood he so desperately wanted? Why did Faustine have to be a part of this at all?

"Ha!" Siegmund threw down his hand in triumph. "I win!"

Faustine squinted at his cards, grateful to give herself something to do besides worry. "No, you don't," she said. "You've got three kings and a four."

"Yeah, so I win!"

Christel was grinning, though. "Not if someone else has four queens."

Faustine laid her own hand on the edge of Siegmund's bed, and accepted their good-natured heckling. Four queens, after all, didn't lie.

Then Faustine said, "Okay, but seriously. I do need to get going soon."

Siegmund made a fart noise in the back of his mouth and Christel sighed enormously. "Just ignore him," they said. "I swear to the Goddesses, he's twelve."

Christel pulled all the cards back together and passed them off to Siegmund, then scooted towards the edge of the bed. "Do you need to take blood from the actual Bloodrune, Faustine?"

Markus hadn't said anything about it, so she prayed she was right when she said, "I don't think so," and wrinkled her nose. "The headmaster said just your arm or something would do."

"Oh, thank the Saints." Christel began unbuttoning the cuff of their sleeve. "No offense, but I didn't want to have to take my shirt off."

"I feel like if you did," Faustine said, "the headmaster would probably have asked Siegmund to do it?"

"Oh, good point." Siegmund folded his arms across his broad chest. "Do you need anything, Faustine?"

"Just the bag I brought." Faustine pointed to where she'd set it atop Siegmund's dresser.

He dropped it in her lap, and Faustine dug around for a moment before pulling out the small, wooden box she'd argued out of Markus. She set it on the bed near Christel, and undid the clasp. There was the syringe, its needle, some gauze, and a small vial of alcohol.

You don't want to disappoint Father, do you? Markus always said, and Faustine mentally scowled at him.

He had also said the syringe would do its thing all on its own, and Faustine just needed to hold it steady. But her hands were shaking violently as she primed the empty cylinder and tugged at Christel's sleeve.

"You okay?" they asked.

"Just, um, nervous." How nice, that Faustine didn't even have to lie. "I'm not exactly a phlebotomist."

Christel's blue eyes were far, *far* too kind. "Take your time."

Faustine squeezed at Christel's arm until their veins stood out against the silvery-pale expanse, and still, it took her two tries to get the needle to go in properly. Sure enough, the mechanics in the syringe, whatever they were, held it in place and began drawing blood up into the small cylinder at the end.

"Damn, that's kinda cool," Siegmund said from over her shoulder. "I didn't know syringes could do that."

"I didn't either," Christel said. "Don't you normally have to pull the plunger-thingy?"

Faustine tried to shrug without moving the contraption. "He said this would probably be easier for me to do."

Siegmund let out a low whistle. "Man, the headmaster is *scary.*"

It's the path that doesn't gnaw at you when you walk it, he'd said.

Was that the feeling in Faustine's gut? A biting ache, where her conscience had once been?

After another moment, the syringe was full, and Faustine slid the needle back out and pressed a wad of gauze against Christel's arm. "Hold onto that a second, would you?"

Christel nodded and pressed the gauze more firmly against their puncture wound, while Faustine snapped the needle off the syringe and fitted both it and the cylinder back into the wooden box.

Professor Valerius' voice suddenly sparked against the back of her mind: *In all things, Faustine, there are hunters, and there are prey. Don't. Be. Prey.*

Her father was a hunter. Markus was a hunter. Professor Valerius and Headmaster Caecillion were hunters. Hell, Siegmund and Christel were even hunters.

But Faustine?

Faustine was prey.

She knew it as she snapped the lid shut on the box, and bid her good-byes to Christel and Siegmund.

She knew it as she hustled across campus with this stolen prize she didn't even *want,* and she knew it when she burst into Markus' office and presented him with the box.

She was prey.

She was prey.

She was *prey.*

And no amount of swords lessons were ever going to change that.

CHAPTER THIRTY

WHEN THE DAY ITSELF arrived, no one was quite prepared.

"Chins up, little owls," Frelia muttered to her homeroom as they stood in the great entrance hall, fidgeting in their formal uniforms. "Your Imperator approaches."

A few more of the Violet Owls straightened up, which Frelia considered to be good enough for government work. Ironfang had, apparently, chosen to arrive in the middle of the day—probably to cause maximum headache—and so the entire population of Silverwood had been forced to run back to their dorms, change clothes, and assemble in the entrance hall.

Frelia would never say, outwardly, that she was grateful Vendrick had made them practice this assembly about a million times, but she was. That was the only reason it worked and looked vaguely presentable.

"Have you ever met the Imperator, professor?" Ellie asked.

Frelia sighed. "Unfortunately."

Ironfang had, after all, been the general responsible for the Imperial victory at Spirits' Fen—the last battle of both the Northern Rebellion and Cillian's life—and for the scar that ran from Frelia's shoulder to her solar plexus.

"*Ellie,*" Owen hissed. "You know she's the General Valerius."

Ellie's eyes widened as apparently, she'd forgotten that. "Oh, Saints, I'm sorry, I didn't—"

"Was Margrave Grimsdalr really as handsome as they say?"

Everyone turned to look at Faustine, who was hiding behind her hands, but she didn't take back the question.

"Cillian?" Frelia wished she could dump this on someone else, and not have to remember. "I guess. He was dumb as a rock, though."

Faustine's brow furrowed. "I thought he was a brilliant general?"

"He was," Frelia said. "He was also a dumbass."

Several of her Violet Owls laughed, to the point that Professor Campagna and her homeroom glared at them from their parade rest twenty feet up the hall.

"That... doesn't make any sense?" Karina ventured.

"Sure it does," Christel piped up. "You've met Siegmund."

"*Hey!*" Siegmund harrumphed.

Frelia was, however, spared further questions by the blaring herald's horn.

"Presenting," shouted Axemaster Ossani, who was their herald for the occasion, "Imperator Elias 'Ironfang' della Luciana, first of his name!"

He was bald, now, his head clean-shaven and greying beard impeccably trimmed, but he filled the shoulders of his formal coat as well as he had any armor, back during any of the wars which had granted him the line of military medals on his left pectoral. He towered over most folks, but Cillian had been able to look him in his grey, fathomless eyes.

Frelia's stomach clenched, and a chill swept across the back of her neck. In her mind's eye, she was standing in a muddy fen in Grimsdalr Territory, and the night was black and full of nightmares.

Ironfang's steely gaze swept across the assembled masses, taking stock of the academy. He halted, for just a moment, when he met Frelia's eye. His expression didn't change, but his posture tensed, his footsteps halted.

Frelia stared him down like a wild boar, her fingers curled around the hilt of her sword. Fury breathed life into her lungs, loud and demanding the Imperator's head. She could lay it on Cillian's lack-of-grave.

Gut the bastard, urged a voice in the back of her head. Saints only knew who it belonged to. *He deserves it a hundred times over for every wretched thing he's done, and even if you're tried and hanged afterwards, at least you'd be in Solivallr with your volchyea.*

She could do it. He was only, what, thirty paces out? Twenty? If she could draw the Grimsdalr Blink behind someone's back, not break eye contact...

No.

Frelia was many things, but suicidal was not among them. She drew in a deep breath, choked down her grief for the thousandth time, and dropped her sword in the face of an unwinnable battle.

It fell back, listless, against her side.

Ironfang continued on through the entrance hall, and Frelia didn't miss that his eye landed on Gellir, Olsen, and Edmund, too. Taking stock of his old adversaries, maybe? Though Olsen had said she'd been too old to fight in the Tyrant's War, that didn't mean she couldn't have been a headache in the Winter War. She'd done *something* to be worth hiring at Silverwood, after all.

By the time Ironfang and his retinue met Vendrick and Magicmaster Marcellius at the end of the hall, Frelia didn't know if it was anxiety screaming at her to do something, her bloodrune, Cillian's ghost, or all three.

"Your Majesty, you honor us with your presence." Vendrick swept into a low, Volsinii bow, and beside him, Magicmaster Marcellius did the same. "I trust the journey went well?"

Ironfang's smile was plastered-on as he turned to face the assembled crowd of students and teachers.

"You honor *yourselves*, your families, and this institution with your upstanding presences." The Imperator's voice echoed into the rafters, and Frelia did her level best not to think about the last time she'd heard it. "I have heard many great things about the classes this year I hope to witness for myself."

His smile was meant to have been magnanimous or something, Frelia was pretty sure, but all it filled her with was a deep sense of dread.

***

Vendrick knew, somewhere in the back of his mind, that he was supposed to fear Ironfang. The Imperator was the most powerful man on the continent, and that was even before one took into account the fact that, physically, Ironfang was an imposing beast of a man. But try as his primal brain might, Vendrick could never quite summon the requisite terror. Most of what he felt when dealing with Ironfang was wariness mixed with anxiety. Maybe some irritation, and a little dread.

Not fear, though.

So when Ironfang strolled right up to the end of the entrance hall with his retinue and a handful of Watchers, Vendrick was still going through event planning in the back of his mind. The dinners, the Victory Day ceremony, the accommodations, the winter ball itself, and Yule.

Once the initial assembly dispersed, Ironfang insisted on taking a tour of the place. Vendrick tried to imply it wasn't necessary—it hadn't changed much from when Ironfang had been a student himself, or even when he'd dropped off Faustine last year—but the Imperator had insisted.

And one did not say no to an insistent Imperator.

"I'm just ever-so-curious about your newest faculty," Ironfang said as they crossed the academic quad with a handful of Imperial Watchers in tow.

The hairs on the back of Vendrick's neck stood on end. "There are several this year," he said evenly. "Roguemaster Olsen, Swordmaster Valerius, and Tacticsmaster Vitellus. What would you like to know?"

Predictably, Ironfang's bushy eyebrow rose. "I thought I saw Valerius."

Vendrick hadn't figured burying her name would work, but it had been worth a try. "Indeed, she's proven an adept teacher despite a few..." He paused, trying to come up with a diplomatic word. "...quirks."

Ironfang's laugh had always grated on Vendrick, but it was somehow worse, now that he was no longer used to it. "I wonder," he said in the kind of tone that meant Vendrick had better have an answer prepared, "how in Hypogia's name did you manage to recruit the Warden of Kaldr?"

"I believe that was Grand Duke Einar," Vendrick said, deceptively light. "His daughter was the Wolf."

There were a few students hurrying across the quad, one of whom actively squeaked at the sight of the Imperator. Her friend curtseyed haphazardly and then dragged her towards Iuvenlis Hall.

Ironfang's smile was razor thin as he watched the students go. "The question stands."

"Believe it or not," Vendrick said, making a mental note to check up on those two students after he was free of Ironfang, "Valerius just showed up one day. Was quite surprised to find me running the place."

"Did she expect to find Headmaster Viril?"

"Frankly, Your Majesty, I don't think she got that far."

That laugh again, this time twice as grating. "Truly, I must know... how *did* she manage to avoid us until the Ascalon Accords were signed?"

Vendrick was out of practice in the Imperator's court, but he knew a slight when he heard one. *All the resources I gave you,* Ironfang said without saying, *and you couldn't manage to track down one measly swordswoman?*

As though Vendrick were a miracle worker, instead of a Spymaster.

"I'm told she dyed her hair and joined a mercenary company until the Accords granted her amnesty," Vendrick said coolly. "Though you're well aware I did try."

It was the least he had owed her, not to allow the Unseen a crack at the Valerius Bloodrune. Vendrick had scoured the continent for all of his bloodruned classmates and their families, trying to deliver them from Ironfang and his Unseen before it mattered. He had turned up scant few of them. To this day, he wondered how many had simply hidden themselves phenomenally or escaped the continent entirely, and how many the Unseen had found first.

"Of course you did," Ironfang said, mock-soothingly. "You always do."

Vendrick refused to allow so much as an eyebrow to twitch as he held open the door to the mess hall. "I suppose it's worked out in the end," he said. "She's turned around our classes' swordsmanship quite nicely."

Not to mention given him the first hope for a decent war strategy in months, but Vendrick couldn't tell Ironfang that.

"The mess," Vendrick added, gesturing to the long rows of tables and benches, "which I'm fairly certain has not changed in fifty years."

Ironfang surveyed the cafeteria with evident distaste. "Is this a school cafeteria, or a mead hall?"

"It's both," said Vendrick, "on graduation night."

The janitor mopping the floor nearby snorted, but Ironfang didn't crack a smile. *Stone-faced as ever,* Vendrick thought, annoyed.

He stewed in that annoyance for a moment as he led Ironfang through another exit door towards Salonia Hall. Why was he annoyed, anyhow?

All the Volsinii were was stone-faced, according to just about everyone who had ever dealt with them. The Imperator was hardly an exception.

"And how is your sister doing, Caecillion?" Ironfang suddenly asked.

Vendrick could feel his blood pressure spiking, and forced himself to remain calm and deflect with every Volsinii's biggest weakness—gossip. "Oh, she's fantastic. Currently visiting our mum up north, last I heard from her."

Ironfang tsked. "Does your mother know how haphazardly you're looking after her only daughter?"

Vendrick held open the heavy side door to Salonia Hall, and didn't mention he was his mother's only son, for that matter. "That would require her to write me."

"That's strange," Ironfang said, "I was under the impression *your* pen was the one out of ink."

Vendrick stiffened as the Imperator brushed past him. "Have you met with her recently?"

"Oh, no," said Ironfang. "We do exchange letters, though. She says to give you her love."

Vendrick leveled as sharp a look as he dared at Ironfang. "What did she actually say? If you don't mind."

Ironfang made a conciliatory gesture like an actor in an opera. "I believe it was something to the effect of, 'tell my son not to blow himself up with grey magic, and for the Saints' sake, would he just get bloody married already.' But that about equates to love from General Deadcut, I'd say?"

Vendrick was unfortunately forced to agree.

"And speaking of," Ironfang said, "which of these classroom's is Valerius'? I must admit, I'm curious as to how well *that* woman handles teaching."

It sang a warning song deep in Vendrick's most primal core. No, *no*, the last thing anyone needed was the retired General Ironfang and the disgraced General Valerius in the same room for any length of time longer than 'goodbye'.

"We *weren't* speaking of Valerius," Vendrick pointed out.

"No?" Ironfang raised an eyebrow.

Vendrick also didn't need Ironfang prying into his personal life—or lack thereof. "In any case, she should be out in the training grounds at this time of day. Though I doubt you'd enjoy trampling through the muddy practice fields to get there, Ironfang."

There was a delicate pause.

"An expert in my preferences now, are you?"

"I should hope so," Vendrick said evenly. "I served your family long enough to know how you take your tea—and your steak."

Ironfang's stare could have burned a hole in Vendrick's frock coat. "I have never appreciated your flippancy, Caecillion."

"And *I* have never appreciated assumptions."

Ironfang stared at him for so long that Vendrick itched to reach for his spellbook, sheathed uselessly at his belt.

"This is clearly my fault," Ironfang finally said with an enormous sigh. "I've left you alone too long."

Vendrick jerked back as though singed. "I beg pardon?"

"While I certainly understand the importance of maintaining a working relationship with one's colleagues," Ironfang continued, as though Vendrick hadn't spoken, "I do worry for you, without your father around to curb your... more questionable attributes."

"Questionable?" Vendrick repeated, more sharply than he'd intended. "Ironfang, do you trust me to keep your secrets, or don't you?"

The words tasted like ash.

"Oh make no mistake," Ironfang said, "I trust you're not stupid enough to tell Valerius things that would get yourself hanged, but I'd imagine it's been a rather lonely decade." A predatory smile curled across Ironfang's impeccably-trimmed beard. "Hasn't it?"

Vendrick had never wanted to incinerate a monarch so badly. Not even when he'd actually done it. "Shall we continue on to the lecture halls?" he said, instead, through gritted teeth.

Ironfang smiled like the cat who'd gotten the cream. "By all means, Headmaster."

CHAPTER THIRTY-ONE

FAUSTINE DIDN'T LIKE BEING in Markus' office on a good day. She disliked it even more when her *father* was involved. When she strode through the door, she could tell by the set of Ironfang's jaw that this was a business meeting, not a family get-together. And here, Faustine had been hoping her father actually *cared* how his children were doing.

She knew better, but some small part of her had still hoped.

"Good evening, Faustine," her father said from where he sat taking up most of the loveseat in Markus' office. "Shut the door."

She obeyed. "Good evening, Father. Markus."

Markus made a face from where he sat across the tea table from Father. He was lounging just like Ironfang, and it made Faustine wonder where they'd thought she'd sit. The ground?

"Now that you're both here," Ironfang said as he poured a measure of wine into his glass, "one of you can tell me—why is a simple task like 'destabilize Silverwood with a few garmur' so difficult for the pair of you?"

Markus' head snapped up. "Father, had I not explained in my letter?"

Ironfang swirled the wine about his glass. "I wish to hear it from the horse's mouth."

Markus' jaw opened and shut a few times like a broken nutcracker, and then he glanced to his sister. "*You* tell him, then."

It's your fault, he left unspoken.

Faustine scowled at him. She knew what she was supposed to say here, but that didn't make it any easier. "It's my fault, Father. I didn't realize Markus had set them loose, and so I helped the professor take care of them before they bit anybody."

Markus rolled his eyes. "Said professor being Frelia bloody Valerius."

"I didn't know she was the *General* Valerius, then." Faustine stared at her feet; it was easier than looking at either of them. "It won't happen again, Father. I swear."

For a long moment, Ironfang didn't say anything.

Then, "And why was your sister not informed of your orders?"

Faustine's head snapped up so fast she heard tendons in her neck crack.

"So that she couldn't muck it up," Markus said. "Obviously."

Ironfang raised an eyebrow. "That went well."

"I underestimated how dense she is," Markus muttered. "It won't happen again."

Faustine squeaked at the indignity. "I'm not dense—!"

"Enough!" Ironfang roared.

Faustine's jaw immediately snapped shut, but Markus' jaw was set nearly as hard as their father's.

"Now tell me," Ironfang continued, "how did Valerius manage to evade you this long, Markus?"

Distaste diffused across Markus' face. "At this point, I believe she was simply overshadowed by the Grimsdalr twins."

Cillian and Thera, the professor called them. Her best friends. She'd told a few stories about them in class, disguising them as "old friends" and never using their family name, until today. But everyone knew who she meant, thanks to Owen.

Faustine didn't know what she'd do if something happened to one of the Violet Owls, and the professor had been dealing with that exact scenario for almost a decade. No wonder she was so surly; she had no one to talk to!

"I suppose he did have that tendency," Ironfang agreed over the rim of his wineglass.

"Though really, Father," Markus continued, "what do we need her for if we have him?"

Him? What did Markus mean, *him?*

"Cursebreaking is an... imprecise art," Ironfang said. "It's unknown how much of their blood we'll actually need."

Spill it all still echoed in Faustine's ears late at night, just like when it had echoed up through the halls of the family villa.

"And to be right honest," Ironfang said, "draugur are terribly unpredictable."

"Too true." Markus made a face into his wineglass. "Now, Father, Valerius does complicate things. She's too observant."

"Then give her things to observe," Ironfang said flatly, as though it were obvious. "Your sister should be an excellent assistant for that."

"However," Markus pressed, and Faustine could tell he was getting annoyed, "I do have good news."

Ironfang regarded his last living son over the rim of his wineglass. "Do you now?"

Markus' smile was as false as he was. "I've procured you a bloodrune."

He stood up and went to his desk, rummaging around for a moment before he came up with a small test tube. He presented it to Ironfang with a flourish like he was casting a spell. Their father took it and held it up to the light.

And there, swirling in the center of the test tube like a horrible, glowing brand, was Christel's bloodrune.

"Well, I'll be damned." Ironfang leaned against the back of the couch, staring at the blood vial intently. "This is the Traust rune."

Markus was practically preening. "It is indeed."

"Well you didn't get it."

Faustine hadn't realized she'd said it aloud until Markus and her father were both staring at her. She wished she could sink into the cushy leather of Markus' office chair, but it was too late to take it back now.

So she added, "I did."

Markus scowled at her as their father studied her for a moment more, and then Ironfang smiled and said something Faustine never thought she'd ever hear.

"Well done, Faustine."

Then he glanced back to Markus. "You still have a bit of the Grimsdalr blood left, yes?"

"I do." Markus was suddenly stiff in his seat. "And, Father, you know Faustine only assisted in—"

Markus' hedging and hawing washed over Faustine like high tide from the sea. *Well done, Faustine.* She'd never heard her father say that, or anything close. Nor her brother, or older sisters. Hell, even her childhood governess had been a stern woman too strict for something as silly as praise.

But her professors said it. In fact, they said it all the time—

When she'd finally stopped stutter-stepping at the start of a duel, Professor Valerius had crowed, *Good, again!*

When she'd caught Professor Marcellius' falling books before they scattered everywhere he'd said, *Well done, thank you, Faustine.*

And when she'd brought Christel to the headmaster when their bloodrune awoke, he'd said, *You've done well.*

Why did it feel so hollow, now?

"Well, I see no use in standing around, here." Ironfang clapped a hand to his knee and rose to his feet. "Let us get to work."

Markus practically fell over himself in his haste to unlock his laboratory, and Faustine's only passing thought was that nobody had offered her anything to drink. They had what they wanted, and beyond that, she might as well be office furniture.

Prey, prey, prey.

Down in Markus' cold laboratory, the horrid smell made Faustine's eyes water. She couldn't tell exactly where it was coming from—the sewer drain, maybe? The furry, half-mangled corpse on his lab table?—but her throat filled with bile and she struggled not to throw up.

"My, my," Ironfang said, studying the incomplete darkbeast. "You've been busy, Markus."

"Of course I have." Markus looked genuinely affronted. "Let me just get that Grimsdalr blood for you, Father."

He scurried over to his supply cabinet and began rummaging around for the mostly-empty blood vial. Ironfang folded his arms as he continued to study Markus' lab. Faustine had no idea what he was thinking—she never did.

"I have been... oof!" Markus cut himself off as he yanked on the stubborn supply cabinet door. "I have been researching the darkbeasts, of course."

"As that was your entire purpose here," Ironfang said acidly, "I should hope so."

"But with Traust blood..." Something distinctly glass-like clinked in the supply cabinet. "...I believe it will be possible to summon Lord Muninn, Father."

Markus beamed as he presented the half-inch of Grimsdalr blood still in his last vial.

"Why stop there?" Ironfang plucked the vial from Markus' grasp. "Why not summon Huginn, Geri, Freki, or the Watcher while you're at it?

Faustine didn't recognize any of those names, but they didn't sound Volsinii. Her father was studying the blood left in the vial with a hungry look in his eye, and Faustine didn't like where this was going at all.

"I..." For the first time in Faustine's life, Markus faltered.

Their father sighed, and put a conciliatory hand on Markus' shoulder. "This is why your sister is the ambitious one."

Furious color crept up Markus' neck, but Ironfang kept right on talking.

"You are correct, however, that the Traust Bloodrune will revitalize Muninn—if you've done everything right to prepare for him." Ironfang held the Traust vial back out to Markus. "So let's see it, then."

Markus swallowed audibly, then nodded and took the Traust vial from Ironfang. He strode over to the mangled corpse on the lab table, and Faustine's jaw dropped when she realized, it wasn't a corpse at all. It was breathing. Faintly, but its chest discernably rose and fell.

Holy shit, what had Markus done?

He was priming a syringe with Traust blood now, and Faustine watched in mute horror as he pulled Christel's stolen blood through a wicked-looking needle.

"Where are you getting your supplies?" Ironfang asked.

"Here and there," said Markus, flicking the newly-filled cylinder. "Nowhere obvious. This amalgam was a particularly unlucky fisherwoman caught in the latest storms."

Faustine's jaw actually dropped at that. She knew that making darkbeasts took a host body—you couldn't create something from nothing, even with magic—but that was why the family Villa had a robust kennel, aviary, and dairy farm. Was Markus...

She swallowed past the lump in her throat.

Was Markus using people?

He was drawing a rune over the mangled corpse, now, the air heavy with the metallic taste of magic. And, yeah, now that Faustine was forcing her brain to make sense of it, that did look like a human heart and lungs in the exposed autopsy-like aperture of the corpse's rib cage. That was probably human bones and viscera in the waste disposal bin, too.

Something tapped Faustine's shoulder, and she yelped. It earned her a stern look from her father, holding a set of lab goggles out to her. Faustine sheepishly took them and snapped them over her forehead. The world was cloudier as Faustine followed her father to the far end of the room.

"Proceed," said Ironfang.

Markus nodded and then stuck the hand with the syringe into the corpse's exposed chest. A moment later, he came away with the empty syringe, and set it aside. Muttering to himself, Markus drew another rune in the air over the corpse, his red-gold magic bloody in the faint runelight of his lab.

For a moment, all was dark and quiet. Faustine counted her breaths as she stared at the monster on Markus' lab table. *One, two...*

It moved.

The mangled, headless corpse began to *move.*

Its skin bubbled over like stew set to simmer, furry building blocks rearranging into something resembling... a bird. Yes, it was definitely a bird the longer Faustine watched it shape itself. The fur was melting into feathery wisps, the mangled flesh at its side molding itself into wings.

Markus skittered backwards as the monster spilled over the edges of the table. Its wingspan was huge, and its feet were bubbling into wicked-looking talons bigger than Faustine's dagger. Flesh molded itself like clay atop the monster's shoulders, until a raven-like head coalesced from the black mess of its innards.

And then Faustine was staring into four, bioluminescent green, avian eyes.

"My lord Muninn," Markus whispered.

The bird cawed, and it was like no sound Faustine had ever heard. It was panic and pain and somehow, inexplicably, reminded her of every night she had spent alone in the Villa della Luciana, hunched against her bedroom door in the darkness while some experimental darkbeast rampaged through the house.

And then Ironfang started to laugh. The deep, belly-aching kind that Faustine had never actually heard from him before.

"Well, I'll be damned," said a thin, reedy voice that came from Ironfang's throat but did not belong to him. "Hello, little brother."

CHAPTER THIRTY-TWO

THE MORNING OF THE worst day of the year, Frelia awoke with a keen, stinging sensation in her chest, as though someone had spent the evening slipping needles between her ribs that stabbed her when she tried to take a breath. She stared at the beams in her ceiling, wondering if she could get out of dealing with today by faking an illness or something. But all of her colleagues would know why, and they'd look at her with pity that ranged from genuine to offensive, and besides, Frelia Helm's Grace Valerius was no coward.

So instead of hiding under the covers or getting very, very drunk, Frelia got out of bed, got dressed, and went to teach.

Her students had no idea there was anything terrible about today—least, not most of them. They chattered about the ceremony later, and what they'd be wearing, and what the mess hall would serve at the feast afterwards. Charcuterie and fish swimming in *garum* and dormice weighed at the table and absolutely *nothing* Frelia would have served for a feast, if anyone had still curtseyed and called her 'Your Grace'.

An old anger bloomed in her chest, followed by a deep, dark hurt that threatened to swallow her whole.

And so that night, when she unlocked the Violet Owls' homeroom to wrangle her kids, she was tense as a drawn bowstring. It didn't help that they were making everyone dress up for this farce of a ceremony, either. It would have been one thing to wear normal clothes and organize her kids like this was a tournament rally or something—it was quite another to dress up, do her hair like she cared what it looked like, and pretend like she wanted to be there.

She was wearing blue, though. As close a shade to the real one as she could bully the dexter in Silverwood Town into making. There was no cutout over her right hip, though—she wasn't stupid, even if dressing up didn't feel right without her bloodrune on display.

"Hi, Professor!"

Frelia was snapped, violently, back to her classroom. Ellie, Karina, and Faustine had arrived, two in perfectly-pressed formal Silverwood uniforms, and Karina in one that advertised she'd at least done her best to iron it.

"I like your hair, Professor," Karina said brightly.

"Thanks," said Frelia, who had braided it up and away from her nape in a style she hadn't worn since before the Tyrant's War. She still wasn't sure why, just that she'd felt like it that evening, and the twists and pins still came easily to her battle-scarred fingers.

"You, um." Faustine swallowed audibly. "You aren't wearing any makeup?"

It was easier to just lie. "Didn't have time."

Ellie's eyes widened. "Do you want to do it real quick? I have some touch-up stuff with me, and your skin tone is close enough to Karina's that it wouldn't look clownish or anything on you."

Part of Frelia wanted to ask the teenager whether the Owls had ever seen their Kaldiri swordmaster wear makeup. She knew the kids just thought they were helping—Volsinii women never went anywhere without something stuck to their faces, especially to something formal.

But the other part of Frelia was so hair-triggered right now that she just wanted to scream that it wouldn't matter in about two hours.

"No." Frelia forced herself to sound even. "Thank you, though."

"Are you sure?" Faustine asked. "It's no—"

"Do not," Frelia interrupted sharply, "question me *again*."

Faustine actively scuttled backwards, and Frelia had approximately half a second to feel bad about it before Christel and Siegmund burst through the classroom door. Their formal uniforms were passable, although Siegmund's was inexplicably covered in white cat hair.

"You look nice, Professor!" Christel called over.

Frelia tried not to sound annoyed. "Thank you, Christel."

Valente showed up a few minutes later, his hair neatly combed and formal uniform perfect in every line. He looked like a miniature version of the general Frelia had seen across many a battlefield, in the war, and she wondered if Valente had grown up attending Victory Day parties like this every year.

She tried not to scowl at him, she really did.

Owen was, as usual, the last to arrive, his uniform jacket misbuttoned. Ellie made him stop and fix it, which Owen did, blushing so hard even his ears were turning red. The Professor part of Frelia's brain wondered whether he'd gotten his shit together to ask her to the winter ball yet (having heard him talking about it with Christel and Siegmund more than once over the past month), but the part of her that had once been General Valerius was too loud for such frivolity.

Across campus, the bells began to toll the hour, and Frelia barked, "Form up."

The Violet Owls fell in line alphabetically, except for Faustine, who stood at their head in her house prefect's half cloak. Frelia drew in a deep breath, her hand curling on the hilt of her sword, and then went to take her place at the head of the line.

***

The Silverwood ballroom had been done up in violently crimson banners and screaming gold accents for the Victory Day ceremony. Frelia's eye watered as she led the Violet Owls to their assigned seats up near the front, a row of chairs half of them had helped put there during this past week. The entire ballroom had been set up for a long night of speeches and posturing and Frelia already had a headache.

The dull pressure behind her eyes didn't let up when the farce of a ceremony began properly.

"Let us take a moment to bow our heads in prayer," said Markus, in a combination of words Frelia was pretty sure had been written for him by Ironfang.

The bastard actually waited for people to do that before continuing. As though he hadn't slept through every single High Holy Day ceremony they'd attended, in school.

"Lady Midnight, we are grateful for your guidance and understanding," Markus said and Frelia couldn't stop the horrified glare she sent him.

Not that he could see it, all the way up on the dais, but seriously? Lady *Midnight,* the understanding goddess? No, that was Lady Twilight, but Saints-forbid the Unseen's little puppet acknowledge Lady Midnight's divine sisters.

It was strange, almost, how easily Vendrick's explanation of cults and cold wars fit right into the bullshit she already knew to be true.

Markus babbled on for a few more minutes in a bastardization of a Triad prayer and ended with how grateful he was for everyone's resplendent presence and if they would please rise for His Imperial Majesty.

Ironfang's broad frame drew all eyes in the room to him like a lodestone in a forge. He was dressed in an impeccably-tailored waistcoat and long, silk coat that probably cost more than Frelia's entire wardrobe. He took stock of Silverwood just like he had the day of his arrival—a general sizing up the opposing side—and stepped up to the newly vacant dais.

The moment their eyes locked, all the blood drained from Frelia's face, leaving her cold, wary, and standing in a muddy field in Grimsdalr Territory ten years ago.

Spirits' Fen was alive with booming cannon fire and mages' lightning, the sulfuric smell of the land threatening to choke them all. Rain smacked against her face and mud caked her calves as Frelia felled Volsinii after Volsinii, slicing and parrying with none of the finesse her father had drilled into her. This was spite, and survival, and nothing short of death would keep her from splitting open that damn hellbeast whose wings blotted out the moon.

"Going somewhere?" called a voice.

Frelia immediately yanked the Valerius Shield up into a defensive guard, bringing up her blade to bear. She had waited all Rebellion for a crack at General Ironfang, and he would not stand in her way now.

"It was fifteen years ago that our brave knights had punched deep into enemy territory," Ironfang began from the podium, without preamble. "Winter was coming, and we were locked in a siege at the city of Skjöldr. If the battle was not decided soon, the brutal Kaldiri winter would decide it for us."

"We have the food to outlast them." Thera thumped a fist on the war table, hard enough to rattle the maps and inkpots spread across the rest of it. "I say let them starve at our gates."

"We only have supplies if they don't poison the Ivory Channel," King Hägen had said—and oh, how strange it was that the boy Frelia had grown up beside was finally king, in the worst possible way. "And I wouldn't put it past them to dump garmur corpses upstream."

Cillian's laugh was dark. "We've given them plenty of the damned things."

"Volsinii aren't built for winter," Frelia said, feeling like her da even as she said it. "If they haven't retreated already, they're going to try to take the city before the first snows."

"Agreed," said Edmund. "There will be an assault."

"We should try to negotiate," Hägen insisted. "Surrender is better than annihilation."

He left unspoken which side would give in—the besieged, or the summer children.

The memory was sharp and intrusive, as though it had been called up by her bloodrune. But that wouldn't make sense—Frelia never saw her own memories, that way.

"And but for the grace of Lady Midnight and the darkbeasts, we would have lost the city entirely," Ironfang continued. "Our beastminders bred darkbeasts just as quickly as the Kaldiri could kill them."

As Cillian's charger rounded the bend to the southern plaza, Frelia counted six garmur already in the city, as well as a few more blasting through the pitch now rolling down the southern gate.

He wasted no time drawing a rune across her shoulders, steering with his knees and lifting Frelia's shield off her back so he could touch her actual body. Frelia felt the familiar tug of his magic behind her navel, even as the press of his fingers was dulled by her armored coat and his gauntlets.

Cillian paused just before completing the rune. "Now?"

"No." Frelia kicked at his horse's flanks.

The charger whinnied and cantered on, its long-legged stride eating up the last of the road at a truly frightening clip. A few more breaths and they'd be in range of the garmr.

"Now?" Cillian's fingers were insistent where they'd paused against her back. "I'll overshoot, at this rate."

For a moment, Frelia said nothing. Even at top speed, she could just begin to make out the garmr's ever-burning green eyes, now zeroing in on the two humans charging at them like suicidal idiots,

"Now!"

Cillian dragged his fingers down sharply to complete the rune, and then Frelia was no longer in his saddle.

"But the Kaldiri made a fatal error," said Ironfang, and he smiled. "They underestimated us."

Frelia wanted to spit in his eyes, and the scar on her chest suddenly spiked with fire.

"They underestimated our resolve, our knights, and the rightness of our cause. When the Queenmakers punched through the southern guard, it would have been a victory in and of itself, but the battle did not end there."

Ironfang nodded to Vendrick, sitting in the front row with his spine stiffer than a snarling dog's, and to Markus, who preened in the attention like a puffed-up bird of prey.

"Princess Octavia, Lady Midnight rest her well, led one last, desperate charge through the city streets. She and her Queenmakers sliced their way through to the heart of the city—Castle Skjöldr."

No, no, no, Frelia did *not* want to hear this. She didn't want to hear how Octavia had killed Hägen and then Markus and Athos del Priore had probably mopped up the Einnaska house knights and Vendrick had probably murdered the remains of the King's Council who weren't actively fighting because that's what his family were for. How Irirangi of the Kingfisher Clan and Roland Sferrazza had probably stood guard at the throne room doors until the rest of the army could reconvene.

"They first downed the Tyrant King's Margravine and Countess," Ironfang said.

Snatches of Thera's burnished, copper hair and wyvern scale-style armor flashed in Frelia's mind. Sticky red pooling beneath her as her blood soaked into the tiled floors of Castle Skjöldr, where she'd run as a child and celebrated her engagement as an adult.

By the time the Queenmakers hit the castle, Geir Traust was already dead, out near the north gate. Blonde hair splattered with blood where someone hacked her head off and stuck it on a pike to stare, unseeing, at the winter sky. Her little sister Ulfhild would obviously survive long enough to have Christel, but Frelia had always figured she'd died there, too.

Frelia mentally scowled. *Bitch should have fought in the Northern Rebellion, then.*

"And when they rounded on the Tyrant King himself," Ironfang continued, "they took his head from his deceitful shoulders."

Frelia had known—in fact, she'd known for years now—that the Volsinii blamed the Tyrant's War on the Einnaska family. On their bloodrune that demanded your obedience whether you wanted to give it or not, especially if you were bloodruned, yourself. In previous eras, they might have even had a half-decent case.

But Hägen?

Hägen would 'have been a fucking cleric, if he weren't the Prince of Kaldr. He'd still trained with them, a white mage in every aspect, up to his elbows in blood in the complete opposite way that an Einnaska King was supposed to be. He had been too kind for his own good, and probably would've been an excellent king in just about any other timeline. Not to mention, he didn't even have the Einnaska Bloodrune. It was rare that it didn't manifest in a direct descendant of the Saints, but it happened.

So the entire Volsinii reason for war was bullshit, and all the Krakenguard had known it.

But what Frelia had wanted to know for fifteen years now was the *actual* reason why the Imperium had slaughtered her homeland. Volsinii had lost the Winter War, sure, but that wasn't why, or they'd have stopped when Traust Territory fell.

They'd wanted something. Land, maybe? Resources? Farmers? Frelia would probably respect the Senate more if they'd just come right out and say one of the usual reasons people went to war, instead of pretending like they were better than it.

"And with his death, the Queenmakers restored peace to the mainland Imperium," Ironfang was saying, "and the brutal Einnaska Kings could suffocate our land no longer."

Wait.

Einnaska.

It was the first actual name Ironfang had used in the entire speech. Probably partially because it was the lynchpin of their propaganda efforts, but if the Unseen were collecting bloodrunes via the Bloodrune Hunters, and King Njal and Princess Reina were dead by the time the Battle for Skjöldr happened, and Markus had been one of the ones to kill Hägen...

There would have been blood that Markus could have collected. Hägen had never manifested the family bloodrune, it was true, but his children would still have the potential for it. Their father was directly descended from Saint Einnaska.

It was as though someone had splashed an icy bucket of dread over Frelia's head. Her blood froze in her veins, and she stared, increasingly unseeingly, at Ironfang up on the dais.

The Unseen had wanted the Einnaska Bloodrune.

And she would be willing to bet anything that they'd gotten it, when Hägen died.

Did Vendrick know? Did he *suspect?* Why hadn't he fucking said something during Gyastfylnacht? Helheim, why was he a fucking Queenmaker, if he knew that? Had he known that back then?

Frelia needed to know whether she ought to strangle him.

"Professor?" whispered Christel at Frelia's left. "You're crying."

"Pay attention," Frelia muttered, dragging her hand across her face to scrub the weakness from it.

Christel didn't say anything else, but they did carefully sneak a handkerchief out of their pants pocket, and set it silently on Frelia's lap.

CHAPTER THIRTY-THREE

FRELIA MANAGED TO GET the Violet Owls to the mess hall without losing her shit, but she was full up on posturing today.

"Faustine's in charge," Frelia said the instant they rounded the corner to the mess hall. "Mind your manners, and all that shit."

"You're not staying for the feast, professor?" Faustine asked.

"I would sooner gouge my other eye out."

The Violet Owls flinched, one after another like a row of purpure dominos, and all Frelia could feel was the eyes of her dead *volchya* on her back.

The night was cold and calm as Frelia slunk across the campus. The oil urns burned so brightly on their pillars that their light left a little halo announcing snow was not far off. It was the sort of bitter, blue cold that Frelia had grown up in, learned to fight in, expected to die in.

It was perfect for beating the shit out of training dummies, so that's where Frelia went. She didn't even bother to change clothes.

Unterhau, oberhau, zornhau, mutieren. Frelia smashed through her training regimen with a fire she hadn't felt in a long time. She could almost hear her da lecturing her from beyond the grave: *it is the Valerius'*

duty to guard king and kin, even at the cost of ourselves. Guard up, little
wolf; you call that oberhau?

She had gotten too comfortable at Silverwood, Frelia realized the
longer she worked. Gotten too used to three hot meals a day, and an
actual bed. Too used to lower-order concerns like getting grades in on
time and whether her curriculum was appropriately paced and whether
her students would focus on class when there were more exciting things
on their horizons.

Nobody was going to die if Frelia Helm's Grace Valerius didn't show
up for work, and what was she supposed to do with that?

There is no peace, the old poem went, *even in death.*

"Well, why the fuck not?" Frelia muttered, just as her bloodrune
activated.

She sheared the training dummy's head clean off, and the
bucket-helmet went tumbling into the dirt. For a moment, she just stared
at it, too tired to deal with reattaching it right then and trying to shake
off the arcane haze her family power always left behind.

"Why not what, sorry?" came a painfully familiar voice from over her
shoulder.

It startled her, and she pivoted to striking range. And there,
half-hidden in the gloom, was Vendrick.

His eyebrows raised slightly as he studied the tip of the bastard sword.
"Good evening to you, too."

All at once, the raw anger fell away, and it left behind a hoarfrost
hollowness that ached like no war wound she'd ever weathered.

No war wound, except for him.

"Hey," Frelia croaked. "Piss off."

Vendrick folded his hands behind his back and Frelia could only see
Ironfang in the movement. "Why not what, sorry?" Vendrick said again.

"I don't want to talk to you." Frelia turned back to the training
dummy and tried to drum up enough fury to cover the gaping holes

he left in her emotional armor. It was like trying to shove your own intestines back inside your gut and calling it surgery.

"I'm sure," said Vendrick, "but what do you take me for, a man who grew up with brothers?"

Frelia resisted the urge to snort, just barely, by stabbing into the headless training dummy. She yanked out the *stechen* strike with all the force left in her, and nearly wrenched the stuffing out of the dummy.

"You seem upset," Vendrick observed.

"Of course I'm fucking upset." Frelia's accent was growing thicker, like falling snow piling atop itself. "I am *always* fucking upset. And it's never going to matter. So go back to your party and leave me to the ghosts where I belong."

He didn't move.

Frelia made an exasperated noise. "Did I stutter somehow?"

"No," said Vendrick, "I'm simply not leaving."

Frelia's hands shook on the hilt of her sword, like the rumbling beneath a volcano on the Rippling Isles, or the low tumble of blood against bone when a garmr was near. She jammed the tip of her bastard sword into the training sand, grasping at the hilt to keep steady.

"You do not owe the dead a debt of misery, Frelia."

She glared at him, half-melded into shadow like he always was, and something so deep and sharp twisted in her chest she felt as if she'd vomit.

"And, let's just get this out of the way—I'm working off assumptions, here," Vendrick added. "But I don't think anyone you've lost would like you to think so."

"Then you know nothing," she hissed.

"Not about fathers," Vendrick agreed, "but friends? I lost those too, in the war. And I can promise you that Octavia Nova would not want me to remain in miserable mourning just because she isn't here to help me organize Clarissa's engagement party or babysit her children."

He exhaled, and the frost of his breath rose like smoke towards the stars.

"Octavia would want me to carry on," he said. "And I doubt I'm wrong in guessing Cillian and Thera Grimsdalr would tell you the same. And so would Hägen Einnaska, Brigitte Konstantin, and your father."

"You have no *fucking* right—"

"You're correct," Vendrick said, so matter-of-factly that Frelia startled. "I don't."

He shrugged at Frelia's silence, and it struck her as the most honest gesture he'd ever made.

"But I'm Volsinii," he added, "and we don't wait around for someone to give us the right to do anything—we walk right up to the Senate and demand it. At swordpoint, if necessary. If we didn't, Ascalon would still be overrun with tenement slums whose occupants cannot vote, and..." He shuddered. "...taxmen.

"So yes, I have no right to stand here and care about your wellbeing. I'm aware. I'm just doing it anyway."

Wellbeing? *Wellbeing?* Was he out of his Saints-damned mind? Frelia's entire person was held together with gauze, booze, and spite—wellbeing was a concern for women who had never seen war, and didn't talk to the dead.

"Now look me in the eye, Frelia Helm's Grace Valerius," Vendrick said, soft as a spider in its web, "and tell me I'm wrong."

The arrogant bastard! Who the hell did he think he was, lecturing her about the dead?

"I died at Skjöldr," Frelia hissed. "And I died again at Spirits' Fen. My ghost has been haunting my life since then, and you think you can just waltz in here and dictate how I grieve?"

"Of course I don't," Vendrick said, fast and hurt as a struck viper. "My point is—you *didn't* die. At any of those battles. You are not a ghost, even if you feel like one."

He detached himself from the shadows of the proving ground and for the first time in Frelia honestly didn't know how long, she saw him. Not the shadows he slunk through or the silhouette he constructed from mages' coats and perfect posture, but *him*. The man beneath all that. The boy she'd known, once.

The ghost of a man who was still alive.

"So fight me," he said. "No swords, no magic, just... you and me. And let's see how solid you really are."

Something in Frelia's chest wobbled. "Are you insane? I'd kick your ass."

"I appreciate the vote of confidence. And I can assure you that, despite everyone's best efforts, I'm still sane."

He curled his fingers into fists and brought them to his chin in a classic boxing stance. His form was passable, despite probably having last had to grapple as a student himself.

"Now are we dueling, or what?"

"Okay..." Frelia let go of her bastard sword, still freestanding in the sand. "But I warned you."

She curled her own aching fingers into fists, and struck.

Vendrick dodged the first punch, his eyes going wide at the sudden assault, but Frelia's next punch caught him in the ribs. He wheezed and brought his arms closer to cover up, but those acid green eyes were bright and clear.

Good. He could take a hit.

Frelia loosed a torrent of everything that had been building in her since this morning—no, before that. Since Spirits' Fen, since the Battle for Skjöldr, since the Tyrant's War had been declared, since Silverwood, since birth. Frelia Helm's Grace Valerius had been a disgrace long before she'd lost her title. She just hadn't known it.

But there was a certain clarity in motion, a peace in occupying the rage screaming in her blood long enough to think. Part of her wanted to smile—grappling was, after all, her first love—but the louder part was screaming the same question over and over and over again:

"What do I do with it, Vendrick?"

Without the icy rage coursing through her and a bastard sword in her hands, Frelia became acutely aware that she was not built for any of this. Introspection, grief, the weight of her ghosts—they would drown her in an ocean of regrets.

Vendrick looked like he knew the feeling.

"What do you want to do with it?" he asked.

It caught her so off guard, she froze long enough for him to land a surprisingly solid blow on her solar plexus. Frelia coughed as breath whooshed out of her lungs, and she struggled to breathe.

"The fuck kind of question is that?" Frelia wheezed.

"All other things being equal," Vendrick said, "what would you do, with your ghosts?"

She stared at him so long, Vendrick almost dropped his guard. She watched him think about it, his hands lowering towards his chin before he stiffened up again.

Words came to her then. Not hers, but her battle brother's: "Take back Kjell," she said quietly, almost like a prayer. "And then the mountain passes, and my family's barrows. And then one day my kids would go sledding with Cillian's on the giant hill behind Valerius Lodge, and my da would teach them how to find the best shields for it. Thera would probably be weaving together druid charms out of the sled dogs' blown-out coats, and Hägen would be trying to help and probably just end up playing with the puppies."

They exchanged blows again, nothing landing, nothing changing.

Then Vendrick said, so gently it hurt, "Frelia, that's not what you do with ghosts. That's what you do with the living."

What's the difference? She wanted to say, but she knew. There would never be a world where that afternoon came to pass, not even if she joined them all in Solivallr one day. Any children she had would never meet their grandfather, their uncles, their aunts, their mother's *volchya*.

Something wet fell across her cheek, and Frelia scrabbled at it with calloused fingers. They came away bloody, and for a moment, Frelia stared at her fist. She'd wrapped her hands before she'd begun training, knew they were red and chapped from the cold, but hadn't realized she'd worn the bandages to bloody ribbons. Blisters and broken calluses stared back at her, accusatory.

A debt of misery you will never pay.

She tried to bring her fists up again, to grit her teeth and fall back into middle guard, but all she saw was something not quite like pain crossing Vendrick's carefully-crafted neutral face.

"Where is Hägen buried?" Frelia asked, before Vendrick could say something worse.

"I don't know."

Frelia's blood froze in her veins and she stared, uncomprehending, at the Imperator's former Spymaster. Oh, this was worse. This was so much worse.

"What do you mean you don't know," she managed after an excruciating moment. "It's your job to know."

"It was my job." Vendrick made a useless gesture with a hand; Frelia could have broken his jaw in the opening. "I was with the rearguard when Castle Skjöldr fell. That's where I ran into you and Cillian, if you'll recall."

"Barely." Frelia had been so hazy with pain by that point, Cillian'd had to hold her in his saddle between his knees and elbows and pray he didn't need to lance something.

"I figured Hägen would be paraded in a Triumph and executed." The softness in Vendrick's voice couldn't dull the sharp edges of his words. "I found out he'd died at the same time everyone else did—via an announcement three days later."

Frelia didn't know what she was supposed to be looking at, anymore, and so she pressed forward, looking for gaps in his defenses she could crash a fist into. "So you never saw his body?"

"No," Vendrick confirmed. "And I've spent a good amount of manpower over the years looking for it—and yours, might I add—because—"

"Of our bloodrunes," Frelia interrupted. "*Ja,* I know."

Her hand went, absently, to her right side, just beneath her ribs. Her father, her best friends, her family, her country—all of them were dead because of the power that slept on her skin and in her blood. She'd led hundreds, if not thousands, to their deaths to defend king and country, sure, but apparently it had also been to defend her.

That... wasn't how it was supposed to go. The Valerius Family was the shield of Kaldr, and always had been.

"Not just the bloodrunes," Vendrick said, and Frelia flinched.

"One life, or two, or three, or three-thousand," she muttered. "How are we supposed to calculate the worth of that?"

"By triage." Vendrick had stopped trying to punch her, now, and his voice was thickening. "Who's causing the most damage? Who has the most likely chance of survival? Who will infect the rest if we don't amputate?"

"Me, apparently." The realization was slipping down her spine and into her pores like acid. "Dammit, Vendrick, what do I do with you?"

He was so startled he missed the next punch she threw and it landed solidly. She froze at their sudden proximity, and Vendrick's hand fell to trap hers against his chest. She couldn't read the look he was giving her, and wasn't sure she wanted to.

"If forgiveness is 'I see all you've done, and I am choosing to see better in you,'" Frelia said to his waistcoat buttons, "and letting go is 'I see what you've done, and I am choosing not to let it hurt me any more,' but everything hurts, and everyone can do better, then... how am I supposed to be anything but angry?"

For a long moment, Vendrick didn't say anything, and Frelia could see the rise and fall of his chest beneath his jacket.

"Grief is the price we pay for love," he said.

Frelia's eye narrowed. "That's from *Men of the Forest.*"

"Well, it's true! Do you think I've wasted a single moment grieving my father?"

It struck her harder than his fists ever had, and Frelia froze. "You... haven't?"

"Of course not," Vendrick scoffed. "He was a brutal tyrant of a man whose faults are too numerous to bother with, at the moment. My point is—"

"You didn't love him," Frelia interrupted, "so there was nothing to grieve?"

Vendrick's jaw snapped shut. "Well I might have put it a bit more eloquently, but yes. Essentially."

For a moment, Frelia stood at the Battle for Skjöldr again, her left eye bleeding down the front of her armored coat, Cillian's breastplate digging into her back as he held her upright. And there, across the smoking battlefield and standing between her and freedom, was Vendrick, in Caecillion purple and with his spellbook in hand.

Don't hold back, she'd written him when war was declared. *I won't.*

"I grieved you," she whispered to her clenched fists. "Cut you from my heart and didn't look back."

"Then you got further than I did." Vendrick wasn't looking at her, either. "I wasn't allowed to grieve you any more than I was allowed to love you."

The world had gone so still she could hear his wild heartbeat.

"Is that why you're here now?" Frelia asked. "To grieve?"

"Oh, no," he said, and Frelia had approximately half a second to feel gutted before he kept talking. "That's because I can't fix that Hägen Einnaska is dead, and I can't fix this bloody mess of an empire, and I can't change what I did in the war or whose side I was on."

Frelia's head jerked up, but he was staring at her so intently she forgot what she'd been about to say.

"I can't do anything about Ironfang being Imperator, or being here, or what he did during the Northern Rebellion. And I can play the spider in this long game of war, but I can't actively change a single thing right now."

His neutral expression cracked up the middle, like Frelia had struck a porcelain mask, and suddenly there was rage and grief there that rivaled her own.

"But I *can*," Vendrick continued, "take a few punches. So that's what I'm going to do until you stop hurting yourself."

"Why?"

"It's the one thing I can do anything about, right now."

"That's your brilliant strategy?" It sounded too simple. "Do one useless thing because you can?"

"And then the next one," Vendrick murmured, nodding, "and then the next one, until all the 'one things' become many, and the Imperator himself fears your next move, because..." He trailed off, and then, inexplicably, smiled.

It was breathtaking, in the haloed lamplight.

"Because...?" Frelia pressed.

He caught her eye again, snared her in acid green and white-hot intention. "The fight is not over so long as you breathe."

Out of all her memories, all her ghosts, all her broken things, the only thing that jumped to Frelia's mind now was that day beside Lake Silverwood in the spring of their third year.

One thing I can fix. Just one.

She tugged him close with shaking hands and sealed their fates.

Vendrick made a surprised noise somewhere in his throat when their lips connected, and then pulled her tightly against him. His kiss was insidiously soft and breathlessly fierce, and Frelia would have been content to drown in it. When she pulled back a moment later, Vendrick stared at her in thunderstruck wonder.

"That's... not quite what I meant," he said.

Embarrassed fire erupted across her face. "Do you want me to stop?"

He tipped her chin up towards him—"Absolutely not."—and cut off the world with another kiss.

He angled her chin experimentally, trying to find just the right way to slot their lips together. He smelled like woodsmoke and parchment, pleasantly earthen and deeply masculine, and Frelia wanted it to live in her lungs. At first, she was annoyed that he kept fidgeting. But then Vendrick found it, and she stilled, her hands now resting on his chest, their end goal forgotten.

To her dying breath, Frelia would have no idea what 'it' was. But suddenly kissing him felt like melting into the warmth of a bath after a long day's ride, or sinking into the cushions before the fireplace in Valerius Lodge during the winter holidays. It was the most natural thing in the world, kissing Vendrick. As if she'd done it a hundred times, a thousand different ways.

As if she'd been made to.

Vendrick's voice was raw when they finally broke apart, and he stared at her like he couldn't believe she was real. "Why the fuck didn't I do that twenty years ago?"

"How the fuck would this have worked twenty years ago?" Frelia pitched her voice lower to mimic him. "'Hey, Octavia, I can't brood until seven-thirty like usual, I have a date with Hägen Einnaska's duchess.'"

Vendrick laughed softly, his breath ghosting across the bare skin of her face. He couldn't mimic a Kaldiri accent nearly so well as she could a

Volsinii, but he tried: "'Hey, Cillian, don't get into any trouble I can't fix until tomorrow, yeah? I'm busy tonight with Octavia Nova's left hand.'"

He swallowed her laughter when he kissed her again. A quick study in all things, Vendrick was already getting better at this, already learning what made her dig encouraging fingers into his back and fit herself closer to him. But there was so much between them, too many layers, too many things unsaid, and Frelia felt a little like she might burst out of her skin.

So she said, "Mine or yours?"

For a half-second, Vendrick tilted his head like a confused dog. Then understanding blossomed across his face alongside a violent blush that was Goddesses-damn charming.

"There's a right way to do this, you know, and I—"

"*Ja,* don't care," Frelia interrupted. "I've decided; let's go to mine."

CHAPTER THIRTY-FOUR

THE INSTANT THE DOOR to her room shut behind them, Vendrick was back on her with such single-minded intent that it made Frelia's brain cease its higher functioning. All she knew was that she wanted his warmth back, *now,* and that Vendrick was shaking, just a little, like he was nervous. His hands shook as they divested themselves of sword, spellbook, and boots.

"Off with these damn things," Frelia ordered, tugging at one of his gloves.

Vendrick's laugh was hoarse and low, and it sent slow, rolling warmth into Frelia's bones. "Far be it from me to argue, my lady."

He put their lips back together as he tugged his stupid leather gloves off, and the instant his hands were free, they found their way to her face. His scarred fingers spread across the contours of her cheekbones, and a sigh escaped from her mouth into his. He tasted like Volsinii wine and ozone, like all the magic he'd ever cast. He traced the rounded angles of her face gently, like a sculptor studying a masterwork, and slid a hand into her hair where he could get around her hairpins.

Then his thumb snagged on the eyepatch strap below her ear, and Frelia's hand snapped up to catch his in a vice grip. "Don't touch that."

"I'm so sorry." At once, Vendrick jerked his hands back in a gesture of surrender.

Frelia searched his face for a moment, but found nothing but sincerity. "It ties here, and here." She tugged it back into its proper place over her ruined eye, and pointed out the knots. "Just... leave those alone."

"I will do that." Vendrick nodded, and he was just looking at her again, like he couldn't believe she was real. "It's whatever you're comfortable with, love."

It's not pet names, Frelia wanted to say, but that one really did sound alright, coming from him. Maybe it was just the accent. She'd figure it out later.

Their next few kisses were shier, quieter—sweet, even. It wasn't a word anyone would have ever used to describe Vendrick Caecillion, and yet, Frelia could think of no other word for him now. The urge to reach out surged through her, to tangle her fingers in his dark, brown hair, and find out exactly what would happen when a man this tightly wound came undone.

Next went their cloaks, her heavy mantle and his dark one. Frelia's dexterous hands made much easier work of his throat clasp than his made of hers, but that might just have been because she was sitting in his lap, now.

She pressed her face into the crook of his neck, trailing hot, open-mouthed kisses down towards his collar. And then one of them slipped, and Frelia squeaked as they went tumbling into her bedding. She was no longer sitting in his lap, but sprawled across his chest too. Their bodies realigned, and Vendrick reached up to push her hair—glaringly, gloriously black once again—out of her eye. He touched his forehead to hers again and breathed with her, for a moment.

"You're magnificent," he mumbled, "you know that? Absolutely stunning."

Frelia rolled her eye. "I am literally already on top of you."

"So?" His bare fingers—blackened at the tips as though stained with ink—traced the curve of her scarred cheek, and down her neck. "I have nearly two decades of compliments I owe you, so I—ah *ha,* I knew that blush had to travel."

He pressed a soft kiss up into her throat, and Frelia hissed his name into the fevered darkness.

He pulled back, just far enough to look at her. "Was that a good 'Vendrick' or a bad 'Vendrick?' I want to learn."

Frelia made an embarrassed, irritated noise and buried her face in the crook of his neck again. "I will end you," she threatened, half-heartedly.

"Got it." He smiled against her cheek. "Good Vendrick."

He pulled her to his chest again, pressing feather-light kisses wherever he could reach, content to simply let her hide in the warm darkness with him.

Frelia should've known better than to take the bait.

"I'd really been hoping I hadn't shot all the nerve endings in my fingers." Vendrick's voice was shadowy silk, right near her ear, and damn it all, she could feel herself falling apart in his hands. "If you ever let me touch you, I wanted to know exactly how it felt."

Frelia pulled away to stare at him, her stomach whirling like she was in free fall off a garmr's back. "You've *been thinking* about this?"

Vendrick's eyes flicked away for a moment, as though he were debating his answer. "Literally every day we've spoken since alchemy class."

Stunned, Frelia began to laugh. A bemused, jagged thing that oh, no, he was going to misinterpret if she didn't catch it fast. "I want to tell you to shut up or I'm getting up," she said hurriedly, "but I've done the same thing."

Vendrick's blooming hurt broke when he grinned again. "Have you, now?"

And then he flipped them.

Suddenly the mattress was pressed against her back, and it was his green eyes staring down at her, half-shrouded in brown hair, his weight bearing down comfortably against her. She should have felt trapped, and yet some deep, instinctive part of her purred with satisfaction.

Had she really just been yelling at him about Hägen Einnaska half an hour ago? It felt like a lifetime.

"So are they?" Frelia asked, tapping her fingers against his ribs. "Shot, that is."

Vendrick's hands spread against her waist, thumbs dragging across the sweat-stiffened fabric in muted wonder that left fire in its wake. "Somewhat, but I'll make it work."

She wasn't sure what possessed her to reach out, to lay a hand against the sharp edges of his cheekbone and murmur, "Good."—except maybe the need to get her tongue back in his mouth.

His facial expression softened, then, its hazier edges falling away into concern as his hand came up to meet hers. "Frelia..." He seemed to struggle for a moment to come up with the words he needed. "...do we need to slow down?"

Frelia was no longer falling apart, it was simply done. Whatever soft underbelly he'd been looking for now exposed, her armor cracked open to expose the spongy, squishy parts within. She would die to a Volsinii in the stupidest possible way, with only herself to blame.

"I started it," she said, somewhat distantly.

A slew of emotions flickered across Vendrick's face, too quickly for Frelia to read, before settling back on that soft concern that felt so out of place when directed at her. He started to say something, but she missed it amongst the first strains of the Traust War Song as they slipped into her mind from somewhere far away.

> *Little wolf, from where do you*
> *hail?*

The hour is late, and thin is the
Veil.
Little wolf, oh, why do you howl?
What have you seen, out amongst
the owls?

The requiem song had rung throughout Valerius Territory when her
warriors had returned from the Winter War—for not all of them did.

"*Frelia, you need to come out of there eventually!*" *Thera shouted from*
just outside her bedroom door.

"*Do not!*" *Frelia's child-self argued back. Her voice was thick with tears*
both shed and unshed, her tiny body still full of more rage than sense.

A heavy thud came from the other side of the door, and then Thera's
voice came from about the same level, through the door—"I know you're
sad, Frey. I am, too."

"*No you don't know!*" *Frelia howled back.*

"*The grown-ups keep saying they're sorry,*" *Thera added, patient as ever*
in the face of the little Valerius' fury. "*But I don't get why. They're not the*
ones who killed Kjeld and Diarm—"

Frelia slammed her fist into the door, and she hoped Thera startled on
the other side. "*Shut up; shut up!*"

"*Frelia!*"

She blinked a few times, and suddenly she was no longer hunched
against the door of her childhood bedroom, but fetched up against a man
she really had no business being so close to.

Merciful Goddesses, that's right. She was a disgrace.

"Frelia," Vendrick said again, much more quietly. "You're safe."

Slowly, tenderly, he brushed the hair from her face again, and the
brazen worry Frelia saw in those eyes was more terrifying than any of her
ghosts. But it was only when he swept a gentle thumb across the arch of
her cheekbone that Frelia realized she was crying.

His voice was velvet soft. "Talk to me, love. I'm here."

And for a thousand reasons, in a thousand ways, Frelia Valerius should not be. Her shield was breaking, unable to hold off one more onslaught.

"Get off me." She didn't feel angry; she felt like broken glass.

And he did, immediately putting space between them. But his facial expression didn't change, and Frelia was suddenly in desperate need of air and space and a weapon. *Where the fuck is my sword?* She shot to her feet with the explosive force that had decapitated many a Volsinii knight, padding barefoot across the room.

Yet somehow, unthinkably, Vendrick was faster. "Frelia..." He pinned her sword to the desk where she'd thrown it. "...are you having a panic attack?"

She froze, but her heart kept pounding in her ears and her instincts kept screaming at her to run. "Is that what this is?"

"I'm not in your head, but it appears so to me." Vendrick's voice was still soft and light, but devoid of the warmth from before—a voice used to soothe territorial wyvern mothers and spooked war horses, not admire a lover. "Why don't you sit down a moment?"

Frelia shook her head. "No, no, no, I need to move, I need to—"

"Frelia," Vendrick interrupted. "You don't need to run from me." His hand twitched at his side, like he no longer knew what to do with it. "I'm not here to hurt you."

"Don't you dare." Frelia flinched away from him.

Pain crossed his expression, more than Frelia had ever seen—or perhaps, more than he'd ever let her see. "Sit down, Frelia. Please."

She staggered, felt the backs of her knees hit the bedframe and collapse her onto the end of the bed. A few moments later, she felt a cloak settle over her shoulders, and then Vendrick was crouching before her at the foot of her bed.

"Focus on your breathing." Vendrick didn't touch her, and it was impossible to sort out whether she wanted him to. "And I can talk about nothing, if it helps?"

Frelia tugged the cloak across her heart, and realized it was Vendrick's. Something in her chest squeezed so hard she saw stars "I don't know if it does or doesn't. I think I've always been alone, when this happens."

"I'm... so sorry," Vendrick said after a moment—though for what, Frelia didn't know. There were too many options.

She couldn't look at him—or anything else in her room, for that matter. The small space was devoid of anything one might consider personal—no half-read books on the side table, no knickknacks or portraits of family or friends. She did have a small, clockwork alarm, but that was the only thing that said someone actually lived here, and it wasn't merely one of the empty dorm rooms.

It was as if a ghost lived here, not a living woman.

"I think I'm done, here," she finally said. "You don't have to stay."

Vendrick made an exasperated, affectionate noise. "In case I didn't make it clear, just now—I'm rather fond of you. Sort of always have been."

It echoed between them.

And then there were eyes burrowing into Frelia's blind side. "I'm... sorry?" she said.

"That's not something you need to apologize for. If anything, I should be."

She snapped her eye shut. "I must be losing it. Am I honoring the dead or drinking myself stupid on the anniversary of the Fall of Skjöldr?" She made a useless, frustrated gesture. "No, of course not, I'm making out with a Queenmaker. What the fuck is wrong with me?"

She wondered why she couldn't hear Cillian's ghost, or her father's, or Thera's. Maybe they were busy haunting other people, for once, or the Traust War Song had calmed them.

Or maybe she just had no idea what any of them would say about this.

"There's nothing wrong with you," Vendrick said firmly. "You're still breathing, aren't you?"

And wasn't that just the problem?

Frelia tried to sift through her thoughts for something to say. But they swirled and eddied around her, as though she'd waded into a stream to catch a fish darting beneath the waters. What had Vendrick told her to focus on, again? Her breathing?

It was one thing for Frelia to leave. She did it all the time—at pubs, after class, around campfires—usually without announcing her departure. It was easier that way, less fuss; Cillian even dubbed it the Valerius goodbye, once upon a time. But it was quite another for everyone else to leave, that way. Cillian had done it; Thera had done it; Hägen had done it; her father, her mother, Diarmuid. Countess Traust and Margravine Grimsdalr. All of her Silverwood classmates she'd graduated with, and then met again a year later across the battlefield.

She hadn't actually said goodbye to any of them.

Frelia shut her eye, mentally tracing over the melody of the Traust War Song. For the twins, and Hägen, and her da, and her mum, and Diarmuid...

Something in front of her creaked. Vendrick was rising, and Frelia shot an arm out to catch him. He startled, and she tugged at him like a child afraid of a storm, so he carefully took up his place again beside her.

Frelia thumped against his arm. "Talk about nothing."

So he did, going on about this project and that gossip with a steadying arm around her shoulders, until the panic bled from her eye and her heart stopped pounding in her throat.

CHAPTER THIRTY-FIVE

FOR THE FIRST TIME in years, Frelia was warm.

She couldn't remember the last time she'd felt properly warm, like this. Childhood, maybe? When she'd slept in a pile of kids and sled dogs during blizzards? Or maybe once or twice as a mercenary, when Leon had passed out in her tent?

Actually, why was she this warm, anyway?

She cracked open her eye, and saw that her cheek was pressed against a suspiciously well-tailored waistcoat. Her eye travelled north, and suddenly last night came rushing back with frightening clarity.

For there, studying her through half-lidded eyes of brightest green, was Vendrick.

"Good morning." His voice was low and hoarse.

"You... stayed?" Frelia realized her hand was curled into the space between two of his waistcoat buttons, and she had to extract it to rub her eye.

He snorted, softly, and there was a smile tugging at his face that threatened to turn her bones to jelly. "Of course I did."

So where did that leave them, Frelia wondered. What horrible thing was going to burst through the door and ruin this moment of perfect calm and warmth? Ironfang? A garmr? The ghost of Grand Duke Einar himself?

But before she could get a word out, Vendrick did something far worse than whatever her mind was conjuring.

He bent his head down and kissed her good morning.

It was a soft, quiet thing. No more than a few seconds of contact. Just a 'hello, my dear' or a 'have a good day at work' that Frelia had only ever witnessed in storybooks and operas.

But still, when he pulled away, she stared at him in outright shock.

"Was...?" He turned violently pink in the pale, early morning light oozing through the curtains on her window. "Was that too forward?"

He was in her bed, tangled up with her in a twin-sized comforter, and would have seen her bloody naked last night if she hadn't suddenly been slammed with a bloodrune memory too awful to dwell on. She refused to think about that memory right now, not when there were a million other things demanding her attention. Like the rise and fall of his breath beneath her cheek, or what they were supposed to do now that the cat was out of the bag.

"You think I'm being ridiculous," he said.

Frelia's resolve broke into a million tiny pieces as she laughed at the utter Volsinii-ness. "I think you're being a *dorchya.*"

There was no disguising the warmth in her voice. Was she still supposed to try?

"I don't think I know that one," Vendrick said. "I presume it's Kaldiri?"

When she didn't answer right away, he tilted his head to study her again. And just looked at her. Like he was seeing something worth studying. Worth learning. Worth staying for.

And what was she supposed to tell the ghosts that clambered in the back of her mind about that?

"Alright," Vendrick said after another moment, a teasing lilt in his tone now. "Keep your secrets. I do love a good cipher and—"

"*Why did you stay?*" The small, pained whisper practically choked her on its way out.

His smile fell. "What do you mean?"

"You know exactly what I mean." Despite how warm it was, Frelia shook like she stood in a blizzard in her home territory without her furs. "If you had just left when I told you to last night, we could have pretended like this didn't..." She didn't have the words anymore. "That *we* aren't..."

Naked, grey-magic-stained fingertips alighted on her cheek, soft as a butterfly wing, and it stopped her cold.

"This was the one thing," he said softly. "Remember?"

That was right. The one thing she could fix right now. And maybe there would be more later, and maybe the ghosts that lived in her would never stop shouting, but this was one thing she could reach out and hold onto.

It had made so much sense, last night. Still did, when she fought down her initial instinct to panic. She was alive, and the ghosts were not. That had to count for something, or else what was the point of it all?

"*Ja.*" Frelia drew in a deep breath. "You're right, but... now what?"

"How about I take you to dinner, once the winter ball is over? Somewhere that's not the mess hall. And then..." He let out a breath as he considered. "I don't know, let's go dancing, or to the night market, or something."

The same tears as last night fell from Frelia's good eye. "Are we allowed to be that normal?"

"I dunno." Vendrick's thumb swept just out of sight, dragging across her cheekbone and taking her weakness with it. "But I'm not going to wait around while the Senate votes on it."

He tugged her closer, but the only place left to go was on top of him. Frelia could feel his hammering heartbeat beneath her fingers as she tried to steady herself again, could feel his hands slide across the curve of her waist and settle there.

"What do you say?" he whispered. "Want to pretend to be normal?"

He held her gaze, but his eyes were soft—too much so. It hurt to look at the hope he carried there, like staring into the sun.

"What about Ironfang?" Frelia asked. "Or Markus? What happens when they find out?"

Vendrick's face twisted as he considered. "Definitely some bitingly witty commentary about my choice in war dogs."

Frelia snorted. "I'm serious."

"So am I," Vendrick said. "They can say what they like, but there's not really much they can do. You've been acquitted, and I no longer serve in the Senate or the royal house. There aren't any rules in the Silverwood annals about professors courting—probably because they've never really needed them—and if it gets to a point where Senators start complaining about the idea of a Kaldiri-born Countess Caecillion, my sister can simply retain the title."

Frelia blinked in surprise. The logic was watertight, but... "How long have you been thinking about this, Vendrick?"

"Eh..." He trailed off. "Embarrassingly long, let's just leave it at that. Don't tell me you never thought about it."

Tell him she'd never thought about how he would look in deer pelts and Valerius blue? How his verdant, green eyes would sparkle in the firelight of the Lodge's great room? How he, Cillian, and her da would probably play chess during blizzards and...

No. She had to stop thinking like she had one foot in Helheim.

"You would have had to have been the Grand Duke Valerius," Frelia said, and then she winced at herself. That was not getting out of the land of the dead, dammit.

He took it in stride, though. "Wouldn't that mean I'd have outranked you?"

"No?" Frelia made a face. "They're parallel titles. Or, well. They were."

Her forehead suddenly thumped against Vendrick's neck as he cradled her there. Frelia tried to breathe deeply, but choked on the stench of burning garmur fur and sulfide.

"Easy, love." Vendrick's voice was smooth and silken, beside her ear. "I've got you."

No, these weren't the same tears as last night at all. They were new ones.

She grabbed at the first thing that crossed her mind. "What time is it?"

"According to your clock, probably time I got back to my own sleeping quarters before it's noticed I'm not in them."

Despite the fact that Frelia hadn't felt a single shred of embarrassment in all the mornings she'd hustled across the Cost Effectives' camp back to her own tent, the implication that it was Vendrick she'd slept with made her face overheat like she'd sat too long in a sauna.

Helheim, she was *so* fucked. Without even the courtesy of actually fucking! She didn't know if that made it better or worse, honestly.

"But, given that everyone already thinks we're sleeping together..." Vendrick shrugged as best he could, laying down with Frelia on his chest. "I can't say it makes a compelling argument to get up, even if I know I should."

A dumb thought bubbled up from beneath Frelia's broken armor, and she laughed. "Well, now they're right."

"On a technicality." Vendrick's hand lifted from her waist long enough to shoo the thought away. "But also, you haven't answered me."

Frelia steadied herself on parchment and woodsmoke, and then raised her head to meet his very much living eye. "After the winter ball, *ja,* "she agreed. "Let's go."

She was spared the effort of stringing together something else to say when he smiled so broadly it would have blotted out the sun. Frelia had never seen him look so... happy. It was bizarre, and so normal, she didn't know what she was supposed to do with it.

"It's a date, then." He tugged one of her hands out from beneath the comforter and pressed a kiss into her knuckles.

Her callouses were still broken and the skin was still cracked, but the bleeding had stopped, at least. Vendrick had let her touch him with these hands? They had to have been rough as cut stone.

"Are these alright?" Vendrick asked, studying her injuries now.

No, no, no, he was going to fuss, wasn't he? "They're fine," Frelia said quickly. "Dealt with worse in the war."

Vendrick sat up, pulling her along with him, but he didn't move to get out of her bed. "Well, we're not in the war. Let me heal them for you."

Frelia blinked. "Can you even do that?"

"Sure, I've got the rune in my spellbook."

"It's white magic, though." Which went against most everything Frelia knew about the man, including his own nature.

"Octavia insisted all the Queenmakers' mages be able to perform at least basic white magic." Vendrick pulled both of Frelia's hands towards him now, and into the early predawn light. "Afraid I'm not much good for anything beyond blisters and fractured shins, though."

He turned her hands over a few times, studying her injuries, her scars. "I think I can fix these. Do you have a first aid kit?"

"Are you seriously going to waste your time on this?"

"It's not wasted time if you enjoyed spending it."

That... was hard to argue with.

This time when he moved, Vendrick actually did get out of her bed, and Frelia's personal space was her own again. She'd apparently slept in the dress she'd worn yesterday—the stitching had dug into her ribs all night—and she itched to change into something actually comfortable and maybe take a shower. But first things first, apparently.

She dug around her closet for a moment before retrieving her travelling pack. She thumped it on her bed and rummaged around for a moment, moving aside spare clothes, a flask, and sword polish that probably needed replacing, before she found the small, orange-and-green pouch that she carried anything medical in.

"Here." She held it out to him.

"Thanks." He tugged her towards her desk chair, told her to stay put, and opened her medical pouch. "Is this an Islander pattern?"

How did he know that? "*Ja,*" Frelia said, suddenly embarrassed. "Leon gave it to me once upon a time. I used to run with his mercs."

"Leon of the Titanheart runs the Cost Effectives?"

"*Ja,*" said Frelia. "He's their captain, now."

Vendrick nodded, somewhat absently, and began to work in the kind of silence that normally made Frelia's skin crawl. His focus was entirely on her ruined hands as he carefully unwound the bandages and unstuck them from her cuts and scrapes. It was more gently than Frelia had been treated in her entire existence—the entire morning was, in fact.

So for once, it wasn't her war instincts screaming in her ears, but garden-variety, nobody-was-dying panic. She should not be letting him this close; should never have kissed him, either. But there he was, standing in her room with a bruise forming on his neck like he or it had any right to be there. Like she'd had any right to put it there.

Maybe he was onto something about not waiting around for someone to hand you rights.

"Why weren't you wearing gloves?" Vendrick asked.

"I haven't had any in a while." There was nowhere to look that wasn't Vendrick—his hands, his face, his concern.

He shot her a look that Frelia felt in her bones. "We're in the middle of winter."

"This time of year is balmy," Frelia said, partially to be ornery and partially because it was true.

"Even so, I'm fairly certain you're not immune to frostbite." Vendrick pulled the last of the bandages away, and set them in a bloody heap on the desk beside her. "Why haven't you gotten a replacement pair?"

"You know what I get paid."

Vendrick shook the ointment bottle a few times to loosen the viscous liquid. "And you didn't say something because...?"

Frelia looked to her stockinged feet. "It's not your problem."

"I'm the judge of that," he said, and Frelia hissed when Vendrick set to cleaning her wounds with a clean wetted bandage. "Sorry. I know it's not the most pleasant concoction, but it beats infection."

Frelia tried not to grimace as he continued. She'd been magically healed more times than she could count, and she could usually see it coming. But Vendrick surprised her when he began to draw a half-familiar rune in the air between them, purple light dripping from his forefingers. It hit Frelia a moment later, astral energy sinking into the popped blisters and jagged scrapes on her hands. Edmund's healing magic felt like sinking into a hot bath after a long day's ride, but Vendrick's was the first bracing wind of winter. It was exhilarating and terrifying, all at once.

He turned her hands over a few times to check his work until, apparently satisfied, Vendrick raised her hand to press a gentle kiss into her scarred knuckles and then set her hand back down in her lap.

"There you are." His voice was so soft as to nearly be lost among the shadows of the early morning. "Good as new."

Frelia flexed her hands experimentally, and was surprised to see them move with their usual, easy grace, but even more surprised to discover that her hands didn't hurt. For the first time in Saints knew how long, her scarred, warrior's hands *didn't hurt*.

"That's amazing," Frelia murmured, staring up at him in unfettered awe as she continued to wiggle her fingers.

He was turning pink again. "It's just a bit of white magic."

Impulsively, Frelia threw her arms around his waist and tugged. He made a surprised noise in the back of his throat as she pulled him off balance.

"Thanks." It was muffled against his chest, and her hands fisted into the back of his shirt. "*Thank you,* Vendrick."

Tentative arms wrapped around her back and held her there, squeezing in return. "You're quite welcome," he murmured into her hair.

CHAPTER THIRTY-SIX

THE TRAINING GROUND WAS blessedly empty when Frelia showed up, just after dawn and dressed for it this time. She tried not to think about anything as she worked. Swords were comfortable; combat training was safe. The aching sting of her bloodrune was familiar, the hoarseness of her voice after trying to sing the Rebellion war song that wasn't meant for a woman's register was normal.

Not like falling apart at the seams and having someone else stitch you back together. Not like trying to make sense of the living and the dead.

Not like kissing Vendrick.

"Professor Valerius?" came a small voice from the training ground entrance.

Frelia glanced over her shoulder to find Faustine della Luciana, dressed in her sparring uniform and nervously twisting the end of her cuffs. "Shouldn't you be with your family, or something?"

Faustine shook her head. "My father's staying through Yule, so he said I should prepare for finals like normal."

"Ah." Frelia turned back to her training dummy. "Understood."

She got four more slashes into her training regimen, such as it was, before Faustine piped up again.

"Professor, can I talk to you?"

Frelia knew that tone and she was in no mood to deal with it today. "You don't want to talk to me about feelings. Go ask Edmund Blightsen."

Faustine's lower lip wobbled.

With an annoyed sigh, Frelia stabbed her bastard sword into the training ground floor. "Are you ill?"

"No, I..." Faustine hugged her arms to her torso, as though that would keep her upright. "I just... I think I did something really bad, and I don't know how to make it right."

Frelia wondered what she possibly could have done to be so terrified of the response. Stolen the answers to the loremaster's history final? It couldn't have been the roguemaster's final—stealing it was the whole point, last Frelia had heard.

Frelia drew in a breath, tried not to take her irritation out on Faustine. "Well, if you wronged someone, the first step is always to take responsibility."

"I don't know how to do that for this." Faustine's voice was little more than a whisper.

"It will look different, depending on what you did," Frelia pointed out.

I can't change what I did in the war, echoed in her ears.

Faustine chewed on her nails. "I've told them I'm sorry."

"It's more than that. An apology is just you acknowledging that you know you've fucked up. I've known Volsinii who are *sorry* for what they did in the war, but it doesn't bring my dead friends back, *ja?*"

Faustine looked at her boots. "Like Headmaster Caecillion?"

Frelia was grateful Faustine was so occupied with the floor; the girl didn't notice her blush. "I was actually thinking of some of the mercenaries I've run with, but yes, I suppose. Him too."

Faustine's head snapped up. "So you worked with them afterwards?"

"Had to." Frelia shrugged, trying to kill her embarrassment by sheer force of will. "Weren't my mercenaries to fire."

"How did you make that make sense, in your head?"

"Some days, Faustine, I still can't." It was the kindest way Frelia could think to put it. "So even if you apologize and admit you wronged someone, what they do with that is up to them."

"But then what do you do, though?"

"You prove," Frelia said, "through action, your remorse and commitment to changing that behavior. Otherwise, an apology is an empty acknowledgement not worth its weight in ink."

I can't fix Ironfang, or the Imperium, or that Cillian Grimsdalr is dead—but I can take a punch.

For a long moment, Faustine just stared at Frelia's bastard sword, freestanding in the sand.

"You don't have to tell me what you did," Frelia said at Faustine's silence, and the teenager squeaked in surprise. "But I would probably be better able to help if I knew."

Faustine bit down on the inside of her cheek, to the point that Frelia could see it externally on the girl's face.

"I took something from someone," she finally said. "Something precious to them. They said it was okay, but I feel awful."

Frelia cocked her head to study the littlest della Luciana, standing miserably in the Silverwood training grounds and begging a Kaldiri expat, of all people, for guidance. "Why would you do such a thing?"

Faustine's voice was so quiet, Frelia almost missed it. "My brother wanted it."

Well. That took it from "Stolen finals answers" or "Volsinii are weird about having sex" territory to "Siegmund's contraband vodka" territory.

"Then I take it back," Frelia said. "Your first step is actually to tell your brother to shove off. *Then* it's to apologize."

Faustine's grey eyes—the same as Ironfang's and Markus'—widened. "I can't do that, Professor. He'd be furious!"

"Just because he's family doesn't mean he gets to walk all over your good sense." Frelia glanced reflexively over her shoulder, before she added, "Have you ever heard the story of the Wild Hunt?"

Faustine carefully shook her head. "Does it have something to do with apologies?"

"No," said Frelia. "Cycles."

Faustine blinked a few times, as if she couldn't comprehend what she'd just heard. "You mean like..." She struggled to voice whatever she was thinking. "How if an Imperator dies, a new one will take their place?"

"Sure, that's one," said Frelia. "There's also life and death, the seasons, the weather. Laundry." Frelia shrugged. "Even the school year. They're all cycles. The same happenings, but different ones, stacked atop one another."

"Okay," said Faustine, slowly, like she was chewing it over. "I guess that makes sense."

"Family is also a cycle," said Frelia. "You're born into one, grow up within it, then leave it one day and start your own. If you have children, you pass down yourself and everything you've learned to them, and then the cycle begins anew. *Ja?*"

"Yeah."

For a moment, Frelia thought about trying to come at it from an angle. But ultimately she was exhausted, and she was anxious, and most importantly, she was a Kaldiri shieldmaiden. The only way out was through.

"You are stuck in a cycle with Markus," Frelia said. "It's probably very old, and formed when you were little. Maybe he'd bully you into doing things he wanted but didn't want to get in trouble for—stealing cake from the kitchen, staying up after bedtime, that kind of shit."

Tears had begun to form across Faustine's face, still round and sweet from the last vestiges of stubborn baby fat, but she did not sob.

"You stayed in this pattern as you grew because it was familiar," Frelia continued. "There is comfort in knowing what lies ahead, even if it sucks. It's normal, and you're used to it."

The fight is not over so long as you breathe. The family task ripped into her mind, unbidden.

"But now you stand on the precipice of something." Frelia's voice had dropped without her consent, low and grieving like she stood at someone's barrow. "And you cannot stay in this cycle anymore. The longer you do, the more it will chafe."

"But what if it ends?" Faustine burst out. "What if it stops, and everything is over, and I have nothing left?"

"They never stop." Frelia shook her head. "A new cycle just begins. That's why I was asking if you knew the story of the Wild Hunt. It's... easier to explain this kind of shit with stories."

"Tell me it!" Faustine seemed to realize what she'd just said, and added, "Please?"

Frelia sighed, an uncomfortable tightness in her chest. She hadn't told this story in a great many years, but here she was, offering it to Ironfang's daughter. Postwar sure was a funny thing.

"It's part of the tale of Heit Reiði." Frelia glanced over her shoulder again, as though anyone else was dumb enough to be out here at this time of day, of year, of eternity. "It was said that, when the Saints sealed Lady Midnight into hell, she cursed them all. 'We will meet again, where the end shall begin, and the first snow will fall twice'."

"That's written in fancy calligraphy in Father's study," Faustine piped up. "I always thought it was just pretty-sounding nonsense."

"That doesn't surprise me," Frelia said, and tried not to sound annoyed. "Heit Reiði is Lady Midnight's story more than it was ever her Sisters'."

Faustine's brow furrowed. "I wonder why no one's ever told me."

"Dunno." As if Frelia needed more incentive to tell the oldest Triad stories. "But anyway, Lady Midnight's curse was three-fold: the Bloodrune Saints' seal would not hold forever, the Saints' children would be cursed to forever bear their traitorous brands, and her retribution would begin with Fimbulvetr, the great winter.

"Lady Daybreak will die first, and the world will be plunged into Ainacht, the eternal night. Fields will lie fallow as crops cease to grow, and brother will turn against sister as humanity slowly starves. Lady Twilight will go mad in this eternal darkness—for there is no dusk without dawn—and when only the fiercest, nastiest warriors remain, the Wild Hunt will devour them, village by village, until the world and all its people belong to Lady Midnight and her children."

Faustine recoiled, and blinked a few times. "That's... dire."

"It will be the end of this cycle," Frelia said. "It's supposed to be."

Why do you think the Sacred Tasks are so important? she wanted to add. *They keep Lady Midnight in hell where she belongs.*

"But after Fimbulvetr," Frelia added, conspiratorial now, "spring will come again. It always does."

Faustine's brow furrowed hard, like when she was trying to grasp a particularly difficult sword maneuver. Then understanding rippled across her face. "Because it's a new cycle?"

"Because it's a new cycle, *ja.*" Frelia nodded. "And as for this person you've stolen from... after you take care of your brother, you'll be free to make amends with them, too, as much as they'll allow for."

Faustine was staring at Frelia's bastard sword again, as though it would help the girl piece together her next move.

"Now." Frelia yanked it back out of the sand. "Did you want to train this morning?"

Faustine blinked a few times, and then finally met Frelia's eye. "Yes, please."

***

Vendrick tried to hold onto the memory of Frelia's skin beneath his fingers as he snuck across campus and back to his quarters in Salonia Hall. It was still predawn, so mercifully the grounds were mostly deserted—particularly after last night's feast. If he weren't so anxious, he'd probably find it soothing to be so alone.

And yet, he wanted to turn back around, march right into Frelia's room, and waste the entire morning doing absolutely nothing more important than learning the precise way their lips fit together and maybe planning where they'd go to dinner.

It wasn't like him.

Vendrick was a paranoid planner and an ex-Spymaster and he did *not* throw caution or responsibility to the wind, ever. What in Hypogia had gotten into him? If she hadn't started it, he'd almost wonder if he'd dreamt the whole thing.

But even in his wildest dreams, he'd have never guessed she'd wanted him, too. Maybe he should have—Kaldiri were brazen in war and politics, why not love?

Er...

He was getting ahead of himself. Better to think on how his brain had completely stopped working when she'd thrown her arms around his middle and tugged, and how his name sounded so harsh, from her lips—the consonants too rough, the "r" flipped between her teeth. But not only had he grown used to it, he sort of liked it her way.

And better to think on when she'd looked up at him, all amber eye through dark lashes, and suddenly Vendrick had been seventeen again with absolutely no idea what he was doing here. She was much too pretty for the likes of him, much too honest and proud and dauntless. She deserved to stand beside a light like Cillian Grimsdalr, who smiled broadly and laughed easily and drew people to him like moths to a flame—someone just as diligent, fierce, and fearless.

Not a shadow from the Volsinii Imperium. Not a Spymaster's son with more blood on his hands than in them.

Not *him.*

Vendrick shook himself a little. He needed to get a grip, maybe take a cold shower. Why was he so miserably considering the past, anyway? He'd never been one for dwelling on previous mistakes; there were always plenty of opportunities to make new ones.

At the top of the stairs to the headmaster's suite, he found the door unlocked. *Again.*

Annoyed, Vendrick raised his right hand to the level of his eyes and breathed in sharply. His violet magic crackled to life at his fingertips, sparking like lightning and pungent like ozone. With his free hand, he turned the doorknob and slipped into his room, already mentally walking through his favorite battle runes.

"*Vendrick dear*, I am so proud of—" The intruder pulled up short. "Oh, for the Saints' sake, brother, it's *me.*"

Vendrick groaned, and pressed his free hand to his forehead. "Clarissa, stop doing this. What on earth do you want at this hour?"

She smiled—a toothy, winsome gesture that usually got her what she wanted. He'd already had enough of her nonsense and he'd just walked in his own door.

"I really *am* proud of you," Clarissa said, still grinning. "Sneaking across campus from an honest-to-the-Goddesses *girl's* room first thing in the morning!"

Vendrick made a strangled noise. "How do you know about that already?"

"This is a *school*, Vendrick." Clarissa rolled her eyes. "The only place rumors move faster is the Imperator's court."

"Oh, aren't you supposed to be in New Ascalon?"

"I *was.*" She laid into the word. "Don't you want to know how mum is doing?"

Vendrick sighed. He needed caffeine if he was going to deal with his little sister this early in the morning. "I presume well enough that you're back here with only mild emotional scarring?"

Clarissa put her hands on her hips. "You know, if I didn't know any better, I'd say you didn't even *miss* me."

"My dear baby sister," Vendrick said, "of course I didn't; you're annoying."

Clarissa laughed and followed him into his kitchen. "Mum's fine, by the way. Her leg still gives her trouble in the winter, but she's not actively ill or anything."

"Capital," said Vendrick flatly, pulling the kettle off the stove and into the sink. "I will be sure to send her a perfunctory Yule card."

It was less than his mother deserved from him, in that she *deserved* a kick in the teeth.

"Wouldn't that have had to go out like three weeks ago to make it there in time?"

"Oh, *no,*" Vendrick said dryly. "Guess I'll have to aim for next year."

Clarissa didn't laugh, and it set Vendrick's teeth on edge. He paused in filling the kettle to look over at her. She was studying him with wide eyes that should have belonged to a kitten or something equally as tiny and cute.

Somewhere in the back of his mind, Vendrick's anxiety began to sing.

"What?" he said. "You said she's doing fine. She hardly needs me to check on her."

Clarissa raised an eyebrow. "You know, I'd have thought you'd be in a better mood this morning."

Vendrick's face lit itself on fire. "I'm not talking about it."

"Oh..." Clarissa's eyes widened. "Did it not go well?"

"What did I *just* say?"

Clarissa leaned forward to whisper, consolingly, "Was it over embarrassingly quickly?"

Vendrick smacked his hands on the countertop. "Get out of my room."

Clarissa snorted. "What are we, fifteen?"

"You certainly seem to think so!" Vendrick shut his eyes and breathed deeply, then looked back at his sister. "It went fine, Clarissa. Better than fine, even. I'm now simply tired, and annoyed, and don't get on with our mum."

She studied him for a moment, consideration glittering in the jadeite green of her eyes. "If it was 'better than fine,' why are you so annoyed this morning?"

"Because I'm *here,* instead of still *there?*"

The joke was out of him before he'd properly thought about it. And Clarissa laughed and teased him about when she was getting a niece or nephew, and all was normal between them as Vendrick continued organizing the component parts for his coffee press.

But the joke wasn't right. He had been perfectly content in Frelia's room this morning, and while, yes, sorry to see her go, he also had things to get on with today. And she'd agreed to get dinner after the winter ball! He had no reason to be as annoyed as he was.

Which was why Vendrick Caecillion, the Viper of Ascalon, smelled a trap.

If he asked her their actual code question, Vendrick would be setting himself up for merciless teasing about his paranoia on top of the whole Frelia thing, and he, frankly, didn't have the patience for it today. But he could still shut up the anxiety a little before getting down to business.

"Clary, how old were we when Mum moved up north?"

Clarissa tilted her head at him, confused. "I was..." A slight pause. "...twenty, so you were twenty-three. Happy?"

"I'm never happy," Vendrick pointed out. "But thank you."

Silence fell for a moment, and then Clarissa said, "Oh, I suppose it's my turn now isn't it?" Her eyes flicked up as she thought for a moment. "What did you get Octavia for her coronation?"

"The portrait of the Queenmakers that's now in my office."

It had been a bear to get everyone to sit for their portion—particularly the then-Princess Irirangi, who already had a foot back in the Rippling Isles in those days—and in the end, Vendrick had never even been able to present it to his Imperatrix. Octavia had died in the Northern Rebellion, so her would-be coronation gift was the last known portrait of the late princess.

And now it hung in Vendrick's office as a reminder of what the cost of failure was.

"It's a good portrait," Clarissa said.

Vendrick sighed. "Listen, Clary—forgive the impropriety, here—but what do you want? I'm sort of busy."

"Alright, dour and serious it is." Clarissa harrumphed and threw herself into one of the chairs at his tiny kitchen table. "Besides the stuff about Mum, I do have actually useful news."

Vendrick's Spymaster ears pricked up as he began carefully spooning grounds into the coffee press. "Regarding?"

"Liberalis Territory, of course." Clarissa shot him a dramatically exasperated look. "From what our spies have gathered, I think the Unseen are plotting *something* there, but damned if I've been able to determine what."

Vendrick scowled at the kettle. "That's not news, that's the inciting incident for what you were down there for in the first place."

"Well, it's confirmed," Clarissa argued. "And it begs the question, why Liberalis Territory? Do they desperately need a vineyard, or something?"

"It's remote," Vendrick pointed out, "a border territory, and right next to a certain tract of land we went to war for, twice."

For a moment, Clarissa was ominously quiet, and all the hairs on the back of Vendrick's neck stood on end.

Then she said, "Can I see your spellbook again?"

Vendrick's brow furrowed. "Why?"

"I want to see if maybe I've missed something about why it would be in Liberalis Territory in the first place."

"Oh, my *war* spellbook?" Vendrick clarified. "I suppose. Watch the coffee, would you?"

He ducked out of the kitchen and crossed the apartment, noting that Clarissa had thrown her bag on his couch like she was expecting to sleep there. He stopped at his personal desk, currently loaded with Silverwood paperwork that was weeks overdue, and stooped to pry open the left hand drawer with the false bottom. He didn't have much use for his war spells at the moment, and so he'd stuck his old spellbook in there for safekeeping.

The heavy leather tome firmly in hand, Vendrick was back in the kitchen just in time to see Clarissa pour boiling water into the coffee press.

"Here." He held the book out to her.

Clarissa brightened and took his spellbook without even fitting the lid onto the coffee press. Vendrick sighed and went to fix it while she thumped the book across his kitchen table and began flipping through its pages.

"So has Talis found out anything?" she asked.

The physician had been among the first to disappear from Ascalon after the war, having never possessed either the time nor inclination for politics. Vendrick had cornered his old friend on his way out of town and presented him with his favorite things—a puzzle and a research grant—and the man had officially been researching the bloodrunes and unofficially researching the Unseen ever since.

"Nothing new," said Vendrick, then he dropped into a cadence that mimicked Talis'. "'They can't just sit ambiently in the air until someone needs them, Vendrick. They're *blood*runes. They live in *blood*.'"

Clarissa snorted. "What do we pay him for?"

Vendrick fell back into his own cadence. "Science that is not quick."

They were quiet for a moment while Clarissa continued scrutinizing his spellbook and Vendrick busied himself finding the cream and sugar she'd inevitably ask for.

"You know Ironfang is going to figure out you're friends again while he's here," Clarissa said without looking up. "I swear, no one can keep a single secret from the man."

It took Vendrick a moment to realize they were somehow back to talking about Frelia again. "He already did." Vendrick pulled a canister out of his cabinet that turned out to be flour. "He'll probably just sigh at me during the winter ball and say something bitingly witty about my choice in dogs."

Clarissa laughed. "So does he know Frelia was the only girl you wrote to after Silverwood?"

"That is blatantly untrue," Vendrick said. "I wrote to you, too."

Clarissa rolled her eyes. "Oh, I don't count."

"Are you not a girl?"

"I'm your sister!"

Vendrick found the sugar in the back of his pantry cabinet and unceremoniously dropped the canister on the kitchen table beside Clarissa. "Finding anything useful?"

Clarissa shook her head. "Just what I expected."

CHAPTER THIRTY-SEVEN

"MUNINN WORKS," CAME A feminine voice from the top of the stairs to Markus' secret lab.

Faustine glanced up to find a dark-haired woman with catlike green eyes descending the stairs like she belonged there.

"Vendrick has definitely figured out there's something up," the woman added, "but he's paranoid, so that's no surprise."

It took Faustine a moment to recognize her, even as the woman offered an elegant wave and Markus grunted the affirmative over the bird-like darkbeast their father had bid him to summon. He was feeding it something that smelled horrible, came in a jar, and Faustine apparently had to hold for him while he scooped it into the monster's waiting beak.

"How much of something?" Markus asked.

It wasn't until the woman glanced to Faustine that she could place her properly—in the Headmaster's Suite, the day Christel's bloodrune had activated.

"I beg pardon," Faustine said, anxiety beginning to worm its way into her stomach, "aren't you Headmaster Caecillion's sister?"

The woman's smile was all teeth, glimmering in the half-light of Markus' lab. "I do play an excellent thoughtless tart, don't I?"

Markus shot Faustine a sharp look. "Faustine, this is Lucia della Trova."

Faustine's jaw dropped. "The prima donna?"

"The very one!" Della Trova's smile—or, well, Lady Caecillion's—was a bit more genuine for a half second before she dropped it. "I'm also a friend of your father's."

Faustine's stomach twisted as she realized what that meant: Unseen. This woman was with the Unseen, and she was wearing someone else's face for them.

"Madam della Trova," Markus added like a put-upon manservant, "this is my younger sister, Faustine."

"A pleasure to meet you, dear," said the woman with Clarissa Caecillion's face. "I've heard quite a bit about you from the Secundus boy."

Faustine blinked. "From Valente?"

"Father has many more supporters than make themselves obvious." Markus sounded annoyed, though Faustine wasn't sure why this time. "*Including* the Secundus family."

No wonder Father kept trying to arrange a marriage for Faustine with that family. Faustine was probably supposed to be a "reward for their service," or a tool to placate someone, or something equally as vile.

Something cold and dreadful slithered into Faustine's stomach. "Were you, er, playing Lady Caecillion when Christel's bloodrune activated?"

"Oh, no darling," della Trova waved Faustine off. "We grabbed her on her way up to New Ascalon. No one will realize for ages—the visit to Governor Deadcut was supposed to be a surprise, and Caecillion never talks to his mum, if he can help it."

She turned to Markus then. "So dear Clary should be in Heit Reiði now, being prepped for Orsina's Ascension ceremony."

Faustine's stomach twisted, somehow, even harder. Their father had been Ascended after the Battle of Spirits' Fen and since then, he'd barely seemed to age, remaining at the height of his strength and martial acuity. Faustine also knew that Markus coveted that power within an inch of his sad little life, and it was what Ironfang was dangling over his head with the darkbeast business at Silverwood. *Do this right, and there may be an Ascension in it for you.*

"Orsina is getting one?" Markus screeched. "What has *she* done lately to deserve it?"

"Driven a Valerius, a Secundus, and a Traust to Silverwood via her hunters?" The way della Trova said it made Markus sound like a complete idiot. Faustine felt like she should have been taking notes, or something.

Markus started to put his head in his hand, but remembered slightly ahead of the motion that he was covered in darkbeast ichor. He harrumphed instead, and dug the spoon he was holding back into the jar of gunk in Faustine's hands.

"So anyway," Markus added, "*Caecillion,* ladies. What has he determined?"

"Not a lot," della Trova admitted, coming around to Markus' lab table. "And lucky for us, Lord Muninn gave us the perfect cover story." She absently scratched the bird-like creature's head. "Guess whose room he was in last night?"

"Ugh," said Markus, "*disgusting.*"

Faustine's jaw dropped, though she regretted it a half second later when the smell hit her. "Was he with Professor Valerius?"

Was *that* why she hadn't gone to the Victory Day feast? There were rules about that stuff, Faustine was pretty sure.

"Indeed." Della Trova smiled, and there was no warmth to it. "So he'll be nice and distracted while we use the winter ball to harvest the rest of the energy this little one needs."

Della Trova scratched under Muninn's chin now, and he cooed like a pigeon who'd just been thrown bread. From an actual pigeon, it would have been cute.

"Will he stay little?" Faustine asked. She'd been wondering about that this whole time.

"Don't be stupid," Markus snapped. "He's just diminished right now. He'll return to his full size once the energy harvest is complete."

Muninn cawed then, loud and piercing. Faustine's heart suddenly ached for home in a way it hadn't in a long, long time. Not the Villa della Luciana, exactly, but the era when Ironfang had been fighting in the Northern Rebellion and the house had been quiet and her mother had been alive. Back when things could be as simple as spice cookies and games of chase-the-dragon.

"We're going to need a way to guard against that." The distaste was so thick in Markus' voice, Faustine wondered how he didn't choke on it.

"Against what?" Faustine asked.

"Muninn is the lord of memory," della Trova said. "He can make you relieve your fondest moments or worst nightmares, but mostly his aura just brings out what's buried in one's core, anyhow. He's really only a problem for the particularly bitter and regretful…" She trailed off. "Ah, I see your point, Captain."

Faustine couldn't stop herself from snorting as della Trova began to pace. Markus shot his little sister a withering look, and Faustine had no idea what possessed her to stick her tongue out at him like they were children, but she did.

"Grow up," Markus muttered, shoveling another spoonful of gunk into Muninn's waiting beak.

Anxiety began to dance in Faustine's stomach the longer della Trova paced Markus' lab. She was examining his instruments and experiments like she understood the purpose behind them, and Faustine wondered just how much of Markus' research was actually the Unseen's.

She was willing to bet a lot of it. Markus wasn't stupid, exactly, but he wasn't a brilliant scientist.

"Della Luciana," della Trova finally said, and her voice was all airy lightness and stained glass, "you've still got that bit of Grimsdalr blood left, right?"

"Yes," he said, "why?"

Clarissa's smile was warm and friendly—it didn't suit the coldness della Trova lent to her eyes. "Ever wanted a bloodrune?"

Markus froze. "I beg pardon?"

"It doesn't take much," della Trova added. "You had, what, a half inch left? Quarter inch? That ought to do it."

"What would be the purpose?" Markus was barely breathing, not daring to hope.

Della Trova shrugged. "The Grimsdalr Bloodrune strengthens one's physical and mental attributes. You'd likely be able to hold off Lord Muninn's aura with it."

Faustine watched in growing horror as Markus excitedly directed della Trova to his supply cabinet and she rummaged around for what she needed. A blood vial, a syringe, some gauze, some other bits and bobs Faustine couldn't name. Della Trova drew the blood Markus had so coveted up and out of the vial with a syringe, where it swirled about the barrel. Della Trova drew a quick, complex rune over the syringe, and her magic glowed orange for a moment before winking out like a dying star.

And then a small, whirling sigil began to glow in the barrel of the syringe.

"They're bloodrunes," said della Trova, giggling at some private joke. "They live in *blood.*"

This is wrong. The thought rang in Faustine's mind as clear as a tolling bell.

Faustine had watched Markus autopsy monsters and sew together new abominations from living flesh. She had watched her father nearly choke a servant to death for trying to clean his office. She had seen Orsina torture a man for information she turned out not to need, and she had seen Galeria callously turn widows out on the street after raising their rents too high.

But this?

This was grotesque. Wholly and utterly *wrong*. As though the sun had risen in the west and their father had smiled a benediction. After what Christel had suffered, how the Professor had to carry herself, what Valente kept hidden, della Trova was just going to stab a needle in Markus' arm because it was convenient? How could it possibly be so easy?

What about the family the professor was always talking about, the history? What about Cillian and Thera, and all of the people who had suffered to give Markus his original vial? What about the stories he was supposed to be told so that he could make sense of the memories the bloodrune would give him?

Would it give them to him? He wasn't actually a Grimsdalr; he was an interloper. A thief. Standing on the shoulders of giants and thinking himself tall.

"Steady now," della Trova said, and it took Faustine a moment to realize she was speaking to her. "It's just a little needle."

Della Trova thought Faustine was horrified because of the *needle?*

"Doesn't..." Anxiety began to chew through Faustine's stomach like an unfed hound. "Doesn't Markus need to, you know, lay up for a few days after that?"

"Oh that's just superstitious Kaldiri nonsense." Della Trova waved her off. "It'll take a few days to seal, sure, but he'll be fine."

The image of Christel, convulsing and foaming at the mouth, flew to Faustine's mind's eye. Of Professor Valerius' horrified expressions, and the headmaster's grim concern.

And Faustine suddenly found she didn't much care if Markus was too sick to leave his room for three days.

"If you say so," she said.

"You needn't believe everything that woman tells you to make her like you," Markus told Faustine.

He made it sound so *reductionist*. As though the only possible reason she would talk to the Professor or value her opinion was because she wanted something. With a jolt, Faustine realized—that was how *he* treated everyone. Tools to be used and thrown away when no longer needed.

Stuck in a cycle with Markus.

Something new began to blot out Faustine's ever-present anxiety. Splotch by splotch, it covered the white canvas of her insides in messy charcoal. It was hot, and boiled in her stomach, and Faustine's hands clenched at her sides.

"Are you ready, then?" della Trova asked.

Markus nodded enthusiastically as he rolled up his shirtsleeve.

Della Trova positioned herself and then slid the needle into Markus' arm. He grimaced, but said nothing as the Unseen woman carefully administered the Grimsdalr blood. Something thick and rancid as manure began to clot the air, and Faustine moved to cover her nose and mouth with her hand. Markus gripped the edge of his lab table with his free hand, his face twisted in pain.

A few moments later, della Trova slid the needle out again and pressed a bandage over Markus' bubbling wound. "There," she said, "that should do it. It ought to erupt naturally as you continue about your business."

"Fantastic," Markus murmured, flexing the hand beneath the bandage.

It had been so long, Faustine had needed an extra moment to understand what this feeling was, burning away the anxiety and fear and Saints-knew-what-else that lived in the bellies of prey.

It was fury.

"Now," said della Trova, clapping her hands together, "about the winter ball."

CHAPTER THIRTY-EIGHT

FINALS WEEK PASSED BY with an uneasy peace. The Imperator didn't barge into Frelia's classes, and that suited the swordswoman just fine. But when the day of the winter ball dawned bright and cold with not a cloud in the sky, Frelia was pretty sure it was an ill omen.

"I don't recall that omen from anywhere," Edmund said. "Also, hang on, I've almost got it."

It was only because of Edmund that Frelia had even had the time to have formalwear made for the damn ball, so she tried not to be too annoyed with him. She'd only knocked because his room was a few down from hers, anyway. But the cleric was having a hell of a time trying to drape all of his various formal sashes and cloaks properly, and had Frelia possessed any understanding of Free City formalwear, she'd have offered to help about twenty minutes ago.

She had never been more grateful for the heavy furs and sedate styles of her homeland. Even if it didn't technically exist anymore, Kaldr's bitter winters didn't care about who sat on the Coldiron throne, and Frelia hoped that Governor Deadcut was having a hell of a time.

It would be the least of what the woman deserved.

"It's from the *Ballad of Hana*," Frelia said. "Before the Kraken shows up, a lot of versions have her staring at a cloudless sky."

"Huh."

After a few more moments of fiddling, Edmund suddenly transformed from a man draped in too much fabric to an elegantly-dressed chaperone. Frelia was honestly impressed with his tailor.

"Well," Edmund said, offering an elbow, "I supposed you'd know the *Ballad of Hana* better than I would. Are you ready to go?"

Frelia rolled her eye—"Let's get this over with."—and threaded her arm through his.

They headed down the hall of the professors' dorm, and greeted colleagues and students alike all the way to the grand ballroom. Edmund gave their names to Axemaster Ossani, who was somehow always stuck as the herald, and Frelia felt a pang in her chest when she heard herself simply introduced as Professor Frelia Helm's Grace Valerius. She had never cared much for the pomp and circumstance of nobility and its responsibilities, but even after all these years, not having Grand Duchess or General before her name made it feel so achingly empty.

Edmund disappeared to find them drinks while Frelia found a good corner to lurk in, and then the students began arriving.

Frelia nodded to her students as they passed her by, their full names and modern titles on display like bejeweled butterflies under pressed glass. Some were dressed in their formal uniforms, starched navy and resplendent silver winking beneath the crystal chandeliers. Others wore something more to their personal taste—girls in fancy dresses and capelets, and boys in formal suits and heavy cloaks, and some folks in whichever suited their fancy for the evening.

Some stopped to chat with her or Edmund before finding their seats for the formal dinner, and near the end of the cocktail hour, the show began:

"Presenting Headmaster Vendrick, Count of Caecillion!"

Vendrick had traded his usual waistcoats and collared shirts for their slightly more expensive counterparts, though the difference appeared to be mostly filigree. He was dressed in the matte black and deep purple that made up House Caecillion's colors, and Frelia couldn't help but be reminded of how well it suited him. It was also the first time she'd properly seen him in over a week, so, well, she might be biased.

"Presenting Watcher Captain Markus, Lord of della Luciana and Prince of the Volsinii Imperium!"

Markus was the strutting peacock to Vendrick's raven, basking in the room's attention the way the school wyverns sunned themselves on the Silverwood parapets in the summertime. His tailcoat was eye-catchingly bright and his sleeves were pompously ruffled brocade. *Look at me,* he seemed to say. *Aren't I dreadfully important?*

From his spot at the head table, Vendrick gave a short speech about how he was grateful for everyone's splendid presence, proud of their accomplishments this semester, and if they would please rise for His Imperial Majesty.

"Presenting His Imperial Majesty, the Imperator Elias della Luciana!"

Ironfang's broad frame descended the stairs with a stiff spine and suspicious gaze, and in that moment all Frelia could see was the soldier he had been, not the diplomat he pretended to be.

Frelia grit her teeth so hard, she felt a tendon in her neck pop.

Though it had been a long time since Frelia had attended a party nice enough to bother with waltzing, multiple forks, and string quartets, she was pleased to discover that her old etiquette knowledge came right back, if only for the teasing it spared her. She would be able to lead her students through their dances when they inevitably pestered her, and she could sit through a four-course dinner without wondering which fork was hers.

She could do this, right?

Frelia might have convinced herself if she hadn't felt something rattle against her bones just then.

She froze, her salad fork poised over whatever wilted green thing she was supposed to be eating. She glanced to the Violet Owls' table, but neither Christel nor Valente seemed bothered. They were still chatting with their classmates and unconcernedly eating, clearly relieved to be finished with finals week.

"Frelia?" Edmund said quietly, leaning slightly into her personal space. "Everything all right?"

"I'm not sure," she said, honestly.

Saints, she missed Cillian and Thera! It was bad enough just being back in the Silverwood ballroom with her ghosts; the lack of titles against their names probably would have stung even worse than her own loss. But they'd at least be able to tell her if she was feeling the rumbling, or just anxiety at sitting half a ballroom away from the Imperator himself.

In school, Cillian had been the driving force of about eighty percent of Frelia's winter ball anxiety. He was constantly asking her, Thera, and Hägen their opinions on everything from the booze he was trying to procure and the dates he was debating asking to the formalwear options he was shuffling through. On more than one occasion, Frelia had told him to shut up via the medium of objects thrown in his general direction. Bastard usually caught them, though.

Their third year, in particular, Hägen had been jittery for weeks about asking Thera, despite the fact that most of the class knew the only reason they weren't courting yet, despite their official engagement, was because the future King of Kaldr was too piss-terrified to ask her. By then, Cillian had also begun harassing Frelia about whom *she* was going with, and so Frelia had skipped lunch more often than not just to avoid them all. Vendrick had begun sneaking food out of the dining hall to pass to her in their alchemy class on Tuesdays and Thursdays, and Frelia had both been grateful and incredibly embarrassed that anyone had noticed.

It was a relief when the place settings were cleared away and the dancing began. At least Frelia could *move,* now. Karina and Faustine almost immediately roped her into teaching them a 'Northern Volsinii' dance, and for a moment, Frelia could almost forget about the rumbling-that-wasn't, traipsing across her bones.

Then a cold wind blew across the back of her neck, and it was all the warning Frelia got before she heard, "Why, *Madam* Valerius, how lovely to see you again."

He put insulting emphasis on her lack of title, and Frelia's spine stiffened as she turned to face him.

"Ironfang," she ground out.

All around her, the Violet Owls stared at their swordmaster as if she'd gone mad. She could feel their eyes on her, tiny, pinprick-like arrows.

But Ironfang's smile was just as sharp, like he knew something the rest of them didn't. "Is that any way to greet your Imperator?"

The Volsinii students immediately dropped into bows and curtseys, their foreign-born classmates following suit a few seconds later. But Frelia stared down Ironfang over her students' heads, immobile and resolute as stone. He was no king of hers.

"Come now, Valerius," Ironfang chided. "Didn't old Einar teach you any manners?"

Ironfang could mock her and strip her of her title, but Frelia would not stand insults to her father. She fell mechanically into as mocking a curtsey as she could muster, then rose back to her full height. Her mind was stuck somewhere between a reeking fen and the polished dance floor.

"There," said Ironfang, indulgent like a doting grandfather, "was that so difficult?"

Frelia wanted to spit in his eyes, and the scar on her chest suddenly spiked with phantom pain. "Been a while, Ironfang. How's the family?"

As if she hadn't killed two of his sons in the war.

Ironfang's glare tightened. "I must admit, when my daughter told me about her new professor, I thought perhaps she'd seen a ghost."

Frelia swore she heard a Grimsdalr laughing on the breeze.

"*Father.*" Faustine blushed an embarrassed scarlet. "Professor Valerius is—"

"I'm additionally surprised Headmaster Caecillion let you keep your name," Ironfang continued, as though his daughter hadn't spoken. "He's usually much more thorough than that. Though I suppose it's been largely struck from the record, hasn't it?"

Frelia almost succeeded in not flinching. Almost. "I doubt he saw the need."

"I'm sure he didn't." Ironfang's eyebrows inched up his forehead. "He was always... particularly compromised about you."

Frelia's good eye narrowed, as though taking aim with a bow. "Odd way of saying we were school friends."

Somewhere across the way, someone giggle-snorted and was quickly hushed by a classmate.

"I still wonder," said Ironfang, and all the hair on Frelia's neck stood on end, "what business does your kind have teaching our children?"

Your kind.

Frelia hated the erasure more than she did the insult. She wished she could goad him into just coming out and saying it.

Kaldr. She was from fucking Kaldr, and she always would be.

"Same as the Imperium folk," Frelia said coolly. "Didn't get eaten by a garmr in the war, needed something to do."

Ironfang's grin was uncanny. "And is there a reason you cannot crawl back to whatever mercenary company spat you out?"

A hush fell across the gathering students, and from her spot in Frelia's periphery, Faustine looked like she wanted to step in. But the girl would only get herself disciplined or worse, and Frelia wasn't cruel enough to subject a child to Ironfang on her account.

"Better food at Silverwood," Frelia said, and Karina squeaked a startled laugh from somewhere to Frelia's right.

Frelia wished she could just duel the fucking man. She would seize the opportunity to bruise the shit out of him, or better yet, hit him so many times her bloodrune would be forced to activate. Frelia couldn't control the stupid thing, but she could goad it into action if she attacked enough times. Statistically, it had to.

"Caecillion tells me you simply showed up at Silverwood, one day," Ironfang said. "Is that correct?"

"I needed a job," Frelia said, "and heard Silverwood needed a swordmaster."

Seems like a match made in some kind of hell, she'd said that day. It still was—in some ways less, in some ways more—but it was the kind of hell they all inhabited together.

Ironfang's smile didn't reach his eyes. It was practiced, remote, and political. "Caecillion and I both have the same question then, it seems. How did you manage to avoid us all these years?"

What was it Vendrick had said, at that faculty meeting? Give the shortest answer you possibly can, and don't offer up any extra information? "Dyed my hair blonde and joined a mercenary company."

"You needn't behave as if you're on trial," said Ironfang, the doting grandfather once again.

Frelia's lip curled. "Am I not?"

This time Ironfang did laugh, and genuinely. "Valerius, my dear. If you were being threatened, I do believe you'd know."

Something rumbled in her bones, louder this time. Like a tiny earthquake was threatening to take her down.

"You know," came a familiar voice from behind her, "as much as I hate to break up a rematch a decade in the making, we are running dangerously low on martial professors."

Vendrick's shadowy presence bloomed on Frelia's blind side, and she couldn't even find it in her to be annoyed about it.

"So I shall have to ask you not to duel in the middle of the ballroom," Vendrick added. "We haven't the budget for janitorial hazard pay, you understand."

"*Caecillion.*" Ironfang sighed like he'd just discovered his warhorse pissing on his shoes. "And here I thought your sister was supposed to be the flippant one."

"We take turns." Vendrick's gaze flicked to Frelia as the students laughed nervously around them. "Also, Valerius, Blightsen and my sister were asking after you. Something about settling a debate they're having."

He offered an elbow, and Frelia knew an exit strategy when she saw one. Part of her wanted to tell him she didn't need rescuing, and the other part of her had been in too many foxholes not to grab a way out when she saw it.

"I go where I'm needed," she said, and slipped her arm through Vendrick's.

"You'll have to excuse us, Your Majesty." Vendrick's smile was wide and predatory as he bowed. "Please, do enjoy your time at the winter ball."

Frelia expected to be called back like a loose sled dog, but instead, Ironfang said, "I'm certain I shall.", and allowed her to be pulled away under the thinnest excuse Frelia had ever heard.

"How the fuck did you do that?" she hissed to Vendrick the instant they were out of earshot.

He didn't look at her, but squeezed her hand where it rested in the crook of his elbow. "Years of practice. Also a genuine need for someone else to break up the argument Clarissa is having with Blightsen."

Frelia's brow furrowed. "About what?"

Vendrick sighed. "I think she was *trying* to simply strike up a conversation, but it's dissolved into a theological debate."

"With *Ironfang* around?" Frelia hissed. "Tell me Edmund isn't that stupid."

She couldn't stop the glance she threw over her shoulder. Ironfang was still talking to some of the Violet Owls, and across the way, Markus was chatting with a few Watchers and Lancemaster Sabine.

"He's desperately trying to get out of it," Vendrick said.

Frelia made a face. "Let me guess, he's too nice to tell her to shut up?"

"It is his best and worst quality."

As they rounded on a terrified-looking Edmund and elegantly-dressed Clarissa, Vendrick squeezed Frelia's hand one more time before letting go.

"I had no idea you were so interested in ecclesiastical literature," Edmund was saying as quickly as he possibly could. "There are a few texts still around, but, the Bloodrune Hunters have, um, mostly..."

"Oh I'm sure," Clarissa said. "I just think it's so *interesting*, you know? Doomsday stories always are. Is the Wild Hunt really supposed to--"

"Bit early for Fimbulvetr, *ja?*" Frelia interrupted. "It's not supposed to snow until next week."

"*Frelia,*" Edmund hissed. "*You are not helping!*"

"Hello, Blightsen," Vendrick said. "I've found your tiebreaker."

"Ooo, what's a fimm-bull-vet-er?" Clarissa asked, sounding the unfamiliar Kaldiri word out slowly, like a child learning her letters.

"Never mind that," Frelia said. "What am I tiebreaking?"

"Ooh, a philosophical question!" Clarissa jumped on the topic change so fast it almost gave Frelia whiplash. "What do you suppose would happen if all the bloodrunes were together in a room again, if everyone were standing on the Saints' original seal? *I* think it would reverse the seal, but Blightsen here seems to think nothing would happen?"

Frelia recoiled so hard she jammed her shoulder into Vendrick. "Ironfang is *right there*, Clarissa!"

"*Thank you!*" Edmund squeaked out. His eyes were wide and he looked ready to bolt.

"Oh it's just a thought project." Clarissa waved off the Kaldiri concern with a flick of her hand. "And it's Lady Midnight-adjacent, anyway, I doubt Ironfang would mind. He might even join in."

Frelia and Edmund exchanged horrified looks, for once in total agreement.

"How about we talk about something that won't get us hanged, *ja?*" Frelia said.

"Capital idea," said Vendrick, and, like any good Volsinii Senator, he changed the subject. "Clary, remind me—what's playing this season at the Imperial Opera?"

Clarissa rolled her eyes, clearly aware of the game but going along anyway. "*Wives and Traitors,* like always. Probably *Children Who Stare,* too, it's been a few years since that one's gone on, and they finally have a proper bass again to play Giacomo. *The Red Fox* should be good though—oh, except, *ugh,* guess who's the *prima donna* this season?"

Vendrick apparently didn't even need to consider the answer. "Hell, it's not Lucia della Trova, is it?"

Clarissa made a face. "Who *else* would it be?"

"Della Trova is a lovely soprano," came a new voice as its owner slid into the conversation. "A fantastic actress, too."

"She's a maudlin hack," said Vendrick immediately, with the kind of vehemence Frelia usually reserved for people like Ironfang. Clarissa even looked surprised.

"Yes, well," came a voice, "I'd say you're a bit biased, hmm?"

And then Markus was strutting into their conversation, swirling lemonade around his glass as though it were wine.

Frelia glanced at Vendrick. "She your ex or something?"

"No," said Clarissa grimly, "she's mine."

"A shame you seem to like opera so much," Markus told her, "if you're going to eschew its most talented rising star."

"How's the lemonade, captain?" Edmund inputted lightly.

Markus' smile was all teeth—"Bitter."—and Frelia didn't like it.

"Oh, Vendrick." Clarissa tugged on his arm like she'd just remembered something. "I keep meaning to ask, can you introduce me to Perseo Ossani? I can see over there he's finally knocked himself loose from Olsen."

Vendrick stared at his sister for a half-second too long before saying, "You've met him."

Clarissa's entire face scrunched up. "I have?"

"Yes," Vendrick insisted. "At Talis Mitri and Hazel Stonebreath's wedding."

"All I recall from that wedding is Talis' spinster aunt passing out in the punch bowl," Clarissa said.

Markus snorted into his lemonade, and immediately glanced around for a kitchen servant to pass it back over to.

"So come on." Clarissa looped her arm through Vendrick's and tugged. "If I'm an idiot who's just forgotten, we can blame Talis' aunt." She barely spared a passing glance for Edmund, Frelia, and Markus. "Ta, all!"

It occurred to Frelia as she stared at Vendrick's retreating back that Edmund was no match for Volsinii politics, and never had been. This minefield would be hers to navigate them through.

"I've been trying to recall," Markus said, giving up on finding staff and simply setting his ruined lemonade onto a nearby table, "do either of you recall the song they used to play last, at the winter ball?"

Frelia clenched her jaw, while beside her, Edmund murmured, "Haven't the foggiest."

She shot him a dirty look. *Coward.* "Grimsdalr Waltz," she bit out.

"Ah, that's right. *Grimsdalr.*" The old Margravate dripped from Markus' tongue with disdain. "How long has it been, again?"

Frelia didn't need to ask what he meant. "Fifteen years since Thera Bones' Defiance died, sixteen for Herja Ancestor's Truth, ten for Cillian Wilds Guardian."

Edmund started to clasp his hands in prayer, and then seemed to think better of it, and dropped them again.

"Kaldiri names are always so... colorful," Markus said. "What was Hägen's, again? Fallen something?"

"Falling Stars," said Edmund, softly. "He was born during a meteor shower."

"And that's *Einnaska* to you, della Luciana," Frelia hissed.

"Is it?" Markus' eyebrow rose. "I thought it was 'dead rebel king.'"

"Technically," said Frelia, "*I* was the rebellion's queen."

Not because she'd wanted to be, that was for damn sure. But in the absence of the entire Einnaska bloodline, the Crown of Kaldr rightfully went next to the Grand Duke or Duchess Valerius.

And there had only been one of those.

Edmund shot her a horrified look that begged her not to poke the Captain of the Imperial Watchers. But there was no polite way to say she'd been forced not to stab the Imperator all evening due to 'decorum,' 'survivability,' and other such nonsense, and so needling Markus was the one thing she could do.

"Oh that's right," Markus said, like he'd just remembered. "You Kaldiri do so love dying for kin and country, don't you? It's a miracle your lot survived as long as you did."

"We survived," Frelia said harshly, "because we fought."

"And poorly, that," Markus pointed out. "Wasn't that the whole problem with King Hägen?"

"I wouldn't know," Frelia said. "I never thought there was anything wrong with him."

Edmund squeezed her arm in silent thanks. No, he was never going to fight a Volsinii again—physically, or otherwise.

"Well you're certainly glib today," Markus said. "Next thing I know you'll be begging me for a dance."

Frelia shot him a look. "Not entertaining suitors today."

"Oh, *Your Grace,*" Markus wheedled sarcastically, putting a hand to his heart, "you wound me."

"My Lord," Frelia snapped, "I outrank you."

She would never turn her back on an enemy, but she would pull on Edmund's arm to sidestep behind cover and bolt for the nearest human shield.

"Are you insane?" Edmund whispered as they hustled across the dance floor. "You can't go bringing up the past like that!"

"He started it," Frelia hissed back. "And it's not my fault he's not a duke."

"Do you think they'll care who started it?" Edmund asked.

Before Frelia could respond, her bloodrune stabbed painfully into her side a half-second before her very bones began to vibrate.

No mistaking it this time. That was definitely rumbling.

"I need to find Vendrick," she muttered.

She left Edmund with Magicmaster Marcellius—who had just so happened to be standing closest to the fiasco with Markus—and bunched her skirts in her hand to properly give chase. Her soft, booted footsteps were lost amidst the chatter and music in the ballroom, and her eye raked the crowd for the telltale black-and-purple.

She spotted it twice over by the refreshments table—once on Vendrick's back, and once on Clarissa's. They were still talking to Axemaster Ossani, whose facial expression was a weird sort of stilted grimace like he needed to take a shit or something.

Frelia slipped past the punch bowl, pausing just a half-second to tell Christel not to tip their hand so much, she could see their flask. The swordsman yelped and nodded furiously as Frelia pressed on.

"...I do recall that, about Mitri and Stonebreath's wedding," Ossani was saying, "but I could have sworn you were discussing some opera with my sister for half the evening?"

"That sounds like a thing I would do," Clarissa said. "Do you recall which one?"

"Oi, Caecillion!" Frelia interrupted.

Vendrick turned a half-second before Clarissa did. "Oh, Valerius," he said, "what can we do for you?"

"Lost a bet," said Frelia. "Come dance with me."

She held out a hand and tried to ignore the waggling eyebrows Ossani was shooting her.

Vendrick colored to the tips of his ears, and tried to cover it by cocking an eyebrow. "And I'm the loss condition, am I?"

Dammit, Frelia didn't have time for this. "I mean," she said, "the bet was with Edmund, sooo...." She shrugged.

Ossani cackled uproariously, and it occurred to Frelia for the first time that maybe he was from Siegmund's branch of the family. "Ah, go on, Vendrick," he said, clapping a heavy hand to the mage's shoulder. "You know better than to keep a lady waiting, and all that."

"I didn't say I required assistance," Vendrick muttered at him, although he still took Frelia's hand and led her out to the dance floor.

For a moment, they simply moved in time with the music as it swelled and shifted. Heartbeat to heartbeat like this, Frelia could almost remember what it had felt like to be close to another person, could almost remember what it had felt like to be warm.

She really needed to stop thinking about the other night.

He hadn't pressed, hadn't prodded, had simply offered an ear if she wanted it. Cillian would have pestered her half to death before he dared admit defeat, and Thera would have talked Frelia around the point until she knew what was bothering the swordswoman without Frelia ever having to say it.

But the twins weren't here anymore, despite their ghosts' clamoring for her attention.

Vendrick was, with his black clothes and dry humor and jade green eyes that saw far too much. They fell into step too easily, too readily, for the sheer number of times they'd been ordered to kill each other.

For the sheer number of times she'd done what she needed to do tonight, if her bones were right and there really were loose garmur nearby.

"We both know this isn't really a bet," Vendrick said quietly, even as their footsteps swept them elegantly across the dance floor. "What do you need?"

There it was again! A violent, rumbling sensation from deep in her bones. Frelia tried to steer them towards it as she murmured, "I've been feeling the rumbling all night."

Vendrick's spine stiffened, and he fought her for the lead as gently as a man could. "You think there's a darkbeast on campus?"

Frelia nodded. "Somewhere close, *ja.*"

For a moment, he stared over her head at the undulating waves of the dance floor. Probably marking wherever the Imperator had gotten off to, or the exits.

Then his gaze flicked back down to hers. "Which direction?"

"I'm *trying* to move us towards it," Frelia muttered, annoyed.

"Oh. My mistake." Vendrick rearranged them towards the far wall, twirling her past students who stared, slack-jawed, at their grim headmaster and cantankerous swordmaster. "How's that?"

"Better," Frelia grunted past the rattling of her teeth, "in that it's actually worse."

Vendrick laughed, but it was quick and short, like he'd realized in the middle of it that he wasn't actually supposed to be doing that in public. "That would be towards the Watchers' Barracks and why am I not surprised?"

Frelia glanced over to where Markus was deep in conversation with his father and Faustine. "Think Markus summoned it?"

"Undoubtedly," said Vendrick. "And I presume you're wanting to go after it, but you shouldn't go alone, Frelia."

Alone.

All at once, Frelia's grief tore from her iron grasp.

She had been doing a bang-up job of ignoring it, all evening. She'd shrugged off Cillian's ghost and the memory of the taste of smuggled whiskey beneath the old ballroom's crystal chandeliers. She'd ignored Hägen's nervous ghost, overthinking his every step, and Thera's moody one, goading her to tell her war stories, truly, the kids needed to know.

Frelia was, as she had been since the fall of the Northern Rebellion, *alone.*

Her sword jangled against her hip as she said, "Well you're sure as shit not coming. They'll notice you're missing."

She flicked a glance towards the della Luciana cabal.

Vendrick sighed, because of course he caught on. He was made of hints and secrets and bits of arcane pocket lint. "You have one hour," he murmured, "then I'm coming after you whether you like it or not."

"I won't need it," Frelia muttered.

As the final strains of the waltz swelled across the floor, Vendrick added, "Do you want to get going, or stay for another one?"

Frelia knew she should move. She should go to battle with sword and shield and the Grimsdalr blink. But his hands were warm against her waist and his eyes were glittering in the chandelier light and she was the shield between everyone she had ever cared about, and the nightmares that lived at the edges of this world. So why would tonight be any different, even if her *volchya* were her students and a defrocked cleric and a former Spymaster and his little sister.

So she said, "Surprise me."

Vendrick's hand tightened pleasantly against her right side as he led her through the transition to a lively quickstep.

CHAPTER THIRTY-NINE

"I AM WATCHING A courtship of *demons*," Markus muttered into his lemonade.

Faustine glanced over to the dance floor, where Headmaster Caecillion was leading Professor Valerius through a lively quickstep. They both seemed slightly softer, around each other, and Faustine was pretty sure she had never seen the headmaster laugh before.

"I don't know, they're kind of... cute? For two very terrifying people?" Faustine ducked her head at the glare that earned her. "Never mind, I see your point."

"Yes, well," said Markus flatly. "If you're finished stuffing your face, there's work to be done."

Faustine self-consciously set down her dessert plate (and she had been good! She had only decided to try half of what she'd initially wanted to) and wiped her hands on her navy blue formal uniform skirt. She tried to quell her furious heartbeat, and failed. Dismally.

This was to be Markus' show tonight. Their father wanted to test his ability to carry out orders. Mostly what that meant was that Markus was even meaner than usual, and their father wasn't going to lift a finger if something went wrong. And Faustine was supposed to be a good girl and say her lines to distract Professor Valerius and Headmaster Caecillion so they didn't check on what Markus or della Trova were up to.

"Clarissa Caecillion is being so kind as to assist us." Markus flicked a glance over to where the woman was still talking to Axemaster Ossani. "I shall inform Father we're moving forward. Stay out of my bloody way."

"Right." Faustine tried to swallow, but it felt like treacle had gotten stuck in her throat. "Okay."

"You needn't confirm yourself twice," Markus muttered as he swept towards where their father was talking to some starry-eyed third-year Red Eagles.

Faustine had made disappearing into an art long ago, and so she slipped around the edge of the dance floor un-accosted. She was supposed to keep Professor Valerius occupied while Madam della Trova snuck away into the grounds, so for the moment, Faustine could watch the dance floor in peace.

And eat dessert, she thought sourly. Why did Markus have to be so cruel, anyway? She definitely could have eaten dessert and kept an eye on the professor.

"Oi, Faustine!"

Faustine froze, and turned to see Christel making their way towards her with a cheerful grin. "Oh, um, hello."

"Siegmund's snuck in vodka. Did you want any? We've been passing it around most of the class."

Ah, well. That explained why some of her classmates had seemed so bubbly tonight. Faustine's stomach flipped at the thought of putting more alcohol in it, given that even the wine they'd served with dinner was weighing her down like a lodestone.

"I'm okay. Thank you, though." Faustine tried to smile genuinely, but she felt like a fraud. "Also, as your prefect, please don't get caught."

Christel snorted. "Look, Siegmund's fun and all, but he's an idiot. That's why I'm in charge of holding onto it."

Faustine gave them a quick once over, noted their formal uniform vest and pants, and couldn't help but ask. "*Where?*"

"It's a secret, obviously," Christel said. "And don't tell your brother, but we totally got the punch."

Faustine's eyes bugged open. "Do you think the professors won't notice?"

"Professor Valerius told me not to tip my hand so much when she passed me by."

Faustine wasn't sure whether she wanted to laugh or cry.

"I like her," Christel added. "I hope she sticks around."

It threatened to bring Faustine's entire dinner back up the way it had come.

"Though I think the Headmaster would try to stop her if she just ran, though." Christel flicked a pointed glance towards the dance floor.

"You make it sound like an opera, or something." Faustine was stalling and she knew it, but at least Christel laughed.

Dinner continued to threaten a return, and Faustine tried to breathe evenly. The idea that this could be the last conversation she'd have with Christel clawed at her insides with heavy, leaden guilt. She didn't want to help Markus and she didn't want to distract the professor and she didn't want to feel like she was going to vomit just talking to her friends.

She wanted—no, that wasn't strong enough. She *needed* something to change.

Across the room, the headmaster bowed to Professor Valerius as the song ended, and she rolled her eye but curtseyed back. He pressed a kiss to the back of her hand before ushering her off the dance floor. It was nothing Faustine hadn't seen a hundred times at various court events, but she suddenly felt like she was intruding on something intensely private.

Christel's brow furrowed. "Are you okay, Faustine?"

"I don't feel well," she said, and that, at least, wasn't a lie.

"Oh, shit." Christel's easy posture fell away. "Do I need to get Professor Blightsen?"

Shit, they couldn't go and alert Magicmaster Blightsen! *He'd* alert Professor Vee. "No!"

Christel flinched at her vehemence.

"I just mean," Faustine tried, "I don't want to bother him at the winter ball."

Christel's brow furrowed further and, like the swordsman they were becoming, aimed for the gut. "Did your brother say something shitty?"

"No," Faustine lied. "I think it was the bouillabaisse."

She was losing sight of Professor Valerius in the crowd. Her verdant blue dress stood out amongst the darker navies and crimson in the crowd, and Faustine *should* get moving. But Christel was looking at her with sympathy and understanding and everything just hurt.

"Want me to find Ellie?" they asked. "Or Karina?"

Faustine started to say she was fine, but stopped. She *wasn't* fine, and if Markus wasn't going to change, then she was simply going to have to. No more running, no more hiding.

A plan began to form in her mind. Slowly at first, but then all at once, the way dawn breaks.

"Actually," Faustine said, "can you get Siegmund? I need your help with something."

***

Vendrick watched Frelia's retreating form with a mixture of things in his chest he didn't feel the driving urge to unravel, at the moment. He'd heard Frelia dismissed as a Kaldiri dog over and over again, but he'd never before considered the possibility of what that would be like to have on his side.

It was harsh, brazen charisma, buttressed by skill, and he fervently hoped it wouldn't get her killed.

With the dancing in full swing, Vendrick was off the hook as a figurehead for the rest of the evening, and remained in the hall largely as a deterrent to students feeling publicly amorous. And there were a few he should probably nudge apart, but frankly? He had bigger things to worry about. A *second* darkbeast was loose on Silverwood's grounds. (Or, well, third, if you counted each individual one from the first day of classes.)

How? How could it possibly have gotten through his wards, *and* the Imperial Watchers, *and* the night patrol?

If Markus hadn't summoned it, Vendrick would eat boot leather.

She'll be fine, Vendrick tried to tell himself as he plucked a glass of lemonade from the refreshments table. Frelia was famous for killing darkbeasts, and he'd personally watched her gut a dozen of the big ones at the Battle for Skjöldr.

A dozen, he thought blackly, *with Cillian Grimsdalr's help.*

The two she'd faced alone at the beginning of the year had broken her arm, and he'd needed to conjure an astral sword for her. She had real steel now, but still no shield, and he didn't like these odds.

Vendrick's Spymaster anxiety began to sing in the back of his mind as he surveyed the ballroom. He watched as the students paired up (and didn't), as Ironfang danced with various students and professors and terrified them all. He saw Blightsen waxing poetic to his students about some landmark or other he'd once painted, and Tacticsmaster Vitellus talking with Roguemaster Olsen, the former gesticulating wildly and the latter watching with an eyebrow in her silver hair.

Vendrick loosed a deep sigh, and took a long sip of lemonade. Despite how he'd gotten here, he *did* love his job, and the students of Silverwood. It felt like a gentler version of the strategizing and planning he'd done for the Crown his whole life. A hobby of sorts while he warred beneath the cover of night.

They would be safe, here. He would make sure of it.

"Vendrick, dear." Clarissa suddenly appeared at his elbow. "Where's Frelia got off to?"

"Said she wasn't feeling well," Vendrick said, wary of the ballroom's listening ears. "She's going to get some air."

Clarissa cocked her head to look at him, and it struck the warning bells already singing in Vendrick's mind. Where had he seen that gesture before? It looked *odd* on Clarissa. Who had she been spending time with, lately, to pick that up?

"Well, shouldn't you go after her?" Clarissa asked. "Loan her your cloak, or something?"

"She's Kaldiri," Vendrick reminded her. *"I'm* more likely to need *her* cloak."

"Oh, you know what I *mean."* She shot him a familiar, exasperated look. "Go do something romantic. You can fix that you never did it in school."

Vendrick shot her a look. "How in the Saints' name would you know that?"

"Octavia told me."

Vendrick wasn't sure how to curse a dead woman without bad luck, but he would find one. Right after he found a way to strangle his sister in the middle of this ballroom without witnesses.

Had she always been this annoying?

"You're not helping," Vendrick said, just as a pink-cheeked Christel Vilulf stumbled over.

"Hey—hic—headmaster!" Christel said, and Vendrick winced. "Can I—hic—talk to you outside in the hall real quick? About... something... real quick?"

Oh, *Saints*, did Christel feel the rumbling too? That had to be why they wanted to talk to Vendrick, specifically.

"Yes." Vendrick pinched the bridge of his nose. "And I shall pretend not to know you're intoxicated if you can pull yourself together enough to give me plausible deniability."

"Thanks." Christel turned even pinker, and hiccupped again.

Vendrick glanced at Clarissa—"I'll be back."—and followed Christel around a few tables and out a side door.

In the sconce lit hallway, Christel immediately straightened up and scurried towards where the hallway bent towards the mess hall. Vendrick's eyes narrowed, but he matched pace, and was just about ready to demand to know what was so bloody important when he turned the corner, and nearly ran smack into Faustine della Luciana.

"Where's Professor Vee?" she asked, and there was no mistaking the terror in her voice.

"She said she wasn't feeling well and is just getting some air." Vendrick's sharp gaze raked the Violet Owls.

Christel, who suddenly looked much, *much* more sober.

Faustine, who had the della Luciana grey eyes the family was so famous for, but with none of the cruel intention behind them. What she did have was guilt—bucketloads of it.

Vendrick's eyes narrowed. "Why?"

Faustine swallowed past an audible lump in her throat. "Because your sister's not your sister," she said, "and if the Professor is going after the darkbeast, she's in a *lot* of danger."

The warning bells in the back of his mind rose to a fever pitch, but before he could say anything, a familiar voice interrupted them from over Vendrick's shoulder.

"You don't seriously *believe* this drunken rabble…" A toe began to tap impatiently. "Do you, brother dear?"

CHAPTER FORTY

FREED FROM THE CONFINES of guilt and glamor, Frelia tore through the halls of the Silverwood Military Institute like the huntress she had always been. Her da and the Valerius Master of Arms hadn't taught her to move swiftly through the trees and steady her breath just for a hellbeast to find her now. But instead of footprints in the dirt or blood on the air, Frelia followed the rattling of her very bones towards her quarry.

At some point during the winter ball, it began to snow, and Frelia watched the heavy flakes fall softly across the parapets and settle into arched doorways. A hard pang of heartsickness crushed her in a vice so strong she struggled to breathe.

Focus, Frelia. There would be time to mourn later. *The fight is not over so long as you breathe, and you have someone to protect.*

It... kind of felt nice, to have a purpose again.

The rumbling led her past Iuvenlis Quad, the academic buildings, the library. It led her down winding sidewalks and up hilly thoroughfares until she stood at the crest of a hill between the Watchers' Barracks and the chapel.

The chapel itself rose majestically skyward, its peaks and parapets stretching towards the Goddesses—or at least, the ones that remained, anyway. Its upkeep had clearly fallen by the wayside since the war, but it still stood, unlike the Church of the Triad itself. Its iron gate was padlocked, as it had been all year and *never* had when Frelia was a Silverwood student herself.

Unease coiled in Frelia's stomach. She had very few happy memories of the chapel as a student, and even fewer now. Mostly, it was just an ever-looming reminder that too many people were gone, Lady Daybreak rest them in Solivallr.

On the other side lay the Watchers' Barracks, the self-contained camp of squared-off brick and stone. It was just a more permanent version of all the Volsinii war camps Frelia had seen the whole war. Buildings, not tents. A tiled plaza, not a tramped-down field.

The unease in her stomach sharpened. She had laid waste to more than one of these damn camps, in the war. Been shoulder-deep in their trenches and scaled watchtower walls to cut the throats of archers before they punched holes in her knights' armor.

Not over, so long as you breathe.

"Ready to go?" came a warm voice to her left.

Frelia startled. She knew that voice better than she knew her own. She whirled on it, only to come face to face with Cillian Wilds Guardian Grimsdalr himself.

For once, he wasn't seated on his warhorse, and had both feet on the ground beside her. His hair was bright, burnished copper in the moonlight, and the shadow of a beard skittered across his blunt jawline. He was dressed in the green of house Grimsdalr, a well-cut tunic and severe work boots that would stand the test of march after march after march. A lancehead glittered just over his shoulder.

Frelia blinked—and *both eyes* blinked. Was that strange? She had the sense it was supposed to be strange. She reached up to touch her face and found... both eyes, exactly where they were meant to be.

"Ja," Frelia heard herself say, as though compelled. "Let's go."

Cillian crept forward, his footsteps light in the crunching snow, and Frelia breathed in the sharp pine smell of a northern winter. The cold air burned her lungs and cleared her sight, and they made their way, sure-footed, down the snowy hill as only children of Kaldr could.

Her teeth were rattling, now, and her war instincts began to sing in the base of her skull. As soon as Hägen gave the all-clear, they would storm this war camp. Frelia would scream the royal war song until her throat was raw, slice through Volsinii knights until her sword arm was numb and her blood pounded in her ears, and kill until she couldn't feel anything, anymore.

Cillian's eyes dug into her, like daggers between her ribs. "Sure about that?"

"I didn't say anything," Frelia muttered back, and anxiety rose in her gut.

"Yeah, you did," Cillian insisted. "You said you're going to go to the Grimsdalr lodge for at *least* a month if we win this."

Frelia was pretty sure she remembered that conversation. But it had been before a different battle, in a different place. Atop a warhorse just before black-furred nightmares broke into Skjöldr itself.

"But there's no way you're going alone," Cillian said, and he smiled.

It echoed in her ears in someone else's voice, someone else's accent.

"And a few dogs," Frelia said. "Maybe a keg."

"Now we're talking!"

Who said you're invited? tried to push its way out of her mouth, but Frelia couldn't voice it. Why *wouldn't* Cillian be invited? Thera, too. And Hägen, Edmund, and Gudrun. And... someone else?

She was forgetting someone. She could sense it, deep within the battle-haze of her mind.

Then Cillian smacked her arm with the back of his gauntleted hand, then pointed across the Volsinii war camp to where a single torch had gone up.

"There," he whispered. "That's the signal."

They locked eyes for half a second—Cillian's were warm, in the frigid darkness, brown and alight with mischief—and then they burst forward together.

Frelia's feet carried her the rest of the way down the hill, and her gloved hands pulled her up and over the outer war camp wall. At the height of the wooden fence, Frelia dragged the rest of her into the war camp, and then jumped.

She hit the ground hard, knees buckling on impact. Her armored coat fell around the tops of her boots a half-second later, and Frelia reflexively reached for the shield at her back as the war camp came alive all around her.

The weight on her back came free, sliding onto her arm like it had always been there. The heavy, enchanted-wood targe was painted woad-blue, the back reinforced with steel and with a small bloodstone inset in the back of the shield boss. Her family's magic, keeping eternal watch over their heir.

With the Valerius Shield securely in its place, Frelia felt balanced for the first time in years.

Years? It shouldn't have been years. She had been fighting just this morning, hadn't she?

Not over—breathe!

The first clash of blade-on-blade was jarring enough to rattle her teeth, and Frelia's bloodrune sang deep in her stomach. She slashed and parried without breaking for thought; muscle and ancestral memory driving her. Frelia's head snapped back when she caught the edge of a woman's shield in the chin, and stars sparked in her periphery.

The second time she made to shield bash, however, Frelia caught the woman's shield mid-strike on the edge of her sword. For a moment, the woman's eyes widened beneath her helmet, but then Frelia twisted the woman's arm in the wrong direction until it snapped like brittle ice.

The woman shrieked, and was quickly silenced with a brutal slash of Frelia's blade. The body fell, and she stepped over it, pressing ever onward. Frelia parried and struck with all her fury, lashing out with the edge of her shield as much as the edge of her blade.

More than once, she caught a blast of black magic with the shield—fire, frost, lightning, even grey magic—as years of training and practice suffused her blood. The Valerius Shield was built for it; where ordinary shields would twist and warp under arcane fire, the enchanted targe was as unbroken as the family who wielded it.

Cillian's laugh drifted across the clamor of war, and it rang wrongly in her ears.

She had learned her letters alongside him and his sister. Gone sledding with them in Kjell when the snow was thick and powdery during Yule. Physically shoved Cillian's nose into his schoolbooks to force him to study, practiced sword fighting in the training ground with Thera until their arms and throats were numb. She knew what his voice was supposed to sound like, and this wasn't it. It was like there were cobwebs in her brain or something.

But even so, she should *know*, shouldn't she? Hell, Cillian had promised to marry her, even, if they decided on political expedience over their personal wellbeing when the rebellion was over.

Rebellion? This wasn't a rebellion; this was a war. Justly waged and hard fought. If the Volsinii stopped fighting, there would be no war, but if the Kaldiri stopped fighting, there would be no Kaldr.

Something in her soul was cracking, like she had stepped onto the ice over Lake Hvita in the spring. Something from deep in those waters was trying to tell her something, desperately slamming its fists against mental armor and years of suppression.

"*Cillian!*" she tried to call, anxious and jittery now.

But what came out was "*Vendrick!*"

The world suddenly whirled around her, a flurry of snow and ice so thick she couldn't see through it.

Vendrick? She hadn't thought about Vendrick Caecillion in... well, realistically, a few days at most. She lived with a deep dread in the pit of her stomach at the thought of staring him down across another battlefield, but Frelia was a Valerius and she did not half-ass a war. She would not weep like a frightened child if she faced him, or beg like the war dog they called her for scraps of affection that should never have been hers to take in the first place.

She would fight. And she would die, if she had to. But she would not break.

The soft memory of waking up in his arms flashed in her mind's eye, just for a second. A half-a-second. The ghost of the sensation of lips against hers and scarred hands on her face.

But that wasn't right; she'd never kissed him. She'd *wanted* to, plenty of times, but never...

Four burning-green eyes burned on the horizon, and it struck Frelia like a bolt of lightning—"Cillian, you're dead!"

The snow stopped. The throbbing in her side stopped. The bruising on her chin, the stuffed-cotton feeling in her ears, the anxiety gnawing at her stomach like a rabid animal.

Everything. All of it.

Stopped.

"Well that's not nice," said Cillian.

His form loomed before her, but it wasn't *right*. She could see that, now. He didn't have the scar over his eye from the Massacre of Kollavik, didn't have grey in his beard like he had at the Battle of Spirits' Fen.

And *she* wasn't right, either. She could blink both eyes, and the Valerius Shield was on her arm, and she wasn't dressed for the Silverwood winter ball.

"And that's not how Cillian talked," Frelia told the ghost-that-wasn't-Cillian. "Who are you? *What* are you?"

Cillian laughed, but it wasn't his laugh. It was wheezier, quieter. No longer an echo pulled from her memory, but something else entirely.

Then he said, "Ready to go?"

And they were back at the crest of the hill overlooking a Volsinii war camp.

"*Ja,*" Frelia heard herself say, as though compelled. "Let's go."

CHAPTER FORTY-ONE

FAUSTINE STARED AT THE rounded features and perfect makeup of "Clarissa Caecillion," and her stomach clenched in abject terror. No, *no!* She couldn't let Lucia della Trova hurt anyone else. She *wouldn't.*

And if that meant siding with the headmaster, then merciful Saints, here went nothing.

"I'm not drunk," Faustine said at once.

"I'm not either," Christel said, "actually."

The headmaster stared at them, his face unreadable, and then glanced over to della Trova.

She shifted beneath his gaze, clearly uncomfortable. "They're children, Vendrick. How would they know?"

He said nothing for so long a moment, Faustine wanted to throw up.

"Clarissa," he finally said, crisply and without looking at her, "do me a favor and remind me—where's that thing you gave me for my eighth birthday?"

Faustine stared at him in exasperated horror. Now was *not* the time to be asking ridiculous questions! For a terrible moment, Faustine wondered if she'd chosen wrong after all.

Della Trova seemed to be of the same mind. "How should I know what you've done with something almost three decades old?"

Something shifted imperceptibly in the Headmaster's face as he said, "Right..."

He was still for a moment longer, and then the hallway came alive with purple, arcane light. Headmaster Caecillion drew a magic rune so fast, Faustine barely saw his fingers move, and then he was blasting dark fire at della Trova.

"Vendrick!" della Trova screeched, scrambling out of the way just in time to avoid being incinerated. "What's gotten into you?"

"I have no idea who you are." The headmaster drew a new rune even as he spoke. "But I know my baby sister knows *exactly* where that gift is."

A knot of grey magic bloomed in the air just before the rune the headmaster was drawing, and it streaked towards della Trova like a tiny shooting star.

"*Hypogia,*" della Trova muttered, and drew her own rune.

The headmaster's magic comet crashed into a tightly-woven wall of arcane energy, and della Trova batted his magic away like an annoying insect.

Faustine had to *do something!* She'd only get in the way during a mage's duel, but there was more than one way to be a thorn in someone's side.

For the first time in her whole life, anxiety didn't gnaw at her as Faustine shouted, "It's Lucia della Trova!"

And then Faustine saw a Volsinii adult get genuinely, outrightly, angry. It lit the sharp angles and gaunt features of the headmaster's face until his eyes glittered like poisoned emeralds.

"Is this the Unseen's idea of a joke?" The headmaster yanked on air, and the shooting star arced sharply around a pillar at the end of the hall and rocketed back towards them.

"Fooled you, didn't it?" Della Trova stepped towards the wall and stretched her shield to the size of a dinner plate, a tea tray, a tea *table,* her eyes never leaving the headmaster.

"I *knew* something was off," the headmaster growled, pulling on the comet like a mad puppeteer. "My little sister would *never* talk about Triad business with Ironfang in the room, would *never* question roasting our mum, and she never, *ever* calls me 'dear' unless it's directly preceded by *Vendy.*"

Della Trova jerked her shield up, but wasn't quite fast enough. The comet ricocheted against the wall opposite her, and then the one behind, and then ripped through her leg as it sped off down the hall.

"You're not as good an actress as you think you are," Headmaster Caecillion snarled over the woman's scream.

Faustine almost missed when his free hand made the Silverwood war sign for 'restrain her' at the small of his back.

"You *bastard!*" All of della Trova's weight collapsed onto her good leg. "Markus della Luciana will have your head for this!"

"No he won't," Faustine said, and both adults jumped. "Where do you think Siegmund is?"

"Siegmund loves a good war story," Christel added, and then glanced to Faustine. "He's been asking Captain della Luciana for all his good ones for the last twenty minutes."

Faustine nodded, and together they drew the daggers they'd been carrying since the darkbeasts had first attacked Silverwood.

"Well, well," della Trova said, "turning traitor for the attention? How 'youngest child'."

That warm, angry feeling from down in Markus' lab was back in Faustine's stomach. "I don't really care what you think," she said.

Della Trova's jaw fell open and her free hand jumped to her heart in mock offense. "I daresay, Faustine, your father raised you better than that."

"Must you make this into yet another opera performance?" The headmaster sounded genuinely annoyed. "I wasn't joking; you're a maudlin, talentless hack my sister could always do much better than."

Della Trova gasped, affronted, and that was when Faustine took off running and slammed her shoulder into the woman's spine.

They fell hard onto the tiled floor, Faustine's dagger flying out of reach in the scramble. Della Trova screeched and raked at Faustine with talon-like nails, leaving long, angry welts down the girl's cheek. Faustine drew back a fist—*thumbs on the outside, for the Saints' sake!* she could hear Orsina saying—and smashed it into Clarissa's stolen face.

"*I.*" She cracked the woman's face into the floor.

"*Am.*" Again.

"*Not.*" Blood began to splatter as the tile cracked beneath the concussive force.

"*Prey!*"

Like makeup washing away in heavy rain, Clarissa's face began sloughing off. It cleared away the austere, Caecillion features, and left behind squared-off ones and a head of icy blonde hair.

Faustine only had a moment to memorize what Lucia della Trova's *actual* features looked like before cracking her head against the ground again.

Della Trova's hand snapped up, clawing at Faustine's face again, she was forced to fall back or lose an eye. Della Trova's hands crackled with golden magic as she dragged herself into a kneeling position. She launched herself at Faustine, and after a short, scrabbling scuffle, caught her arm around Faustine's throat.

Faustine's nails dragged uselessly at della Trova's pale forearm, and the woman's other hand buzzed with golden magic as it pressed into the side of her face.

"Drop the Singularity," della Trova hissed. "*Now.*"

Headmaster Caecillion stared her down with visible hate in his eyes, his comet floating somewhere near his left ear. "You're not going to kill Ironfang's daughter."

"If she wants to turn traitor, I certainly will!"

"Let *go!*" Faustine shouted, pounding her fist against della Trova's side.

Della Trova suddenly choked, and Faustine wrestled away the stinging, grey magic needles. And there was Christel, their knife in della Trova's kidney and their arms around her throat.

"Don't touch my friends," Christel said.

Light winked out to Faustine's right as the headmaster's comet disappeared, and he began drawing another rune in the air before him. Purple astral energy began to coalesce around della Trova's throat and wrists, just like the astral sword he'd conjured at the beginning of the year for Professor Valerius to fight with.

For a moment, Faustine just stared at the magic as it tightened around their prisoner. This was the right thing, and she could feel it in her bones. *No more lying,* she thought, *no more sneaking, no more of Father and Markus' schemes.*

But still, her stomach twisted into knots.

"Keep a firm hold on the prisoner and don't let her out of my sight," the headmaster ordered. "We've a swordmaster to find."

CHAPTER FORTY-TWO

FRELIA'S HEAD WAS SWIMMING.

It usually happened around the fourth time Cillian flung her at a garmr with the Grimsdalr blink rune, and if her math was right, she'd already felled six today, putting her total at a completely absurd ninety-one killed in the Tyrant's War. It made perfect sense that her head was swimming and a headache was blooming between her eyes and...

No. Something isn't right.

She was fighting knights now, her sword slick with blood. Her sword-arm had long since gone numb, her shield-arm deadened. Though the Valerius Shield had saved her life on countless occasions even just today, the bloody thing was *heavy*.

She stepped over the dead—some in deep Valerius blue or mossy Grimsdalr green, some in virulent Volsinii crimson or somber Caecillion purple—as she battled the living.

Caecillion.

Dammit, what wasn't she remembering? It dug into the back of her mind and refused to let go.

It wasn't until the Volsinii Knights began retreating that she snapped out of battle-numbness and took a moment to scour the battlefield. That wasn't right; the Volsinii didn't retreat. Unless—and she barely dared to think it—the Krakenguard had managed to take out their Princess, or something. Was it possible this was over, after all?

No.

They weren't retreating; they were *regrouping*. Their beastminders were calling new orders to the remaining garmur, and Frelia cursed that she'd run out of arrows hours ago. Her aim with magic had never been quite as true. Taking out a beastminder or two would have been helpful, right about now.

An arrow whizzed by her cheek, scoring a long welt. Frelia cast about with wild eyes, bringing the Valerius Shield back defensively against her chest. She found her mark a moment later—a knight atop a swooping wyvern, already nocking a second arrow.

"Where the hell are Thera and the wyvern corps?" Frelia growled, already on the move.

"I don't know!" Cillian shouted back, and she realized he'd looped his warhorse back around towards her.

"Arrow!" Frelia ordered, unslinging her bow from across her shoulders.

"I'm out!"

"Fuck!"

A second arrow pinged against the Valerius Shield, hard enough to bruise her deadened arm.

Cillian pulled up short some ten feet from Frelia, yanking his last javelin from its notch in his saddle. He pulled back to throw as Frelia forced her hand into casting position, and began to draw the wide, looping arcs of the ancient lightning rune as familiar to her as her own skin. They released the projectiles within seconds of each other, and the knight above spurred her wyvern into a spinning maneuver that made Frelia want to vomit just looking at it.

But somehow, she'd nocked a third arrow during it, and Frelia barely saw the release. But she heard the twang of the bowstring, and apparently Cillian did, too; he urged his charger into a sharp canter. Frelia was forced to fall back out of his way or be trampled.

She heard the sickening, fleshy *thunk* as the arrow burrowed into Cillian's leg, and cursed the wyvern knight as she sailed back out of range.

"You *dorchya!*" Frelia's confused numbness turned to irritation; war was no place to play the hero. "Get to a healer, *now!*"

Cillian grimaced as he snapped the arrow shaft and tossed it aside, leaving the arrowhead embedded in his leg. "You seen one lately, Frey?"

Come to think of it, no, she hadn't. Their white magic corps should have been by, by now. *The wyvern corps, the white magic corps...* where *was* everyone?

Everyone...

Wasn't everyone at Silverwood?

"You're dead!" she shouted at Cillian, and the cycle began again.

"Ready to go?" he asked amidst a world of whirling, silvery snow.

"*You're not him!*" Frelia shrieked, holding desperately onto that fact with a white-knuckle grip. "The Valerius Shield is gone and I only have one fucking eye!"

They stood atop the crest of a hill, looking down on a Volsinii war camp, and Frelia howled like the wolf they called her.

This happened every single time she remembered the truth. Not-Cillian would reset the world, and they would fight through some of the worst battles of Frelia's life while she forgot she'd already survived them. Already lost most of them. She would shield-bash her way through knights and garmur and Silverwood friends and all the while, a dead man fought beside her.

"Cillian." Frelia's sword slipped from her grasp as she reached out to grab hold of his face. "Listen to me. You. Are. *Dead.*"

He had to know that. *She* had to hold onto that. The dead had to stay in Helheim where they belonged so that the living could...

So that the living could do what? She thought, desperately trying to remember.

Stubble scraped across Frelia's hands as Cillian spoke. "Not yet, I'm not."

"Yes, you are," Frelia insisted. "For ten years, I have fought without you. And without Thera, and Hägen, and everyone else. I..."

Even here in this unending cycle of death upon death, Frelia couldn't find the words to tell that dead that she was fighting alongside Volsinii, now. Just one of them, technically, but the result was the same.

"Move forward!" Frelia burst out. "The living are supposed to move *forward!*"

"Did you hit your head on that last charge?" Cillian reached out to feel around her hairline for bumps or bruises. "You're not making sense."

"You don't believe me," she said, and her hands fell away from his face.

He cocked his head to study her. "Of course I don't. I'm still breathing."

That's right. He was *breathing.*

"And the fight is not over so long as you breathe," Frelia murmured.

She stared at Cillian for a long moment, and something began to unspool across her mind.

She had known for a long time that she was a patchwork of everyone who had ever loved her. She had her mum's eyes, her da's swordsmanship style, Diarmuid's place in the world, Cillian's awful sense of humor, Thera's work ethic, Hägen's war song, Edmund's stories of the Triad, and Leon's inability to turn down a cold beer. She had been ripped apart and stitched back together more times than she could count, and her body bore the scars. Those, too, were signs someone cared enough about her to piece her back together again—even if it was just herself.

But she had no worldly idea what part of her patchwork came from Vendrick. Nor who she'd be if she allowed him a bigger patch. And maybe she was just terrified that whoever that Frelia would become would be no longer recognizable to the ghosts she'd left behind.

But she *had* to leave those ghosts behind—in Helheim, where they belonged—before they consumed her. She saw that now, as clearly as she saw her only path forward.

"Frey?" asked the ghost with Cillian's face.

"I'm breathing." Frelia stooped to pick up the sword she'd dropped.

Cillian nodded. "Right. And we're going to win this, and you're going to go to Grimsdalr Lodge for a bit, and then we'll take back Kjell. And then the mountain passes. And then your family's barrows. And then your kids will go sledding with mine on that giant hill behind Valerius Lodge, just like we did."

He smiled as he painted a picture of the future he would never see, and Frelia's resolve almost broke free of her grasp and swallowed her.

"I promise," he added.

Almost.

Frelia shut her eyes—"Don't make promises you can't keep."—and swung.

The bastard sword whooshed through empty air, and Frelia's eye snapped open.

Just the one.

They no longer stood on the crest of a hill overlooking a Volsinii war camp, but one overlooking the forests of Valerius Territory. Frelia knew that if she turned around, she would see Valerius Lodge in all its unburned glory. A proud manor of stone and heavy timber, its roofs peaked to run off the snow and its approach swept and shoveled at all hours.

But she had to stop looking back. All that remained of her ancestral home were a handful of ashen cross-beams and piles of stone, and she *knew* that. So no matter how desperately she wanted to hold the memory of her childhood in her hands, she couldn't.

There was nothing there to see.

"That's not very nice," Cillian said.

"That's not how he talked!" Frelia slashed again, crosswise, and watched as her sword slid through his body without resistance. "Cillian would be making fun of me for 'always saying the nicest things' or flirting with him or something."

She could almost hear the echo of him—the *real* him—in her ears. But she squashed it down and wrapped both of her hands around the hilt of her bastard sword. The Valerius Shield disappeared from her left arm as she fell into middle guard, as though it had never been.

As though she'd lost it after the Battle of Spirits' Fen and fought for ten years now without it.

"He did not go into battle without his horse..." Frelia slashed again through the ghostly figure before her. "...and he did not laugh during war..." Reversed thrust and tried again. "...and the last time I saw him, he had a scar over his eye from Kollavik and grey in his beard..." Side-stepped around his unmoving person, and readied to thrust again, low, from the Fool's guard. "...and if I told him something, he would *fucking believe me!*"

Frelia dragged the tip of her blade skyward, and would have slashed him cleanly in two from groin to crown, if he were real.

But the ghost-who-wasn't-Cillian merely cocked its head at her, and cawed like a raven.

The sound vibrated against her bones, and the world became a whirl of silvery-grey snow once again.

"You're a garmr!" Frelia shouted over the blizzarding winds. "I'm supposed to be tracking you!"

The world froze.

"No I'm not," came a tiny voice from behind her.

Gripping the hilt of her bastard sword tightly, Frelia turned to find Cillian's child-self standing knee-deep in snow. He was wearing the wolf hat his aunt had knitted him for Yule one year, and he was bundled in pelts and furs and carrying a linden shield almost the entire size of him.

Frelia stared in mute horror.

"Do you want to go sledding?" Child-Cillian asked. "I brought you a shield!"

He held out the linden shield with a beaming grin. His front tooth was missing, from where he'd knocked it out horse training as a child and it hadn't grown in until years later.

The fucking monster pretending to be her best friend had dug *deep* into her memory for that detail. It would pay for that, feather by bloody feather.

"No, little one," Frelia managed. "You need to go home, now."

Child-Cillian jutted out his lower lip. "But we just got here!"

Frelia's fingers tightened around the hilt of her sword. It was one thing to run a sword through a man, but a child? How was she supposed to kill a child?

Frelia didn't realize she was crying until the tears froze to the one side of her face. "You need," she pressed, "to leave."

"Sled with me," child-Cillian insisted, shoving the linden round shield at her again.

Frelia's knees gave out, pitching her forward into the snow. Ice seeped into the nicest dress she owned, but she barely felt the biting cold. She stared at the young face of one of her dearest friends, and the voice that came from her throat was not her own.

Or, well. It wasn't her own anymore.

It had been, once. When she was very young, and her da and Diarmuid were still alive. It was the tiny voice that had chased her brother up and down the halls of Valerius Lodge, and shrieked with laughter out in the forests and fields of her home territory.

"I'm sorry, Cillian," said Frelia's child-self.

The bastard sword had become a dagger in her tiny hands, and she thrust it forward with all the might in her child's body.

It sank this time, biting deep into Cillian's stomach. It was his brown eyes that stared at her in horrified betrayal, but it was ichor that was black as pitch running from the wound in his stomach and dribbling from his lips.

"But you're dead," Frelia-past and Frelia-present both whispered, "and I'm not."

And then it was an adult who knelt in the snow between the Silverwood Chapel and the Imperial Watchers' Barracks.

It was an adult whose bloodrune reverberated so hard against her bones she wanted to vomit as she rose to her feet.

An adult who wrapped her fingers around the hilt of her very much real, very much steel bastard sword and drew it.

And it was an adult who stared down four green eyes on the horizon, set into an avian face fifteen feet off the ground.

The garmr cawed as it spread its wings wide enough to blot out the moon, and it was a sound Frelia knew well. It was pain, and it was loss, and it was grief and rage and a thousand dead knights. It was dyeing your hair blonde to hide, and it was wearing blue to piss off the Imperator himself.

"*Muninn,*" Frelia growled, and she lowered the sword into middle guard.

CHAPTER FORTY-THREE

VENDRICK TORE THROUGH THE Silverwood grounds, expecting to chase footprints in the snow and hoping to death he'd just have an earful on the other end about how it hadn't been an hour. Faustine and Christel struggled to keep up, dragging della Trova between them, but they didn't complain.

She did, however.

"Do you have any idea what the Unseen are capable of?" della Trova shouted at his back.

Vendrick regretted not taking the extra moment to gag her with astral energy when he'd had the chance. Her arms were bound, but he wasn't about to stop to draw another rune now. Frelia's footsteps went clear across campus.

"They'll flay you alive and use your bones as science projects!" della Trova added. "Whatever you're thinking of doing to me, it isn't half so awful as what they'll do if I fail."

"Can you shut up?" Christel muttered, but they were visibly pale in the moonlight. "Also headmaster, keep going right, I can feel the rumbling that way."

"You've already failed, della Trova," Vendrick said as he followed Christel's directions. "Now it's simply a matter of death or dishonor."

"No I haven't." Della Trova shook her head maniacally. "The ritual can still succeed."

"Oh, we're talking *rituals,*" Vendrick said. "Fantastic, what kind?"

"Give up, Vendrick." There was no longer mocking confidence in della Trova's voice, but something quiet and desperate. "If you interrupt them, you'll kill everyone you take with you to do it."

"No need to concern yourself with my fate," Vendrick interrupted. "I'm your ex-girlfriend's dour older brother, remember?"

"What ritual, della Trova?" Faustine's voice trembled, but she said it anyway. "You don't mean the Ascension, do you?"

Della Trova spluttered for a moment like a fish yanked out of Lake Silverwood. "You little bitch!"

"Left, now!" Christel interjected.

"What do you mean 'Ascension,' Faustine?" Vendrick pressed as they moved on.

"It's what they did to my father," Faustine said, shaking so hard she was making della Trova move, too, "he was never the same afterwards and my mother never came back."

Vendrick's stomach twisted, and he forced himself to keep moving. "Where is my *sister,* Lucia?" he demanded.

Silence fell as they dragged their prisoner towards the Watchers' Barracks, broken only by the crunching footsteps of boots on snow.

"You're going to need to torture that out of me, Vendrick—excuse me—*Vendy,* dear," della Trova said. "I'm not saying a word."

Vendrick refrained from pointing out how many words she had, in fact, been saying. He could practically feel Christel and Faustine's eyes on his back, asking without asking if their prisoner were serious. If it were something he would realistically do. It was almost a relief to pass the chapel fence and get a clear look at the Watcher's Barracks, in that at least he wouldn't have to answer those accusing stares.

Of course he would. He would do anything necessary for victory.

The relief was short lived, in that there was *not* a lecture about leaving a Kaldiri shieldmaiden to her work waiting for him.

Frelia knelt on the crest of the hill, frozen in place and locked in a staring contest with a monster from legend. The enormous, raven-like darkbeast was taller than the chapel itself, and the arcane energy in the air was so thick Vendrick wouldn't need any of his own to cast. He could simply pull from the air around him.

"What the hell?" He held up the Silverwood hand sign for 'halt' with his left hand while his right immediately started to draw.

"What are you *doing?*" della Trova screeched. "They are in *communion!*"

Vendrick was so startled he actually looked away from his rune to search della Trova's face. It was beaten bloody, but he'd made sure there was no danger of concussion.

"What?" Faustine asked. "You mean like they're talking?"

"Lord Muninn is feasting on her memories," della Trova snapped. "It is an honor."

"And we *shouldn't* rip her out of it?" Christel added with enough sarcasm to drown a small animal.

Vendrick just stared at della Trova. "Were you always this insane, or is this new?"

"She sounds like every other Unseen," Faustine offered, shifting her weight from foot to foot, "for what that's worth."

"Noted." Vendrick turned back to his rune. "Keep her secured."

He got two lines further into the Singularity rune before Frelia recoiled away from the creature so violently Vendrick could see it across the field. She got to her feet a half-second later, drawing her sword and settling into a sword stance Vendrick knew very well.

"*Muninn,*" she growled.

"How does she know that?" Faustine asked in naked admiration.

Frelia's head jerked towards the source of the noise, and she startled a second time to find them all standing there. Disbelief warred with horror in her eye.

"You said an hour!" Frelia jabbed a finger at him.

Vendrick was so relieved he could cry. "Change of plans!" he shouted back. "Now do what you do best!"

Frelia grinned, and though it looked almost like she hadn't meant to, it was the most beautiful thing Vendrick had ever seen.

"*How did you break out of communion?*" della Trova shrieked.

"Who the fuck are you?" Frelia shouted back. "Actually never mind, I'm dealing with the Goddesses-damned garmr first!"

I love this woman shot through Vendrick's mind a half-second before the darkbeast cawed in what he could have sworn was affront. As though, really, it was *right there.*

Frelia shuddered at the noise, but shook herself and began to draw a jagged, looping rune with her free hand. Vendrick abandoned his half-drawn singularity rune and began working through the one for dark fire instead, holding off just before the last stroke.

He would only have one shot, if she cracked its ribs open.

Cries of alarm went up behind him as Frelia disappeared from sight, but Vendrick kept his eye trained on the raven-like monster's breast. He wondered, somewhere in the back of his mind, how the hell Frelia could aim the Grimsdalr Blink. He really ought to ask her.

Muninn took off with a single beat of its great wings, and suddenly Frelia was falling through empty air.

"*Shit!*" Christel hissed.

Vendrick knew he didn't have a rune to catch her or arrest her fall, but he flipped through his spellbook for one anyway. *Clarissa would have one,* he thought, sourly. There was too much ground to cover to do it physically, either, and all he could do was watch in horror as Frelia scrabbled at the open air, and began to fall. And then another, even louder howl pierced the frozen night a half-second before the back wall of the chapel erupted outwards in a shower of stone and masonry.

An enormous, wolf-like garmr pounced through the opening it had created.

It bounded across the hill in loping strides, and though snow had begun settling across its furry pelt, Vendrick could still see vast, old wounds slashed across its flanks. His stomach sank as the garmr pushed off the crest of the hill, going airborne and snatching at Frelia with its massive jaws.

It caught her by the cloak like a mother cat yanking a kitten to safety by the scruff of its neck.

Oh thank the Saints warred with *wait, fuck!* in the back of his mind, while dread unlike anything he'd ever felt crashed into Vendrick. Everything he had ever built was tumbling down around his ears, and he was powerless to stop it.

CHAPTER FORTY-FOUR

FRELIA STARED INTO THE fiery green eyes of a second Goddesses-damn garmr, and a very old fear blossomed in her stomach. The thing was massive, bigger than a carriage and twice as stocky, and she was the only melee fighter in this battle.

We're going to die, aren't we?

The same hopelessness that had threatened to swallow her during the war crept into Frelia's heart. She was going to join Cillian in Helheim after all and she was never going to be able to tell Vendrick that—

Fuck, its eyes are wrong.

She wasn't sure where the thought came from, but it was true. The wolf-like garmr's eyes were fiery, effervescent green just like every other garmur's she'd ever encountered, but it was just a ring around a familiar, muted brown.

Familiar? She stared hard into the garmr's unnatural gaze, trying to place where she'd seen it before.

Wait.

All the breath left Frelia's lungs, and she was rendered incapable of a single thought beneath the rumbling in her bones. Her sword was heavy in her hands, and her instincts screamed at her to *run, dammit!* as she dangled from the creature's claws.

"You don't... want to fight that one." Vendrick's voice pierced through her panic from somewhere very far away.

"Why not?" Frelia shouted back without breaking eye contact with the beast.

Silence, and then:

"It's Thera Grimsdalr."

The beast dropped her then, even as Muninn screeched overhead and Frelia took off running.

She could not have heard him right.

"The fuck you mean it's Thera?" Frelia shouted.

"The, er, Unseen experimented on her." Vendrick was doing that Volsinii thing where they shifted their weight because they wanted to run. "I brought her with me from Ascalon when I left the Imperator's service."

"They did *what?*"

Her throat tightened as she met Vendrick's eye, across the hill. She almost missed it when the wolf-garmr—when *Thera*—sank her teeth into Muninn's clawed foot and jerked the raven around.

In the frigid moonlight, Vendrick seemed hollow, somehow. Lesser. More like the boy she'd learned to brew poisons beside than the grim-faced Spymaster who had ordered the deaths of hundreds.

It didn't make sense.

Nothing made sense.

Frelia had grown up beside Thera. Learned her letters, her numbers, the war songs beside her. Had suffered through having her hair braided and clothes stolen and endless rounds of sparring. Thera was her sister as much as Cillian was her brother. Frelia should have *known*, somehow, what had become of her.

Besides, the Grimsdalr were born to stand as the bulwark of the Northern Wilds. Theirs was the Bloodrune of the Sentinel, made to kill garmur. This was blasphemy, heresy, *desecration;* the guardians of the Northern Wilds couldn't be turned into garmur...

Could they?

Frelia grasped for something, *anything* to make it make sense. "Thera died at the Battle for Skjöldr."

"Presumed to," said Vendrick.

"Then why the fuck didn't you tell me one of the Grimsdalr twins was alive?"

"One, because I am a wretched pile of secrets," Vendrick shouted, "and two, what do you propose either of us do about it, exactly?"

That wasn't how Vendrick did business. There was something deeper here, something worse.

It was then that Frelia felt it—a visceral pain in her gut that made her battle scars feel like nothing, made losing the war feel like nothing. She almost wondered if they'd crossed the border into Helheim itself, it was so desperately cold. Her hands itched to spill the blood that the twins couldn't, to impress upon this monster that they *had not won.* This fight was not over.

Frelia was still breathing.

From overhead, Muninn cawed again, and the echo was deafening. It had managed to kick Thera down the hillside, its taloned leg spouting ichor. By some miracle, Frelia's fingers were still wrapped around the hilt of her sword. There would be time for accusations later.

Fight. Breath. Now.

She drew up to cast the Grimsdalr blink, as fast and accurately as she dared. Muninn was diving, now, its great feathery wings outstretched as it veered sharply downwards with grasping talons.

Blue light dripped from her fingers as Frelia dragged them through the air in front of her chest. One looping line, another, *another*, a jagged one sharply down the center. When it didn't immediately spark, Frelia's stomach lurched in fear she'd miscast. But then the once-familiar jerk of magic sparked behind her navel, and she no longer stood on the hilltop.

The world whizzed past her, crystalizing into a hazy blue, kaleidoscopic tunnel centered on those twin sets of blazing green eyes. Hideous laughter tore from her mouth as she realized, she'd already killed her best friend, today. What was a demigod?

Frelia sliced into Muninn with the force of a cannonball, her bastard sword scraping a raw line of ichor across its wing. Wind ripped past her face at screaming speed, and her sword stuck in the junction between wing and neck. For a moment, Frelia clung to the Guardian of Traust Territory with steel and claws of her own.

Then the bastard sword which had carried her through the Northern Rebellion, through countless missions with the Cost Effectives, through this post-war hell she should never have lived to see, cracked.

Blood dripped into Frelia's eye and she stared, horrified, at the crossguard a half-second before it broke away from the blade entirely. And then she was falling, caught in the slipstream behind the enormous raven, barreling towards the ground.

She was pretty sure she was laughing, but she couldn't hear it past the roaring in her ears. *Leave it to Lady Twilight's raven to finally get the best of you, eh?* She could almost hear... *herself* say, actually. Normally that kind of thing would have come from Cillian's voice in the back of her mind, or maybe her da's.

But those memories were dead, so the thought was her own, and it startled Frelia so much she stopped laughing. The world still whipped by at a dizzying speed, the ground looming larger with every moment, but she could just make out the glint of something grey-gold and metallic embedded into Muninn's back.

The *Ballad of Hana* suddenly screamed in the back of her mind—
Now only the dead see the end of war,

but even fewer keep accurate score.
Oh, I'll tell you a tale that you'll wish weren't true—
Of Midnight's hell-children that our Hana slew.

—and Frelia *needed* that sword. More than life, more than air, more than solid ground beneath her feet. She would use Saint Hana's sword to slay the monster her ancestress had never managed to.

Frelia spread her arms and legs like wings themselves, trying to steer her fall towards the damned raven. It didn't do much to slow her down, and so Frelia went with the next best thing—

She drew the Grimsdalr blink.

As fast as she dared, she drew the sigil on the back of her opposite hand to keep it in place. Looping arcs and jagged lines came together into one arcane sigil that burned into the skin of her hand.

And then she was dragged through the crystalline, kaleidoscopic tunnel again by her left hand, like something was pulling her towards a building across the way. Her shoulder wrenched at the force of the blink, and blood was smearing in her eye and turning the whole world a hazy red. She smashed through to the Waking World shoulder-first like a fireman with a burning door, crashing squarely into Muninn's back and snatching fistfuls of feathers.

The garmr cawed again, and this time, Frelia felt no pain.

It pulled up mere yards from the ground, flapping its great wings and trying to shake off its newfound parasite. Frelia dug her fingers deeper into the creature's greasy feathers, and her eye raked its back for the tell-tale gleam of Hana's sword.

There! So deep in the garmr's mantle as to nearly be buried, Frelia could just make out a hilt and crossguard.

She dug her hands as deep into Muninn's feathers as they could go, and dragged herself, hand over hand, towards the blade. It was agonizingly slow going. Her hand slipped and she was dragged halfway down Muninn's back before she caught hold again.

"Frelia!" shouted Vendrick from somewhere in her periphery.

"Need Hana's sword!" she shouted back, risking lifting a hand to point at it.

He fell silent, and Frelia focused on her hands. She wished for a hatchet, a dagger, a Goddesses-damned arrow—anything to help her make purchase on these oily feathers. A trail of light caught in the corner of her eye, and Frelia flattened herself against Muninn's back to get a look at it.

One of Vendrick's Singularity pellets was whizzing past her like a tiny comet. It illuminated the inky black sheen on the raven's feathers for a moment before burying itself in Muninn's back.

The raven roared in horrified pain, but it was no longer an eldritch echo. Muninn was a normal garmr, in normal garmr pain. Frelia watched in stunned amazement as the Singularity pellet ripped itself out of Muninn's back north of the sword, and then, like a deft sewing needle, dug back in across the way.

Vendrick was *sawing a chunk off the garmr.*

Frelia glanced down to the fast-moving ground below. After some quick mental math, she drew in a breath and loosened her grip. She let herself slide down the monster's back and fall the final yards to the ground.

She smacked into the ground hard enough to knock the wind out of her lungs, and Frelia stared through the red haze up to the cloudless sky for a moment, trying to catch her breath.

Something heavy smacked down near her, and Frelia jerked upright. The smell of garmr blood and rotting meat hit her full force, and Frelia's eye watered as she dragged herself to her feet to go after it.

And there, deep-seated in a sawed-off chunk of garmr flesh, was the Sword of Hana. Frelia's triumphant *"Ha!"* rang out across the hillside a half-second before she put her boot to the disgusting, fleshy lump and yanked.

The old blade came away from the decaying tissue, as sharp and shiny as the day it had been forged. The hilt fit comfortably in Frelia's hand, the runes familiar as they stared up at her from the crossguard.

A replica had hung in her father's study for Frelia's entire life. It had nothing on the real thing.

And as she flung ichor off the enchanted steel and brought it up to middle guard, her bloodrune sang with rightness.

CHAPTER FORTY-FIVE

MUNINN WAS FALTERING. THE headmaster had sawed a chunk out of its wing and Professor Valerius had scraped a line of feathers and skin off its other shoulder. And now the professor had pulled a sword out of a disgusting wad of darkbeast flesh, and was readying to go at it again.

"*Heel!*" shouted a familiar voice that turned Faustine's insides to ice.

And Muninn froze—well, as much as it could while beating its wings to hover above the ground. After the shrieking of the darkbeast and the sizzling of arcane runes, the sudden, windy silence on the hilltop was deafening.

"*Vendrick Caecillion,*" Markus shouted, "*what is the meaning of this?*"

Faustine cringed and felt the instinctive urge to hide behind Christel or della Trova. No, *no,* she couldn't let him ruin this like he did everything else!

"About time you showed up!" della Trova shouted.

Professor Valerius, however, said, "Oh, you can fuck off, Markus." and finished the rune she'd been drawing.

She disappeared from sight for less than a second, and when she snapped back into view, it was accompanied by the stench of ozone and an arcane snap Faustine felt in her bones. The Professor cleaved into

Muninn's breast, and the monster shrieked as her sword cut deep into purplish tissue. They plummeted together, Professor Valerius hanging onto her sword for dear life.

Faustine's stomach twisted as black fire ricocheted off the headmaster's fingertips and into the hole in Muninn's chest. It danced along organs and necrotic tissue, and forced Professor Valerius to drop to the ground.

Muninn crashed into the side of the hill, and all was silent for a moment but for the crackling flames.

Markus began, "How could you—!"

But stopped, suddenly, when the Professor's sword was aimed at his throat. "How dare you," she seethed, "pervert Muninn for your own selfish goals!"

She swung, but Markus ducked out of the way just in time. "I have no idea what you're talking about," he said.

"Do you think I don't know my own stories?" the professor screeched. "That I don't recognize Lady Twilight's raven, the Guardian of Traust Territory, the Lord of the Slain?"

Oh no, those sounded like stories, Legends, even. Faustine's hands twisted into fists. This raven truly was grotesque, and her brother even more so for what he'd done to it.

"Why are the Kaldiri so macabre?" della Trova muttered.

Christel hit her in the arm, just like when they were telling Owen to shut up in the middle of class.

"I. Know. My. History." The professor was rounding on Markus again, surefooted as a huntress in the snow. "I am Kaldiri; I learned the old tales before I was even off my mother's milk. I know my place in the Waking World, Markus della Luciana."

She raised her sword again. Quick. Fast. Brutal.

"It is opposite *you.* "

She swung, and this time Markus was ready for it. He drew a short, sharp rune in the air between them, and then Professor Valerius was blasted backwards with enough arcane force to knock her into Muninn's smoldering corpse.

Faustine was torn between running after her and holding onto della Trova. That hit looked bad, and no matter how many darkbeasts she killed, Professor Valerius was still human. She still bled, still hurt, still could die.

Arcane light bloomed at Headmaster Caecillion's fingertips, but apparently he needn't have bothered. The wolf-like darkbeast that had caught the professor the first time was back, bounding up the hill with snarling jaws wide and ivory teeth glinting.

"Stay," barked Markus.

The darkbeast froze mid-step, skidding to a halt a stone's throw from Markus' smug face.

"Well, well, Vendrick." Markus clicked his tongue reprovingly as he strode over to the wolf-like darkbeast. "I knew you were up to something. Stealing from the Imperator, are we?"

Faustine blanched. "That... *thing* belongs to Father?"

"It's a darkbeast, you insufferable snit," Markus snapped. "To whom else would it?" He pitched his voice louder to add, "Hello, Grimsdalr! I presume you missed me?"

All four of the beast's green eyes narrowed at Markus.

Grimsdalr? Faustine thought. *Like the Blink rune?* How could Markus possibly know whom this darkbeast had been built from?

Unless...

Unless this was the one he'd lost, all those years ago. Markus always said it had been stolen, but he'd never said by whom.

"Yes, hello!" Markus added. "It's been a while. How have you been, you wretched thing?"

Faustine stared, wide-eyed, at the monster. "Markus, I don't think you should be taunting it."

Already her mind was whirring through what Professor Valerius had said about darkbeasts at the beginning of the year. *Guardians of Helheim, Lady Midnight's Children. You know. Monsters.* If it attacked, would it stop at just eating Markus? Or would they all be dead?

"What was the point, Markus?"

All eyes went to the Headmaster, who had not one, not even two, but *three* of those comets swirling around the space behind his head like a frightful halo.

"Those are incisions on her flanks," the headmaster added, jabbing a finger at the darkbeast. "Daily, repeated incisions, and likely blood draws. But why? Darkbeasts do not require medical treatment."

"I need not answer the likes of you," Markus snapped, although he didn't move to draw a rune to fire back at the headmaster.

But Faustine knew. If that darkbeast supposedly belonged to the Imperator, then it was for the Unseen. And if it were what remained of Thera Grimsdalr, and the blood Markus had been given to work with at Silverwood was theirs...

There was only one reason. One, horrible little reason.

"For her bloodrune," Faustine said. "That's the only reason the Unseen do anything."

"Oh, that's right—Captain Markus, dear," della Trova piped up, "your little sister here thinks herself a hero."

Markus' colorless eyes turned to Faustine. "She always has. It never gets her anywhere."

He began to draw something in the air before him, but abandoned the rune when one of the headmaster's comets came zipping across the hill towards him. Another comet zoomed over to sit at eye level with della Trova, and she stared at it with horrified distaste.

The headmaster stalked across the hilltop just as surely as the professor had, his short, leather boots silent in the snow. "Where," he said, low and dangerous, "is my sister?"

The statement was the flag atop a mountain of pain, and it struck Faustine hard in the stomach. That was what concern sounded like, what care did. And for his sister! Not even a spouse, or a pawn, or particularly beloved pet, but a sibling.

In that moment, Faustine made her choice.

Markus' eye flicked between the headmaster and his remaining comet. "Perhaps you should have kept a closer eye on her."

The headmaster's hand rose to the level of his eyes, and purple arcane light rippled across his fingers like static lightning. "You have one chance remaining."

Markus raised his own casting hand. Red-gold light bloomed at his fingertips a half-second before he cried out in pain. He clapped a hand to his eye and reached out, blindly, to steady himself against something that wasn't there.

"Well," della Trova muttered, "that's deeply unfortunate."

The headmaster was staring in consternation, frozen mid-strike. When Markus stood up again, it was as though someone had taken a knife to his eye and drawn the whirling sigil Faustine had seen in the barrel of the syringe. The Grimsdalr Bloodrune. Blood and fluids ran down his face and into the collar of his immaculately-pressed shirt.

Faustine squashed the urge to feel sick.

"You *fucking zychnik.*"

Like a specter from the mists of the north, Professor Valerius rose shakily from where she'd been thrown before Muninn's smoking corpse.

"You weren't satisfied with stripping us of our titles..." Her footsteps were heavy, now, and war was on the horizon. "...our lands, our families, our *volchya*, our entire way of life—you are stealing our bloodrunes?"

From where it stood, frozen under a beastminders command, the wolf-garmr who had once been Thera Grimsdalr howled. Faustine could hear the pain of a thousand sleepless nights in it.

How could she not? It was the sound of her own grief, too.

"You have no right to the Grimsdalr blood archives!" the Professor screeched. "No right to their memories, their stories, their wounds—you fucking thief!"

She was down to just fists, now, but she swung with the fury of a god. Markus' eye widened and he jerked out of range, his wounded eye screwed shut.

"*I will bleed them from you myself!*"

Her eye was wild, tears and snot streaking down her ichor-splattered face as she dissolved into shouting in Kaldiri, and it was in this moment that Faustine could finally see why Father had always called her unhinged. But she didn't look that way to Faustine. She looked upset, and hurt, and like something deep in her had broken, but she didn't look crazy.

She was the farthest thing from crazy.

That's it.

Faustine's feet picked up speed without her say-so, and suddenly she was skidding across the hilltop and straight at her brother.

"Oh, don't be so dramatic," Markus snapped. "It isn't like I—oof!"

He cut himself off when Faustine's shoulder connected with his solar plexus.

They went toppling to the ground, scrapping like children in the dirt. Despite Markus easily having forty pounds on Faustine, she unbalanced them and got her hands around his throat and pressed, hard. He coughed and spluttered, and overhead, the darkbeast roared again.

Faustine glanced up just in time to see Roguemaster Olsen pelting across the hill.

She dodged the comet the headmaster threw her way, knives slipping between her fingers as she went. The Roguemaster flung them without stopping to aim, and Professor Valerius was forced to fall back. Another dagger buried itself in the headmaster's shoulder, followed by one in his left arm that sent his spellbook toppling to the ground. Then the Roguemaster slammed feet-first into where Faustine and Markus still scrabbled on the ground, and slid one dexterous hand into Markus' coat pocket.

"Don't envy your lot," Roguemaster Olsen said, and then she kicked at Faustine's ribs.

Faustine recoiled with a startled grunt as bright pain flared across her chest. She wheezed as the Roguemaster kicked at her again, and then she and Markus both winked out of sight a moment before the headmaster's comet blasted at nothing.

This time when the world fell silent, it was as gentle and all-encompassing as the snow.

CHAPTER FORTY-SIX

VENDRICK STARED IN HORRIFIED understanding at the space where Markus had once been. The Roguemaster was, apparently, Unseen. That was the only reason she would be assisting this complete fiasco in the first place.

"Faustine," Frelia croaked, "you okay down there?"

"Been better," the girl wheezed, although she sat back up. "But I'm alright, I think?"

"Good," Frelia said. "Get a look at Vendrick's wounds."

She was worried about him? No, there was no time for that now. "I'm fine for the moment," Vendrick muttered, stooping to pick up his spellbook. He winced when it jostled the knives.

"Er," said Faustine, "don't we need to get those knives out of your back?"

"Not yet." Vendrick tried to hide his grimace. "I'll bleed out without a healer."

He watched, ready to send his singularity flying, as Frelia staggered towards the wolf-like darkbeast. It blended into the shadows and was half covered in snow, but there it was, unmistakable and nightmarish.

Frelia breathed in frost, and reached her scarred hand out with visible, shaking effort.

The darkbeast stared at her for a long moment, all four eyes unreadable, its presence looming. If Thera were truly in there, she was a long way off.

But then the darkbeast nuzzled Frelia's scarred fingers like some sort of nightmare dog, and fell onto its belly, staring intently.

And a voice, so soft, so easily missed, came from deep in its throat: "Fre... li... a...?"

"This is madness," Frelia told the darkbeast, reaching out to stroke its snout as tears and snot streaked down her face. "Sheer, stark raving madness."

Vendrick's heart twisted.

"Madness was stealing her from the Unseen in the first place!" came della Trova's reedy voice.

Frelia and Thera both turned to glare at the woman, still bound by Vendrick's astral chains.

"*Really,* Vendrick," della Trova added. "What in Hypogia were you thinking?"

"I was *thinking,*" he said coldly, yanking the dagger out of the meat of his left arm, "that when I was asked to review laboratory procedures some Saints-forsaken evening, I would find mages poring over tomes and perhaps titrating blood samples or something.

"And I was thinking..." He flipped through his spellbook for a few moments before settling on a page. "...of a woman I had once known birthing a child in that compound, alone, and of the possibilities of how that came to pass, or what became of the little one."

He felt Frelia's horrified stare land on him, but still, Vendrick had more:

"And I was *thinking*—" He drew a jerky healing rune in the air before him, and then the skin on his arm began to knit itself back together. "—that *this* is not the Imperium I bled for."

He snapped his spellbook shut, and shoved it into his belt holster. With his newly-healed arm, he drew his Singularity pellets to him. They snapped to at his arcane call like angry fireflies.

He shouldn't so much as be considering what he was about to do, with two students staring at him in horror, but one of them was Ironfang's daughter and the other had a bloodrune and had already seen too much. And Vendrick was pretty sure that, one way or another, this would be his last night as Silverwood's Headmaster.

He couldn't spare them witness, but he could spare their involvement. They needed a healer, anyway.

So he said, "Frelia, would you kindly assist me?" and plucked a Singularity point out of the air around him.

Frelia's shoulders tensed, but she parted from the darkbeast with an apology scratch to its muzzle and stalked past the smoldering corpse of Muninn. "There's the Imperial torturer," she muttered. "Wondered where he'd been this whole time."

"Oh, but *Frelia dear,*" della Trova called, her voiced pitched just slightly lower—more like Clarissa's, "I thought we were friends?"

Vendrick gestured for Frelia to take Christel's place, and Frelia shooed her student away and yanked della Trova's arms so far back out of position they were in danger of breaking.

"Your mistake," Frelia hissed.

"Go on, Christel," Vendrick said, flicking a glance sideways. "Why don't you and Faustine go find Professor Blightsen and bring him here?"

The swordsman's eyes flicked between Frelia, della Trova, and Vendrick, and there was fear there, thick and dark. It made bile rise in Vendrick's throat, but this was a *child!* Of course there was fear.

Christel stared at him a moment longer—"I'm sorry, headmaster."—and then they grabbed at Faustine's arm and the two headed back down the hill.

Part of Vendrick wanted to ask what for, and part of him knew it was better not to know.

"Oh, how paternal," della Trova mocked.

"Shut up." Frelia's hands tightened in place. "What do you need, Vendrick?"

"Hold her mouth open."

The Singularity pellet rippled ever-so-slightly in the air as Vendrick waited for Christel and Faustine to get out of sight. The grey magic was practically feral in his hand, a devouring, demanding beast as sure as any darkbeast.

Frelia grabbed hold of della Trova's jaw and wrenched the woman's mouth open. She braced her other arm around della Trova's neck, and then glanced back to Vendrick.

With a sigh, Vendrick shoved the singularity pellet into della Trova's mouth. "Bottoms up."

For a moment, she struggled against his gloved palm, spittle flying and dark foam leaking down her chin. Not for the first time, Vendrick wondered if his victim would simply choke out of spite.

But then della Trova swallowed, audibly, and stopped straining.

"Well, now what then?" she said. "You torment me to death, or something?"

Vendrick drew a sharp, arcane line it the air before him, and the singularity pellet burned brightly enough that its outline stood out against della Trova's pale skin. She gasped, and then her fingers curled in on themselves in stubborn refusal.

"Something like that," he said. "But since you're already well aware of what I'm capable of, how about we skip the half-hour of fingernail-pulling and go straight to the part where you spill your bloody guts."

He loomed closer, magic crackling around his hands and in his hairline.

"My *sister*, della Trova," he insisted. "What have you done with her? What's the ritual Ascension Faustine is so afraid of? And where is she?"

"And who the fuck are you?" Frelia muttered.

"Oh that's right, you've never been introduced," Vendrick said, unable to keep from sounding like a Count no matter the circumstance. "Frelia, this is Lucia della Trova, Clarissa's ex-fiancée. Della Trova, Frelia Helm's Grace Valerius, the Silverwood Swordmaster and renowned darkbeast-killer."

"That... explains how she wore Clarissa's face," Frelia muttered.

"I am an *actress!*" della Trova snapped, although she was pale and her eyes were going glassy.

"Okay, that too." Frelia twisted della Trova's arm further in the wrong direction. "Now answer him."

"Burn in hell," della Trova coughed.

Vendrick sighed and drew another tail on his singularity rune. The pellet burned even more fiercely in della Trova's chest, right between her lungs.

"Are you *trying* to die?" Frelia asked.

"It's better than the alternative." Della Trova was turning faintly green. "I mean it, Vendrick. Give up this little war of yours, and maybe you can live a long and happy life elsewhere."

"So that, what," Vendrick said, "your lot can continue stealing bloodrunes in peace? Ironfang can torture innocents until their minds break and they turn into..." He gestured to where Darkbeast-Thera was staring at them across the hilltop, as still as stone. "...well, that?"

Della Trova coughed, spraying the front of her Caecillion-purple gown with blood and spittle. Unseen blood, apparently, had streaks of green interwoven into the usual rust red. That was disconcerting.

"You know I loved her, right?" della Trova's voice was very small.

"Spare me the sob story," Vendrick said. "I'm not interested in how you're justifying this to yourself."

She stared at him with something new in her eyes. Beyond revulsion, beyond disgust, what della Trova looked at Vendrick with now was fear.

"You're a monster," she whispered.

"Always have been."

He reached up to draw another tail on his Singularity rune, and della Trova finally broke.

"Stop! *Stop*, no more!" della Trova was thrashing in Frelia's grasp now, trying desperately to escape the swordswoman's hold. "You'll kill everyone you take to go get her. You know that, right?"

"That's my business," Vendrick said. "Tell me where she is, della Trova."

"Not without a guarantee you won't just turn me over to Ironfang," della Trova said hurriedly.

"Done," Vendrick said. "Make yourself scarce after we're done here, and we can call it even."

Della Trova tried to get a look at Frelia for long enough that the latter caught on. "Sworn on the grave of my father," Frelia muttered.

Della Trova slumped in Frelia's grip, a pathetic lump just like Vendrick had always known her to be. "Serpentbrook Hold," she croaked. "They're holding her there until the new moon."

Frelia's brow furrowed and she glanced back to Vendrick, but his blood had gone cold. The moon was a waning crescent in the sky overhead, and Serpentbrook Hold was far, *far* to the north. They'd never make it.

"For what purpose?" Vendrick hissed.

"The girl was right." Della Trova sighed. "It's meant to be Orsina della Luciana's Ascension ceremony."

Vendrick's fingers itched to draw more tails on his Singularity rune, but he stayed his hand now that she was talking. "Why my sister?"

"Any runeless person would do to power the Ascension," della Trova said. "But not for unbalancing you and leveling the playing field."

Shit, this really was all Vendrick's fault. But there was no time to dwell on it now; he had more pressing questions. "What does an Ascension do?"

"It'll turn della Luciana Hypogean, if she survives." At the blank look della Trova got, she added, "Kin to the Old Ones."

Frelia looked at Vendrick for some sort of translation, but he had none. "Old Ones," he repeated. "Really."

"This is what I *mean,* Vendrick," della Trova said. "You have absolutely no idea what you're dealing with."

"So enlighten me," he said.

She harrumphed, annoyed. "The bloodrunes are just a tool," della Trova added, exasperated. "A way to speak with them, since they don't talk like we do. The Old Ones have had their eyes on the Waking World for a very long time."

Frelia apparently gave up on waiting for Vendrick. "So what's an Old One?"

"The..." della Trova paused. "...Goddess species, I guess? Hypogeans are a step down from that."

Vendrick had seen and done a lot of awful things over the years, but he had never once considered literally divesting himself of what made him human.

"So what does one gain by losing one's humanity, exactly?" he pressed.

"Transcendence," della Trova said. "Dominion. Mastery over death. Old Ones can't really die, you know, they just sort of..." She made a popping noise with her tongue. "...drop off the face of the world, for a while. But they always come back."

"Then what do creatures that powerful care about us?" Vendrick asked.

"I think they're just... curious," della Trova said. "We're incredibly fragile, comparatively. Maybe they think we're cute; I don't know."

They eat people! Vendrick wanted to shout, but Frelia was ahead of him.

"Wait a minute," she said, "does that mean all the garmur I've killed have come back?"

Della Trova laughed, hollowly. "No, they're on the same level as Hypogeans."

Some of the horror left Frelia's eye "Thank the ever-loving Goddesses."

"Great." Vendrick's faced pinched. "So how does Clarissa... power this, you said?"

"They'll combine della Luciana's life essence with the blood of a runeless person, and a vessel for divine power." Della Trova spoke to the sky, as though that made it any easier. "It's some ancient magic I haven't the head for, and if Her Grace survives, she'll Ascend. But either way, Clarissa won't."

No, that wasn't an option. There *had* to be a way.

It struck him, a moment later, that there was a Queenmaker at Serpentbrook Hold, last Vendrick had heard. "And is Athos del Priore still himself?"

"So far as I know," della Trova said.

"Then one last thing." Vendrick's voice was devoid of emotion, and he gestured for Frelia to let go. "How long were you Clarissa?"

"Not long," della Trova admitted. "Just since she went to visit your mum."

It was so... personal. Most of what Ironfang did was just business. But this? This was designed to get under Vendrick's skin, and Saints damn him, it was working. Vendrick had stolen Thera Grimsdalr out from under the Imperator's nose because what the Unseen were doing to her was an affront to science, magic, and medicine, and this?

This was cruel for its own sake in the exact same way.

The mask that served as his face cracked, and he ripped the Singularity pellet from della Trova's chest with a savage burst of arcane energy.

Della Trova choked as blood poured over her abdomen. "You... swore...!"

"That we wouldn't turn you over to the Imperator," Vendrick growled. "Not that I wouldn't kill you."

He sent the Singularity pellet back into the gaping hole it had left in her chest, and then squeezed his hand into a fist. The comet burst, and a blast of grey magic ripped through della Trova's broken body.

She did not move again.

Frelia eyed him warily. "Easy, Vendrick."

He spoke through gritted teeth: "Is this how you feel every time someone brings up a Grimsdalr?"

"...*Ja,*" said Frelia. "Pretty much."

He tried to regulate his breathing, tried to bring his demons to heel and regain his composure, but it was like trying to hold water in his cupped hands.

"We need to do something about—" He began to glance to Frelia, only to find a sword at the level of his eyes.

"No more lies, Vendrick." Though there were blood, tears, and ichor splattered across her face, Frelia was as clear-eyed as she'd ever been. "Why is Thera here, and why is she a monster?"

CHAPTER FORTY-SEVEN

VENDRICK STAYED SILENT so long, Frelia began to wonder if she'd end up having to kill him after all. He studied her like a wild beast, but all the anger had drained from his features and been replaced by something bleak and hopeless.

"If you think everything out of my mouth is a lie," Vendrick finally said, "this... whatever we are... will not last."

He was right, damn him, but Frelia's war instincts were still screaming too loudly for her to care. "You didn't answer me, oh pile of secrets." Frelia spoke through gritted teeth. "*Thera*. How did she get here?"

The Imperator's former Left Hand shut his eyes, until only Vendrick remained. "Do you recall Roland Sferrazza?"

Frelia had only the vaguest memory of the cavalier general from the lance classes she'd taken as a student. "He led your cavalry, *ja?*"

Vendrick nodded miserably. "He guarded the Unseen's laboratory, after the war. So when I took the job at Silverwood, I told him to get them to release Thera. I didn't care how."

Frelia drew in a harsh breath. "That's... really sloppy, coming from you."

"I was finished with politicking," was all Vendrick offered. "The Unseen liked to pretend that their experiments were science, but they were nothing of the sort." Vendrick dragged his gloved hand through his hair. "They were cruelty for the simple sake of being cruel, and I would not stand for it any longer."

He might have just gutted her. It would have hurt less than knowing the Imperial Torturer had a breaking point, and that point was on the back of her unblood sister.

"So what did Roland do," Frelia managed, "to get Thera out?"

"Lied through his teeth," Vendrick said, and Frelia winced. Roland Sferrazza had been a knight in every sense: chivalrous, courteous, talented. "Told them the Imperator had ordered it, and I supplied the paperwork. He took care of the rest."

Frelia could just barely picture Roland's shaking hands leading the wolf-like beast out of the mouth of hell.

"But he panicked." Vendrick dragged that gloved hand down his face. "Halfway here, he started getting jittery, asking what exactly my plans were."

Frelia's stomach dropped into her boots. "He was talking to them, wasn't he?"

"I don't know," Vendrick whispered. "I had to kill him."

They stared at each other for a long moment, the disgraced Kaldiri swordswoman and the lonely Volsinii grey mage. All around them, snowflakes swirled like so many tiny stars, borne aloft by the wind of a garmr's dying breath.

Vendrick broke first, glancing back towards where Thera still sat, scarred and unmoving. "Don't look at me like that."

"If you hadn't done it..." Frelia didn't know where to look, anymore. "...you and Thera would both be dead."

"I said *don't.*" His voice cracked on the word.

"And what should I be looking at you like?" Frelia challenged. "A monster out of Helheim?"

"What else would I be?"

"No, Vendrick, *I* am hell," Frelia pressed, trying to make him understand. "You're..."

She faltered.

Vendrick wasn't hell. He was the furthest thing from hell. He was laughter and late night cheesecake and terrible jokes and awkward flirting. He was strategies to take back her legacy and plans for the future and a burst of healing fire in the shadows of the early morning.

And kissing him felt like coming home.

Vendrick *was.* That was the thing. He had always been a part of that patchwork quilt of herself, ever since she'd met him all those years ago in their alchemy class. No wonder she couldn't pick out which piece was his; there were too many.

"I'm *what?*" he pressed.

"Breathing," Frelia got out.

He stared at her for a long moment, and as the wind bit into them and the Guardian of Traust Territory smoldered, Vendrick reached for her hand.

"And the fight's not over," he said, as though it finally struck him properly, "so long as we breathe."

Frelia nodded, suddenly exhausted.

"I know I have no right to ask," he said quietly, "but will you come with me to Serpentbrook Hold?"

Frelia didn't want to be the bearer of bad news, but she wasn't one to lie to spare your feelings, either. "We'll never make it before the new moon."

Instead of crumpling or accepting reality, Vendrick said, "Yes we can."

"How?"

"At the beginning of the war, I developed a transportation rune that would allow me to instantly appear in Octavia's vicinity." Vendrick spoke so fast his words tripped over themselves. "But as the war dragged on, I also made them for the rest of the Queenmakers. So if Athos is still himself, I'll show up right behind him."

Frelia's eye widened. "Well shit, Vendrick! I can..." As quickly as it had bloomed, her excitement died. Even if they got there in time, they would then be fighting out of the middle of a fort of hostiles. "Wait, then we'd just be loose in enemy territory, and I'm not stealthy or good at anything but destruction."

"I know." Vendrick squeezed her hand tightly. "But I have a plan, and I'll need your help."

"Why me?" Frelia dragged bedraggled hair out of her eye as she stared at him in overwhelmed confusion. "And why did you bother to follow me out here, anyway? What do you need me for that you can't handle?"

He studied her for a moment, and then he snorted, drew in a deep breath, and said, as casually as he might ask about relatives or students, "Because I love you, you fucking *dorchya.*"

Frelia froze over completely, absolutely dumbstruck.

"How do you know what that means?" she got out.

"*Dorchya?*"

Frelia nodded, numbly.

"I asked Blightsen. It's a good word. I needed one for 'I care deeply for you, but you're being an idiot.'"

Frelia stared at him, stunned beyond all recognition. "You... you can't..."

She couldn't even get the word out.

Though mercifully (or not, depending on how you wanted to look at it), Vendrick knew what she meant.

"Merciful Saints, don't tell me you hadn't figured it out before now? Even after the training ground?"

"Uh..."

"I snuck food into an alchemy lab for you!" Vendrick snorted amused frost. "One of the stupidest things I've ever done, honestly, but I knew you were skipping lunch because you couldn't deal with Hägen and the Twins."

Each word was a tiny dagger aimed directly for her heart. "You remember that?"

"I remember a lot of things." Vendrick was on the verge of laughter. "Like fixing your potions when you weren't looking, standing up to Markus della Luciana on your behalf, and sparing your life at the Battle of Skjöldr."

"You did *what?*" She knew she'd passed out by the time Cillian got them out of the city, but she had no memory of *that.*

"How else did you think Cillian Grimsdalr managed to escape a crackshot grey mage, exactly? He was a fantastic cavalier, certainly, but I was standing at point blank." At the look she continued to give him, Vendrick only gave a short, very tired laugh. "I don't know how much more obvious I could've been, besides throwing rocks at your window at three in the morning, or something."

"You can't..." Frelia finally found her voice through the fear curdling her blood. "...love me, Vendrick."

"I can, I do, and deal with it."

"No, no, no." Frelia needed to impress upon him what a colossally stupid idea this was. "I mean, *don't.* If you do, you'll die. Like everyone else."

Understanding cracked over Vendrick's face, and he too softened, just a little. Just enough to break them both.

"I'm not going anywhere." He drew her into a hug so fierce, Frelia felt her spine crack in three places.

"I mean it, Vendrick," Frelia tried to warn him, half-muffled against his soaked waistcoat. "I am hell to love."

"That's fine," Vendrick said. "So am I. We're two of a kind, that way."

The night was dark and cold, up here in what had once been Konstantin Territory, and Frelia's heart ached for a home that no longer existed. But maybe...

Maybe she could build another.

Her hands came around Vendrick's back, slid beneath the dagger still buried in his shoulder, and tugged him close. They stood there for a long, overtired moment, the wolf and the viper, sharing body heat and understanding in the depths of a blue, Kaldiri winter.

"Yes," said Frelia quietly. "I'm coming with you. But first, we have bodies to take care of and you have a knife in your shoulder."

He nodded. "You take care of the darkbeast, and I'll get della Trova?"

Frelia sheathed the Sword of Hana. "Deal."

"What is that, by the way?" Vendrick asked. "Its aura is brilliant—strong but stable, and very, *very* old."

"It's Hana's." Frelia grinned, and pointed out the runes across the hilt that spelled her ancestor's name. "As in, *the Ballad of*, and the Saint, the kraken-killer and founder of my house."

"That's a relative of yours?" Vendrick paused. "You know what, actually, I'm not surprised. I take it back."

Frelia glanced to the shadowy man beside her, and to the sword in her hands, and then the grin of a much younger woman spread across her round face. Somewhere over her shoulder, Vendrick's breathing came a little easier.

"Help me start a pyre," Frelia said. "Ghosts can't sneak up on you if there's a fire burning."

Somewhere, far to the right, Garmr-Thera began to laugh.

"My dear lady," Vendrick said, "you've read my mind."

Frelia snorted, and then her eye fell back to Thera. "So what do we do with her?"

"That's an excellent question," Vendrick said. "However, I do have a theory I want to quickly field-test, here."

He turned towards where the garmr sat on its haunches in the shadows of the churchyard.

"Grimsdalr!" he called over. "I need you to bark once for yes, and twice for no."

The garmr stiffened, its ears pricking up.

"You've never needed to eat in this form, correct?" Vendrick asked.

Garmr-Thera barked once.

"Really?" Frelia asked.

"I used to bring her things," Vendrick said. "Usually cattle, or an inordinate amount of fish. And she'd eat at first, but eventually I'd come back to find everything just... hacked up and pushed around, like a picky child trying to make it look like she ate something."

Frelia snorted at the mental image.

"So if you don't eat, Grimsdalr," Vendrick continued, loudly enough for his voice to carry, "is that why you haven't healed?"

The garmr cocked its head at him, a confused dog.

"Oh... I see where this is going." Frelia's stomach twisted. "Garmur don't eat cattle or fish. They eat people."

"Precisely." Vendrick nodded, grimacing himself. "So what happens if you eat della Trova, Grimsdalr?"

Thera's entire beastly form recoiled.

"You can't tell her to risk Saint Háski's Rot like that!" Frelia said at once, but even as she spoke, it landed wrongly in her own ears.

You couldn't be a cannibal, after all, if you weren't the same species.

"She certainly doesn't have to," Vendrick said. "I can simply burn della Trova's corpse, I just..."

He cut himself off as Garmr-Thera rose to her feet as slowly and deliberately as a siege cannon. She lumbered over to della Trova's still-cooling form and stood over it, inert and staring. A deep whine resonated from somewhere in her throat.

"...had a theory," Vendrick finished, much more quietly.

For a moment, none of them moved. Not swordswoman, not grey mage, not monster.

And then the garmr's thick, mottled tongue reached out to lap at the blood soaking into the snow. A moment later, one of the smaller wounds on Thera's flank began to bubble as though doused in acid. She howled, and Frelia swore she could hear the echo of Cillian's voice somewhere deep within it.

And then the wound sealed, leaving behind a faint, pinkish scar.

"I knew it," Vendrick said grimly. "Della Trova's mad if she thinks the Old Ones are interested in humanity out of curiosity. We are a *food source.*"

As if to reply, Thera's beastly jaws clamped down over the entirety of della Trova's remains, threw back her head, and crunched. More of the virulent, unhealing wounds slashed across her sides began to bubble over as Thera chewed.

"Nothing less," Vendrick muttered, "and nothing more."

The horror of what the garmur were had long since washed over her, but sometimes, even General Frelia Helm's Grace Valerius could only stare at the monsters the Volsinii had loosed on her people, and try not to be sick.

"You know," Frelia said numbly, "when I said we were a match made in some kind of hell, I was being facetious."

"No, you weren't," said Vendrick softly beneath the cracking of bones and sinew in a garmr's teeth. "You were dead on."

Also by Evelyn Hyde

Want more of the Wolf and the Viper?

Prequel: A Dark and Ancient Evil
Available for free when you <u>sign up for the newsletter!</u>

Book 1: Some Kind of Hell
You are here!

Book 2: Bring Down the Sky
Available from Amazon

Book 3: Hour of the Wolf
Coming Soon

Book 4: Last Queen of Kaldr
Coming Soon

ABOUT THE AUTHOR

Evelyn Hyde is an indie author, editor, and the founder of Tag Your S#@!. She is a Midwestern native with the tragically Ohio penchant for leaving the surface of the Earth by any means necessary, but no head for NASA. When not at work, Evelyn can be found in her kitchen experimenting, digging into a new story in whatever form it takes, or annoying her loving husband. She is also an excellent Game Master.

You can find her at https://evelynhydewriter.com/

If you want to hear about all her latest novels, new works, and nonsense (and psst get a free copy of *A Dark and Ancient Evil*, the prequel novella to The Wolf and the Viper Saga), you can sign up for her newsletter on her website.

AUTHOR'S NOTE

When I first sat down to start writing this series, it was in the middle of the pandemic. I was working a day job in medicine (which was exactly as stressful as you're thinking) while the regulations on how to handle Covid-19 were changing daily. But slightly *before* that, I had started taking swords classes. Those obviously had to stop during social distancing, but I remember standing there, listening to my instructor tell me how to swing an LED saber (totally legally distinct from a lightsaber, in case anyone asks), and thinking:

Man, it would be hilarious to have a grumpy-ass swords teacher instructing a bunch of kids.

My instructor, thankfully, was not that. But that's how Frelia was born.

She was raised by the Writer Coven, my kick-ass writer group without whose help this series would not exist. Jill, Becca, and Phoebe, I'm grateful to you all from the bottom of my heart. I promise to continue warning y'all when I'm reading a gory chapter this week, and to never stop making "that's my indie band" jokes.

Frelia was then babysat by good friends and excellent betas, so a huge thank you goes out to Heidi and Anna (the incomparable Gaydies), Deb, Matt, Becky, Jared, Felia (no relation to the MC), Tim, Alex, and Mike.

Your signed copies are in the mail, friendos! (Except the Gaydies'; you'll get yours at DnD, statistically.)

Frelia was schooled (buh dum tss) by two fantastic editors, Kezia Kynaston-Mitchell and Heather Rubert, both of whom made excellent suggestions and not only didn't flinch at wild hairs like "What if I made them fight memories, but it's a literal monster?", but genuinely told me to go for it. Thank you to you both, as well.

Frelia was also carried by my sweet husband, Jack, who enthusiastically encouraged me when I started talking about book stuff (or complaining about how book stuff is hard), and our dog, Roy, the Husky/Chow Chow mix whose Husky half demands walkies.

All. The. Time.

Without his husky derpiness, this book would also never have been written and revised, because walking a dog three times a day really gives a woman time to think. And listen to audiobooks, podcasts, and power metal.

I also want to thank the artists who brought Frelia to life—Maria Spada for her awesome covers, Shivnath Productions for the beautiful map, and Alex Spreier for his lovely and expressive bloodrune art.

None of them will likely ever see this, but I also wanted to thank the writers who watered the garden of my soul and helped to grow my own voice, story, and work. Shout out to Hajime Isayama, Kentaro Miura, T. Kingfisher, Dan Abnett, David R. Slayton, Aaron Dembski-Bowden, Silvia Moreno-Garcia, and Andy Weir. Thank you, with everything I have in me, for your art.

Lastly, I thank *you,* dear readers, for giving Frelia and Vendrick the chance to let you into their world. For cheering on Faustine's growth and teenager-ness. For your admirable restraint in not punching Markus whenever he opens his slimy mouth. And for your unending enthusiasm. This author's note is for you, too.

If you're curious about what I'm up to, there are link to my newsletter, website, and social media on my bio page. I'd love to hear from you there, or via reviews on Amazon, Goodreads, and the rest. Reviews are like magic to a writer—*the fuck you mean someone read my book and liked it enough to tell other people?*—and I'm grateful for every single one. Yes, even the ones that say the book is "just okay," because, hey, I don't just read the five star reviews on Amazon, either.

Finally, I will leave you with the biggest irony of this series: It was not lost on me that the book I named *Some Kind of Hell* was rewritten fifteen times. I think those rewrites were worth it, though, and I hope you all do, too.

So keep safe until we meet again (hopefully in the next book)!

-Hyde